The Divorce Planner

by

Angela Lam

The Divorce Planner

Cover Art by *Kristian Norris*

The Wild Rose Press, Inc.
PO Box 708
Adams Basin, NY 14410-0708
Visit us at www.thewildrosepress.com

Publishing History
First Mainstream General Edition, 2019
Print ISBN 978-1-5092-2610-8
Digital ISBN 978-1-5092-2611-5

Published in the United States of America

Victor led Darcy up onto the stage.

A spotlight shone on them.

She stood on wobbly legs, staring into the crowd, but the bright light made distinguishing any faces impossible.

Placing his hand in his interior breast pocket, he curled his fingers around something. Kneeling on one knee, he grabbed one of her hands.

As beads of sweat burst against the crown of her forehead, she swayed like a palm tree caught in a tropical storm.

With soft eyes, he held up a ring.

The diamond shone like a tiny star. Tightening her throat, she blinked back tears. This proposal wasn't happening. But then she remembered Victor's promise to give everyone something to talk about. They will talk about this event for years, she thought.

"My darling Darcy," he said, loud enough for the silenced crowd to hear. "Will you marry me?"

The spotlight glinted off the diamond, blinding her with its radiance. For a long moment, Darcy wondered if the crowd suspected the ruse. A rush of feelings flooded through her, from the anxiety of being found out to the bliss of being falsely wanted. Heart pounding, she held her breath.

Victor gazed up at her.

She could stare into those kind brown eyes forever. Releasing her breath, she smiled. "Yes, I'll marry you."

Praise for Angela Lam

"Angela Lam excels at placing people in an immediate social world, showing both their insecurity and their resilience. She explores the boundaries of individual experience, moving along the sometimes blurred, sometimes rough edges, of relationships. The deeper questions of failed relationships haunt this novel."

~Mary Clark

Dedication

To Kevin

Acknowledgements

First and foremost, I would like to thank my editor, Leanne Morgena, who believed in this story. I have grown as an author from her knowledge and insight.

Thanks also to my daughter, Rose Turpin, for her editorial advice. She helped shape the initial story, streamlining the middle to allow for a surprising new ending.

Special thanks to Doug Greenberg for his friendship and legal expertise.

Thanks to Kis Gross. For the first time in my life, I have someone close to me who understands the artist's life.

Finally, and most importantly, I would like to thank Kevin Gross who has welcomed me into his heart and his life. His presence is the reason why I can devote so much of myself to my writing. I am grateful for his patience, encouragement, love, and support. Thank you, Kevin, for reminding me every day I am living happily-ever-after.

"It's not the beginning but the ending that's hard."
~A. Non Emus, Relationship Expert

Chapter 1

When she noticed her daughter's number, Darcy should have not picked up her phone, but she pressed the speaker button anyway. She drove in afternoon traffic to the attorney's office to meet her client, Monica, for the three o'clock mediation with her soon-to-be ex-husband.

"Mom, I need to talk to you," Joyce said.

Joyce's voice sounded tinny against the wind as it whipped through the open windows of Darcy's ancient sports sedan lacking air conditioning. She refused to roll up the windows when her back stuck against the seat from Sonoma County's summer heat.

"Then talk." Darcy took the exit for Highway 12 in Santa Rosa.

"I'm getting married, and I want you to plan my wedding," Joyce said.

The driver ahead slammed on the brakes.

"Oh, no!" Darcy shoved her foot on the brake and honked her horn as her vehicle slid to a stop. Her heartbeat raced in her chest, and beads of salty sweat streamed down her forehead and dripped from her nose.

"Mom? What's wrong? Are you all right?"

"I'm fine," Darcy snapped. She didn't know if she felt shock or anger as Joyce's words slowly withered like a dead flower in her mind's eye. "You're getting married?"

"To Tyler. You met him a while ago. The last time we visited."

Hoping to see more of her twenty-eight-year-old daughter, Darcy relocated from Southern California to Northern California. But she only made one trip to San Francisco in the three years she lived here. "And you want me to plan your wedding?"

Traffic started moving again. Darcy gripped the phone tighter, hoping no highway patrol officers lurked nearby to give someone a ticket. "I'm a divorce planner, not a wedding planner."

"You're the best party planner," Joyce said. "Remember when you planned a pony sleepover?"

A reluctant smile spread across Darcy's face. "Yes, you were seven." A divorce changed everything a year afterward, and their mother-daughter relationship never fully recovered. "You wanted those tiny pastel horses as decorations."

"What a wonderful party! I'm sure you can make my wedding even better than that. We'll have—"

"Why?" Darcy exited the freeway and turned down the city street toward the attorney's office. She breathed in deeply and steadied her voice in an attempt to reason with her daughter. "You're too young, too ambitious, and too smart to settle down."

"Statistically, it's best to marry when you're between the ages of twenty-eight and thirty-two," Joyce said. "Couples of those ages are least likely to divorce."

"Statistics don't mean anything, sweetheart." Why couldn't her daughter follow her heart? she thought.

"Yes, they do," Joyce said. "You're more likely to get divorced if you live together and have a child first, which is exactly what you and Dad did. I've never lived with Tyler although we're buying a house before the wedding, and I've no intention of getting pregnant before the wedding. I should be married forever."

"Forever is a long time." Too long, Darcy thought.

"Not long enough when you're in love. I know you've built your career against marriage, but I want you to put it aside for one year. Planning my wedding is the only thing I've asked of you since the divorce, and it's the only thing I'll ever ask."

"That's not true." Darcy slipped into a parking spot. "You asked me to pay for school, including your ridiculously expensive master's degree."

"I prefer to think of my tuition as an investment."

"Well, I never realized any return on my money."

"Are you asking me to pay you back?"

Joyce's exasperation surprised Darcy. Her grip loosened on the phone. Repayment wouldn't be bad, Darcy thought. She could move into her own place. She turned off the engine. "I'm asking you to be grateful."

"I am grateful. I'm so grateful I'll pay you to plan my wedding."

Grabbing her briefcase, Darcy stepped into the blazing sunshine and locked the car doors. She thought about her own wedding as a twenty-two-year-old college graduate with a one-year-old daughter toddling around the garden, picking grass and putting it in her mouth. Darcy had asked her mother to care for Joyce so Darcy could gather her girlfriends to help with the last-minute adjustments to her wardrobe.

Too poor to splurge on anything, Darcy wore her mother's wedding dress tugged tight around her post-pregnancy middle. Her freshly washed hair kept falling out of the bun one of her girlfriends pinned to make room for the veil. Worst of all, her eyes itched and watered from allergies, which challenged the strength of her waterproof mascara. But those details faded against the spark Darcy felt for her boyfriend, Nathan, who sported good looks and athleticism. What he lacked in ambition, he made up for in the kitchen and the bedroom, serving up food and affection equally appealing.

That Darcy earned more than him didn't matter. He could stay home and tinker in the garage, designing gadgets he might one day patent into something useful, while she worked as an event planner for a big Los Angeles firm focused on exclusive clientele, including the occasional celebrity. Darcy being the breadwinner didn't matter until the part-time nanny became Nathan's full-time lover. The life they had created dissolved so quickly Darcy sometimes wondered if it had existed at all.

Now, she struggled to contain her fears so she wouldn't spoil her daughter's same romantic illusions. How could she fight against her nature? After all, she thrived in helping people rally legal aid, housing, child support, and career options. She loved planning freedom parties to celebrate the finalization of divorce. She could not imagine drumming up the same level of enthusiasm to help her daughter pick out fine china she would never use and select a five-thousand dollar dress she would only wear once.

"Mom?"

Joyce's tender, yet pleading, voice rankled Darcy's resistance. "Okay, okay, okay. I'll help you plan your wedding."

The thrilling shout of victory from Joyce's mouth

washed away Darcy's hesitation. But as soon as she ended the call, darkness rushed back in and flooded Darcy with doubt. How could she make my daughter's dreams of happily-ever-after come true when she only knew how to undo the knots of unhappily-ever-after? Darcy wondered.

****

At three o'clock, Darcy stepped into the mediation offices of DeSoto & DeSoto, registered with the receptionist, and took a seat in the waiting area.

Five minutes later, Monica dragged her ten-year-old son by the arm into the waiting area.

Joey kicked his legs and screamed.

Dark-haired Monica swatted him with her hand.

Joey twisted and turned to struggle out of his mother's grasp.

The receptionist fumbled with her phone, staring wide-eyed at the commotion.

Tensing her shoulders with dismay, Darcy frowned. From what she remembered, Joey suffered from autism and developmental delay. He tuned out the world and threw tantrums like a two-year-old. Although he wore a freshly washed, striped shirt and denim jeans, he smelled like he spent the last hour rolling around in a pig pen. Probably because he needed his diaper changed.

With her puffy eyes and worn-out clothes, Monica looked exhausted from the non-stop work of caring for a perpetual toddler, who grew bigger and stronger but not any smarter. Darcy met Monica through Legal Aid and agreed to help her organize her divorce from beginning to end. A year of battling back and forth between Monica and her soon-to-be ex-husband led them to the point of court-appointed mediation. Darcy didn't want Monica to reschedule this appointment, but she couldn't imagine Monica negotiating a settlement agreement with her son screaming and kicking in the same room. "Where's his respite worker?"

"Sick," Monica said. "I called for backup, but In Home Support Services didn't have someone available."

Darcy shuddered. How could anyone live a normal life with a disabled child without professional support? "Not even for an emergency?"

Monica struggled to pin her son against the carpet like a wrestler. "They don't consider mediation an emergency."

Darcy stood and waved her hands to get Joey's attention.

Screaming, Joey broke free of his mother's grasp and flung his arms and legs against the floor. "Song!"

"He needs his music." Monica shook her phone. "But the battery is drained."

Darcy grabbed her phone from her purse. "What type of music?"

"His favorite band is Puddle of Mudd."

After searching the tracks of alternative rock music on her phone, Darcy selected "Psycho."

The jarring beat and odd lyrics instantly calmed the boy. He dropped to his knees like a rag doll.

Holding the phone above her head, Darcy knelt.

The mediator called Monica's name.

Monica grabbed Joey's arm.

Shaking her head, Darcy waved an arm. "You can leave him with me."

"Are you sure?" Monica raised her eyebrows.

"Yes." Her phone was fully charged, but she hoped her patience lasted. "We'll be fine."

Monica bit her lower lip.

Since Darcy had known her, Monica seemed stressed all the time. Now Darcy knew why. Caring for this unpredictable child dismantled the endurance of the most patient parent. "Your attorney will support you. I'll stay here with Joey until the meeting is done, okay?"

The worry lines on Monica's forehead erased. She touched Darcy's shoulder. "Thank you."

"You're welcome." Pride pulsed through Darcy's body. Who else could step in and help a divorcing parent of a disabled child so they could finalize their divorce? Not an attorney, not a judge, and not a CPA. Only a skilled, creative, and resourceful divorce planner could.

The song rattled on and on.

Pleased with her decision to download the music from the DJ she dated for three weeks, Darcy smiled and knelt on the scratchy carpet.

Joey rocked back and forth near the row of chairs. He stared at the ceiling, lost in his own little world of music.

Darcy relaxed into the song with Joey, letting her shoulders slump forward and her heartbeat slow to the beat of the drum.

****

That evening, Darcy stood in front of her closet, searching for the best dress to wear to the Legal Aid Gala when her phone rang. Without glancing at the caller ID, she swiped her thumb across the screen. "Hello?"

"I can't believe you. You'll ruin the wedding."

The caller spewed hot venom over the line. Darcy lurched with fear and dropped the black dress she held. Her ex-husband seldom called following Joyce's high school graduation. Her pulse galloped in her chest and sweat beaded along her forehead.

"Nathan, I'm not ruining anything." How dare he assume she volunteered for the job? She curled her hand into a fist. "Joyce asked me to plan it."

"You didn't have to say yes. But you'll never change. You will always do whatever she says, won't you? She's still the tail wagging the dog."

Shame at the truth behind his statements heated her cheeks. She shook her fist in the air. "I don't know why you're complaining. The wedding is not yours."

"Because I don't want our daughter getting it into her mind she can just walk away if this marriage doesn't work out."

"Just like you walked away?" Darcy placed a hand on her hip and took a step back.

"I didn't walk away. You did."

The weight of failure descended on her shoulders. "I wouldn't have if you hadn't started an affair with Tanya."

"I didn't have an affair with Tanya. We didn't start dating until *after* you moved out."

"She moved into your bedroom three days after I left." Darcy swept an arm across the dresses, skirts, and blouses in her open closet. "She even wore the clothes I forgot to take."

"Darcy—"

"Don't *Darcy* me. You have no right to call and yell. I have every right to hang up right now, but I won't because you're the father of our daughter." Darcy took a deep breath and exhaled to the count of three. She stooped to retrieve the simple slip dress she wore to every special occasion. Tonight, the dress looked as tired and as uninspired as she felt.

"I'm sorry," Nathan said. "When she called and told me, I kind of flipped out. I had hoped she would go with our wedding planner."

"*Your* wedding planner?" A fresh wave of shock knocked the wind out of her. She sank on the edge of the bed and clutched the dress to her chest like a security blanket.

"Tanya and I are getting married this fall. We could get a two-for-one deal if our wedding planner took care of both weddings."

A strange blur danced through Darcy's vision. The room spun and pointed her in a new direction. Why hadn't Joyce mentioned her father's wedding when she called? Did she think she could spare her mother's feelings by shielding her from the truth? After all, as long as Tanya and Nathan lived together, Darcy could dismiss Tanya as a shack-up girlfriend, a casual fling, or a person of no consequence. Once they married, Tanya's status elevated from disrespected floozy to regarded wife. Tears pricked Darcy's eyes. "Why are you guys getting married after all these years?"

"Feels right."

The pain of betrayal squeezed her chest. In the eight years they had been married, Nathan's mantra was, "Think. Don't feel." Had Tanya's involvement over the years transformed him? "You're not a very feeling person."

"Okay, so it's practical, too. Easy estate planning.

Nothing to think about if one of us dies."

Over the years, Darcy worked with enough attorneys to know the ins and outs of family law. "That's just an excuse. All legal stuff can be taken care of through a trust."

"Why do you care if I want to marry her?"

Darcy sobbed. Their marriage had been a marriage of convenience, necessity, and moral rectitude, since they shared a child, but the marriage had not been full of love. Tears spilled down her cheeks. Her throat tightened. "I guess what you're saying is she's The One."

He laughed. "You're bitter, aren't you? You became a divorce planner to get revenge every day through your clients."

She shook her clenched fist. "That divorce business kept a roof over your head with all the child support I paid you."

"And now look where it's gotten you…a room in someone else's house."

"At least, I'm doing what I do best."

"Good for you. Bad for Joyce. You should have told our daughter you didn't want to plan her wedding. You're not good at starting a marriage, only ending one."

Darcy crumpled the soft dress in her fist. Why couldn't Nathan just leave her alone? Why did he always taunt her? The hatred in the back of her throat tasted like bile. She mustered enormous strength to bite her tongue and stop arguing for another five minutes. Outside her closed bedroom door, she smelled hickory smoke from the barbecue chicken Sam grilled in the backyard. Linda's laughter burst like tiny bubbles over a joke Sam must have said. Her roommates, a long-time married couple, always seemed so compatible. They danced back and forth between their differences like a beautiful waltz.

Darcy thought of her clients who struggled with a rollercoaster of emotions as they negotiated how to divide child custody, spousal support, and shared assets. She then thought of her best friend, Betty Barnes, and her husband, Chuck, and their second-time's-a-charm marriage full of unconditional love. Her thoughts circled to Joyce and all her enthusiasm for marriage, in spite of having parents who presented the reality of the darker, more cynical side of love gone wrong. Finally, she thought of her marriage. She always played and failed in the traditional role of wife. She should let him alone with his opinion and change the dynamics of the situation. "Congratulations to you and Tanya. I wish you both only happiness. Now, if you don't mind, I'm going now to get ready for an event."

"Okay," Nathan sighed. "I'll let you go."

As soon as he hung up, delightful silence filled the room.

Chapter 2

After she finished her conversation with Nathan, Darcy ditched the tired dress and slipped into a splashy sapphire sequined gown she reserved for New Year's Eve. With its plunging neckline and high slit skirt, she felt twenty years younger. A glimpse in the full-length closet doors confirmed her judgment. Fifty looked like the new thirty.

At the convention center, Darcy stepped underneath an archway of red and white balloons shaped like a heart. The theme of the event matched the name of the sponsor, "Desire Our Hearts." Dozens of couples—men in their tuxedos and women in their evening gowns—swarmed the check-in desk. The clash of floral perfume and musky cologne tickled Darcy's nostrils. To prevent an unpleasant sneeze, she wiggled her nose.

Darcy usually attended these events with Betty who volunteered as a divorce attorney with Legal Aid, but Betty missed tonight's event in favor of attending one of Chuck's senior softball tournaments. Sometimes, Darcy questioned Betty's excessive devotion to Chuck. What other wife insisted on being a ball girl at her husband's games? Who else worked double time during the week in the hopes of making partner so her husband could retire early? Darcy blushed. What gave her the right to criticize Betty's relationship? After all, Darcy's only attempt at marriage ended in divorce.

Fidgeting with the clasp on her clutch purse, she glimpsed Victor Costello, another attorney at Betty's firm, in the main ballroom. He always looked good, but tonight he seemed spectacular. His black hair swept in a wave above his forehead. He wore a classic tuxedo with a ruby red bow tie. The tailored suit emphasized his broad shoulders, narrow waist, and long, lean legs. But Victor's kind smile dazzled Darcy the most.

He lifted his glass and winked.

Warmth invaded her chest with the brief acknowledgment. She had only met Victor a handful of times, but their professional encounters always left her feeling welcomed. Since she dreaded feeling alone, Darcy appreciated his attention tonight.

"May we have your credit card information for bidding purposes?" the check-in clerk asked.

With a sigh, Darcy fumbled in her clutch for her credit card. She wished she didn't have to relinquish her credit card information. If she didn't, then she would be dismissed from the event.

"Did you bring a guest, Ms. Madison?" the clerk asked.

"He's already checked-in." She motioned to the ballroom.

The clerk chuckled. "A little impatient, isn't he?"

"Better impatient than late." Darcy laughed. Before sauntering into the air-conditioned ballroom, she grabbed her auction paddle and a glass of champagne. She shimmied past couples circling the silent auction tables to Victor, who stood talking to a server carrying a tray of crab cakes.

"Want one?" Victor plucked a crab cake off the

tray with a napkin and offered it.

Darcy nibbled the crispy, spicy crust and tender, flaky center. "Mmm…delicious."

Before he smiled, Victor gave her the once-over. "I thought coming in a tux would be overkill until you arrived." He lifted his glass of champagne. "Nice dress."

"Thanks." Darcy touched the neckline. "I usually wear it on New Year's Eve."

"I'm glad you're wearing it tonight."

The compliment rippled up her body and filled her with pleasure. She glanced away and blushed.

"Are you here alone?" Victor glanced around the room.

"Yes." She cocked an eyebrow. "And you?"

"Not anymore." He offered his arm. "Let's mingle."

As she stared at his arm, apprehension clenched her stomach.

He chuckled. "Afraid of seeing me outside the office?" He leaned closer. "I promise to be a complete gentleman," he whispered.

His reputation as an excellent attorney earned him the designation as one of the top forty professionals under forty by the *North Bay Business Journal*. She remembered reading the article last year, taking note of his interest in antique collecting. His memorable quote left an impression. "I enjoy the quality found in vintage wine, turn-of-the century furniture, black-and-white movies, and the wisdom of older people." His reputation of being conscientious and compassionate with his clients, but swift and merciless in the courtroom, intimidated even Betty, the best attorney she knew. "I'm not scared of you." She lifted her chin.

"Good." Again, he offered his arm.

She drained her glass of champagne, plunked it on an empty tray, and linked her arm through his.

With a smile, he directed them through the crowd, stopping every now and then to talk to someone they both knew.

Judge Newman, a portly man with a wicked sense of humor, nudged Darcy in the elbow. "You surprised me, Madison. For all those years you've been coming with Betty, I had you pegged for a lesbian."

She forced a titter. She hated when men assumed her lesbian status because she seldom dated. "I hope your judgment doesn't extend to the courtroom, or your caseload will evaporate."

Victor squeezed her arm closer. "Darcy's a tough woman, Your Honor. A guy from the Special Forces of the Leagues of Disillusioned Divorcees is needed to break through her resistance."

Judge Newman narrowed his gaze. "You don't come from that League, Costello. You're the only family law attorney I know who hasn't been married or divorced."

"I didn't say I was the guy."

Judge Newman pointed to their linked arms. "You're together now?"

Flashing a tight smile, Darcy waved her auction paddle. "I won him in another auction. He's mine for tonight." She pecked Victor's cheek.

The muscles in Victor's jaw flinched.

Judge Newman glanced back and forth between them. "You guys make an interesting couple, whether you're together or not." He stomped off to the silent auction tables.

"Let's not mingle anymore." Darcy turned toward the dining room tables. "Deflecting the rude comments I always get because I'm single is exhausting. People don't understand I never want to remarry. They just assume things."

"Ditto," Victor said. "Just because I'm thirty-seven, people think I'm a confirmed bachelor. I used to be called the George Clooney of Sonoma County."

"George Clooney is married now." Darcy cocked her head to the side, wondering how he could be ignorant of the celebrity's current status.

Victor raised his eyebrows. "Not when people compared me." He led them to their table and slid back the chair.

She waited for him to scoot her chair close to the table before she placed her auction paddle beside her plate and waved for a server to bring her a drink. The clock against the wall stated the time as seven. Dinner was served in a half hour.

"Would you like to browse the auction tables with me?" he asked.

"No, thanks." She waved her hand in dismissal. "I never bid on anything."

"I didn't say *bid*. I said *browse*."

"Why browse if you can't bid?"

"People spend most of their shopping time browsing."

"Not me. I have a list. I go in, and I come out. No extras."

Narrowing his gaze, he frowned. "You're not a typical woman."

She shook her head. Oh, life would be simpler as a

typical woman, she thought. Primp, pamper, shop, and repeat.

"The service here is terrible." He stood and touched her shoulder.

A frisson of electricity zipped through her body.

"Let me get you something from the bar," he said. "I hear their appletinis are good."

She shifted in the chair.

His hand remained on her shoulder.

The heat of his skin against hers tingled. "Please, no appletinis. I don't like sweets. If you're getting us martinis, make mine gin, extra dry, with two olives."

His hand fell from her shoulder. "Why two?"

The shock of cold air on her bare skin rippled through her. She craved the comfort of his tender touch. "So the first olive doesn't get lonely."

He winked. "You, my dear, are a man in a woman's body."

She stiffened. Was he complimenting her or disparaging her? To refrain from asking, she bit her lower lip.

With purposeful steps, he wove through the crowd.

Heat flamed her cheeks. She glanced away and fiddled with her auction paddle. She's not on a date. She's working. Nothing else.

"What's the look of petulance for?" He placed her gin martini with two olives on the table and sat.

"I failed to come up with a clever remark to your comment I am a man in a woman's body."

"You can't work at being clever. Humor comes naturally." He patted her hand. "Don't worry. You've been mighty clever tonight. Your banter with Judge Newman thrilled me." He nodded toward the martini.

"Try your drink."

She sipped the martini and sighed. It tasted as cold and stark as a starless sky in winter. The sharp aftertaste lingered on her tongue, begging for another sip. Why couldn't her life be as perfect as that?

"I take it you like it," he said.

"Of course, I do. It's perfect." She admired his thoughtfulness. "Like you."

He stood, turned his chair, and straddled the seat.

She pinched the skin between her eyebrows. "Why are you straddling the chair like a cowboy?"

He stood, turned his chair, and sat with his legs crossed. "I wanted to prove a point."

"You're an uncouth imbecile?"

"No. I'm not perfect." He leaned back and crossed his arms over his chest. "Don't place men on pedestals. We'll fall and bruise our egos. We're actually very fragile."

She laughed.

When he frowned, the lines cupping the sides of his mouth deepened. "I'm serious. That's why I'm not married. Every woman I've met treats me like a superhero. They want me to rescue them." He pointed to his chest. "I can't even rescue myself. I'm a hopeless boy trapped in a man's body."

She swallowed, ashamed of the fire of desire sweeping through her body. "I'm sorry."

"Don't worry," he said. "We all have our issues. You're gifted and talented at working with basket cases. Like the woman who attempted suicide when her husband left her for her brother. You swept into the situation and found her the help she needed. Did you know she's now a psychologist specializing in posttraumatic stress disorder, and she's engaged? Last week, I met with her and her fiancé to write a prenuptial agreement. She kept talking about how you saved her life and how grateful she still is. That's why I can tell you anything. I respect you." He flashed a wide smile. "Even though you're a man trapped in a very attractive woman's body."

Confident in the compliment, she laughed. A soft glow of satisfaction incited her, and she smiled. How delightful to know Sonya recovered from depression and transformed her life.

By the time the first course arrived, Darcy relaxed enough to ignore her physical attraction toward Victor and just enjoy his company. Sure, he lacked Betty's enthusiastic retelling of courtroom dramas and softball escapades, but he entertained her with his quick-witted banter and chivalrous hospitality.

Before dessert, the auctioneer announced a raffle for a $50,000 Desire Our Hearts diamond ring. Tickets cost one hundred dollars each. Volunteers walked from table to table selling tickets. The beautifully cut diamond sparkled in a white gold setting. Darcy shuddered when she thought of the plain yellow gold wedding bands she and Nathan wore for eight years. Would she still be married if she sported a two-carat princess-cut diamond ring? Or would she struggle to pawn it once the marriage ended?

"Would you like to buy a ticket?" the young lady asked.

Darcy stared at the facets and marveled how each one reflected a tiny rainbow. As a young girl, she thought rainbows meant magic and magic meant miracles and miracles meant anything she wanted to happen could happen. She shook her head. "No, thank you," she mumbled.

"The money helps a good cause," the young lady said.

"I know, but I can't." She cringed, ashamed of her financial situation.

"I'll buy you a ticket." Victor removed his wallet and handed the young lady his credit card.

"No, don't." She grasped his wrist to stop the transaction.

Frowning, he yanked away his arm. "Please, what woman doesn't believe diamonds are a girl's best friend?"

She glanced around to see if anyone was listening. Confident she would not be overheard, she leaned closer. "A man trapped in a woman's body."

"Touché." He flashed a crooked smile. "But I'm still buying you a ticket." He placed the red raffle ticket in the palm of her hand.

A bolt of energy zigzagged up her arm. She curled her fingers over the ticket and held it against her heart, secretly hoping she might win. If she wore the ring, people would constantly ask about her engagement. Some would react like Judge Newman and say, "Aren't you lucky lesbians can marry?" She cringed. If she won, then she would lock the ring in a safety deposit box until she died. She uncurled her fingers and gazed at the crumpled ticket. What a waste of money, she thought. She wished he spent it on more gin martinis.

"Why the sour face?" he asked.

She hesitated. "What will I do if I win the ring?"

"I don't know." He shrugged. "Keep it, I guess. Or donate it to someone who really wants it." He caught her gaze. "Maybe your lesbian lover." He winked.

She picked up her auction paddle and swatted his arm.

He lifted his almost-empty martini glass for a toast. "You really are clever."

"Not as clever as you."

Wagging his head, he shook his finger. "Now, now, don't be a man and turn this into a competition. Just take the compliment like a lady."

Darcy sighed. She never took anything graciously. "Maybe you're right, and I am a man trapped in a woman's body."

Victor leaned over and kissed her lips.

Her whole body flooded with excitement. "Why did you do that?"

"To see if you would turn into a man." His gaze swept over her body. "You still look like a woman to me."

Biting her lower lip, she could taste the bitterness of his martini on her tongue. She wanted him to kiss her again.

He finished his drink.

After dessert, the auctioneer walked onto the stage to announce the winner of the diamond ring. He plunged his hand into a silver bucket and withdrew a ticket. He read the winning number.

She checked the numbers on her ticket, her palm sweating. She lost. Sighing, she handed Victor the ticket.

Again, the auctioneer read the numbers.

Victor studied the ticket and frowned.

"Are you disappointed?" she asked.

He held her gaze a moment longer. "Not really."

"And why is that?"

"I only bought one ticket. The odds were stacked against us."

"But one ticket is all we needed."

"Sometimes, winning takes more than just one try."

"I hope you don't say that to your clients." Yawning, she slid back the chair.

"Are you leaving?" He stood.

"Yes." A flash of disappointment descended over her shoulders. "I think I'll go."

"Let me walk you to your car."

"But you'll miss the live auction and the dancing."

He offered his arm. "I'd rather spend the time with you."

A touch of kinship united them.

She wove her arm through his. How delightful to find someone who enjoyed her company as much as she enjoyed his.

Matching strides, they walked around the tables of guests. A few people stopped them to comment on how cute a couple they made.

She blushed from the compliments.

He nudged open the double doors.

A gust of cool summer air blasted against her face. She shivered.

He tugged her closer. "Would you like my jacket?"

"No, thank you. I'm parked over there." She waved toward the left.

They strode over to an ancient sports sedan.

Darcy unlocked her door and tossed her clutch inside. As she turned to say good night, she trembled with anticipation. Would he kiss her again?

Standing in silence, he gazed into her eyes.

A flicker of desire lapped at her feet and licked up into her belly. She had never seen eyes so big, so bold, and so beautiful. Oh, why wouldn't he kiss her?

Finally, he pulled her into his arms and squeezed her. His tender lips brushed against the tangle of her hair. Every fiber of her body melted against his firm muscles. Waiting, she held her breath.

"Good night," he whispered.

No kiss? "Good night." She stumbled out of his arms and grabbed the car door for balance as she sank onto the car's cracked leather front seat.

"Drive safely," he said.

The excitement from the evening deflated like a leaking helium balloon. She closed the door and fumbled with the ignition. She backed out of the parking spot and glanced in her rearview mirror.

He strolled to the convention center with his hands thrust into his pockets.

Fighting against the impulse to brake and shift the car in reverse, she clenched the steering wheel. After all, she couldn't invite him to her place to spend the night. She lived in a rented room in someone else's house. Humiliation slapped her face. What was she thinking? She was too old for him anyway. She shuddered and sped away, desperate to save herself from the heartbreak of falling in love.

Chapter 3

On Monday morning a little after eight o'clock, Darcy strolled into Katie's Koffee. The whir of the espresso machine and the clatter of plates competed with the shout of customers' names announcing completed orders. The sugary sweetness of freshly baked pastries enticed Darcy, but the temptation lost against her desire to maintain her weight.

The barista called her name.

Darcy picked up her cappuccino and scanned the room, looking for her best friend.

With her head bent over her phone as she texted, Betty sat at a table beside the window overlooking the main street.

Darcy sighed. In the three years she had known Betty, Darcy had never seen her without her phone. Sometimes, Darcy wondered if Betty slept at all. The woman and her phone seemed inseparable. "Hey." Darcy sat next to Betty.

"Hey." Without glancing up, Betty continued texting.

Darcy sipped the foam off the top of her cappuccino and stared out the window at the passing traffic. In a couple of hours, she would be sitting at a conference table with Monica for moral support as she finalized the last steps of her divorce. Darcy wondered how sitting with her daughter at such a table in the near future would feel. Oh, why did she have to be so cynical? What if Joyce beat the odds and celebrated her silver wedding anniversary?

Placing aside her phone, Betty glanced up. Her wide brown eyes appeared larger through her glasses. She brushed away the black bangs from her forehead and squinted. "Are you all right?"

Darcy flashed a tight smile. "Just peachy."

"Uh-oh." Betty pulled a frown. "What happened?"

Darcy bowed her head. "My daughter wants to get married. And she asked me to be her wedding planner."

Smiling, Betty squeezed Darcy's hand. "That's great news!"

Tension knotted in her stomach. She shook aside Betty's hand and spread her arms wide as if to encompass the entire room. "She's ruining her life."

Betty deepened her frown. "Not every marriage ends in divorce. Yeah, sure, fifty percent do, but look at Chucky and me. We've been together since the millennium, and we're still going strong."

She didn't want to remind her friend over sixty percent of second marriages ended in divorce and just because her marriage hadn't ended yet didn't mean it wouldn't. She took another sip of her bitter cappuccino and sighed. "I just wish she'd tamper her enthusiasm about the whole venture."

Gasping, Betty widened her gaze. "Why should she? Don't you remember the excitement of planning your own wedding?"

"Not as well as I remember planning my divorce."

"Not everyone ends up miserable." Betty patted the back of her hand. "Time to let go of the past and embrace the future." She raised her mocha. "Here's a toast to your daughter's happily-ever-after."

Darcy sat immobile. She thought of the drudgery of living daily with a man who she thought she loved but who didn't love her enough to refuse the advances of another woman. Would her daughter suffer the same fate? Or was her marriage to Nathan an anomaly?

Betty nudged her foot underneath the table. "Don't be a party pooper!"

"I'm not." Darcy twisted a napkin in her lap. "I just don't believe in the fairy tale any longer."

"One more reason to plan your daughter's wedding." Betty pointed at Darcy's chest. "Time to get back the spark."

Acres of numbness stretched inside her. "I don't think I ever felt the magic."

Betty's phone rang. She glanced at the screen and furrowed her brow. "I'm sorry, but I have to take this call. Don't go anywhere. I'll be back." She stood and exited the coffee shop.

Cradling her cup of coffee, Darcy observed the other patrons at the counter pouring cream and dumping packets of sugar into their cups. Maybe she harbored resentment because her entire business revolved around the unprofitable, revenge-driven divorce industry instead of the overpriced, hope-driven wedding industry. Betty might be right. A shift in focus could bring a fresh perspective and revive her bank account.

A persistent ringing jolted Darcy out of her thoughts. She glanced at the unknown number on her phone. "Hello?"

"Darcy," a man said. "Great time at the Gala. Too bad we didn't win the diamond ring."

"Victor?" Darcy almost choked on her breath. Her

heartbeat stuttered in her chest. Could he be calling to ask her on a date? "How did you get my number?"

"Not many divorce planners are listed in the directory," he said. "I called because I have a referral."

"Oh, right." She slumped forward. Why had she envisioned him asking for a date? She fumbled in her purse for a pen and grabbed a napkin. "I'm listening."

"Here's the situation. He's a stay-at-home dad. She's an executive wife. Lots of money. No time. Need to divorce fast. Keep things quiet. But I can't handle my client who's emotional and full of high drama. I need your help with the non-legal stuff. Are you interested?"

She jotted down a few notes. "How much is the wife willing to spend?"

"I don't know." He laughed. "I represent the husband. But I figure since she's letting him stay in their house in Petaluma while she works and lives in San Jose, she'd be willing to pay any amount of money to get rid of him."

Thinking, she tapped the blunt end of her pen against the table. Could she work with a self-indulgent, spoiled stay-at-home dad? "I'm not cheap. I donate my services to Legal Aid, but I still need to pay my rent."

"He put up a twenty-thousand-dollar retainer for my services."

Tingling raced through her body. With a few clients like him, she could stop living off savings and start saving for a house, she thought.

"Oh, and one more thing," Victor said. "He's high maintenance."

The higher the maintenance, the higher the price, she thought. "I'll call him immediately."

"Good. I knew I could count on you." Victor

recited Gary's number and ended the call.

With her hands on her hips, Betty stood beside the table. "Who called?"

"Victor." Darcy tucked the napkin with Gary's phone number into her purse. "We attended the Gala together." Heat flamed her cheeks when she met Betty's gaze. "Well, not together-together." She waved her hand and glanced at the floor. "Anyway, he called because he has a referral."

"That's great. You need the business." Betty grabbed her mocha and leaned down for a hug. "I'm sorry, but I have to go. Change in court time. But tell me quickly, did you enjoy the Gala?"

Darcy wrapped her arms around Betty and squeezed her friend. She smelled of floral soap and felt as soft and comforting as a teddy bear. "The food lacked imagination. The band played songs I didn't know."

"But you had fun?"

Releasing Betty, Darcy shrugged. She didn't want to confess she enjoyed the evening and Victor's company. She didn't want to admit to anyone she found Victor to be a good man with good looks and good potential. "I know you have to go, but tell me about the softball tournament."

Betty jumped up and down like a cheerleader. "Chuck's team won!"

"That's wonderful!" She smiled. "I'm glad you attended."

Betty's phone beeped. She shifted her weight and scowled at the screen. "I really have to go. See you here same time next week." She stalked away a few feet then paused and turned. Narrowing her gaze, she pointed with her mocha. "Promise me, no raining on your daughter's parade, okay? She might only get married once. You need to keep the wedding special."

As if swearing to testify before a jury, Darcy raised her hand. "I promise."

****

Later that night, Darcy nudged a shopping cart down the cereal aisle of a twenty-four-hour grocery store. Her cell rang in her purse. When she recognized Joyce's caller ID, she clenched her teeth. Oh, no, Darcy thought. What does she want?

A throbbing headache pulsed against her skull. She held her breath, not wanting to respond to the insistent ringtone. How could she talk to Joyce calmly after she argued with Nathan about planning the wedding and after she promised Betty she would be joyful in the midst of her dismay? Why plan a wedding when she had enough problems planning a divorce?

The phone stopped ringing. Exhaling, she relaxed her shoulders and scanned the row of cereal boxes for something without too much sugar.

Seconds later, the phone rang again.

She ignored the sound.

After a brief pause, the phone trilled again.

Tension bristled across her shoulders. She seized her phone and swiped her finger across the screen. "Hey, sweetheart." She parked her cart against a shelf full of frosted flakes.

"Mom, Tyler and I have chosen the tenth of June as our wedding date. I know it's technically less than twelve months away, but I'm sure we can find a venue. What do you think of the places I've sent you?"

A tangle of nerves tightened in her gut. Sure, she

read the emails her daughter forwarded about wedding venues, but she only clicked on a few links before the possibilities overwhelmed her: church or secular, indoor or outdoor, hosted or no-host bar, buffet or formal dining. How could she narrow it down? She squeezed her cell phone against her ear. "I haven't had time to look. I thought we could browse the venues together."

A sigh whooshed. "Mom, of all people, you know you have to call in advance to make reservations to preview a place. Why haven't you made any calls?"

Because she had been working every day, including the weekend, and that's why she was shopping at eight-thirty when she should be home enjoying dinner like most people, Darcy thought. She tightened her stance. "Okay, I promise I'll take a look tonight and make some calls tomorrow." She tapped her foot. "Am I going to these places alone? Or are you coming up? If you want a say in what I decide, then I'll need to know when you are available."

"This weekend," Joyce said. "I made reservations at a bed and breakfast to see if the place is a possibility for our honeymoon night."

"Is Tyler joining us?" Darcy met him once and could not remember much about him.

"He can't since he's working in Washington DC," Joyce said. "Send me an email with the venues we have appointments for. I want to make sure we see as many places as possible within the two days before I make my decision."

For Darcy, a weekend of just the two of them felt as refreshing as a glass of lemonade after a hot afternoon by the pool. Since Joyce graduated from

Stanford, they'd spent little time together. The wedding planning almost didn't matter. "No problem." A tingle of anticipation prickled her skin. "I'm looking forward to spending the weekend with you."

Chapter 4

When she drove up to a five-thousand-square-foot, single level villa on a five-acre hobby vineyard in Petaluma on Wednesday morning, Darcy sighed with longing. Her dream home! The house perched far enough west to gather the fog bank from the coast every morning and far enough south to avoid the tunnel of wind blowing through the city every night. Gary, her soon-to-be divorced client, lived in the home with his two children.

After brief introductions, Gary led Darcy through a tiled foyer into a great room next to a gourmet kitchen. A wonderful aroma of eggs, cheese, and onions filled the room.

Darcy took a seat at the breakfast bar and glanced around the gourmet kitchen. Oh, what she would give to own a five-burner gas stove and a stainless steel refrigerator full of her own food and not cluttered with her roommates' leftovers. A pang of envy clutched her chest, and she glanced away, ashamed of wanting something she could never have.

Gary's children, four-year-old Paul and three-year-old Patty, played trucks and dolls, respectively, on the veranda while their father prepared breakfast.

"Mimosa for the young lady." Gary set the champagne flute on the bar. "And two fruit smoothies for the kids." He set the smoothies on the table in the breakfast nook.

The children glanced up, carried their toys inside, and shut the French doors. Paul climbed up on the bench seat and used a spoon to scoop out the fresh strawberry garnish. Patty dipped a straw into the glass and sipped.

They behaved well for preschoolers, Darcy thought. She wondered how much to attribute to Gary's parenting style and how much to credit their genetic temperament.

The timer on the oven dinged. With an "I Love The Chef" oven mitt, Gary removed an egg-and-cheese casserole and placed it on top of the stove to cool. He took a swig of his mimosa and chased it with a gulp of black coffee.

When Darcy thought of the self-indulgent house husband, she imagined a super fit man who spent his days working out like her ex-husband. The fantasy dissolved into the reality of an overweight and out-of-shape, middle-aged, bald man moping with depression. His gray eyes reflected the looks shared by other stay-at-home parents who worried how they would manage a household, find a job, and care for the most important people in their lives while undergoing a stressful divorce.

"I hope you like onions." He gestured toward the casserole. "Paul and Patty love green onions with their eggs."

"Green onions are better than green eggs and ham." Paul tossed back his head, shaking the brown bangs from his wide forehead.

"Sing that song, Daddy." Patty bounced up and down, her auburn pony tail swaying from side to side.

Gary cleared his throat. "La-la-la-la-la," he began. "Green onions beat the jar of jam and made it to the frying pan where eggs and cheese and spices roast. Would you like some on your toast?"

Paul and Patty giggled. "Sing it again, Daddy!"

Gary sang the ditty once more.

Paul and Patty joined him. When the song ended, Paul and Patty swung their feet underneath the table and said, "We're going to sing the alphabet. A, B, C, D, E, F, G. I love you. Do you love me?"

"H, I, J, K, L, M, N, O, P," Gary sang. "Hugs and kisses from Daddy."

"Q, R, S. Where's Mommy?" Patty placed a hand above her eyes and swept her gaze around the room.

"T, U, V. She's with me." Paul pointed to his chest.

"W, X, Y, and Z." Gary's eyes watered. "Next time, tell her to see me." His voice broke.

A crinkle inched across her scalp. Was she a guest star on a twisted episode of a preschool television show?

"I want some eggs." Patty jumped off the bench and raced over to the kitchen island. She wrapped her arms around Gary's legs and squeezed him close.

Gary patted her head.

Rushing over to his father, Paul flung his arms around them both.

Gary wobbled back and forth with a smile on his face.

The children giggled.

As soon as the children released him, Gary cut the casserole and placed their servings on pink and blue plastic plates.

The children carried their full plates to the table

and ate in silence.

Gary placed a healthy serving of casserole on white china and offered it to Darcy.

The green onions added just enough punch to the firm eggs, and the gooey cheese melted in Darcy's mouth. What a great cook! No wonder his CEO wife married him.

"When the kids are done, I'll let them watch a half hour of TV so we can talk business." Gary took his plate and sat between Paul and Patty.

Darcy remained seated at the kitchen bar, although she craved another helping of the casserole.

Like a mind reader, Gary stood, sliced another serving, and placed the egg casserole on her plate. He refilled her mimosa and poured himself another cup of coffee before sitting with his children.

After breakfast, the children stacked their plates in a pile, and Gary carried them to the kitchen sink where he let them soak in sudsy water. He turned on the TV to PBS and led Darcy to the adjacent study. "Daddy and Darcy are talking about helping Daddy take care of things while Mommy's gone. If you need anything, just come in, okay?"

Without glancing away from the TV, the children nodded.

Gary shut the door to the study. Morning sunlight slanted through the blinds and fell like a spotlight on the mahogany table in the center of the room.

"You're incredible." Darcy took a seat. "If my ex-husband had been half as talented with the children as you are, we would not have needed a nanny, and we might still be married."

A straight line creased his face. He slumped into a

chair, buried his face into his hands, and sighed. "When does the loneliness go away?"

Concern washed over her. She patted his arm. "How long have you been separated?"

He dropped his hands, lifted his face, and shrugged. "She left us here six months ago to work on location three days a week. Four months ago, she started coming home only on the weekends. Two months later, her visits trickled down to every other weekend. Last month, she stopped coming home at all. This week, a stranger served the papers while Paul and Patty attended preschool."

Gasping, she widened her eyes. "The kids don't know?"

He wagged his head from side to side. "I can't break their hearts."

"They must know *something* is wrong."

"They think Daddy is having a hard time with both of them in preschool. That's why they think I kept them home today and made their favorite breakfast."

"You have to tell them the truth eventually." Darcy ruffled through the papers in her briefcase and removed a sheet of resources. "I have counselors you and the children can talk to, including those with sliding fee scales if you don't have insurance."

"Money's not the issue. We have plenty." He sniffed back the tears. "The problem is everything else: my wife, my children, my family, and my future."

"I understand." She touched his elbow. "Right now, you feel like your life is over."

He folded his arms on the table, buried his head into the space they formed, and sobbed.

With the practice of someone who often witnessed

men reduced to tears, she patted his shoulder.

His sobbing escalated.

Glancing over her shoulder at the door, she worried the children might hear him. "You will be all right." She squeezed his arm. "I've worked with hundreds of divorcing people, and everyone feels better in the end. Every single one. You just have to trust me and trust the process, okay?"

He lifted his head and wiped at his swollen eyes with the tissue she offered him. "You must think I'm just a big baby. No wonder my wife probably left me for a real man."

"That's not what I think." She opened her arms to encompass the room. "You're a talented father who has captivated the hearts of his children. What's not to love?"

"I'm old." He stared at his stomach. "I'm fat. I'm balding. I never graduated from college. I can't balance a checkbook or change the oil in a car."

"You are healthy." As she spoke, she curled each finger toward her palm. "You bake a great egg-and-cheese casserole. You entertain your children as you teach."

Sighing, he slumped against the chair. "I sound like a woman trapped in a man's body."

Recalling Victor's compliment about her being a man trapped in a woman's body, she flinched. Gary's self-depreciating remark reflected his fragile self-esteem just as much as Darcy's bravado reflected her calloused wisdom. Gary and Darcy mirrored two sides of the same coin. Her heart softened with compassion. "You sound like a man going through a divorce." She slid the set of papers across the table. "I'm here to help.

My services are grouped by packages or as a la carte. I'm not cheap, but I do deliver what I promise. These former clients are my references. Feel free to contact any of them."

Gary shuffled through the papers.

"Any questions?"

He pointed to the list of packaged services. "I can get all of these options for this price?"

The premium package included unlimited phone calls and emails, both day and night, during the entire divorce, up to and including a year after the final judgment. When she began her business twenty years ago, she hesitated to include such a generous offer until she realized she exclusively provided the service. All of her competitors coordinated appointments with vendors for every service listed, but none of them doubled as a paid friend, which people most needed.

"Even if you decide not to hire me, I recommend you start taking better care of yourself so you can continue to nurture your children. That means talking to a counselor, seeing a psychiatrist for anti-depressants, and beefing up your exercise routine, and possibly adding a little meditation."

"What about sex?" He pouted.

Darcy inhaled sharply. After all these years, people's request for sexual services startled her. She searched in her briefcase for another sheet of paper and slid it across the table.

Gary scanned the list of escort, massage, and other professional, sexual service providers before shaking his head. "I don't want to pay for it."

"You can search dating sites. I've heard favorable things from clients who've found partners online."

Tears welled in his gray eyes.

Darcy tensed her shoulders. Please, don't have another meltdown, she thought.

The door swung open, and two sets of feet scampered into the room. Paul and Patty flung their arms around their father and shouted, "Let's play."

"Daddy will play with you both after he's finished." A smile creased his face and a twinkle glimmered in his eyes.

"When are you going to be done?" Paul tilted his head and widened his eyes.

"Soon," he said.

"How soon?" Patty asked.

"Five minutes." He held up his hand and wiggled his fingers.

"I can count to five minutes," Paul said.

"I can, too!" Patty said.

"Why don't you both go into the great room to do your counting?" Gary suggested.

The children bounded out of the room without shutting the door.

Gary stood and nudged the door closed. "I'll accept the premium package, but I want you to add one more service."

Darcy stiffened her back. Please, no sex, she thought. Anything but sex. Of course, she fantasized about getting romantically involved with some clients, but none asked for a sexual favor, and she never offered any.

He narrowed his eyes. "Revenge."

Smiling, she relaxed her shoulders. "Deal!" She shook his hand. "Happiness is the best revenge."

Chapter 5

Searching for possible wedding venues after work on a Thursday afternoon, Darcy sat cross-legged on the living room sofa with her laptop propped between her knees. Through the open window, the scent of freshly mown grass drifted on the summer breeze. She typed into the search engine: wedding venues, Sonoma County. A list of possibilities filled the screen.

Click. A tab opened to weddings on the golf course. She scanned the offering. Nope. Joyce didn't like sports.

Click. A tab opened to weddings at wineries. She scrolled through the photographs of luscious vineyards against the backdrop of mountains. How romantic. She searched for a list of local wineries to make appointments for this weekend.

Her phone rang.

She lunged for the phone on the coffee table, and the computer slid from her lap. "Hello?"

"Good news," Monica said. "My ex signed."

For a moment, Darcy's breath caught in her throat. Had she heard Monica correctly? "He signed?"

"Yes, he did. I have a copy of the notarized documents. We just have to wait six to eight weeks for the judge to sign, and then the nightmare will be over. I'll be officially divorced."

"Congratulations! I'm so glad it's over." She

recalled Monica's patience as she endured countless setbacks over the last year, from struggling to find an attorney through Legal Aid to battling with an unreasonable man who felt entitled to everything. Relief flooded her. She swung her legs off the sofa with excitement. "Let me throw you a divorce party to celebrate."

Monica squealed. "How many people can I invite?"

"As many as you want since I'm paying." She did not worry about the expense. From experience, only a handful of loyal friends would show up to enjoy a quiet dinner. Most people, especially married couples, believed divorce spread as infectiously as the swine flu.

"Thank you, thank you, thank you," Monica said. "I can't wait to celebrate!"

"The party will be so much fun." Much more fun, she thought, than planning her daughter's wedding.

****

The next morning, Darcy met Gary at his residence to review the next steps in his divorce. With the children at preschool, the house echoed with silence. Gary led Darcy to the patio. He poured a splash of brandy into his coffee.

When he waved the bottle at her mug, she shook her head. She needed clarity this early in the morning. In the near distance, the sun shone through the emerald leaves of the hobby vineyard. The dusty air hinted at the upcoming grape harvest. Darcy glanced up at the peek-a-boo clouds then down into Gary's deep-set, gray eyes. Those eyes seemed as troubled and depressed as they had a couple of days ago. A pang of empathy squeezed her chest. Gary would have looked like an unkempt man if she had not witnessed his housekeeper ironing his laundered clothes. "Did you call any of the counselors I recommended?"

He shook his head. "I started crying every time I talked to them so I just gave up."

"I can arrange appointments if you sign a medical directive." She reached into her briefcase and withdrew a sample document. "Most insurance companies allow you to have someone manage your case, regardless of whether or not you're in a health crisis."

"Okay." With a pen, he filled out the form and scribbled his signature.

She tucked the document in her briefcase. On her notepad, she wrote, *Make appointments for anti-depressants and talk therapy.* "How are the legal plans coming along?"

He shrugged. "I'll finish my response this weekend. I just need someone to take it to Victor."

"I'll do it." She jotted a reminder on her notepad and glanced at the To Do list she began for him. "Have you started your Income and Expense Declaration or your Schedule of Assets and Debts?"

"No." He folded his arms on the table and buried his head.

She patted his shoulder. "I know divorce is hard, especially at first, but trust me, the process gets better."

As he sobbed, he shuddered.

She removed her hand and stared across the hobby vineyard. She sighed with longing. When she sold her townhouse in Los Angeles and moved to Sonoma County, she envisioned owning a home like Gary's. From listening to his sobs, she suspected owning a piece of paradise did not guarantee happiness. "Do you have family nearby?"

He shook his head and stared with red, swollen eyes. Snot dripped from his nose. "I have no one," he sobbed, "except the kids. My parents are ashamed of me. My siblings don't understand. They're all happily married and blame me for the divorce. They say I couldn't keep her interested."

She nodded. "The alpha female always wants an alpha male."

He slammed his fist against the table. Coffee sloshed inside the mugs. "Damn it, Darcy. I'm not a beta male. I'm a human being."

Why had she made that callous statement? She leaned away from his spark of anger. Not every high-powered, career woman needed a domineering man. Subservient men like Gary balanced the relationship, preventing the tug-of-war for control most couples experienced. What could she say to repair her faux pas? "You're amazing with your kids."

"Not enough for her." He wiped the snot on his shirt sleeve and swept his arm across the backyard. "She wanted more. More money, more glamour, more power, more prestige, more everything."

What more could a woman want with a property like this? "Is she seeing someone else?"

He shook his head. "I don't know, and I don't care, but I wouldn't be surprised if she hooked up with a younger, handsomer man." He stood and pointed to his stomach. "Look at me. I'm old and out-of-shape and homely. Who wants to be married to that man?"

She glanced at his balding head, his saggy jaw, his man boobs, and his beer belly. Yes, Gary could not double as Mr. Olympia or James Bond, but he loved with all of his heart. What woman wouldn't want to come home to that man? Kathleen and countless other women like her, Darcy thought, herself included. Embarrassment flushed her face. How could she reassure him when she shared his soon to be ex-wife's sentiment?

"It's not fair." Gary clenched his fists on the tabletop. "I never thought I'd be in the prime of my life and alone with two small children who haven't even started elementary school. I have another fifteen years of loneliness ahead of me. I just want to curl up and die."

A sharp intake of breath caught in Darcy's throat. No matter how unattractive she found him, she couldn't let him commit suicide. "The depression is talking, and not you." She cupped a hand over his rough fist and squeezed until the muscles in his hand relaxed and his fingers uncurled. "You have to keep it together for the children."

Moisture blurred his gray eyes. The hard lines around his mouth softened. "What about me?"

Darcy laced her fingers with his and held up his hand to show a united front. "I'm here for you. That's why you hired me. My job is to do anything you need to help you successfully make it through to the other side. You won't be lonely forever, and you have tons of things beside your children to look forward to and enjoy." She took in a deep breath and exhaled. "Look around you." With her free hand, she gestured to their exotic surroundings, from the flagstone patio and the black, wrought iron safety gate surrounding the pool and hot tub with the tropical theme of palm trees and tiki torches, to the lush vineyards ripening with grapes which would, through a process over time, become a fine merlot. The quiet serenity of the backyard enveloped them with peace. "See the beauty of this place? I don't know if you'll keep this house or not, but right now, it's yours. Enjoy it. Most people spend their whole lives working to own something like this, and they never achieve it." Her voice thickened with tears.

Gary blinked his eyes. He squeezed her hand before releasing it. "You're right." He forced a smile. "I've been lucky."

Darcy nodded. "You still are lucky."

He deepened his smile. "I'm lucky to have hired you."

A glow of satisfaction swept over her body.

****

"Knock-knock," Linda said. "You have company."

Darcy opened her bedroom door and peered at Linda, a social butterfly with the energy of a two-year-old and the vocabulary of a teenager. At sixty-five, Linda could retire but she preferred to work part-time at the salon she once managed. She wore her dyed burgundy hair in a beehive and dressed in decades-old clothes. Although Darcy still felt awkward living with someone unrelated, she loved how quiet and respectful Linda treated her. Darcy wondered who would visit on a Friday night, since she spent most Fridays with the five other members of her Books and Booze Club discussing literature and drinking gin martinis until the restaurant closed. She expected Joyce tomorrow morning. "Who is it?"

After flashing a grin, Linda popped the chewing gum in her mouth. "She wants her visit to be a surprise."

Darcy frowned, hoping none of the members of her book club decided to show up. Since she spent all of her free time booking appointments for possible venues for Joyce's wedding, she hadn't finished reading *Frankenstein.* "I'll be right out." Darcy closed her bedroom door. She slipped into a pair of jeans and a light sweater, grabbed her battered paperback, and shoved it into her purse. I need a drink, she thought, swaggering down the hallway and rounding the corner into the foyer.

"Surprise!"

When she spied Joyce, fresh from work in her business suit and heels, standing before her, Darcy dropped her jaw. "Baby!" She flung her arms around her daughter and hugged her. Joyce smelled as sweet as peaches and felt as thin as a paper doll.

Joyce giggled. "Oh, Mom! I'm glad you're as happy to see me as I am to see you."

Darcy stepped back and studied her daughter. Joyce had the same beach-blonde hair and sparkling blue eyes as her father with Darcy's high cheekbones and broad bone structure. She wondered if her daughter worked so much she forgot to eat. Darcy wrapped an arm around Joyce's shoulders. "I assume you've both made introductions."

"Oh, yes." Linda smiled. "We were talking about how you're planning her wedding."

"That's right." Joyce squeezed together her palms. "We plan to find the perfect venue tomorrow."

"Have you eaten?"

"No." She pivoted. "Have you?"

"I haven't." She placed a hand over her grumbling stomach. "Let me call my book club to let them know I won't be there tonight, and then we'll leave for dinner." She envisioned hot rolls slathered with lots of butter to pack a few pounds on her scrawny daughter's frame. "I know the perfect place."

Chapter 6

"Mom, I can't eat anything here." Joyce shook her head.

A cool evening breeze tunneled between them as they stood on the sidewalk outside Bella Mia, an Italian restaurant in Railroad Square.

"What's wrong with the food they serve?" Darcy pointed at the menu in the window.

Joyce threw up her arms. "I don't eat meat or gluten."

A brief scan of the items confirmed her suspicion. "They serve more than veal parmesan and pasta. They also offer salads and eggplant." Grabbing her daughter's hand, she tugged her into the comfortable lobby.

A hostess seated them in a booth where the dimmed lights and pungent scents of oregano and basil created an illusion of romance and comfort.

Before browsing the menu for items she thought her daughter could eat, Darcy ordered a glass of the house red wine. The last time she dined with her daughter had been years ago when Joyce started working for Price Waterhouse in San Francisco six months after receiving her CPA license. They'd eaten at a tiny Japanese bistro. She didn't remember what either ordered. Placing her menu on the table, she leaned forward. "Are you sick?"

"No." Joyce crossed her arms over her chest. "I just don't believe in eating red meat because it messes with the quality of my skin. Gluten bloats my stomach." She narrowed her gaze and pointed. "If you stopped drinking alcohol and eating red meat and gluten, you wouldn't have a menopot."

She sucked in her gut. "I don't have a menopot."

A brief chuckle loosened the tension. "Seriously, Mom, you need to take better care of yourself. Eating pasta and drinking wine won't keep you healthy."

She expelled a lengthy sigh. Whenever she complained about their daughter's behavior, Nathan always said, "Don't let the tail wag the dog," but Nathan's advice never helped. Darcy continued to allow Joyce to say whatever she pleased. After a long week, she just wanted to relax and not spend the next hour arguing with her daughter. "Where do you want to eat?"

"Any place serving sushi."

Oh, the irony. She shook her head and chuckled. "You won't eat cooked meat, but you'll eat raw fish?"

"Fish is more sustainable."

The vanity of the younger generation amazed her. Keep a flat stomach and poison your offspring, she thought. "What about all the mercury leading to autism in newborns?"

"I'm not pregnant so I don't have to worry about autism."

"But when you decide to get pregnant, you'll have built up all this toxic mercury in your system from eating fish, and you'll end up with a baby born with autism."

Joyce widened her gaze. "Stop scaring me."

She took another sip of wine. "I'm being realistic."

"You're being a Debby Downer."

Restraining an impulse to shake some sense into her daughter, Darcy leaned forward until her chest dug into the edge of the table. "I'm being protective because I'm a good mother."

Joyce leaned back. "You're smothering me."

The server stopped by their table and plucked a pen and notepad from his apron. "Have you both decided yet?"

"Yes." Joyce placed her menu face down on the table. "We'd like the check for her wine."

With the pen poised over his notepad, the server bent. "No dinner, ma'am?"

She shook her head. "Not unless you serve sushi."

"We don't have sushi, but we have a great halibut tonight with a light broth sauce and steamed vegetables."

Oh, good luck convincing her cooked fish is better than raw fish, she thought. To avoid glowering, she cupped her glass of wine and stared at her hands.

Joyce heaved a sigh. "Okay, I'll try the halibut. But I don't want any dressing on my salad, okay?"

The server nodded and took her menu. "Excellent choice. You won't be disappointed." He turned to Darcy. "And you, ma'am?"

"I'll have the lasagna," she said with a wide smile. "And another glass of the house red, please."

Joyce bit her lower lip.

"I know you want to scold me," Darcy said, once the server left. "But I'm your mother. I'll always be your mother. You have no right to tell me how to live."

"I know." She rearranged her silverware. "You're the captain of your own ship. I just wish you wouldn't sail it into the rocks all the time."

She crossed her arms on the table. "What's that supposed to mean?"

Grabbing the napkin, she placed it on her lap. "It means you shouldn't be living like a college student in someone else's house when you're five years away from being old enough to move into a retirement community. You shouldn't be wasting your time on a business which produces negative cash flow just because you like helping people with their divorces. Go back to school and finish your law degree. You only have two years left."

She wished she never let Joyce prepare her taxes when she started out. Then she wouldn't know anything about her finances.

The server returned with another glass of red wine and a basket of toasty bread.

After she grabbed a slice, Darcy slathered it with butter. She bit into it before her daughter could wince. "I'm happy."

"You'll be even happier to know Dad is getting married to Tanya in October." She rummaged in her purse, withdrew a cream-colored envelope, and slid it across the table. "You're invited to the wedding. Bring a guest."

Dread blanketed her shoulders. She squinted at the envelope and pointed to her chest. "Why would he invite me?"

"Because I asked him to." She pointed to her chest, and then opened her arms. "I want both of my parents at my wedding. Think of this wedding as a trial run. You can practice behaving nicely to each other."

She grabbed another piece of flaky bread and

buttered it. If she couldn't fill her heart with love then she could at least fill her belly with food. "I can't go." Wiping her hands on her napkin, she swallowed a soft, doughy bite. "I don't like Tanya, and I don't approve of him marrying her after all these years."

"Stop being cynical about love and relationships." She sipped from her glass of water. "Just because you refuse to date doesn't mean you can't be happy for those of us who do find our perfect mate."

She scoffed. "No one's perfect."

Shaking her finger, Joyce narrowed her gaze. "An imperfect person is out there who's perfect for you."

"Yeah, right." She snickered and gulped another mouthful of tart wine. "I've spent the majority of my working life helping those imperfect people untangle themselves from each other."

Joyce curled her fingers around her water glass, squeezed her eyes shut, and muttered under her breath. "You're impossible."

She leaned forward to speak softly. "No, I'm practical."

"You're practically driving me crazy."

Darcy glowered.

Joyce leaned back against the booth.

How could she get her daughter to drop the subject so they could enjoy each other's company? What if she said the opposite of what she desired? Would Joyce react with defiance and unintentionally give her mother what she wanted? She took a deep breath and pointed toward the restaurant's entrance. "You can leave any time."

"I'm more stubborn than you are." Joyce squared her shoulders. "I'm not leaving until you see the error of your ways."

The server returned with two salads—one without dressing and the other smothered in Italian vinaigrette.

"Can't we just eat in peace?" Darcy stabbed her drenched salad and shoved the soggy, salty mess into her mouth.

A long moment of silence stretched between them.

Finally, without saying a word, Joyce poked her salad with a fork and crunched a tomato.

By the time the main courses arrived, harmony stitched between them. They discussed neutral topics like the weather. Neither of them mentioned anything that might trigger a reaction in the other.

Darcy wondered how long the truce would last.

****

"I'm hot and tired." As she sat shotgun in Joyce's luxury sedan with the air conditioning vents directed at her flushed face on Sunday afternoon, Darcy stank with perspiration and despair.

Joyce still smelled like coconut oil and hope.

They had spent the better part of two days, speeding from one winery to the next. What a struggle to find the perfect location for Joyce's wedding. Each winery showcased a different flaw: too remote, too expensive, too homey, or too glamorous.

Joyce didn't care about the caliber of the wine but only the standard of the facility and whether or not the venue permitted sparkling water to be served.

On the other hand, Darcy wanted a place where the sun shone on the red-tipped leaves of the vineyards and the wine tasted like heaven.

"You shouldn't be complaining." Joyce signaled for another turn. "You haven't spent the better part of your weekend being disappointed."

"I just want to go home, curl up in bed, and read *The Scarlett Letter*." Especially since she missed last week's reading, she wanted to be sure to finish the assignment for the upcoming week. She gazed at the view of the city from Fountaingrove Expressway.

"You can do that after I find the perfect place to get married." She gunned the accelerator, and the luxury sedan swerved up Thomas Lake Harris Drive.

Maybe she could reason with her daughter. After all, she worked with numbers. "It's getting late, and you have a long drive home. Why don't you just come back next weekend?"

Tightening her hands against the steering wheel, Joyce swerved up another steep embankment showcasing the city views. "Because another two days with you, and I'll be one of those children who files for divorce from her mother."

"You can't divorce me." She laughed. "You're already over eighteen."

She gritted her teeth, causing her jaw to twitch.

"Don't do that." She slapped her daughter's knee. "You'll ruin the orthodontia I paid for."

She flashed a sideways glance. "I don't know why you're always so self-righteous about money. Dad and Tanya paid half."

Shaking her head, she stared at the oak trees dotting the hillside and the tiny buildings nestled against the skyline. "I paid them spousal *and* child support, which means I paid for everything."

"That statement's not true. Tanya has a job, and so does Dad. She's a nanny, remember? After you left, she took on other clients. She raised half the children in

Beverly Hills."

"While your dad wasted her money." She wagged her head, recalling the days her ex-husband spent in the garage tinkering with his designs. "Is he still working on developing some device to save the world?"

Joyce narrowed her gaze. "He's an inventor."

"Who failed more times than Edison." When would Joyce admit her father was a failure who could never financially support himself? Why did she insist on ridiculing her mother instead?

"I can't believe you." She slapped the steering wheel. "Whatever happened to believing in genius?"

Darcy leaned her forehead against the hard, warm window. "I stopped believing in your father when he stopped believing in me."

"You never had a hobby you wanted to turn into a career, so don't compare apples with oranges." She turned left through the steel gates leading up to the tasting room and drove past a wall full of face masks.

A shiver of truth snaked up Darcy's spine, as she recalled what the author Sandra Tsing Loh wrote, "If underneath the masks we wore, most of us were just silently enduring."

"Oh, look!" Slowing almost to a stop, Joyce tapped her mother's shoulder and pointed to the left.

A life-size sculpture of the word, LOVE, nestled in a clearing. Darcy didn't understand her daughter's enthusiasm over a word sculpture. "Reno has another one which says BELIEVE."

"I bet a lot of weddings happen there."

"I doubt it." Darcy shrugged. "The sign is located in the middle of the Truckee River walk downtown. How many couples want a full audience of strangers watching them exchange vows?"

"This location is different." Joyce sped to the pinnacle and parked the luxury sedan.

Darcy opened the door to a blast of heat and stretched her tired legs.

"Look at this place." She twirled with outstretched arms. "I feel like I'm in heaven." She ran to the tasting room door and spun. "Hurry, Mom! They're closing."

Darcy shuffled up the steps and cupped her hands around the glass doors to peer inside. When the tasting room clerk noticed her, Darcy waved.

The clerk walked over to the doors and opened them. The short, dark-skinned young woman with a ponytail wiped her hands on a dish towel. "I'm sorry, ma'am, but we close at four thirty."

Darcy glanced at her watch. "It's four-twenty-five. We only need five minutes to speak with the event planner to book a wedding for next June."

The clerk's gaze widened. "Our event planner isn't working today."

Sighing, she rummaged in her purse and handed her a card. "Please, have her call me."

The clerk read the card and frowned.

"Ignore the title." She pointed to the card. "I might be a divorce planner, but I'm also planning my daughter's wedding. May we come inside to see the venue?"

She glanced around. "Sure, but please look quickly. I don't want to get in trouble with my boss for letting you inside so late."

The plaque on the wall beside the glass doors stated a capacity of two hundred fifty people. That room should be large enough, Darcy thought. Joyce never had a lot of friends.

Butterscotch-colored leather sofas flanked a coffee table facing a massive stone fireplace. A tasting bar nestled in the corner. From there, the room opened into a light-filled dining room full of floor-to-ceiling windows showcasing the views of the Russian River valley. The room smelled clean with wax and lemon polish.

Joyce danced around the room, running her fingers over the furnishings. Tiny fairy lights dangled from chandeliers. On the west side of the room, floor-to-ceiling glass doors opened onto a wrap around deck overlooking the valley. She skipped outside. Leaning against the railing, she pointed south. "You can almost see the bay."

The dry air smelled of oak trees and vineyards. Darcy sighed. This place must cost a fortune, she thought.

"Look, Mom! You can see the LOVE sculpture from here."

Stepping onto the deck, she followed her daughter's pointing finger to the sculpture they had first seen from the road.

The clerk gestured to the French doors. "The back patio has a space for a band and dancing."

Darcy and Joyce walked around the deck to the platform for dancing. Several tables and chairs could be set up to accommodate dozens of guests, if needed. If not, enough space existed for a full orchestra.

Joyce clasped her hands over her heart and jumped up and down. "I want to get married here."

"Do you have a date?" the clerk asked.

"The tenth of June," Joyce said. "But if it's

booked, I'll take the next available weekend."

The clerk wrote the date on the back of Darcy's card. "Zoey, our event planner, will call you tomorrow morning. I don't have her card, but if you don't hear by noon, just call the main line and ask to speak with her."

"Thank you, Angelica," Darcy said, noticing the clerk's name tag. "You've been most helpful."

Joyce hooked arms with her mother and skipped back to the luxury sedan. "I don't want to go yet," she said. "The setting's so magical here. I want to stay until the moon rises."

Darcy scoffed. She wanted to go home, curl up with a good book, and a glass of wine. "If we stay any longer, I'm sure they'll call the cops and have us towed."

She narrowed her gaze. "I can't believe you're stealing my joy."

"I'm sorry." Since the divorce, she squelched her daughter's happiness with reminders of how things could go wrong.

"Sit with me." Joyce scooted over on the hood of the luxury sedan and patted the space beside her.

Darcy dropped her purse and climbed up beside her daughter. Their shoulders brushed. The sunset would be spectacular from this vantage point. The guests would enjoy the open air dance floor, the wrap-around deck, and the beautiful oak trees and vineyards. The summer breeze would whip through the dining hall and cool the guests who stayed inside. Oh, yes, plenty of wine would be served for everyone. Of that, Darcy would be sure, even if she had to foot the cost. Plus, photos of the bride and groom standing before the LOVE sculpture promising to honor and cherish each other for the rest of their lives would prove memorable.

Closing her eyes, Darcy sighed. If only all marriages progressed perfectly after the exchange of wedding vows, then she would be out of business. That prospect wouldn't be bad, would it? She could transition to becoming a wedding planner and take pride in getting newlyweds off to a great start. Like her daughter.

Joyce rested her head against her mother's shoulder. "I'm so happy we found this place," she whispered.

"Me, too." She kissed her daughter's forehead. Please, let the date and time be available, she thought. Joyce must not be disappointed.

Chapter 7

Darcy drove through thick morning fog until she spied Gary's estate home. Her cell phone rang. Fumbling, she placed the call on speaker. "Hello?"

"This is Zoey, the event planner at Paradise Ridge Winery. I'm sorry to be calling so early, but my work hours are seven-thirty to four-thirty," the woman said.

"No problem." She nodded. Knowing her daughter's impatience, she preferred having the event planner call sooner rather than later. "I'm looking to book my daughter's wedding at your facility on June tenth next year."

Through the speaker, Zoey shuffled papers and tapped on a keyboard. "I'm sorry, but the date is booked."

A dart of panic raced through Darcy's chest. Try another date. "What about the week before or after?"

"We're booked."

She careened into Gary's driveway and slammed the brakes. Cutting the engine, she seized the phone from her lap, and removed the call from speaker. A sharp intake of breath calmed the rising fear in her voice. "What do you mean you're booked?" She stepped out of the car into the cool, misty air smelling of new earth and fertilizer and stalked up the driveway toward the house. She promised to pick up Gary's response, which included the Income and Expense

Declaration and Schedule of Assets and Debts, from the mailbox before meeting Betty for coffee at eight.

As she typed, Zoey hummed. "Unfortunately, we only have dates available in August."

Oh, my goodness, what would Joyce say? She raked her fingers through her hair. Calm down, she thought. A solution has to be found. With the back of her hand, she wiped the perspiration off her forehead. Think like a divorce planner who can't get the mediation date the client wants. Negotiate for the win. She took a deep breath and smiled. "My daughter has her heart set on getting married in June. Can't we work out something?"

Zoey coughed. "Well, two weekend dates are booked without a deposit. If we don't receive any money by the end of the week, then I can call you back."

She perched on the cold, hard cobblestone steps and opened her purse. "I have money now." She removed her credit card. "How much do you need?"

A bright laugh punctured the tension. "I understand you're eager, but I have to call the clients first to see if they are ready to make their deposit."

"Call them. I'll give you ten minutes. If no one can pay to reserve then the date is ours." Without waiting for a response, Darcy hung up.

The front door opened. "I thought I noticed you on the video surveillance." Gary wore a long, terry cloth robe cinched at the waist and fuzzy teddy bear slippers. He waved toward the kitchen. "Want to come in for some coffee?"

"No, thank you." She shoved her credit card into her wallet and shut her purse. "I'm just here to get the paperwork. I have a meeting with a colleague for breakfast."

"Here." He opened the mailbox and removed a manila envelope.

"Thank you." Standing, she tucked the envelope under her arm. She cocked her head and studied Gary. His breath didn't reek of booze, and his eyes no longer appeared red and swollen. "You're looking good this morning. Did you enjoy the weekend?"

"After you left, I made an appointment with a therapist." He stood taller. "My first appointment is today after I drop off the kids at preschool."

"Good." One less item off her To-Do list, she thought. Shifting the paperwork from underneath her arm, she wrapped him in an embrace.

He held her tightly against his chest and mumbled. "I couldn't go through this process without you."

A thrill of pleasure swelled within her whenever a client took her advice. She patted his back. "I'm glad I'm here to help."

When he stepped back, tears glinted in his eyes.

"You'll get through this divorce, and you'll be stronger because of it." She squeezed his hand. "I'll call you this afternoon to see how you're doing, okay?"

He nodded.

She waved the manila envelope. "I'll make sure Victor gets this paperwork today."

"Thank you, Darcy."

Her smile softened. She loved feeling the satisfaction of helping someone in need during the darkest moments of divorce. "You're welcome."

As soon as Darcy steered into the parking lot of Katie's Koffee, her phone rang.

"Ms. Madison, I have good news," Zoey said. "The weekend of June tenth has opened. What time will the venue be needed?"

She dumped out her purse on her passenger's seat to look for her wedding planner notebook. "It's an afternoon wedding with the reception starting at six and ending around nine."

"And the officiant is?"

Had they decided on an officiant? She couldn't find any notes about priests, rabbis, or reverends in her wedding planner notebook. "Do you have any recommendations?"

"No, ma'am, we're not allowed to give referrals. I'll leave the question blank for now. How about the caterer?"

Flipping through pages of the wedding planner notebook, she scanned the information. "No one at this moment. The bride and groom wanted to secure the venue first."

"Charlie's BBQ and Pacific Connection cater a lot of our events."

She tilted her head and tapped her lower lip with a pencil. "I thought you aren't allowed to give referrals."

"I'm not referring anyone," she said. "I'm just stating they've catered several events here."

Darcy's phone beeped. "Hold on a second. I need to see who is contacting me." She held the phone away from her ear and gazed at Betty's number. She swiped her finger across the screen. "I'm in the parking lot talking to a winery coordinator for my daughter's wedding. Please order me a cappuccino, and I'll be inside as soon as possible."

"I've already ordered for you," Betty said. "How

much longer will you be?"

"I need to answer a few more questions and place a deposit."

"Well, hurry up. I have a nine o'clock, and your cappuccino is getting cold."

Darcy switched lines. "Thank you for waiting." Elevator music piped over the line. Zoey had placed her on hold. With her free hand, she shoved items back into her purse.

"Hello?" Zoey said.

"I'm back," Darcy said. "I'm late for another appointment. How much longer do we have?"

"Not much longer. I just need to know if a band or a DJ will perform."

"Either or." She rested the pencil against her chin. "We haven't decided on anything yet. We just want to place a deposit today to secure the date."

"Okay, but call me back as soon as you have decided on the other vendors. We must know who will be here, what time they will be showing up, and if they need any assistance setting up or taking down."

She heaved a sigh of frustration. Could this process take any longer?

"So, today, I will need from you a deposit of five thousand dollars. Thirty days before the event, the balance of five thousand dollars will be due. You can pay by credit card."

She gasped. Ten thousand dollars for a view, she thought. Her wedding venue cost nothing since the event happened in her backyard. Maybe she should ask Gary if he would rent out his house for a weekend. But maybe the divorce would be finalized by then, and he might have to sell to even out the assets and liabilities.

She had his statements in the manila envelope. Should she peek and see? No, that behavior would be rude, intrusive, and unethical. Besides, Joyce promised to pay for the wedding, even if Darcy charged the deposit on her own credit card today.

She hoped she had enough left on the available balance. As she rattled off the numbers, the expiration date, and the three-digit security code, she crossed her fingers and said a silent prayer. A nerve-wracking moment of silence stretched over the phone. She fiddled with the pages in her wedding planner notebook to distract the bolts of worry lighting her mind.

"Thank you for your deposit, Ms. Madison."

A wave of relief washed over her. She placed her hand on the wedding planner notebook and offered a prayer of thanksgiving.

"On behalf of Paradise Ridge Winery, I thank you for your business."

"Good-bye." Darcy ended the call. She finished restoring her purse to its rightful order and jogged over to the coffee shop.

Tapping either a text message or an email, Betty hunched over her phone.

Darcy sank into a chair and took a sip of her lukewarm cappuccino. She placed a five dollar bill on the table. "Thanks for ordering."

"Well, that call took forever." Betty glanced up. "Keep the five. You need the cash more than I do."

Heat rushed to her cheeks. She wished she never admitted to Betty she did not own a house.

"How's the wedding planning going?"

"Just peachy." She sighed. "We have the venue, but everything else is up in the air."

She flashed a smile. "You're very organized and resourceful. The rest of the wedding will come together."

"As easily as a divorce comes apart?" She arched her eyebrows.

Placing aside her phone, Betty grabbed her mocha. "You've just been in the business too long." She wiped a bit of whipped cream from her upper lip with a napkin. "Trust me. If you started organizing weddings, you wouldn't feel frustrated."

"Can you believe a venue costs ten thousand dollars?" Darcy shook her head.

Betty shrugged. "How is that cost different than a ten-thousand-dollar retainer fee?"

For a few seconds, she thought about this fact. Of course, most divorces cost several thousand dollars in attorney's fees, regardless of whether or not the couple settled in mediation or court. She removed the paper collar from her too-cool cappuccino. "I guess you're right."

"Of course, I am." She slid her eyeglasses farther up the bridge of her nose. "You've just become bitter about love."

Darcy glanced over at the line of customers and wondered if she should order a fresh cup of coffee. A couple near the back of the line stood close but not too close. They didn't touch, but their eye contact made it clear they could if they wanted. She wondered about their status: a romantic couple or flirty co-workers or friends with benefits. How did the phrase "friends with benefits" ever get started? Who considered sex a benefit? Like health insurance or a 401k plan. She didn't know, but she suddenly cared. What made strangers evolve into acquaintances then friends and later lovers and finally life partners? How did couples make their relationship work over and over each and every day until death?

"Earth to Darcy." She waved a hand in front of Darcy's face.

Blinking twice, she then focused on Betty's brown eyes. "I'm sorry. I'm just puzzled about how long term romantic love works."

She sipped her mocha. "It's different for everyone."

"Not everyone finds love." She thrust her lower lip into a pout.

"If you're not looking for love, love won't find you."

Darcy shook her head and glanced away. "I tried online dating sites and blind dates. Love is just not worth the effort. I'm old and exhausted."

"You're burned out because of your profession."

"And you're not?" She lifted her empty palms and shook her head. "Clearly, you're more involved than I am with your mediation and court dates. I'm just in the periphery, organizing things." She shoved her hand into her purse, withdrew Gary's response, and slid it across the table. "Can you please give this paperwork to Victor?"

Betty frowned at the manila envelope. "Why don't you deliver it?"

Darcy stammered for a quick response. "You work in the same office." She didn't want Betty to know of her fear of seeing Victor and feeling an undeniable attraction.

She narrowed her gaze. "I'm not your errand girl."

"I didn't say you were." She chewed on her lower lip. Why couldn't she just admit her feelings for the man? Surely, Betty would not tease her, would she? "I just thought having you take it would be more convenient for everyone."

"Not everyone. Only you." She finished her mocha and dabbed her mouth with a napkin. "Besides, I'm not going into the office today. I'm in court."

Darcy wondered what would happen if she and Victor ever dated. How could they make their relationship work if they both dealt with the ending of love and never its beginning? Maybe Betty knew. She had been married to Chuck for fifteen years. Darcy touched her friend's wrist. "Tell me one thing before you go."

Betty lifted her eyebrows. "Yes?"

"How can you keep love alive with your husband when you go into the battleground to end it for other couples day after day?"

"Easy. Love is dead by the time I show up," Betty said. "My job is to make sure everything ends fairly. That's all." She grabbed her jacket and empty cup. "I have to go. Call me later this week, okay?"

Darcy nodded. She could not imagine giving love a second chance even if she stopped being a divorce planner and started planning weddings instead. For her, love equaled failure. She never again wanted to fail. But she also wanted to feel alive, as alive as she felt every time she thought of Victor.

As she drove across town for her next appointment, she heard her phone ring. She pressed the speaker button and placed the phone on her lap. She should buy a headset, but she couldn't afford anything other than food and rent. With one hand, she struggled to roll up the window so she could hear the caller's voice.

"Did we get the venue or not?" Joyce asked.

Embarrassment burned Darcy's face. She had been distracted and forgot to call. No wonder her daughter sounded worried.

"Yes, we have the tenth of June, just as you wanted." Beads of sweat erupted along her hairline. She wished she could afford to fix her air conditioner. Oh, why had she footed the bill for the deposit on the winery this morning? When would she stop placing her daughter's needs before her own?

"Mom? Are you there?"

"Yes, I am." She braked at a stop light. "I placed the deposit on my credit card."

"Mom, I already told you, you're not paying for my wedding. Tyler and I are will reimburse you for the expense. How much was the deposit?"

She accelerated with traffic. Her hands gripped the steering wheel. Oh, why was wedding planning so different than divorce planning? At least, with her clients, Darcy received a retainer upfront. Why couldn't Joyce have been so generous and left her credit card information with her? "The deposit is five thousand dollars now and five thousand thirty days before the wedding."

"Good job negotiating the price. I thought it would be much higher."

Relief rinsed over her body.

"Tyler and I are sending you a check for seventy-five thousand dollars. That's our wedding budget. Whatever's left after the wedding's planned is yours."

Darcy gasped. How could her daughter and her

fiancé afford to spend so much on a one-day event? She needed to stay focused and remain grateful, because if she planned things right then all of her financial worries would cease to exist.

****

"I just want to drop off this paperwork for Victor." An hour after her phone call with Joyce, Darcy slid the envelope with Gary's response paperwork underneath the glass partition of the receptionist's desk and prayed she would not have to speak with him.

The older woman with long painted nails glanced at the envelope. "I think Victor has something for you, too." She rifled through a stack of papers on the counter. "Do you have a minute? I'll go see if I left it in his office."

She breathed quicker. Nervousness quivered her legs. Leaning against the counter for support, she pretended to admire the framed artwork on the walls. What could he have left for her?

"Darcy?"

She spun toward his voice. Victor stood in the doorway, wearing a blue suit and a white shirt unbuttoned at the collar. His tousled black hair fell over his forehead. His dark eyes sparkled like wet stones, and his smile glowed.

"Good to see you." He motioned toward the hallway leading to his office. "I have a few referrals. Want to discuss them?"

A hummingbird of heartbeats hammered her chest. Perspiration moistened her palms. Why hadn't she told Betty the real reason why she wanted her to deliver Gary's response?

"I know you're a busy woman, so I won't take up

any more time than you can spare."

"Sure." Striding along the hallway, she fumbled with the strap on her purse.

He held open the door and gestured for her to step inside his office.

As she walked past, she caught a whiff of his musky cologne. She struggled against the impulse to wrap her arms around his neck and bring his face toward her lips for a long, deep, and satisfying kiss. Instead, she took a seat, crossed her legs at the ankles, and placed her hands in her lap.

He sat in a leather executive chair and handed her a sheet of paper across the mahogany desk. "Here are a good mix of men and women in various stages of separation in need of your services. None are as loaded as Gary, but they are all financially capable of paying for a divorce planner." Leaning back, he placed his fingers in a steeple beneath his chin. "By the way, how is Gary?"

"Terrible." She shuddered. "I've never seen a guy worse off."

"I'm glad he's working with you. He needs someone organized, detached, and willing to take control." He leaned forward and tapped the envelope by his phone. "One more week, and he would have missed the deadline. His estranged wife could have settled without giving him what he deserves."

"I think things will get better once he gets on anti-depressants."

He frowned. "Don't anti-depressants take six to eight weeks to become effective?"

"A divorce takes a lot longer to finalize." She scanned the names on the sheet of paper he had given her. "You sure do have a lot of clients."

"I work a lot longer and a lot harder than anyone here." He glanced away. "I love my job more than anything else."

She relaxed her shoulders. "I feel the same way about what I do."

"Ah, a kindred spirit." He widened his smile. "I enjoy helping people in tough times. I'm sure you understand."

"Definitely." She nodded. "I wouldn't be a divorce planner if I didn't make a positive impact in others' lives."

He held her gaze a moment longer before he glanced at the clock. "I have an appointment in ten minutes. We should get through this list." He cleared his throat and pointed to the first names. "Chloe and Theo have been married thirty years. Chloe's an architect. Theo's a general contractor. Two adult children. One house and one vacation timeshare worth next to nothing. But they have retirement accounts to be split and a shared business to divide or sell."

"Who would I be calling?"

"Both."

"I can't." Resistance tightened her shoulders. "I never represent both sides of a divorce."

He pinched the space between his eyebrows. "Why not?"

"Representing both parties compromises my fiduciary duty."

He crossed his arms over his chest. "Aren't you objective?"

She braced her legs, ready to stand and leave if she could not convince him she did not discuss the feelings she had for her clients. "I am objective, but I'm also human."

Pausing for several seconds, he frowned. After a long moment, he released his folded arms and nodded. "I understand. Please, call the wife. I'll find someone else to help the husband."

The phone rang. He picked it up on the second ring. "Yes? Okay. Thanks for letting me know." He hung up. "I guess we don't have to rush. My noon appointment just canceled."

Growls erupted from her stomach. She placed a hand on her belly. "Excuse me." This morning she had not eaten anything with her cappuccino.

A smile spread across his face. "Want to grab lunch?" He winked. "My treat."

Butterfly wings fluttered in her stomach. Could she behave with the same professionalism she struggled to maintain in the office? Or would she succumb to drowning in a tsunami of attraction? Another grumble of protest from her stomach betrayed a greater need. "Sure, lunch sounds wonderful."

Chapter 8

"Let's eat across the street," Victor said. "Their sandwiches are good."

Darcy stood beside him at the crosswalk, waiting for the light to change. Bright, hot sunlight beat down on her shoulders. Cars honked as they wove through the clot of traffic. A stranger jostled her shoulder, angling to be the first to step off the curb as soon as the light changed.

Victor grabbed her hand to help her navigate across the street.

A jolt of electricity shot up her arm and sent a bolt of heat throughout her body. How could he be so strong yet so gentle?

After they stepped onto the sidewalk, he released her hand.

He's so thoughtful and so kind, she thought. A flutter of heartbeats swept across her chest. He's also sexy and successful. She swallowed a lump in her throat. "Is this a date? Or are you just a gentleman?"

"A gentleman." He grinned and winked.

A hot splash of desire sizzled her body. She glanced away, unable to meet his dark gaze. At the café, the smells of hot pastrami and fresh coffee wafted through the air-conditioned room.

A server led them to a small table.

Victor scooted back the chair for Darcy to sit

before he settled in the chair across from her. He placed the napkin in his lap. "I recommend the turkey sandwich, but any sandwich is good."

She browsed the menu. When she glanced up, she caught him staring. Heat invaded her face, and she touched her chest. "Is something wrong?"

Shaking his head, he smiled. "We had so much fun at the Gala."

A whiff of his woodsy cologne propelled her back to that magical night when he placed his hand on her shoulder. This lunch is not a date, she reminded herself. Focus on business. She arranged the silverware on the table. "Did you get any referrals from the event?"

"I get referrals all the time." He shrugged. "I don't keep track of where they come from." He lifted his eyebrows. "How about you?"

She glanced at her lap, her skin prickling. "I get all of my referrals through attorneys like you."

The server served them two glasses of water. "What would you like to order?"

"I'll have the turkey sandwich." He nodded toward Darcy.

Without registering the words, she scanned the menu. "Umm…I'll have the turkey sandwich, also."

"Good choice." He deepened his smile. "You won't be disappointed."

After the server left, Darcy removed the list of referrals from her purse and set them on the table. "Where did we leave off?"

He grasped the list.

Their fingers brushed.

Pleasure danced across her skin.

Gazing at the sheet of paper, he pointed to the next

set of names. "This couple has been married six months with no assets to divide. The husband wants someone to plan a trip for him and his buddies to Vegas. Can you do that?"

"Of course." She loved planning Freedom Parties. "How much does he want to spend?"

"Call him." He took a swallow from his glass of water. "I don't know his budget, but his net worth is somewhere in the high millions."

She whistled soft and low. From experience, people with enormous wealth often made great sacrifices in their personal happiness to maintain their fortune. "Why are they divorcing?"

"Something about a disagreement over how to set up a living trust."

Nodding, she jotted notes on a pad of paper. "The marriage died from greed."

He shook a finger. "Don't be so quick to judge. The wife signed a prenuptial agreement allowing him to keep all of his wealth, but she wouldn't sign a living trust. He wanted to leave out her children and any future children they might have together in order to divide his estate among a host of former girlfriends, including a hooker he spent one night with during his senior year of college."

How absurd, she thought. She clenched her pen. "Why would he have the contact information for a hooker?"

Shrugging, he set aside the sheet of paper. "I didn't ask. Honestly, I didn't want to take the case—it's a slam dunk anyway—but I couldn't say no to the insane amount of money he offered."

"I wish I had wealthier clients." A sigh escaped her

lips. "I could buy a place of my own, and my daughter could stop nagging about my college lifestyle."

He folded his arms on the table. "You don't have real furniture in your rental?"

"That's not her complaint. She wishes I didn't rent a room from a couple."

"Understandable." He leaned forward. "So, why are you doing it?"

She hesitated. Should she tell him? Or should she keep things focused on business? His casual demeanor and sincere interest allowed her to soften her stance and open up. She leaned closer to whisper, "When I moved from LA, I sold my house and used the proceeds to pay off my daughter's college loan. I thought I would find tons of work up here, but the demographics are different. Too many retired couples who love each other. Lots of single college students. The miserable folks who are married don't have the discretionary income to afford my services."

With lips pressed together, he nodded. "We'll change that scenario."

The server delivered their sandwiches.

They both leaned back to make room for the large plates on the table.

She bit into the warm turkey, firm avocado, and gooey cheese.

"Good, isn't it?" He swallowed a bite.

With a full mouth, she nodded then swallowed. "You have great taste."

"I pride myself on quality." He glanced down at the list of referrals. "The other couples are your garden-variety cases of infidelity, boredom, and neglect. But they are all busy professionals who can appreciate and afford your services." He nudged the sheet of paper across the table with his elbow. "Who else sends you referrals?"

"Betty. She's in your office and working on making partner. We've been friends since I moved here." She folded the paper and tucked it into her purse. "A few attorneys at other firms sometimes send clients my way, but Betty has been my staple...until you."

Dabbing his mouth with a napkin, he averted his gaze. "So, when you have enough money from your clientele to afford your own place, what are you buying?"

She widened her eyes and broadened her smile. "An estate like Gary has. Have you seen his property?"

Lines creased his forehead. "Mediterranean home? Vineyard?"

"Yes, that's it."

He grimaced. "The house is overpriced, in my opinion, although the grapes bring in an income and allow for an agricultural tax deduction."

Clasping her hands against her chest, she gazed at the ceiling. "The home is peaceful and beautiful in the way I imagine heaven."

"Ah." Smiling, he nodded. "You're a romantic."

"Aren't most women?"

Again, he wagged a finger and shook his head. "If I remember a former conversation accurately, you aren't like most women."

She gulped. What else did he remember?

He finished his sandwich and placed his crumpled napkin on the empty plate. Leaning back, he folded his arms across his chest. "I live in a condo on the Town Green in Windsor above an Indian restaurant. My bedroom smells like curry."

She wrinkled her nose. "How do you do it?"

"I'm hardly home, except to sleep."

"That's how I am, too." Darcy's phone rang. She glanced at Joyce's number on the caller ID, her heartbeat jolting into a gallop. "Do you mind if I take this call? It's my daughter."

Smiling, he waved a hand. "Go ahead."

She shifted in her seat to maintain a bit of privacy. "Hello, sweetheart."

"Mom, why haven't you responded to my email?"

Her daughter's harsh tone started her. "What email?" She checked her account last night and did not remember any email from Joyce.

"I sent you a message about an hour ago. We need to schedule caterers and florists and a ton of other services for the wedding."

She clenched her jaw. Did her daughter expect her to check her email every hour on the hour? Didn't she know Darcy had another job? Or did the whole world revolve around Joyce?

"Mom, I need you to do some research and select the top three vendors in each category for Tyler and me to visit."

Sweat beaded against her forehead when she considered the length of the list. "How much time do I have?"

"Don't you know? Every bridal magazine I've read insists we should have everything booked within the first month of selecting a venue."

She relaxed her shoulders. Four long weeks stretched ahead like an oasis. "Take a deep breath and calm down." She lifted and lowered her hand to mimic the rhythm of breathing. "I'm at a business lunch. I'll check my emails tonight and respond by tomorrow morning."

"I thought you were making time to plan my wedding during your work day."

A knot tightened in her stomach. "You're not my only client."

"But I'm your daughter. Doesn't that mean anything?"

She modulated her voice into a lullaby. "Of course, being my daughter means something, sweetheart. But I can't neglect all of my other clients and just focus on your wedding."

Joyce grunted. "I'm calling you back at four o'clock. If you haven't taken the time to read my email then I'm firing you."

She tightened her grip on the phone. A headache bloomed between her temples. "Then what? Hire Dad's wedding planner and move the venue to LA?"

Joyce gasped. "Who told you about Dad's wedding planner?"

"Your father since I do not speak to that scumbag woman he'll be calling his wife."

"Be nice. I don't talk about you that way with Tanya."

"Well, you might after you fire me tonight."

"I'm only firing you if you don't make time for me."

Shaking her head from side to side, Darcy laughed. "I spent this morning getting Paradise Ridge Winery booked, even though your date wasn't available. You didn't even say thank you."

Joyce heaved a sigh. "You're being petty."

Darcy gritted her teeth. "You're being a bridezilla."

"I want everything to be perfect." She sobbed. "I'm only getting married once."

"You don't know that. Tyler could be the first in a long line of ex-husbands." A stab of guilt pierced her chest.

"Stop being cynical!"

"I'm being realistic."

The server removed their empty plates and placed the bill on the table.

"I have to go." Darcy eyed Victor. She hoped her unprofessional behavior didn't detract from an otherwise pleasant luncheon. "My business meeting is almost over. I'll call you from the car. Just give me ten minutes." She ended the call and tossed the phone in her purse. "I should have never agreed to plan my daughter's wedding."

Slightly frowning, he placed a twenty on the table and stood. "Ready to leave?"

She glanced at his long, lithe frame in the tailored suit and imagined the tight muscles underneath the fabric. She gestured to the vacant seat, hoping he would sit and they could resume talking. "An hour hasn't passed. We don't have to hurry."

He pointed to her purse. "But you need to call back your daughter."

"It's not urgent," she lied.

"Your voice sounded urgent."

"She's just a bride anxious about everything." And it's probably my fault for indulging her, Darcy thought.

A crease deepened in his forehead but a smile remained on his face. He offered his hand. "C'mon, I'll walk you to your car so we can talk a little bit longer."

She placed her sweaty fingers in his palm.

He curled his hand over hers and helped her to her feet.

Relief swept through her body. She had no idea why his touch calmed her nerves and settled her thoughts. She only knew she always wanted to feel as relaxed as Victor made her feel.

Opening the door, he ushered her outside into the blistering heat. "I couldn't help but overhear the tension in your voice. You sound worse than some of the couples I work with in litigation. Why did you agree to help your daughter plan her wedding?"

She shrugged. Since the divorce, she orbited her daughter's life like a satellite. She missed the daily milestones and celebrated only the major events. "I thought planning the wedding would help us bond."

He snickered. "Sounds like you don't agree on anything from the way you were fighting."

Pressing the button to activate the crosswalk sign, she ignored his comment. "Thanks for lunch."

He placed his hand on the small of her back and directed her across the street.

When they stepped up on the sidewalk, she resisted the urge to turn and kiss him.

"Good luck with your daughter." He tucked his hands into his pockets. "She sounded a little frazzled from what I could hear."

"Do you have any children?" She arched an eyebrow. Maybe he has more parenting experience, she thought.

He shook his head. "No children, no ex-wives."

"Oh, that's right." She snapped her fingers. "You're the George Clooney of Sonoma County."

Striding beside her, he stared at the sidewalk. "If I remember correctly, you said George Clooney is now married. And I, for the record, remain single."

She unlocked her car door and tossed her purse on the front seat. A shot of hot air blasted out. "Well, if you ever change your mind, please don't call me to be your wedding planner."

He chuckled. "Oh, don't worry. I won't. I'll only call you if I'm planning a divorce."

After Victor left, Darcy rolled down her car window and took out her phone to return Joyce's call. But the thought of facing another of Joyce's verbal assaults stopped her, and she dialed a wedding planner in Los Angeles she used to associate with when she attended event planning seminars.

The phone rang three times before someone answered, "Bridal Dreams Come True."

"May I speak with Gloria? It's Darcy Madison."

A few moments later, a woman squealed on the line. "Oh, Dee, it's been so long. Are you moving back to the area?"

"No." Darcy sighed. "I'm planning my daughter's wedding, and I need some advice."

Gloria laughed. "Dee, you'll need a bottle of aspirin, a prescription for tranquilizers, and a sleep aid."

Frowning, she fiddled with her pen. She had expected something more technical like how to find the best florist in five steps or less. "I don't think Joyce will go the medical route."

"I'm not talking about her," Gloria explained with a laugh. "You'll need them. Trust me, after thirty years in this business, if I didn't take a pill to go to sleep and a tranquilizer to remain calm while awake, I would have quit years ago and joined the circus."

"There aren't any well-known circuses left."

"Then I'd be so crazy I'd wander the streets looking for one."

She rubbed her forehead. "Maybe I should quit and tell her to hire a real professional."

"Don't. You girls have never been close. Invite her to the next wedding expo, and let her go wild with the vendors."

"I can't." She sighed. "I checked and the next local one isn't for months."

"I'm sorry. You'll have to do things the hard way and research. Make sure to read the reviews on any bridal message boards you can find from the locals." She exhaled. "I'd help you more, but I'm so far away I don't have any contacts where you live."

Darcy's phone beeped with another caller. "I have to go. I'll call you back and chat when I have more time."

"Of course," Gloria said. "Always good to hear your voice."

Darcy switched to the other caller. "Hello?"

"More than ten minutes have passed," Joyce said.

She grimaced. Joyce's sharp tone of voice suffocated her more than the stuffiness in the hot car.

"Did you read my email? I just have a couple of minutes to talk before I go into my next meeting."

Treat her like a divorcing client, she thought. Keep a friendly demeanor, and don't get involved. The wedding is her show, and not mine. Flipping to a blank page in her wedding planner notebook, she forced a smile. "What are the theme colors?"

"Peach and purple. I wanted lavender, but Tyler

wanted a more masculine color, so I decided on purple."

"Good compromise." She would need flowers, wedding favors, and table decorations in those colors. "What type of food do you want to serve at the reception?"

"No meat."

"What about fish? One possibility is The Pacific Connection."

"No fish. Tyler and I are thinking we'll serve local, organic vegan food."

She sighed. For the next four weeks, she had her work cut out.

****

Amidst the chatter of happy couples and the smell of sizzling steaks, Darcy stepped into Ophelia's Bar and Steakhouse on Friday night. She strode to the back of the restaurant where her Books and Booze Club met every week to discuss literature. Pushing the swinging door, she stepped into the dimly lit wood paneled banquet hall. She sat next to Charlotte, a recently graduated art and history student, and gave her a quick squeeze. She glanced around to see if all six book club members had arrived at the round table. The air smelled redolent with pepper and gravy. She rubbed her nose to stifle a sneeze.

A server placed a double gin martini next to Darcy.

"I took the liberty of ordering," Charlotte said.

"That's so sweet." Darcy smiled with appreciation. Why couldn't her daughter be as thoughtful as the young lady beside her? Sometimes, she wondered if Joyce had been swapped at birth, but then remembered her ex-husband's attributes and regretted her decision to have an only child. A sibling might have created some balance and maybe even prolonged the marriage.

Darcy turned off her cell phone, placed her battered copy of *The Scarlet Letter* on the table, and took a long, delicious sip of her drink. She looked forward to a night of banter about anything other than weddings or divorces.

The server served tonight's meal: platters of smoky chicken wings, tangy cheese quesadillas, and oily fried onion rings.

Charlotte plucked an onion ring from the platter. "I'd like to go first and discuss the theme of forbidden love."

Raising his hand, Lucas, a photographer who wore his long blond hair in a pony-tail, glanced around the table. "Can we compare and contrast forbidden love with romantic love and familial love?"

"Forget love," said Anita.

Darcy cringed. She didn't know what to think of the sixty-five-year-old diva with a penchant for pool boys and boxed chocolate candy. Anita preferred to read romances but could not find a book club which shared her passion. Darcy marveled how the woman managed to steer every discussion toward sex.

Anita nodded. "Let's discuss adultery."

Picking up his paperback, Barry, the leader of the group, flexed his biceps. He worked at the library while studying for the bar exam.

"I think Anita's right." Barry placed a thick finger on a line of text. "We should start with the theme of adultery. What causes spouses to cheat? How frequently did couples commit adultery during the colonial times? Is adultery relevant now?"

Lucas took a swig from his bottle of light beer. "If Hester Prynne and Arthur Dimmesdale shared the same public humiliation for adultery then they both would be exiled."

Eric chuckled.

After living most of his life in Las Vegas as an Elvis impersonator, Eric retired in Oakmont where he preferred to read military war stories. He joined the Books and Booze Club after a disagreement with one of the members of his senior book club.

"I doubt Dimmesdale would have gotten off easily." Eric frowned. "Those Puritans would have punished him for knowing better. Society always assumes men know better."

"That's right." Darcy selected a chicken wing. "Society has been that way since the beginning of time. God punished Adam because he listened to Eve and ate the apple."

"If reliable birth control and legalized abortion had been available then no one would have known anything," Anita said.

After swallowing a mouthful of beer, Barry filled his plate with chicken wings. "I think Darcy's on a roll. The God-fearing colonials believed no one should have sex outside of marriage."

Charlotte pointed with a chicken wing. "Having sex with someone you love should not be a sin."

"What if you're already married to someone else?" Barry lifted his empty palms and raised his eyebrows.

Charlotte shrugged. "Hester could have been a widow. After all, everyone thought her husband died at sea."

"Sex with someone other than your spouse is adultery." Eric shook his finger. "When you're not married, sex with anyone is fornication."

"Both types of sex were still a sin." Barry stood and opened his arms. "Doesn't anyone know anything about history?"

"I do." Charlotte stood and lifted her chin. "The only sexual morality existed behind closed doors between a husband and a wife."

Darcy didn't want to talk about sex and sin. She wiped her greasy hands in a cloth napkin and shook her head. "What about that poor child, Pearl? She grew up wild and uncontrollable without a daddy."

"I don't think Dimmesdale would have been a good father." Barry sat and shook his head. Waving a beefy arm, he sighed. "He behaved like a weak boy, not even a boy man, just a boy."

"What is the definition of a boy man?" Lucas tilted his head. "How is it different than a girly man?"

Barry tugged on Lucas's long pony tail. "A girly man wears his hair like you do and dresses in bright colors and smears eyeliner on his face. A boy man pretends to be a hero, hiding behind something greater and more powerful than he is. In Dimmesdale's case, that power is God and the Church."

Charlotte sat, finished her glass of chardonnay, and poured another. "Either way, I'm glad women aren't punished for having sex with anyone anymore."

"You must be referring to the United States and Western Europe." Eric grabbed a quesadilla. "Tons of places still exist where women aren't afforded sexual freedom. They're either slaves to men's desires or stripped of all pleasure. Like those poor African girls who get their clitorises circumcised."

The server set another drink before Darcy and placed one more platter of appetizers on the table.

Oh, the horrors of womanhood. Darcy shuddered. Ironically, the global atrocities released her from the grip of wedding planning. She took a sip of her martini and sighed. How wonderful to disappear into a conversation about imaginary people with imaginary problems. The alcohol warmed her body, and the conversation warmed her soul.

All the talk about adultery steered Darcy's thoughts toward sex. She couldn't remember the last time she slept with someone. Why didn't she miss it? Dizzy from the booze, she opened her mouth. "Sex is overrated."

A smile lit Anita's face. "You, my dear, have never had good sex."

She lifted her glass. "Never good enough to feel guilty." She wondered if Nathan had felt guilty the first time he had sex with Tanya.

Charlotte nodded. "Why punish yourself for doing something wrong? We're human. We make mistakes."

"This book isn't about forgiveness." Barry bent the spine of the paperback and set it against the table so he could grab the mug of beer.

Lucas widened his gaze. "Well, maybe it should be."

All the chatter about guilt sparked a flicker of pain in Darcy's gut. Her thoughts drifted back to the wedding planning. After reading the email, she'd called Joyce at four o'clock and left a message on voice mail. Afterward, she called a few of the vendors to add to the list, but most had closed for the day. Instead of searching online for alternatives, she shut her computer and left for her book club. A spasm of fear squeezed her. What excuse could she give her daughter the next time Joyce called for a report on caterers who specialized in vegan cuisine?

Maybe she should eat something more than chicken wings to stop the swirling thoughts in her head. But the spicy, greasy wings tasted so good with the crispness of her martini. If she drank too much, she could always call her roommates for a ride home. "You know what I hate most about this book. The people never take into account someone's intention. Hester didn't intend to become adulterous. She didn't intend to become a single mother. If everyone didn't focus on actions and results then they could forgive people with good intentions."

Eric crossed his arms over his beer belly and chuckled. "That's why they say the road to hell is paved with good intentions."

I have no hope for redemption, she thought. For how could she gain her daughter's love and respect when she always did everything wrong, no matter how much she intended to do things right? Gulping her drink, she slammed the empty glass on the table. "My place in hell is confirmed."

Chapter 9

Consumed by guilt, Darcy spent the following week calling every catering company in Sonoma County. She discovered three caterers who offered appropriate menu selections. Two bakeries sold gluten-free wedding cakes, but only one also offered dairy-free frosting. Finally, she located several locally grown, organic wines, but Paradise Ridge only permitted their vintages to be served.

During their weekly meeting, Darcy sat beside Gary on the veranda, sipping iced tea in the late morning sunlight. They were supposed to discuss strategies on how to prepare for the legal battles once the mediation date had been set. But Gary had asked Darcy how her weekend went and she lamented about her struggles planning Joyce's wedding at the winery. "We sell our grapes to Paradise Ridge," Gary said.

A cool breeze ruffled her hair. "My daughter doesn't drink and neither does her fiancé. They're into a healthy lifestyle. The wine at the reception would be for people like me."

Gary shrugged. "I don't think I could make it a week without drinking. Maybe I should cut back. Maybe my wife wouldn't have left if I led a healthier lifestyle."

"She left because she chose to leave. Not because of what you ate or drank." Darcy wagged her head from side to side. "Besides, your diet doesn't matter anyway. In the end, we all die."

With one week left until her deadline, Darcy spent every free moment listening to bands and interviewing DJs. She found a blues band, a jazz band, and three DJs who could play either 90s grunge, 80s rock, or 70s disco. Next, she located two local florists who provided photographs of potential wedding bouquets and arrangements for both the ceremony and the reception. Lastly, she browsed through online catalogues for potential bridal gowns and bridesmaid's dresses.

On the day of her deadline, Darcy compiled her list and sent it to Joyce in an email. She turned off her laptop, crossed her fingers, and left her rented room to see Betty for breakfast. Tension knotted at the base of her spine. Oh, please, let me receive a thankful text message from Joyce, she thought. I want this wedding planning to end.

****

In spite of juggling wedding planning with divorce planning, Darcy could rely on two things every Monday—coffee with Betty and lunch with Victor.

As she stepped into Katie's Koffee, Darcy peeked at her phone. No call or email or text from Joyce. She heaved a sigh. Maybe her daughter was too busy settling into her work routine to bother reading the list Darcy sent. She tucked her phone in her purse and started to order her usual cappuccino before she noticed pumpkin spice lattes on the menu and changed her mind.

Coffee in hand, Darcy navigated around the crowded tables until she found Betty sitting in their usual spot by the window. Settling into the hard wooden chair, she breathed in the scent of nutmeg and cinnamon before taking a long sip. "Mmm…I'm so happy all the coffee shops start serving their fall drinks even when the weather is still balmy."

"My favorite is the salted caramel mocha." Betty licked the sweet whipped cream from the top of her drink. "But I'm sad, too, because fall is the end of the softball season for Chuck."

Darcy frowned. "I thought he played year-round."

"He used to play fall ball, but the cold temperatures bother his knees too much."

Smiling, she nudged Betty's leg underneath the table. "I guess you both can stay home and curl up by the fireplace drinking hot chocolate."

"Oh, wouldn't snuggling by the fire be nice?" Frowning, she shook her head. "I bet I'll end up working. I need more billable hours to make partner." She bit into a cinnamon walnut scone and dusted the crumbs from the table. "I've been at the firm the longest, but sometimes I feel like I'm competing with Victor because he works so much."

"Don't worry about Victor." Darcy waved a hand. "He works because he has nothing else to do."

Betty leveled her gaze. "How would you know that tidbit of information?"

"He told me." A tinny vibrating sounded from Darcy's purse. Jolting upright, she fished out her phone and checked the screen with a trembling hand. No calls, no texts, and no emails just a calendar reminder of her next appointment. She exhaled and relaxed her shoulders. Joyce should have responded by now. Had she sent the list to the wrong email address?

Betty rapped her knuckles against the table. "When

did you talk to Victor?"

She shrugged. She met with Victor so frequently her heartbeat no longer stuttered in her chest and her knees no longer buckled whenever someone mentioned his name. "We talk all the time."

"He told you he's not working to make partner?"

She nodded. "About four weeks ago during lunch."

Leaning forward, Betty narrowed her gaze. "Why did you have lunch with him?"

She widened her eyes and scooted her chair back. The movement jostled the legs on the table, and her full drink splashed over the rim. She blotted the sticky spill with a rough napkin. She didn't think Betty would have objected to her lunches with Victor. "We had to discuss a referral he gave me. You were here when he called, remember? You said you were happy because I needed the business."

Betty squinted through her glasses. "You didn't tell me the rest of the story."

"Why is it a big deal?" Darcy crumpled the napkin in her fist. "Are you objecting to our friendship?"

She shifted in her seat, her eyes tiny slits. "How often do you see him?"

Heat rushed to her face. She felt like she was a defendant on trial and Betty was the plaintiff's attorney. If she gave the wrong answer, she might be implicated in a crime she did not commit. Inhaling deeply, she straightened her spine. "We have lunch every Monday."

"Every Monday?"

At the sound of Betty's voice, the people at the next table turned their heads and stared.

"Are you two dating?"

"Oh, my goodness." Darcy threw her napkin on the

table and stood. Betty's interrogation had gone too far. "Why would Victor be romantically interested in me?"

"Because you're smart and attractive, and he's always admired you." She tossed up her arms. "Remember that suicidal client you had? No one could convince her to keep living except you. Victor still talks about it."

Darcy blushed. Victor admired her? She sat and reached across the table to take Betty's hand to reassure her. "You're my best friend. If I was dating anyone, I would tell you. Victor and I have working lunches. We discuss the clients we share."

Betty withdrew her hand and tapped her nails on the table. "How many clients has he referred?"

Swallowing, she sensed the waves of Betty's jealousy. "Not that many clients."

Several moments passed. "How many?"

She felt pinned against a wall, the guilty verdict one gavel strike away. She averted her gaze and mumbled. "Five."

Covering her mouth with a hand, Betty gasped. "Five?"

Darcy glanced away. She usually had one or two referrals from each of the ten attorneys she worked with until Victor starting sending his clients. Was Betty more concerned about Victor stealing Darcy's friendship or encroaching on her chance to make partner at the firm?

"That's three more than I referred." Betty shook her fist. "Where does he get them?"

Exhaling with relief, Darcy shrugged. At least, she wasn't endangered of losing Betty's friendship. "I don't know his secret."

"Find out." Betty slammed her empty cup against the table.

Darcy jumped in her seat, startled by the abrasiveness of her friend's reaction. Was Betty that desperate for clients? "Don't you have enough work?"

Betty slumped against the chair and crossed her legs. Averting her gaze, she sniffed and rubbed her nose. "I need more billable hours before the end of the month, or I can kiss my chance of making partner goodbye."

Was that a tear sparkling in the corner of Betty's eye? Pain clenched in Darcy's chest. She would not allow Victor to destroy Betty's chance at partner. She lifted her hands in defeat. "Okay, I'll ask him today at lunch." She did not want to strain her friendship with Betty. She already had enough stress with her daughter.

Later that morning, Darcy sat in bumper-to-bumper traffic on Mendocino Avenue. The crisp fall air blew through the rolled-down window. She glanced at the clock on her dashboard. Eleven-fifty. If traffic didn't pick up, she would be late for her lunch date with Victor.

At the next stoplight, a truck rolled up beside her. A chorus of honks surrounded her. Darcy glanced at the smiling couple dressed in a tuxedo and a wedding dress. JUST MARRIED and J + C within a huge pink heart filled the side windows. The truck inched forward. On the back window, pink spray paint read, "Honk if you believe in love."

Darcy did not honk.

Ten minutes after twelve, Darcy opened the door to the café. A blast of tepid air accosted her. She glanced around until she noticed Victor's bowed head above the booth in the back of the crowded room.

He lifted his head and met her gaze. Smiling, he waved.

Smiling back, she listened to her heartbeat slow along with her breath. Every time she saw him, she felt her muscles relax. As she strode toward the back of the café, the scent of hot chocolate and fresh bread enveloped her. A growl erupted from her stomach. "Sorry I'm late." She hung her sweater on the back of the seat. "I ran into terrible traffic."

"No worries." Victor's brown eyes glittered. "I ordered for you."

"What did you order?" Darcy sipped her glass of water and unfolded her napkin.

"Pastrami on rye."

She laughed. "You're starting to know what I like."

"Ah, I know you much better than you think." He pointed. "I know why you like to eat what you eat." As he spoke, he curled each finger toward his palm. "You eat chicken when you're feeling fine, salad when you're down, the special when you're excited, tuna salad with extra pickles when you're angry, and the pastrami when you're flustered."

She widened her eyes. "How did you know I'm flustered?"

"Because you were late."

She took a deep breath. She didn't know Victor cared enough to translate her moods. "So, tell me, what's new this week?"

"I have to subpoena bank records from Gary's wife." Victor sipped from his glass of iced tea. "She could be hiding accounts."

"I'm not surprised. He said she's always been

private."

He nodded, and his smile turned into a frown. "Secretive is not the same as private. The former suggests malice or ill-intent. The latter suggests discretion."

Darcy's phone trilled in her purse. Joyce's caller ID flashed on the screen. She hitched her breath and felt her gut clench into a knot.

"Who is it?" Victor asked.

"My daughter."

Victor waved his hand. "Go ahead and take it."

Darcy answered the phone. "Hi, sweetheart, I'm in a business meeting. Is this call urgent, or may I call you back?"

"You *never* call me back," Joyce said. "I'm *always* leaving you messages."

Darcy bit her lower lip and tightened her grip on the phone. She didn't agree with Joyce's black-and-white thinking, but she also didn't want to fight in front of Victor. "Okay, talk."

"I'm responding to your email. When are the appointments scheduled with the caterers? I need to know in case Tyler gets a break from Congress and can fly back to taste things."

"I haven't scheduled anything yet." She modulated her voice. "I did what you asked and compiled a list of three choices per category."

"You were supposed to setup appointments and confirm days and times."

Oh, really? She lifted her eyebrows. "That's not true. You said I had three weeks to come up with a list." Shifting in her chair, she faced the wall for privacy. "Your job is to go over the list and tell me what you like and what you don't like. Then I'll set appointments."

A moment of silence occupied the airwaves.

"All right," Joyce said. "Go ahead and order the gluten-free wedding cake with the dairy-free frosting. Three layers should be enough. Tyler wants the eighties DJ. I like Grohe's floral arrangements the best. We already decided against the wine. We'll serve sparkling water instead."

"Okay." Relief flooded through her. "We only need to find a caterer and a wedding dress. I can schedule appointments next weekend. Will your bridesmaids be coming up?"

"No, they're not," Joyce said. "You just have to schedule the caterers. I already have a wedding dress."

"You do?" Darcy sucked in her breath, feeling an invisible punch to her stomach. Out of all the tasks, she anticipated wedding dress shopping with her daughter.

"Yes, I do," Joyce said. "It's yours."

Darcy gasped. "You can't wear that dress. It's bad luck."

"I don't believe in superstition. I've had the dress hanging in my closet ever since you left. As a little girl, I fantasized about wearing it every day. I tried the dress on last weekend, and it fits. I just have to take in the waist a little bit."

"That's because you're so skinny from not eating meat."

"My BMI is perfect. You were a little chubby."

"Of course," Darcy snapped. "I had given birth."

"You can lose twenty-five pounds in less than a year."

She squared her shoulders. "You can. I can't."

"That's not my fault," Joyce said. "Anyway, you neglected to include wedding favors. Tyler wants something classy, but I don't want those candied almonds in netting. So, can you please spend this week finding something which will please both of us?"

Sighing, she thought her daughter ought to realize a wedding favor reflected the couple's interests and not a wedding planner's guessing game of whether to order the traditional candied almonds in netting tied with a standard couple's name and wedding date embossed on a ribbon or a donation made in honor of each guest to the couple's favorite charity. Oh, well, let's not start another argument, she thought. She scribbled a reminder in her wedding planner notebook. "Sure, I can."

The server set their meals on the table—the hot pastrami on rye for her and the turkey club for Victor.

"And Mom?"

Joyce's voice sounded far away, as if she spoke from inside a tunnel. "Yes?" Darcy glanced over at Victor. She tensed her jaw. How much of this conversation had he overheard?

He pursed his lips.

Guilt swept over her, and she turned away, hoping to end the conversation soon.

"Please, RSVP to Dad's wedding this week. I don't want you to miss the deadline."

With her free hand, Darcy snatched a napkin off the table and shoved it into her lap. "I already told you I'm not going."

"But I told everyone you'd be there. Attending Dad's wedding will be a great opportunity to get ideas on things we should and should not do for my wedding."

She snickered. "I can stay home and watch romantic comedies for that information."

"Why won't you attend?"

Picking up a salty fry, she snuck it into her mouth. "I never liked Tanya."

"She'll be my stepmom."

"Yes, I know, you love her because she raised you while I worked day and night to provide for you *and* your father for two years until the court ordered your father to get a job. Then I still ended up paying the mortgage until you were in high school and he had enough to buy me out."

"Go to therapy and get over it. You need to move on. Coming to this wedding would be a perfect first step."

How dare she speak with the authority of an expert? Didn't she realize how agonizing watching your former spouse pledge undying love to another woman felt? "I'm *not* going."

"If you don't go to Dad's wedding then don't bother coming to mine."

The line echoed with silence.

I can't believe she just gave me an ultimatum, she thought. She tensed her shoulders and clenched her jaw. "Joyce?" Darcy glanced at her phone. An angry pit settled deep at the bottom of her stomach. "She hung up. My own daughter hung up on me."

Victor straightened his lips into a line. "I don't know how you plan divorces and a wedding. I have a hard enough time juggling prenuptial agreements with marital settlement agreements."

Darcy tossed her phone into her purse, bit into her

peppery pastrami on rye, and chewed. She didn't want to let her daughter get the better of her, but she didn't want to keep fighting either.

He finished the first half of his turkey club sandwich and washed it down with a gulp of iced tea. "You know what you should do?"

She narrowed her gaze. "Don't say what I think you're going to say."

He deepened his smile. "Listen. I don't have kids. So, I can't even pretend to know what being a good parent is. But I'm a son. I would want both my parents present at my wedding."

"We *are* both attending her wedding." She shoved a fry into her mouth. "That's not the issue. She's wants me to go to her father's wedding. And I won't."

He reached across the table and touched her arm. "You should go."

Warming against his touch, she stared at his fingers on her sleeve. How dare he tempt her? She yanked away her arm. "No, I'm not going. I don't like any of the people who will be there. I don't want to be subjected to anyone's scrutiny, especially my ex-husband and his new wife."

A crooked smile played at the corners of his lips. "What if you attended with a guest?"

"I don't have enough money to hire an escort as my date."

Shaking his head, he chuckled. "I'm not referring to an escort. I'm talking about me."

"You?" She widened her eyes. The angry pit in her stomach dropped into a freefall of excitement.

"Yes, I think attending would be fun. We both hate weddings as much as most people hate funerals. I don't know any of those people, so I won't care what they think. I clean up quite nicely. I can turn a few heads, maybe even the bride's head, and that benefit alone is worth my presence." He leaned a forearm on the table and winked. "Don't you think?"

When she swallowed the half-chewed fry, she almost choked. If she attended the wedding with Victor as her alleged date, then she would show her ex-husband she could attract a younger, more successful man. "I'll consider your offer." She sipped from her glass of water. "But the wedding isn't local. It's in LA, and the event's next month. The last weekend before Halloween."

"No problem." Victor waved a hand. "I have airline miles I need to use before the year ends, and I'll reserve my own hotel room for the night." Shoving aside his plate, he folded his arms on the table and leaned closer. "So, what do you say? Is it a date?"

She twirled the straw in her glass of water. She liked Victor, from his good looks to his sharp intelligence. Plus he could hold a conversation with anyone. Attending the wedding with him by her side would remove the sting from seeing people who she hadn't seen since she moved here. A little jealousy from other women, including the bride, wouldn't hurt. Most of all, Joyce would be happy. Nothing made Darcy happier than seeing her daughter happy.

She shook his hand. "Okay, let's do it." A flush of warmth invaded her face. Could she maintain her composure in front of family and friends with Victor as her date, or would she succumb to the weight of the fantasy and allow her romantic feelings to finally overshadow their budding friendship?

Chapter 10

On Friday night, Darcy sat at the round table with the Books and Booze members discussing *Romeo and Juliet*. The soups and salads had already been served, and most of the members already drank their first alcoholic beverage of choice.

Darcy hated the play. When Juliet schemed with the nurse to secretly meet Romeo, Darcy tossed the paperback on the waiting room floor in a mediation office and stormed outside for a break. When Juliet visited the apothecary for poison, Darcy clutched the book in her lap in a public restroom and counted to five so she would not scream.

"Romeo's and Juliet's deaths were unnecessary." Without waiting for Barry, she launched the evening's discussion. "If divorce had been legal, Juliet could have schemed with her nurse to hire someone like me to orchestrate the entire process so no one would have known she had been married to Romeo."

"Oh, I disagree." Barry bent the spine of his paperback. "Legally, the marriage could have been annulled. But Juliet didn't want the marriage terminated. She wanted to be with Romeo forever, because she thought she loved him."

"Amen." Anita lifted her glass of merlot for a toast.

Barry clicked his bottle of beer against her wine glass.

With her heartbeat racing, Darcy opened her mouth. "How stupid young love is! Always thinking the future will be better than the moment. Sacrificing everything to save face against impossible ideals!" She threw up her arms. "No wonder the play ends in a double suicide."

"That's why the play is called a tragedy." Lucas tugged on his pony tail. "A tragedy ends with a death. A comedy ends with a wedding. Doesn't anyone remember Aristotle?"

Charlotte lifted her glass of chardonnay. "Love is tragic."

In an attempt to regulate her breathing, Darcy gulped a mouthful of air to keep herself from choking. She placed her hands against her chest until her heartbeat fluttered into a normal rhythm. Why was she so upset over a play? Who cared if couples died for love? After all, the play was make-believe, and not a documentary. Why not join the others and toast to love? With a steady hand, she lifted her martini glass and tapped the rim of Charlotte's wine glass. "To love."

The server delivered plates of prime rib, barbecue chicken, hamburgers, and New York steaks.

Barry cut into his rare steak. "*Romeo and Juliet* is about impossible love."

Shaking his head, Eric set down his dripping hamburger. "Am I the only one who sees the play differently? *Romeo and Juliet* is a story about the origin of gang violence. That's why they remade this play into that movie, *West Side Story*. If they were remaking it today, it would be called *The Bloods and Crips*. It's about territories and belonging—"

"—and how true love conquers all." Anita

swallowed the last of her merlot and poured another glass.

Charlotte nudged Darcy. "She's had too much to drink."

Darcy giggled. "No, she hasn't. She's an incurable romantic."

Eric clicked the side of his glass with his fork. "Can we read *Heart of Darkness* for next week?"

"What's it about?" Anita squinted.

"A trip to the Congo where everything goes wrong."

"A comedy of errors?" Anita arched an eyebrow and took a sip of merlot.

"No." Eric pointed a fry. "More a tragedy of common sense."

Groaning, Anita waved her hand. "I think I'll skip next week."

Eric slapped his hands against the table. "We can't always read everything you choose. It's a group. We need to consider each other's suggestions. No one has agreed to any of my suggestions since *Lord of the Flies* one year ago."

Charlotte shuddered. "I didn't like the scene where those boys killed the pig. It still gives me nightmares."

Standing, Eric flung his napkin on the table. "If we don't read *Heart of Darkness,* then I'm leaving the group."

Barry motioned for him to sit. "Let's nominate another book and vote for one or the other. Okay?"

Darcy raised her glass. "How about *A Doll's House*? I'm craving some Ibsen."

Anita lifted her chin. "That suggestion reminds me of my favorite novel. I nominate *Valley of the Dolls*."

"That book is not a classic," Barry said.

"It's a best seller."

"Not the same thing."

Lucas raised his hand. "How about *A Portrait of an Artist as a Young Man*?"

Eric shook his head. "Barry said we nominate one more book, not two."

"Yes, that's what I said." Barry nodded to Eric. "So, the vote will be between *Heart of Darkness* and *A Doll's House*. How many vote for *Heart of Darkness*?"

A tick of panic alerted Darcy. With the wedding planning, she lacked the time to indulge in reading. Ibsen's plays she knew by heart. Holding her breath, she glanced around the table.

Eric and Barry raised their hands.

"How many vote for *A Doll's House*?"

Charlotte, Darcy, Lucas, and Anita raised their hands.

"Okay." Barry lifted his arms. "*A Doll's House* wins." With his elbow, he nudged Eric. "I'm sorry your nomination lost. I really don't want to read a feminist play either."

Relief snaked through Darcy's body. One more item was marked off her to-do list.

****

On Saturday morning, Darcy raked up small piles of brittle orange and gold leaves in Sam and Linda's front yard and scooped them into the green yard waste bin. She loved the burn in her leg muscles from squatting and standing as she cleaned the yard and the pleased look of satisfaction on the faces of Sam and Linda who didn't have to hire a gardener.

The crisp, cool air contrasted with the vibrant

warmth from the exercise. When she finished, she would freshen up before driving to Healdsburg to meet Joyce and Tyler for their visit with caterers. Tomorrow, they planned on shopping for a photographer.

"Darcy, your phone is ringing." Holding up the trilling cell phone, Linda stood on the porch.

She wiped the sweat off her forehead with the back of her hand and grabbed the phone. "Hello?"

"I got the final judgment in the mail today," Monica said. "I'm divorced."

"Congratulations!" Darcy smiled. "Time for your freedom party."

"I would love to," Monica said, "but I've lost all my friends. There's no one to invite."

"Yes, there is." Darcy straightened her spine. "I'm coming. The two of us are having dinner this week. Pick your favorite restaurant. I'll make the reservations and order your favorite cake. We're celebrating your new life."

She sobbed. "Thank you, Darcy. You don't know how much this party means. Everyone else thinks something's wrong with me for wanting to throw a party. They say I'm a sick person. Even my mother said she doesn't want to talk to me anymore because I'm going to hell. That's why I didn't abort my son, even though I knew he might to be born disabled, and I wish I had. Life would have been so much easier. I wouldn't have gotten a divorce, because I would've had the time and energy to be a better wife to my husband. But I listened to my religion and ignored my heart." She sniffed. "Don't get me wrong. I love Joey, but I wouldn't have missed him if he hadn't been born. Am I a bad mother?"

Darcy sighed. How many times had she wished Joyce, a normal child with all the typical little problems, had never been born? She could not imagine raising a disabled child and being married to Nathan. The amount of courage, strength, endurance, and patience seemed unfathomable. "No, Monica. You're not a bad mother. You're just an honest one."

****

From across the elegant, formal dining room, Darcy spotted Joyce and Tyler waving. Scents of fresh bread and coffee filled the room with a pleasant aroma. The low chatter of patrons mingled with the clatter of silverware.

She smiled and waved back, weaving around the white linen-covered tables full of people until she arrived at the one in the back by the window.

Tyler stood and walked around the table to pull out her chair so Darcy could sit.

"Thank you for being a gentleman."

"It's been a long time since I've seen you, Ms. Madison." Tyler's blue eyes sparkled. His golden brown hair fell in a wave over his forehead. He folded his lean, tanned arms on the table.

"Call me, Mom," Darcy said.

"Okay, Mom." Tyler flashed a crooked smile, and the dimple winked.

No wonder Joyce wants to marry him, Darcy thought. How wonderful to wake up to his smile every morning.

"We've already ordered." Joyce unfolded her napkin.

"But I haven't looked at the menu." Darcy pinched her eyebrows together, wondering how exotic and expensive the dishes might be. "I thought you would wait for my opinion."

"Don't worry. We have excellent taste. Everything is organic and locally sourced," Tyler said.

Joyce clapped her hands. "You'll love it."

When the server set down trays full of polenta surrounded by sautéed vegetables, asparagus covered in mustard-looking sauce, and salads full of nuts and berries, Darcy widened her gaze. Who ate this type of food?

Joyce slid the plate of polenta toward her mother. "Try it."

Forcing a spoonful of the polenta into her mouth, Darcy chewed. The mushy mess tasted like cardboard. She swallowed it like medicine and grimaced.

Tyler leaned closer. "What do you think?"

"Not flavorful enough." Darcy washed her palate with iced water and reached for the salt shaker. "I know you both are vegans, but I don't understand why you won't serve one meat dish for the rest of us who aren't."

"Most of the people we know have food allergies. No gluten, no dairy, no food dyes, and no preservatives." Tyler ticked off each item on his fingers. "We figured we can't go wrong with fruits, vegetables, and beans."

"Thank goodness you aren't serving wine, because I don't think anyone knows what type of wine goes with this food." She pointed to the asparagus.

"Don't make fun of us, Mom. Dad's not serving alcohol at his wedding." Joyce leaned closer and whispered, "Is that the reason why you're not attending?"

She sat straight and smiled. "Actually, I sent in my RSVP last week."

Joyce parted her lips, but no words escaped from her mouth.

Tyler raised his glass of water. "That's great, Ms. Madison, I mean, Mom. Are you coming alone or bringing a date?"

Uh-oh, Darcy thought. She didn't mean to discuss the topic any farther and hardened her smile into a mask. If she stated the facts, she wouldn't be lying. She clutched the napkin in her fists. "I *am* bringing someone."

"You don't have to bring Betty." Joyce wrinkled her forehead. "I know the plane ticket will cost a small fortune, not to mention the hotel room. I'm just happy you're coming."

"I'm not bringing Betty." She released the napkin in her lap. As she thought of showcasing Victor as her date, she smiled. "I'm bringing a man."

Joyce gasped, her eyes as wide as teacup saucers. Placing a hand on her chest, she leaned forward and whispered. "Meeting men online is dangerous."

"I didn't meet him online." She deepened her smile. "I work with him."

"Ah." Tyler nodded. "A classic workplace romance."

Joyce frowned. "I don't remember you mentioning any man you work with. You only talk about Betty."

"I work with tons of divorce professionals." She extended her arms wide to encompass the room. "I just talk about Betty because she's my best friend."

Tyler crossed his arms and set them on the table. "Tell us about this man you're dating."

111

"There's not much to tell." She cocked her head. "He's a family law attorney specializing in divorce. He's never been married nor had kids. And he's just as jaded about love as I am."

"You're lying." Joyce shook her finger and narrowed her gaze. "You don't date. You stay home and read books and drink martinis. I bet this guy doesn't exist."

She pinched her lips tight. Victor did exist. They worked together. "No, I'm telling the truth."

"What's his name?" Frowning, Joyce crossed her arms over her chest.

"Victor." Why the twenty questions? She felt she was a teenager who had just started dating.

"His *full* name."

"Victor Costello. I don't know if he has a middle name."

"That's interesting." He leaned back. "I attended San Jose State University with a man named Victor Costello. Track and cross country. Best sprinter I ever met. How long have you been dating?"

"A couple of months." Perspiration beaded against her neckline. She hoped Victor wasn't the same man Tyler knew. How awkward would that situation be?

"That's wonderful." He smiled.

Joyce pursed her lips.

Wrapping his arms around Joyce's shoulders, he kissed the top of her head. "Aren't you happy for your mother? After all these years, she's found someone."

Joyce lifted her eyebrows. "Do you have a picture?"

A lump thickened her throat. Darcy fumbled with her phone, her palms slick with sweat. Didn't she take some photos from the Gala? Or download any from the newspaper when the article appeared? As she scrolled through the images, she held her breath. She found an out-of-focus picture of Victor sitting next to her at the dinner table engaged in a conversation. "Here." She relaxed her shoulders as she handed the phone to Joyce.

Joyce squinted at the fuzzy photo.

Tyler leaned over Joyce's shoulder. "I can't tell if it's the same guy I know, but it could be."

Joyce's mouth dropped open. "My mom can't be dating the same guy you attended college with. He's too young for her."

Tyler shook his head. "Like I said, I can't tell from the picture." He handed back the phone to Darcy. "I'm sorry she can't be happy for you, Ms., I mean, Mom."

"That's not the issue." Joyce clutched the sides of her head. "How can someone who's against love be dating?"

"Stranger things have happened." She scrolled through a few more photos and handed the phone to Joyce. "See the dead raccoon on the side of the road? Someone stopped and tied a Get Well Soon balloon to his leg."

She shook her head. "It looks altered."

"No, this picture is mine." She touched her chest. "You know I don't know enough about computers to touch up anything."

She laughed. "You're right. Otherwise, the photo of you and Victor wouldn't be so blurry."

"Exactly." Relieved, Darcy exhaled. How she wished Victor was an older man. Everything would be so much easier, she thought.

Chapter 11

On Monday morning, Darcy and Betty sat at their usual table by the window at Katie's Koffee, drinking their pumpkin spice latte and salted caramel mocha, respectively.

After a sip of the hot beverage that smelled of nutmeg, Darcy leaned across the table and brushed Betty's forearm with the tips of her fingers. "Guess what?" She widened her eyes. "I'm going to my ex-husband's wedding—and I'm bringing Victor as my date."

Betty spat a mouthful of salted caramel mocha across the table. Coughing a few times, she gasped. "You're what?"

Darcy grabbed a napkin and rubbed the sticky chocolate splatter from her shirt. "I'm attending Nathan's wedding"

"With Victor?"

She nodded, grinning.

Gazing up at the ceiling, she shook her head. "Why?"

A thrill of excitement swept over her body. "Victor said attending the wedding as my plus one would be fun." A smile brightened her face. She crossed her arms on the table and leaned forward, daydreaming of waltzing across the dance floor in Victor's arms. "He's the perfect date. He's young, good-looking, and successful." She leaned back and sighed. "What better way to make everyone jealous?"

Tears welled in Betty's eyes. "He's ruining my marriage."

Fear plummeted in Darcy's stomach. Betty had the best marriage of everyone she knew. "How is Victor ruining your marriage?"

Betty removed her glasses and dabbed at her eyes. "He's up for partner, and he'll probably get it. Chuck keeps complaining I work too much, and I'm not there for him emotionally when I am home because I'm too worried about money and the future."

"You working too much and Chuck's complaints are not Victor's fault." She wagged her finger. "Besides, they can't make him partner. He hasn't been there long enough."

Betty sipped her mocha and wiped the whipped cream from her mouth. "Duration at the firm has no impact on whether or not you make partner. Billable hours matter. And he has tons more than I have."

Darcy hugged her friend and patted her back. "You and Chuck have been married a long time. You can make it through this rough patch, can't you?"

"Chuck asked if we could go to marriage counseling," Betty whispered through Darcy's hair.

Oh, no, Darcy thought. She tightened the muscles in her lower back. Releasing Betty, she sank into the seat. Marriage counseling failed to save most marriages, including hers. Could Betty avoid it? She racked her brain for a solution. "If Chuck saves money, then can you work less?"

She gulped back more tears. "You don't understand. Chuck can't save money, so we decided I would try to make partner. I thought things were going well, but Chuck now says he'd rather be poor and spend more time with me."

Darcy held her friend's hand for reassurance. "That's what Chuck wants. What do you want?"

"I don't know." She averted her gaze and shrugged. "I don't have a problem with money. He does. As soon as new softball gear comes out, he buys it. We must have a dozen bats at three hundred a piece sitting in our den. Not to mention the jerseys and the hats and the turf shoes. I think his gym membership is more expensive than our dental plan."

"You sound upset...and resentful. What about him? Can he work more hours?"

She shook her head. "How much he works is pointless. He's salaried."

"Can you find a way to earn more and work less?"

She sighed. "I don't know. We've tried all of those home-based businesses from multi-level marketing to essential oils, but nothing brings in as much money as my attorney's fees."

Darcy released Betty's hand. She took a sip of her drink and thought of other alternatives. "Have you any investments?"

"You must be joking." She widened her gaze. "I told you how Chuck lives. Day by day, in the moment, like a child."

"What about you? You must have something saved."

Betty drained her mocha and slammed the cup on the table. "I spent all my savings on him. Traveling to those tournaments isn't free, you know."

Darcy shrugged. "I guess you're going to marriage

counseling."

Betty stared at her empty cup. "I guess I am."

A rush of despair washed over Darcy when she noticed Betty's defeated face. She recalled the last days of her own marriage as she sat in a therapist's office, confessing troubles she thought she would never have in a marriage she thought would always last. She clutched Betty's hand and fiercely squeezed. If Betty and Chuck could not save their marriage, then what hope existed for any of the couples she knew?

****

That afternoon at the café, Darcy sat across from Victor, waiting for the server to bring their order. She placed her napkin on her lap and fiddled with her silverware, thinking about her earlier conversation with Betty.

"Will you please stop fidgeting?" Victor motioned to her hands on the silverware. "You're making me nervous."

The fork tumbled from her hand and clattered against the table.

He pursed his lips into a straight line. "What's wrong?" He placed his hand over her wrist.

A tremor of pleasure rippled up her arm from the heat of his skin. She gazed into his soft brown eyes and tugged away her hand. "I know it's none of my business, but have you been nominated for partner?"

He chuckled, releasing her wrist. "Is that all you're worried about?"

She furrowed her brow. "Yes, it is. Betty thinks you're her competition, and she'll lose."

He frowned. "I'm only building my clientele so I can start my own firm one day." He held her gaze.

"But, please, don't tell anyone. This information is confidential."

She hated when people were meddlesome, giving unsolicited career advice, but she needed to say something to intervene. "Can you stop building your clientele until after Betty makes partner?"

"You women get hysterical over nothing." He lifted his empty palms and shook his head. "Betty works hard. She's been with the firm forever. I don't know why she thinks she won't get it."

"She doesn't have as many billable hours as you have."

"So?" He waved his hand. "I work longer and harder than everyone else."

Frowning, she twisted the napkin in her lap. "Why don't you have a life outside of work?"

He crossed his arms over his chest and scoffed. "Like you?"

Straightening her spine, she leaned forward. "I have my book club and my daughter's wedding. Don't you have any hobbies?"

A broad smile creased his face. "The only hobby I have is sleep."

"We need to change that fact," she said.

"I'm happy the way I am."

She threw up her arms. "You're ruining my best friend's life. She's working way too many hours to make partner. If she fails, she will have lost her promotion and her husband."

He pointed at his chest, his eyes wide. "Why are you blaming me?"

As she exhaled, she shook her head. How could she divert his attention from work long enough for Betty to make partner? She had to think of something, anything, to distract him. "Do you like to read?"

He nodded. "Legal briefs, trade magazines, business journals."

"Join my book club. We read the classics. We meet every Friday night at Ophelia's Bar and Grill. You'll work less and spend more time with me." Although she did want to spend more time with him, she bit her lower lip and hoped he didn't notice the last phrase.

He chuckled. "I can't just stop working so your friend can make partner."

Relief wound through her body, and she exhaled. Thank goodness, he didn't think she liked him romantically. Tapping her finger against her chin, she continued thinking of another plan. She lifted her finger and widened her eyes. "I have an idea on how you can cut back your hours without jeopardizing your long-term plan. If you're starting your own firm, I'm sure you'll be recruiting associates. Tell your new prospects you're full with clients and refer them to one of the attorneys who will be working for you. Leave at five each night and go grocery shopping for dinner. Spend two hours cooking and a half hour eating and another half hour cleaning up. Read a couple of chapters from the assigned reading. Attend the book club every Friday night. Start living." She slumped against the chair and gulped a breath.

He twisted his lips into a crooked smile. "I'm touched you think so much about your friend's welfare, but I'm not the only attorney at the firm. Someone else could still beat her out for partner. What will either of us do?"

Closing her eyes, she sighed. Why did everything

have to be so difficult? When she opened her eyes, the server had delivered their food—turkey sandwiches. She gazed at her plate and then up at Victor. She needed something more appealing to occupy his time. "Do you know how to dance?"

He tucked a leaf of lettuce between two pieces of turkey. "I don't like dancing."

"What will we do at my ex-husband's wedding?"

"Drink until we get drunk."

"Impossible." She sipped from her glass of water. "From what my daughter says, they aren't serving alcohol."

He lifted his eyebrows. "Why not?"

"They want people to remember the event."

"That's what photos are for."

"Exactly." She bit into her tender turkey sandwich layered with tart cranberry sauce, chewed, and swallowed. "At least, we agree on that item."

"We agree on a lot of things."

"Like what?"

He pointed to their sandwiches.

"Not enough." She shook her head.

Swallowing a bite of sandwich, he wiped his mouth with a napkin. "I'll make sure Betty gets promoted on one condition."

She arched her eyebrows.

"Stop bugging me about your book club."

She opened her mouth. "That's it?"

He flashed a crooked smile. "What else do you want?"

For him to spend more time with her, she thought. A burning desire fanned her face, and she glanced down at her tangled hands in her lap. When she lifted her head, she met his gaze. A rush of heat flooded her veins, tensing every muscle in her body. "Umm," she mumbled. "Nothing." Why couldn't she stop thinking of him romantically?

****

While Gary met with his accountant in the library to discuss the financial state of his divorce, Darcy sat in the family room, watching Paul and Patty perform their latest song-and-dance routine.

The children held hands and sang, "This Land Is Your Land."

They are simple and peaceful and full of love and happiness, she thought. Ah, what I would give to be a child again. She clapped as soon as the song ended. Sometimes, she enjoyed the "extra services" part of her contract. Supervising Gary's children was easy since they were so well behaved.

Climbing up on the sofa next to her, Paul and Patty snuggled close. "Do you think our mommy will like it?"

How would she know what their mother would like? Didn't the children know that not all working mothers shared the same sensibilities? Of course not, she thought. They're only children who miss their mother. Who *was* their mother? From what she had been told, Kathleen worked as an executive at a Silicon Valley technology firm. Gary and Victor portrayed her as a woman who cared more about her employees than her family. During their divorce, Nathan painted Darcy as a heartless career woman who didn't care about fighting for full custody of their daughter. Unbearable pain ripped through her body with the memory. "I don't know."

"We can practice again," Paul said.

He had Gary's round face and soft gray eyes, but his voice sounded firm with determination.

Patty snuggled up against Darcy's arm.

Her hair smelled of strawberries.

She gazed up into Darcy's eyes. "We need to sing the very best song in the whole wide world."

"Why?" Darcy knitted together her brows.

Patty stared at the floor. As her lower lip quivered, she hugged her legs to her chest. "Because that's how we're going to get Mommy to come home with us."

Hadn't anyone told the children about the divorce? Darcy clenched her hands.

Patty sniffled.

"Come here, sweetheart." Compassion thawed her heart, and she tucked Patty closer.

The little girl shivered.

Darcy squeezed her shoulder and kissed the top of her head. Oh, how she wished she could lie to the girl to spare her from the pain. "Tell me, when are you seeing your mother?"

"This weekend," Patty said. "Daddy's going to take us."

Why would Gary subject his children to false hope and empty promises? He needed to discuss the visitation process with her or Victor first, so they could devise an age-appropriate action plan for the children. She raised her eyebrows. "He is?"

Patty nodded. "Daddy has to stay at a hotel, but we get to stay at Mommy's house."

And the visitation rotation begins, she thought.

Gary padded into the family room. "Does anyone want some hot apple cider?"

"Me!" Both children raised their hands.

Gary glanced from his children to Darcy. "What about you?"

"Sure." She stood. "Let me help you."

In the kitchen, Darcy cornered Gary by the refrigerator. "Why didn't you tell me you're taking the kids to San Jose this weekend to see their mom?"

Blood flushed his cheeks. "I—guess—I thought—"

"No, you didn't think." She shook her finger. "Your kids are practicing a song they learned in preschool. They believe if they sing the song perfectly, then their mother will come back home. When it doesn't work, they'll blame themselves for her leaving the family. You can't let the children think it is their fault their family fell apart." She stepped closer and narrowed her gaze. "Didn't you discuss any of this situation with your therapist?"

As he placed it on the stove, Gary fumbled with the pot. "She said the children need to see their mother."

Darcy leaned a hip against the counter. She didn't want to come across as a pushy know-it-all, but she wanted to impress the importance of keeping the children truthfully informed. "Did she recommend how you approach them about the visit?"

Gary searched the cabinets and set three mugs on the counter. "She said I should tell them Mommy and Daddy are not getting back together, but they can see Mommy every now and then."

Relief flooded through her. She stepped away from the counter and placed her hands on her hips. "Have you told them?"

He rubbed his damp eyes and sniffled. "I don't want to talk about it." He turned his back toward her.

She crossed her arms over her chest and waited. If she touched him, his reserves might break into an avalanche of tears.

Wiping his eyes on a dishtowel, he continued to snuffle.

"I don't know if your therapist informed you, but your children's mental health can be impacted by what you tell them." She touched his shoulder. "You're a great father, but you're also under an incredible amount of stress. You might suffer from a lapse in judgment if you don't have someone knowledgeable guiding you." She stepped closer. "What did you tell them?"

Pivoting toward the stove, Gary stirred the apple cider. "I told them we are driving to visit Mommy this weekend."

She leaned forward, sniffing cinnamon rising with the steam. "Did they ask why you had to stay at a hotel?"

He wagged his head.

"Do they know you both aren't getting back together?"

Silently, Gary stared at his feet.

Frustration simmered within her. "Why are you allowing them to have hope?"

Tears burst from his eyes.

Folding him into her arms, she let him sob against her shoulder. He smelled of apple cider and baby powder. She rubbed his back. "Please let them know Mommy isn't coming home with them, no matter what they do," she whispered. "You must tell them before they go away this weekend."

Gary clutched her for a long moment before releasing her and stepping away. He turned off the stove and poured the steaming apple cider into three mugs. He handed one mug to Darcy and carried the other two mugs into the family room.

Singing another song, the children bounced on the sofa cushions. "Do you think Mommy will like that song better?"

"All your songs are wonderful." Gary set the mugs on the coffee table and placed his arms around his children. "I have something important to tell you, so listen very closely. I know you're excited about seeing Mommy this weekend, but when we leave on Sunday, she is not coming home with us."

Patty widened her eyes. "Why not?"

"Because Mommy doesn't live here anymore." Gary squeezed her shoulder. "Daddy and Mommy are getting a divorce."

"Why?" Paul frowned.

Gary twisted his hands in his lap. "Because Mommy wants to be in San Jose, and Daddy wants to be in Petaluma."

"But can't we take turns living in San Jose and in Petaluma?" Patty asked.

He hardened his mouth into a tight line. "No, we can't."

"Why?" both children asked, their eyes wide and mouths agape.

"Because…" Gary's voice broke, and he stared at his hands. "Mommy doesn't love Daddy anymore."

The children burst into tears.

Gary rubbed their shoulders until their crying muffled into sniffles. "Things will be all right," he said. "Darcy is here to help us."

Why did Gary mention her? Darcy tensed her

shoulders, forcing a smile on her rigid face.

Paul glanced up and narrowed his gaze. "She's not Mommy."

A hot flicker fanned through her. The children needed to see her as a friend and not an enemy. She turned toward Gary, silently willing him to say the right thing.

"You're right," Gary said. "She's not Mommy, but she's here to help."

Patty sat on her heels. "Why has Mommy stopped loving us?"

Gary widened his gaze. "Oh, no, sweetheart, that's not what I said. Mommy still loves you and Paul."

"But she doesn't love you?" Patty tilted her head.

Gary nodded.

"Why?" Patty asked.

"I don't know." Gary gazed at the carpet and shook his head.

Darcy cleared her throat and touched both children on the shoulders, determined to steer the conversation toward happier territory. "Your father is the luckiest man in the world because you both love him." She gestured toward Gary. "Show him how much you love him."

Paul and Patty exchanged glances before they tackled their father on the sofa.

Gary's gloom erupted into a fit of giggles in the arms of his children.

Deep satisfaction coursed through Darcy's body, although a pang of regret pierced her heart because her daughter never loved her the way Gary's children loved him.

****

Later that night, Darcy curled up in bed to read *Madame Bovary*. What a long Monday! Between dealing with Betty's marriage crisis and Gary's divorce announcement, Darcy looked forward to disappearing into an imaginary world. She slipped on her reading glasses and cracked open the spine of the book.

Deep into the scene of Madame Bovary's wedding, Darcy jumped at the sound of her phone ringing. Who could be calling this late? She grabbed the phone off the nightstand. The caller ID showed Joyce's number. "Is anything wrong?"

Sniffling sobs greeted her.

"Mom, Tyler and I got into a fight registering at Best Wedding Gifts," Joyce said. "I told him I just wanted something classic like a gold rim around the plates. He insisted on paisley. When we finally agreed to go with plain white, we couldn't agree on how many place settings. Tyler said we needed only eight. I suggested we order twelve. He doesn't realize our families will be expanding over time. Eight is not enough."

In her mind, she calculated the total number of people in the immediate family: Tyler and Joyce, Tyler's parents, Nathan and Tanya, and Darcy and Victor. "I think you're overreacting. Eight is enough."

"Eight is not enough. What if we want to invite another couple to Thanksgiving? That's ten people. What if we have children? That's twelve people."

"You'll be fine with eight place settings." She rubbed her forehead. Why couldn't her logical daughter think with reason? "Other couples go to their parents' houses for Thanksgiving. Children eat from plastic plates for many years."

"You don't understand." Joyce sobbed. "Tyler first said he didn't care about the details of the wedding, and now he wants to help plan everything. He's ruining my wedding."

"Your wedding?" How could her daughter be so selfish? "Don't you want his input? After all, he's getting married, too."

"No, I want the wedding of my dreams."

Sighing, she placed the book face down on her lap. Who cared about place settings and patterns? She needed to remind her daughter about the importance of marrying the man of her dreams. "Listen, Joyce. Marriage is full of compromises. If you can't compromise about the wedding plans, then how will you compromise about career conflicts, childrearing challenges, and unexpected catastrophes?"

She sobbed louder.

"Is that what happened between you and Dad? You couldn't compromise?"

Darcy thought back to the early days of her marriage. At first, she only cared about Joyce. Later, she only cared about her career. Finally, she forgot to care about what mattered most—her marriage. "Of course, our inability to compromise contributed to our divorce."

"Did Dad want to plan the wedding?"

She thought about the small event held in her mother's backyard. The informal gathering didn't require reservations, down payments, or gift registries. "No, he didn't. But he wanted to plan other things like where we lived, where we traveled on vacation, and what school you attended. If I didn't agree, I always railroaded him into surrendering to what I wanted when

I should have listened more."

"But Tyler and I have always agreed on everything." She sniffled. "Why are things different now?"

Darcy thought about Madame Bovary's wedding. Even a century ago, planning a wedding consisted of picking a location, inviting guests, and preparing for the festivities from what to serve for dinner to what type of wedding cake to have for dessert. Nowadays, bridal magazines, television shows, and online videos complicated the task even farther. Why not abandon the wedding and elope? Save the money for a down payment on a house or a deposit for the inevitable divorce. "I think you're both under a lot of stress. Planning a wedding comes with tons of pressure. And it brings out various personality traits in different people."

"I don't like these personality traits in Tyler."

"These personality traits are part of his character. You can't change them." Darcy stretched her legs against the smooth percale sheets. "At the very least, you need to resolve these conflicts before you're married and the only alternative is divorce."

"Divorce is the last resort," Joyce said. "For some cultures and religions, divorce is not even an option."

Closing her eyes, she rested her head against the wall. "Are you saying you'll stay married to Tyler even if you're both miserable?"

"That's what premarital counseling is supposed to prevent."

She winced. What revolutionary changes in the field of psychology had transpired to make counseling more effective in preventing divorce? If she asked Joyce, she knew the question would inflame the situation. "Do whatever you want with your relationship, your wedding, and your life. I'm here to support you."

A moment of silence united them.

"I'll bring up this situation in counseling," Joyce said, "and listen to what the priest thinks we should do."

Priest? she thought. What priest does counseling? "I thought you were seeing a psychologist."

"Tyler and I are seeing a priest for premarital counseling. He's Catholic, remember?"

She tugged a sheet over her legs and thought of her former clients who filed for divorce over religious differences. Would Joyce have to attend Mass with her future children even if she didn't believe in a god? "Doesn't the Catholic Church prohibit getting married anywhere except inside a church?"

"We're hiring a non-denominational minister for the ceremony, but we're attending premarital counseling from Father Ahern through Tyler's church."

What a compromise! "I guess hope exists for the marriage after all."

After the call ended, Darcy placed her hand on the paperback and wondered if she would ever love someone enough to set aside her belief to never remarry. What type of man could convince her to embrace a life together?

Chapter 12

On Saturday night, Darcy slipped into her standard black dress and sling back heels and drove over to Bella Mia to meet Monica for her Freedom Party.

The hostess led Darcy to a booth in an intimate corner away from the kitchen and the bar.

Darcy placed a small gift-wrapped box on the candlelit table and ordered a bottle of champagne.

A few minutes later, Monica arrived dressed in a floral sheath and stacked heels. She smiled, her cheeks flushed. No more tired eyes or sadness tugged at the corners of her thin lips.

Darcy stood and hugged her so close she could feel her heartbeat and smell her lily of the valley perfume.

"Thank you so much for planning this event." Monica slid into the booth and glanced wide-eyed around the room. "This restaurant is where my ex-husband and I had our first date. I've come full circle, ending what began in this restaurant twelve years ago."

Oh, happy coincidence, Darcy thought. A moment of pride rushed through her.

The server uncorked a bottle of extra dry champagne and poured two glasses.

"Here's to new beginnings." Darcy lifted her glass, her standard toast to all Freedom Parties. After saying the same words hundreds of times, she felt the tired monotony of starting over again instead of the usual flush of excitement at the next life chapter. Was planning Joyce's wedding rubbing away at her stubborn belief that singlehood was best?

"To new beginnings." Monica clicked her glass for a toast.

They drank half the bottle before their salads arrived.

Monica talked about how she felt ecstatic the first few days after receiving the final paperwork, but how her co-workers and family discounted her feelings, accusing her of being mentally or emotionally ill by celebrating the end of what others would consider the greatest achievement of their lives.

Darcy listened and nodded, having heard the same arguments from other men and women who felt vindicated by their divorce, and not defeated. She remembered her own divorce twenty years ago and how she walked away from her beautiful house and her beautiful daughter. Alone in bed at night, she often cried. Sometimes, when she struggled to support two households on one income, she questioned her decision to leave rather than stay married to a man she no longer trusted.

Through experience, she knew the thrill of victory rushing through Monica's body at this moment would wear off after a couple of months. If asked, she would bet a thousand dollars Monica would call her around the holidays in tears, sobbing about her sorrow and regret over the divorce. She would have to comfort her, reassure her, support her, and encourage her to work through the final stages of grief and on toward the next phase of her life as a single person once again. By providing her with the support she never had, Darcy hoped to lessen Monica's feelings of helplessness, loneliness, and unhappiness. Darcy removed a crepe ribbon from her purse and a pair of scissors. "I have a little ritual I conduct with my clients to help them find closure. I'll hold up the ribbon and have you cut it in half to symbolize breaking the ties of your marriage and embarking on a new life."

Squealing, Monica snipped the ribbon in half.

"This gift is also for you." Darcy slid the card-sized box across the table.

Monica fingered the delicate packaging before removing the silver ribbon and tearing apart the white wrapping paper. She lifted the top of the box and cradled a necklace with a silver owl perched inside a hollowed-out heart.

"The pendant symbolizes following the wisdom of your heart." Darcy touched the owl.

Monica's eyes filled with tears. "Thank you." She hugged Darcy.

"You're welcome," she whispered.

The server slid a plate of manicotti before Monica and a plate of lasagna before Darcy.

The food smelled of basil and oregano. Pouring the rest of the crisp champagne, Darcy ordered another bottle. "So, what's next for you?"

Monica smiled. "I'm going back to school after the holidays to finish my degree. I'm three semesters away from my bachelor's. Then I can move to Silicon Valley and find a job at a high-tech firm and finally support my son the way he needs."

"Good for you."

They finished their dinner.

A group of servers gathered around their table.

Their server placed an individual-sized cake on the table with the words, "Happy Divorce!" written in blue block letters. A single candle glowed in the middle of the cake. Clapping their hands, the servers sang the Freedom Party song Darcy wrote,

"You've got your life back once again, Bella Mia!
No more sleepless nights, no more petty fights
Only happy days in your long, wise life, Bella Mia!
No more ball and chain, no more spouse to claim
Only freedom and your own last name, Bella Mia!"
A few of the neighboring patrons clapped.

Darcy flushed with pride. "Make a wish." She pushed the cake closer to Monica.

For a moment, Monica closed her eyes. When she opened them, she leaned forward and blew out the candle.

"Don't tell me what you wished for." She wagged her finger. "Otherwise, it won't come true."

Laughing, Monica spread her arms wide. "I already have everything."

Not everything, Darcy thought. For the first time since her divorce, Darcy felt something was missing.

Chapter 13

The following night, high winds howled through the neighborhood. Listening to the rattling windows, Darcy tossed and turned. Finally, she drifted off into an unsettled sleep. She woke from a loud explosion. Sirens screamed in the distance.

Her phone rang. When she picked it up, she noticed Victor's phone number. Why would he call at four-thirty in the morning? She answered, but no one responded.

Someone knocked on her bedroom door. "The sky's on fire," Sam said.

Fire? Stumbling out of bed, she cinched her robe around her waist and shoved her feet into slippers. She opened the door and followed Sam to the kitchen where Linda stood by the TV watching the newscaster report on the Tubbs fire sweeping over Fountaingrove.

"Sonoma County is waking up early to the worst fire this county has seen in a century," the newscaster reported. "Around ten o'clock last night, high winds carried a spark from a wildfire in Napa to Santa Rosa. By one o'clock this morning, hundreds of homes had caught fire."

Darcy held her breath. Shooting flames lapped up a subdivision of million-dollar homes in spite of firefighters spraying a constant stream of water. Panic raced through her chest. "Do we need to evacuate?"

Linda offered Darcy a cup of coffee. "Not yet. The Nun's fire is still over the hill from us on the south side and the Tubbs fire is too far north. But if the fire crosses the ridge and enters Annadel State Park, then we'll be asked to leave."

Darcy drank the bitter coffee and set the empty mug on the counter. "I'm going outside." As soon as she stepped onto the porch, she wrinkled her nose at the smoke singeing the cool autumn air. From the north, above the roofline of Sam and Linda's house, the sky lit up with plumes of crimson flames. "The whole world looks like the apocalypse." She covered her mouth and coughed. "The air stinks like a barbecue without meat." Smoke stung her eyes and irritated her nose. Crossing her arms underneath her breasts, she listened to the pop and fizzle of electrical transformers exploding and sirens blasting. She grabbed her phone to call Joyce, but she had no dial tone. Darting into the house, she shut the door and ran into the kitchen. "Does the land line work?"

Sam handed her the phone.

She keyed in her daughter's phone number and waited. Each long ring took several heartbeats to complete. "Hello?"

"Joyce, it's Mom. We're having a wildfire. The authorities haven't asked us to evacuate yet, but I'd rather be safe than sorry. May I stay with you until the fires are contained?"

"Of course," Joyce said. "My apartment's tiny, but there's room on the couch."

"Thank you. I don't have cell coverage for some reason, so you might not be able to contact me. I'll leave as soon as possible."

"Be safe," Joyce said.

Darcy wondered if she had enough gas to drive fifty miles south to San Francisco. She handed Sam the phone.

"You're overreacting," Sam said. "They'll have the fire contained by tonight."

With her heartbeat racing, she stared at the TV screen. A wall of flames incinerated a forest of trees near a house. The scene panned to the local hospital. Doctors and nurses pushed patients in wheelchairs and boarded them onto buses to transport them out of the county. Finally, the cameras showed a mobile home park scorched to ashes. Firefighters hosed water on the blaze to prevent the flames from crossing the street to an ammunition store.

Did Victor call because of the fire? "I need the phone again." Darcy opened her palm and wiggled her fingers.

Sam frowned, offering the phone.

Scrunching her forehead, she dialed his number and waited.

He picked up on the second ring.

"Victor, it's Darcy."

"Are you all right?"

She heard panic in his voice. "I'm fine."

"Have you evacuated yet?"

"I'm going to San Francisco to stay with my daughter." She clutched a fist to her chest. "What about you? Are you okay?"

"I'm fine," he said. "I'm in Windsor. The fire has to travel much farther north to affect me."

"I'm leaving." She ran her fingers through tangled hair. "You can't reach me. I don't have any cell coverage."

"That's because the fire destroyed the cell towers in Fountaingrove. You'll get coverage again once you leave the county."

A shiver of panic raced through her. Fountaingrove burned. No more Paradise Ridge Winery. She must find a new wedding venue for Joyce. No time to worry. "I'll call when I get to my daughter's house. Have you heard from Betty?"

"She's been evacuated. She's staying at her husband's brother's house for now."

What if Sam and Linda's house burned? She gulped. Where would she live? She felt her heartbeat gallop. As she hung up the phone, Darcy nudged away the thought. She downed another cup of coffee and started packing. With trembling hands, she shoved the essentials of her life into a suitcase. "Won't you leave?"

Sam and Linda shook their heads.

She hugged them goodbye. After tossing the luggage into the trunk, she jumped into the driver's seat and turned the key in the ignition. The engine purred. She shifted into reverse and backed out of the driveway, barreling down the street. As she merged into southbound bumper-to-bumper freeway traffic, she slowed to a stop. Hurry, hurry, hurry, she thought. Gripping the steering wheel tighter, she glanced up into the rearview mirror at the blazing sky. Had she left too late?

****

With increased traffic, the one-hour drive to San Francisco extended into two-and-a-half hours. Darcy slid into a parking spot three blocks from Joyce's apartment. She stood and arched her back, aching from the long drive. Cold, damp, foggy air prickled her skin. As cars sped past, honking at jay walkers and cyclists, the smells of garbage and exhaust burned in her lungs.

As soon as she left Sonoma County, cell coverage resumed. She called Joyce to let her know she had arrived safely.

"I'm at work," Joyce said. "A private gated walkway is to the back of the building. I left the key under the doormat. I'll see you tonight after work, okay?"

"Okay." She trembled from the shock of the events leading up to her evacuation. From her trunk, she lifted her suitcase and wheeled it up the sidewalks to Joyce's apartment, a pink-and-white Painted Lady Victorian with lace curtains in the windows. She stepped into the open kitchen, dining, and living room space overlooking Alamo Square Park. The apartment reminded her of the studio she rented outside Beverly Hills following her divorce.

After kicking off her shoes, she padded barefoot to the living room and turned on the big screen TV to watch the latest news on the fire. No areas of containment were announced. The newscaster stated the fires continued to spread.

In spite of her fear, she felt hunger tug at her stomach. She stalked into the kitchen and peered into the refrigerator. The crispers brimmed with fruits and vegetables. The door contained several bottles of water. After careful consideration, she grabbed a bottle of water and a bowl of grapes. Tucking her feet underneath her hips, she perched on the sofa. While munching, she stared at the wall of fire threatening to burn down the community she had called home these past three years. Shock and numbness spread through her body.

During the first commercial break, she called Victor. "I'm safe in San Francisco. How are things in Windsor?"

"Same," Victor said. "My mom's been evacuated, though. I invited her to stay with me, but she can't climb stairs."

"Where is she?"

"She took the first flight to Texas. Her house burned down, so she'll be staying with my sister indefinitely."

"Unbelievable." Sweeping hair off her forehead, she whistled soft and low. "I'm so glad she's safe."

"Me, too," he said. "But I'll miss her. We used to have dinner every Sunday night."

How sweet, she thought. She curled her lips into an involuntary smile. "I hope you will see her again soon."

"So do I." He sighed. "Now, I have one more reason to visit my sister."

She stared at the flames fanning across the TV screen. "Have you heard from anyone else?"

"Just clients," he said. "And you?"

"No one." As she speculated about the safety of her clients and book club members, she felt a shiver run up her spine. "I should start making calls."

"How is Joyce treating you?"

She snickered. "She's not home yet, so we haven't had the chance to strangle each other."

"Be kind," he warned. "Emotions run high during a crisis."

"I'll do my best."

"If things get bad between you two, you can

always stay with me…unless you can't climb stairs."

Smiling, she leaned back against the couch cushions. A warm glow filled her body. "I appreciate the offer."

"I mean what I say."

"I know you do." Feeling her face flush, she bit her lower lip.

"Take care," he said.

"I will." She nodded. "Goodbye."

For the next several hours, Darcy texted and called everyone she knew.

Betty responded first with a brief phone call. "Ten people are now at Chuck's brother's house," she said. "Chuck's ex-wife even showed up. I told him just one of us could stay, so he turned her away."

"You didn't?" She gasped. "I know you don't like her much, but turning someone away in an emergency is kind of mean."

"She has a boyfriend who is safe in Petaluma," Betty said. "Why does she have to run to her ex-husband? Because Chucky still takes care of her, and his devotion makes me sick."

Oh, boy, Darcy thought. Crises unleashed the worst in people.

Next, she called the members of her book club and her favorite clients. She wrote down their statuses in her wedding planner notebook:

Barry—safe in downtown Santa Rosa

Anita and Eric in Oakmont—no mandatory evacuation yet

Charlotte—safe in Rohnert Park

Lucas—mandatory evacuation from Northwest Santa Rosa near Coffey Park

Monica—no power in Rincon Valley, voluntary evacuation

Gary—safe in Petaluma

Sam and Linda—still at home, still safe

Afterward, exhausted from rising early and drained from the initial rush of panic, Darcy turned off the TV and curled up on the couch to take a nap. But her restless body buzzed with the threat of imminent danger, and her mind wandered toward worst-case scenarios. After an hour, she abandoned all hope for rest, turned on the TV, and watched the latest destruction from the fires. Anxiety knotted her chest.

When would Joyce come home?

By evening, the pink and gold lights of the setting sun dimmed into soupy grayness.

Joyce jangled her keys in the lock and entered the kitchen with her arms laden with grocery bags full of fresh vegetables. "Mom, are you here?"

Before enveloping her with a big hug and kiss, Darcy greeted her daughter by grabbing the bags and setting them on the quartz counter. "It's so good to see you."

"Of course." Joyce kissed her mother's cheek. "How long are you staying?"

"Until it's safe to return home." She pointed to the TV. "Coffey Park subdivision has burned. The fires are coming up from the east and the south. People in Sonoma, Glen Ellen, and Kenwood have evacuated. If the fires worsen, the residents of Oakmont must evacuate. My book club members, Anita and Eric, will need shelter. Victor's mom already lost her home. This fire is crazy." Grabbing Joyce's hands, she led her to the sofa. "I have bad news. Fountaingrove has burned.

Paradise Ridge Winery is gone."

Eyes wide, Joyce gasped. "I can't believe it. We placed a ten-thousand-dollar deposit."

"I'm sure they'll refund us if the records exist."

Joyce stood. She paced back and forth across the hardwood floor. "The fires destroyed my wedding venue! Now, where will I find a location for the wedding of my dreams?" She spun and outstretched her arms. "How could this disaster happen?"

Shaking her head, she sighed. "No one knows how the fires started. Some speculate the high winds caused downed power lines that created sparks that flew from one county to the next." She spread her arms. "All I know is Mother Nature is out of control."

Joyce sank on the sofa, buried her head in her hands, and sobbed.

Sitting beside her, Darcy rubbed her daughter's back. She felt her ribs through the dress suit. Didn't she eat? Maybe Darcy could whip up something to put a little bit of meat on her bones. "How about I make some spaghetti? You used to like my homemade sauce."

Joyce lifted her head and narrowed her eyes. "How can you think of food when I have no place to get married?"

"You're overreacting. Victor's mom has no home. Thousands of other homes have burned to the ground. Hundreds of people are missing. Pets have been separated from their owners. You and I are lucky to be here—alive and well. If we're to have enough strength to overcome this catastrophe, we need to take care of our bodies, nourishing them with food, water, exercise, and sleep."

Joyce shook her fist at the TV. "I don't care about

everyone else's problems. My wedding venue is gone."

Full of disappointment, Darcy opened her mouth. "Where is your compassion? I didn't raise you to be so selfish."

"You're right. You didn't raise me." Joyce stood. "Dad and Tanya did."

Darcy sank back against the sofa, feeling as if she had been slapped in the face and punched in the gut at the same time. "I did the best I could under the circumstances."

Joyce scrunched her face and shook her fist. "You cared more about work than you cared about me."

Tired of the same tirade, Darcy swung her legs off the couch and stood. "I worked to provide a roof over your head. I gave so much money I had no place to live. I had to visit you at restaurants or parks until I could afford to move into a two-bedroom condo." Tears brimmed in her eyes. "I *am* your mother. I deserve to be treated with respect, whether you like it or not." Trembling, she grabbed her luggage and wheeled it toward the front door.

"Where are you going?" Joyce asked.

"Anywhere but here." Darcy slammed the door, feeling like she no longer belonged in her daughter's life. Perhaps, she never had.

Chapter 14

Darcy sat in the dim motel bar, drinking a gin martini with two olives, while reports of the fire played on the TV above rows of liquor bottles glinting like amber and crystal jewels in the electric light. She spent the last hour driving north to Novato before checking into the last motel room available. Then she stalked across the parking lot through the cold, smoky air to the bar for a hamburger and fries and as many gin martinis as she could stomach.

For the third time since she arrived, she checked the blue glow of her phone. No messages. No missed calls. Flinching, she shoved the phone into her purse. Why didn't she exist outside her daughter's immediate, self-serving needs?

"Another?" the bartender asked.

She stared at the two olives in the empty glass. Two, so they wouldn't be lonely. Why was she alone? Victor had offered her a place to say. Why didn't she call him? "No, thank you." She placed her credit card on the counter.

Stumbling on wobbly knees, she wandered outside the bar and stomped through the gravel parking lot. The dark sky, singed with smoke, enveloped her in a smothering choke hold. She coughed. Fumbling with the key, she flicked on the light to the dingy room, kicked off her shoes, and closed the door. She hoped the drowsy effect of the alcohol would knock her into a senseless slumber, but she stayed awake, eyes wide, worrying about her relationship with Joyce and the love she had for Victor.

****

Suspended in a bubble of firestorms, text messages, phone calls, and news updates, Darcy huddled in the motel room over the next five days, waiting for Joyce to contact her. Everyone around her continued with their lives—going to work, enjoying time with family and friends—while she read each service alert, waiting for the all-clear sign to return home. By the sixth day, first responders contained thirty percent of the fire. At least, the wind had died. As far as Marin, haze from the wildfires veiled the sky. Breathing the smoke-filled air felt worst than inhaling a pack of cigarettes.

On Saturday evening, Nathan called. "Are you still coming to our wedding next weekend?"

Darcy sat in the motel bar, drinking a gin martini, waiting for her daily hamburger and fries while she watched the latest updates on the TV. "I told our daughter I would be there. I keep my promises, remember? I'm not cruel and heartless like our daughter who won't call to see if I'm still alive."

"Well, that issue is between you two. Don't get me involved. Joyce is pretty upset her wedding is ruined. I suggested she and Tyler get married down here where it's safe."

"You must be kidding. You're always involved." She snickered. "LA is not immune to wildfires. What about the Santa Ana winds?" She tore her napkin to shreds. "You should be a better father and tell our daughter to call her mother and apologize for being so selfish as to think her wedding is more important than the twenty-three lives lost and the five thousand one hundred homes and businesses destroyed."

The silence on the phone rattled like a cage. "Are you there?" she asked over the din of the bar.

"I'm here."

She balled up the shredded napkin in her fist. "Since Joyce isn't talking to me, you can talk to her on my behalf and tell her let's wait to see what's left standing in Santa Rosa before moving the wedding to LA."

"Okay, I'll tell her, but I'm not sure she'll listen."

After ending the call, she received a text from Victor.

Will you come over for dinner tomorrow night?

The words glowed with meaning. Over the past six days, she had been in constant contact. His texts always left her wondering whether or not she should accept his offer and stay with him in Windsor.

Sam and Linda, who ignored the voluntary evacuation, urged her to return home. She dreaded driving through the smoky air, risking a mandatory evacuation with the fires only thirty percent contained. What if the winds changed direction and blew flames down the hills surrounding Sam and Linda's house? No, she decided, she'd stay until officials declared the area safe. In addition, she received daily updates from Betty who worked fourteen hour days in the downtown law office to avoid dealing with Chuck's extended family. She also heard occasionally from the members of her book club, who struggled with their family battles during this crisis.

She stared at the text. He must be lonely with his

mother out of state, she thought. The bartender placed a plate of hamburger and fries before her and pointed to her empty glass. "One more?" She tucked a crisp, salty fry in her mouth and nodded.

Moments later, the bartender returned with her gin martini. He glanced at her phone on the counter. "Boyfriend?"

Feeling betrayed by her wishful thinking, she blushed. "No, he's just a friend from work."

Her phone beeped with a text from the county's emergency services.

—Mandatory evacuation lifted in Santa Rosa—

Sighing, she felt a shiver of anxiety. She would have to return tomorrow and witness everything first-hand she had seen on the news.

The bartender placed her tab next to her plate and leaned against the counter. "I say you go out with him. He's interested if he's texting on a Saturday night."

Pointing to the cell phone, she bristled. "It's an alert to let me know the mandatory and voluntary evacuations have been lifted. I can finally go home."

Her phone beeped again with another text from Victor.

Do you prefer chicken parmesan or chicken marsala?

The bartender peered at the screen and snickered. "I'm telling you he likes you. No guy volunteers to cook for anyone unless the lady's special."

"He misses his mother." She picked up her hamburger. "She used to have dinner with him on Sunday nights until her house burned, and she moved to Texas."

Drying his hands on a dishtowel, he nodded. "His

interest is even more serious than I thought. You rank right up there with his mother."

Blushing, she chewed a bite of the juicy hamburger. After she swallowed, she wiped her hands on a new napkin and typed:

—I don't like chicken—

A few moments later, he responded.

I'll make beef wellington instead

The bartender pointed to her phone. "That dish takes three hours to make. He likes you."

A hot bolt of lust flickered through her. He likes me, she thought. A cold blast of fear paralyzed her. What if he's like Gary and loves to cook for anyone? She tucked her phone into her purse and shoved a fry into her mouth. "I'm old enough to be his mother."

The bartender chuckled. "If my mother looked like you, I'd still live at home."

She blushed. Why was he flirting? Feeling uncomfortable from the attention, she paid her bill and packed up her remaining food to go. She didn't want to escalate the conversation with the bartender anymore than she wanted to consider the possibility of a romance with the man who provided the most business leads. No one needed to know, late at night, she often fantasized about Victor before falling to sleep.

In the privacy of the motel room, she flipped on the TV to the news and crossed her legs on the bed and finished eating her hamburger and fries. She lifted her phone from her purse and stared at the series of texts. With her head swimming from the booze and the bartender's flattery, she stopped worrying about the meaning behind the messages and quickly typed.

—Okay. What time?—

Nine seconds later, he responded.

Six-thirty. Here's my address.

She clutched the phone to her chest, the possibilities between a friendly dinner and a budding romance toggled back and forth in her mind. What if Victor was attracted to her? Could she return the affection without falling in love?

****

Darcy drove through Santa Rosa on Sunday morning, and ashes fluttered like dirty snowflakes against her windshield. A thick haze blanketed the remaining trees lining the freeway. Smoky air filtered through the vents of her ancient sports sedan, even though she switched the ventilation system on recycle.

When she turned into the quiet street where she lived, everything on the surface seemed the same, from the manicured lawns to the white picket porches. She parked on the street and unloaded her suitcase.

At the front door, Sam and Linda waited.

"I don't know why you left." Sam followed Darcy to her car to unload the rest of her belongings. "We weren't in any danger."

Linda pointed to the southern hills. "I was only scared once when smoke came over the ridge."

"We didn't know the firefighters started a backfire to stop the flames from spreading into Annadel Park," Sam said. "The backfires worked. We're safe as can be."

Linda hugged Darcy. "We missed you."

"It's good to be home." Darcy squeezed Linda's soft, fleshy back. As she realized her landlady cared more about her than her daughter, a bittersweet wave of belonging flooded through her.

****

That evening, Darcy drove north on Highway 101 to Victor's condo where she agreed to meet for dinner. To the left, buildings crumbled in blackened heaps along the freeway. The red pointed roof of the Puerto Vallarta restaurant looked like a melted red pot of clay smothered over a pile of black ash. To the right, the Fountaingrove Inn, once a stately hotel of stone masonry, collapsed into charred ruin. Hundreds of feet above, the Hilton Hotel toppled into blackened rubble. Husks of cars, spines of trees, and powdery white towers of chimneys without houses lined the road parallel to the freeway. Farther north, acres of burnt vineyards scarred the landscape.

Shock propelled through Darcy's body. As her breathing slowed, she tightened her hands on the steering wheel. How could the city where she lived look like the remains of hell?

Eventually, the landscape transformed from burned buildings and charred trees to the picturesque images of commercial buildings, shopping malls, and subdivision homes found in travel magazines. She breathed in deeply, her hands relaxing against the steering wheel. The remaining buildings blanketing the green spaces comforted her. She turned off the freeway into downtown Windsor and drove through the quaint streets to Victor's home. She parked in front of a row of shops and ascended the staircase between a deli and an Indian restaurant where the scent of curry overpowered the smoky air.

On the second knock, he opened the door. "Welcome to my humble abode," he said. "I'm so glad you agreed to join me for dinner." He enveloped her in an embrace.

She melted against his tight, firm body, feeling safe.

With a quick peck on the cheek, he released her. He wore an Antique or Not? T-shirt with the long sleeves rolled up to his elbows, faded denim jeans, and a pair of sheepskin slippers. He placed her purse on the credenza and hung her jacket in the hall closet before ushering her into the living room crowded with heavy antique furniture. Photographs of Victor and his sister at various ages hung between black-and-white photographs of other relatives on the amber-colored walls. A picture window overlooked the parking lot. From below, the scent of curry seeped into the room.

"I don't know how you can live above a restaurant." She scrunched her nose at the smell of curry.

He shrugged. "I just need someplace to sleep."

She pointed to a black-and-white photograph of a woman who sat with her head tilted to one side. She had the same eyes as Victor. "Is that your mother?"

"Grandmother." He smiled. "She would have liked you."

Kicking off her heels, she curled up on the sofa and tucked her feet under her hips. "How's your mom?"

"Fine." He sat next to her. "She's lucky her young neighbors helped her escape or she would have died. I'm very grateful. I had the couple over for dinner the night before I invited you. They made me regret being single."

"Why?"

His eyes glistened with tears. Turning away, he sniffled. "Being alone during a crisis is hard."

Recalling the nights she spent alone in the motel, she nodded. Why hadn't she come over? "At least, you get along with your mother." She pointed to her chest. "Look at me. I have an ex-husband I hate and a daughter who takes me for granted. If you ask me, that's worse than being alone."

"You're not alone." He met her gaze.

She shivered. Why did he look at her like she was the most precious item in the room? Uncomfortable with the intensity of desire, she shifted on the sofa. "May I help cook anything?"

"No, the food is done." He grasped her hand. "I just didn't want to rush things. But if you're hungry, I'll serve you now."

Gulping, she stared at their interlocking fingers. A flicker of lust fanned through her body.

He scooted closer. "Did you enjoy your week with Joyce?"

Resentment reared within her. Tugging her hand away, she stood. "We had a fight over Paradise Ridge Winery burning. I left the first night and stayed in a motel in Novato the whole week."

"Why didn't you come here?" Standing, he wrinkled his forehead. "I said you could stay."

"I couldn't impose." As a brush of intimacy shivered through her, she feared falling in love. She ran her fingers through her hair. "I'm not family."

He waved an arm toward the wall of pictures. "See my family? My grandparents and my father are dead. My sister and my mother are in Texas. Who else is around to protect and cherish?"

Tears threatened to well in Darcy's eyes. A week had passed since her fight with Joyce. Why hadn't her daughter called? A tear trickled down her cheek. She turned toward the picture window. A pink and orange sunset blazed across the blue sky. Why would he want to protect and cherish her? "We're just business colleagues."

"We're friends." He gripped her shoulders until she faced him. "Friends are family you choose." He widened his dark eyes. "I choose you. Won't you choose me back?"

Staring at his full lips, she struggled against the urge to kiss him and tell him she had chosen him the moment she noticed him at the Gala. "I guess we're friends."

He squeezed her shoulders and smiled. "Let's eat."

In the kitchen, Darcy sat at the small round table and waited for Victor to serve the beef wellington, mashed potatoes, and green beans. Everything smelled savory. She beamed, radiant with appreciation at how much work he had invested.

He poured two glasses of red wine.

She lifted her glass for a toast. "To friends."

Clicking his glass against hers, he winked. "To us."

Sipping the woodsy wine, she buried her face behind the glass to hide the desire flaming her cheeks. How could she be his friend when her body wanted so much more?

Chapter 15

Betty and Darcy stood in line at Katie's Koffee during the Monday morning rush hour. They chatted, catching up over the week from hell where the fires destroyed not only the physical landscape, but the emotional landscape of everyone's lives. Betty escaped through work, holing up in safety at the downtown office whereas Darcy hid at a cheap motel, worrying about how to reconnect with her clients to replace the lost income for the week. The smells of coffee and pastries filled the air, reminding them both of simpler days when families didn't war over territories in the houses left standing and the biggest worry anyone had didn't involve survival against a natural disaster.

Betty ordered a caramel mocha and a blueberry muffin.

Darcy ordered a cappuccino and a cinnamon walnut scone.

"We're together." After signaling the server, Betty removed her wallet and turned to Darcy. "My treat."

She frowned. They always paid Dutch. "Are you sure?"

Smiling, she nodded. "Yes, I'm paying."

They found a table at the back of the coffee shop. Frost from the cool morning covered the window in a light film.

Darcy shivered, clutched her cup closer to her face,

and breathed in the warm aroma.

Betty licked the whipped cream off her mocha. "Guess who made partner?"

She gasped. Had she heard correctly? "You made partner?"

Chuckling, Betty deepened her smile. "Yes, my hard work finally paid off."

"Congratulations!" She stood and embraced her friend.

"Don't be so proud of me yet." She squeezed and released Darcy. "They offered it to Victor first, but he refused."

"He did?" Darcy leaned back in her chair. Victor had kept his word.

"I'm so happy I don't have to worry anymore." She laughed. "Chuck and I will retire in comfort."

Smiling, she patted Betty's hand. "How thrilling. Let's get together this weekend to celebrate."

Leaning forward, she crossed her arms on the table and frowned. "Isn't this weekend your ex's wedding?"

"Oh, my goodness, you're right." Darcy slapped her forehead. How could she have forgotten? "I guess I should buy a new dress."

Betty threw up her hands. "You haven't shopped yet?"

Shaking her head, she took a sip of bittersweet coffee. "I haven't done anything except RSVP. Victor's taken care of everything else. He wanted to charge the expenses on his card to earn frequent flyer miles, so he can fly for free to see his mother and sister in Texas. I told him I would pay my half once the bill arrives."

Betty clenched her napkin. "Are you nervous?"

"No," Darcy lied. When she thought of witnessing

the exchange of marital vows between two people she did not like and spending the entire day with Victor, she felt her calm demeanor crumble. "Should I be?"

"I would be." Betty tilted her head to one side. "When did you last visit everyone?"

Nibbling on the sweet cinnamon scone, she thought for a while. "I guess around three years ago."

"I know what you need to do." She slapped the table. "Buy something stunning. Maybe an off-the-shoulder dress in a rich color like burgundy or a tea-length gown in sparkling silver."

"The wedding colors are blue and gold." Darcy sighed. "My daughter wants me to wear gold, since she's wearing blue."

Betty wrinkled her nose. "You don't look good in gold. The color washes out your skin tone." She picked up her muffin and pulled at the paper cup. "What's Victor wearing?"

She shrugged. "A standard tux, I assume."

She lifted her eyebrows. "You guys haven't talked about your outfits?"

"What's there to talk about?" Lifting her hand, she curled each finger toward her palm as she discussed the itinerary. "He's picking me up on Saturday morning. Our flight leaves at seven a.m. Victor wants to sightsee since he's never been to Los Angeles. We can check in at the hotel at three. The wedding starts at five. The reception is from seven to midnight. We'll probably leave at ten p.m. since our return flight leaves at six the next morning, and we both need some sleep."

"That schedule's very tight. Why don't you stay an extra night and return on Monday?"

She frowned, thinking of the business she lost since

the wild fires. "We have to work."

Tapping on her phone, Betty brought up the airline's website. "If you're returning to the Schulz Airport, a flight on Monday leaves at six a.m. You'll get here by eight-thirty and can make your first appointment at nine." She handed her phone to Darcy and pointed to the flight details.

Nudging the phone across the table, she chuckled. "Tell it to Victor, the workaholic."

Betty tucked the phone in her purse and picked up her drink with determination. "I will."

She considered spending an extra day with Victor without work or a wedding, and a warm feeling buzzed through her. She hoped Betty convinced Victor to stay another day. Maybe their business-like arrangement would transform into a romantic interlude, and they would become much more than friends.

****

Early on Saturday morning, Darcy woke to knocking.

"Someone's here to see you," Sam yelled through the door.

Darcy rolled over and clutched her head. Oh, shit, the wedding, she thought. "Tell him I'll be right there." She struggled to sit.

"He's in the living room with a cup of coffee," Sam yelled. "Have a safe trip."

Darcy grabbed her bottled water from the nightstand and gulped down two aspirin for her headache. She tied her robe around her waist and shuffled down the hallway to the bathroom. Stopping in the doorway, she gazed at the back of Victor's head as he sat on the couch, facing the picture length window in the living room. The incandescent light from the lamp illuminated his figure. Part of her wanted to go and wrap her arms around him. The other half wanted to slither away, close the door of her bedroom, and go back to sleep.

Instead, she ducked into the bathroom, turned on the hot water, and took a two-minute shower. She towel-dried her hair, brushed her teeth, wiggled her hips into a pair of jeans, and tugged an old sweater over her head. Thank goodness, she had packed her suitcase the night before and Sam made coffee. She wheeled her luggage into the living room on her way to the kitchen. "Want a refill?"

Victor glanced up at her with a crooked smile. "Long night?"

"A little too much booze," she said.

He glanced at his watch and frowned. "We don't have time for a refill. I'll buy you a bloody Mary on the plane."

Stopping, she set the luggage against the wall and placed a hand on her hip. "What about coffee?"

"Booze is better than caffeine." He grabbed the handle of her luggage. "Trust me. I drank through law school. I had a hangover when I took the bar exam… and passed. Thanks to a bloody Mary and an egg sandwich."

Sighing, she rubbed her temples. "That thing about college. Where did you get your degree?"

"Stanford Law School." He frowned. "Why?"

"My daughter's fiancé thought he knew you, but he didn't go to Stanford."

He laughed. "Is that why you're hungover? You were worried I might know your daughter's fiancé?"

"I don't want to be embarrassed or humiliated at this event." She wagged her finger. "I would rather stay home and be disowned by my daughter."

"Trust me. We'll be unforgettable." He cradled her fingers in his hand. "Let's go."

Imagining the longest day of her life, she groaned.

****

Halfway into the flight, Victor put aside his magazine. "Let's agree on our story."

Darcy straightened from where she had been leaning her head against the window and glared. In spite of the bloody Mary, she hadn't lost the headache. Earlier, she asked the attendant for two cups of coffee, hoping the caffeine might take the edge off the pain between her temples. But the extra liquid only forced her to occupy the cramped bathroom every ten minutes. Now, she just wanted to close her eyes and sleep, not concoct an elaborate story about their imaginary love affair for people she hadn't seen in three years and who she probably wouldn't see for at least another three years. "Why didn't we plan our story sooner?"

"So I'll remember more," he said. "I crammed for finals. I crammed for the bar. I cram each time I go to court. I thrive on last-minute detail loading."

Glancing up, she groaned.

He clapped his hands. "Okay, let's start with the basics of what you told everyone."

"I only told my daughter and her fiancé about you." Closing her eyes, she recalled the details. "I said pretty much the truth, except for the part about us dating since August. We work together. You're a divorce attorney." She opened her eyes. "I think that's it."

"Boring," Victor said, frowning. "We need to spice up the story a bit." He tapped his chin. "How in love are we?"

The attendant stopped beside their aisle. "Any trash?"

"No," he said. "But we'll have another set of crackers and another coffee, right?"

She shook her head. "I'll wait to eat once we land. I don't think more coffee will help."

After the attendant left, Victor leaned closer. "What happened last night to make you so miserable?"

She bit her lower lip to stop the well of emotions from bubbling up inside of her. "I got into a fight with Anita in my book club over *Madame Bovary*."

"Ah, I see." Victor nodded. "The dreaded book club."

Darcy glowered. "Anita declared Madame Bovary the first liberated housewife because she took control of her life through her sexuality. I disagreed. Madam Bovary suffered as a victim of circumstance and social order. She committed adultery to find a bit of happiness because she could not get divorced and live on her own and have sex with whoever she pleased. The women's movement had not started. The sexual revolution wasn't imagined. Anita insisted Madame Bovary succeeded as a heroine. I believe she failed. After all, she might have found happiness if she learned to speak up and show her husband what she needed. Then she wouldn't have died of boredom."

"I agree," he said. "No one should die of boredom, especially if one has an opportunity to sizzle. Like the story of how we met and started dating."

She widened her gaze. This revelatory news about

Victor piqued her interest. She shifted in her seat to study him closer. "You've read *Madame Bovary*?"

"Summary Guides." He waved a hand. "I had no patience for the entire book. Too many passages described the scenery."

Alert, Darcy leaned on the armrest between them. "So, what do you think of Madame Bovary? Is she a romantic heroine or a pathetic victim?"

"Neither," he said. "She had romantic ideals, but almost everyone does when they're younger. She's not a victim. Remember when she confided in the priest about her moral dilemma, but the priest wouldn't listen or take her seriously? That disclosure took as much effort and courage as having an affair. After all, she could have become pregnant with another man's child. Sure, you couldn't prove it with DNA testing, but women burned at the stake for having a baby who looked like a man other than one's husband."

"Burning at the stake is from *The Scarlet Letter*," she said, feeling impassioned by his insight in spite of the last blunder. "How can you practice law when you confuse the facts?"

"I read those books so long ago. I'm surprised I remember anything." He frowned. "Besides, I'm thinking about all women during that time period and how they suffered." He shuddered. "I don't understand why anyone would want to spend their Friday nights discussing how women have been abused throughout history."

Releasing her grip on the armrest, she fell into her seat. "I stormed out of the club early to go drink at the bar next door. I had to call Sam to pick me up."

"Sam's a good man." He nodded then lifted his

eyebrows. "Why isn't he taking you to the wedding?"

She widened her gaze. "He's my landlord and is married to Linda. They've been a couple for over thirty years."

"Oh." The wrinkles in his forehead smoothed. "I mistook him for your live-in boyfriend."

She grumbled. "He's not my type."

"What is your type?"

"I don't have a type." She rubbed her forehead and stared at the back of the airline seat.

"You just said you did."

"I lied to get you to stop asking me."

Smirking, he leaned closer. "Lying didn't work, did it?"

Delighted by their playful banter, she smiled. She searched for a clever response, but she could not focus on anything other than the proximity of their lips. A little flicker of yearning caught her off guard. She scooted toward the window but not before catching a whiff of his musky aftershave. Why did he have to smell so good?

Over the loudspeaker, the captain announced the plane would land in twenty minutes.

"We better refine our story." Waiting for her response, he folded his hands in his lap.

She ignored him, choosing to stare out the window at the endless clouds.

"So, how in love are we? Do we hold hands? Kiss?" He leaned closer. "Or are we reserved with occasional risqué banter?"

His hot breath against her ear triggered a wave of excitement. Tonight, she could live out her fantasy as Victor's girlfriend. A shiver of possibilities left goose bumps on her skin. How intimate did she want to get? Did she want his hands all over her body? Or did she want to be near him without touching? How about a tasteful compromise? She turned. "I like lots of affection, but I want you to come across as the perfect gentleman."

"Ah, that's easy." He tucked a loose strand of hair behind her ear.

A frisson of lust rippled through her.

"Are we dating?" he asked. "Or are we engaged?"

Engaged, she thought. Would anyone believe her since she vowed to never remarry? No, they wouldn't. "We're just dating."

He shook his head. "No one just dates." He placed an elbow on the armrest between them. "Let's be a couple."

Heat flamed her face.

"I want to hold your hand and let the world know how much you mean to me," he said.

"And how much is that?" A stammer of heartbeats invaded her chest.

He gazed for a long moment, his pupils dilating into black obsidian stones, before leaning over for a kiss.

Beneath the flame of his passion, she melted. How long would the charade last? She wanted to savor every moment.

He released her. "You're a wonderful kisser."

"Why, thank you." She blushed. "Should we rehearse our relationship?"

Laughing, he patted her knee. "We don't need to rehearse. We're great actors."

Coldness seeped into her body. She wanted to

practice being his girlfriend. She wanted to kiss him forever.

"I see the frown lines on your forehead." He squeezed her hand. "Don't worry. Tonight, everyone will think we're the perfect couple." He raised her hand to his lips for a kiss.

Sighing, she wished they were a real couple.

****

Darcy leaned on the registration counter of the Empire Luxury Estates. So far, the day had already been long. After the plane landed, their luggage circled baggage claim for forty minutes. The free shuttle arrived a half hour late. They rode to Manhattan Beach to find a good place to eat, but the restaurant they chose didn't serve breakfast past ten o'clock. She suppressed her craving for steak and eggs and settled for a grilled cheese sandwich on sourdough bread and another round of coffee. Afterward, they arrived at the hotel to check in, but the concierge told them to come back in an hour. Now, the registration clerk couldn't find one of their room reservations. "What's taking so long?" she asked.

"We're booked because of the wedding," the clerk said. "I'm sorry, but you'll have to share a room."

Victor folded his arms on the counter. "How big is the room?"

The clerk opened a brochure. "They're all the same except for the number of bedrooms. Each unit has a living room with a sofa and a big screen TV, a mini refrigerator, coffee maker, and balcony. I have your reservation as a one-bedroom suite."

Darcy placed her hand on her chest to stop her galloping heartbeat. Oh, why hadn't she shopped for a negligee?

"Can someone sleep in the living room on the sofa?" Victor asked.

"Definitely," the clerk said. "Most even have fold out beds."

"What do we have?" he asked.

The clerk typed on the keyboard. "You have a fold-out sofa bed and a queen-sized bed."

He turned toward Darcy. "You take the bed. I'll take the sofa. Okay?"

Disappointment invaded her body. Why pretend to be a couple if they had to sleep alone?

"I'm sorry." He raised his empty palms. "I thought I had booked two rooms."

She deepened her frown. Why did he have to be a gentleman and offer up the bed? Embarrassment flushed her face. Why couldn't she stop fantasizing about running her hands over his body while lying naked beside him?

He lifted his eyebrows. "Please, forgive me." He squeezed her hand. "I promise to make it up."

A current of pleasure increased her lurid thoughts. Ashamed of her fantasies, she tugged away her hand and shrugged. "Mistakes happen. You're forgiven."

Leaning over, he brushed his lips against hers.

Heat rushed through her.

He turned toward the clerk. "Okay, we'll take the one-bedroom suite."

"Good," the clerk said. "I'll need a credit card to cover incidentals and your IDs, Mr. and Mrs.—"

"Costello." He handed the clerk his credit card and his driver's license. "And this is Ms. Madison." He waved away the credit card Darcy removed from her purse. "I'll get the extra charges."

"Thank you." Darcy slid her license across the counter for the clerk's inspection.

"Here are your keys." The clerk handed them two cards and two passes. "Show these passes to the staff person at breakfast, which is served in the dining room from seven to ten on Sunday. These passes also allow you to receive one free drink during happy hour in our bar. Enjoy your stay."

Victor dragged both suitcases to the elevator with Darcy striding beside him. When the doors of the elevator slid closed, he slumped against the glass wall. "For a moment, I worried you'd react like a real girlfriend and hold my error against me all night."

Interest widened her gaze. Real girlfriend?

"Lucky for me, you're not a typical woman." He wrapped his arms around her and whispered through her hair. "I want tonight to be magical."

As the glass elevator overlooking the atrium ascended to the fifth floor, she softened her body against him. What a dazzling night awaited them!

The doors parted.

He tugged out of her embrace and strode down the hall to their suite.

She jogged ahead, slid the key card into the slot, and opened the door.

After he wheeled Darcy's suitcase into the bedroom, he returned to the living room, sank into the sofa, put his feet up on the coffee table, and turned on the big screen TV.

Did he follow the same routine at home? She slipped into the bedroom area and unpacked her belongings into the dresser drawers and the closet.

"What will you wear?" he asked from the living

room.

A buzz of excitement zipped through her. She showed him the dress she bought at a consignment shop, hoping he liked it.

He waved her closer.

She dangled the dress on its hanger.

Touching the fabric, he frowned. "Gold? Good god, who suggested this dress?"

"The colors of the wedding are blue and gold. My daughter is wearing blue. I'm supposed to wear gold."

"You'll look like a disco dancer in this dress." He crossed his arms over his chest and shuddered.

She groaned. Betty was right to suggest an off-the-shoulder gown in a jazzy earth tone. "I thought you were too young to know about disco."

"Social media," he said.

If she didn't wear the dress, then what would she wear?

He stood and strolled over to his garment bag. "I brought along a present. From Betty." Unzipping the bag, he removed a sapphire blue gown with ruches around the waist. "Try it on. I think this dress will look better."

Wow. What a rich color. I'll upstage my daughter, she thought. She stared at the dress a moment longer before she exchanged her gold dress for the blue one. Slipping into the bathroom, she shut the door. The dress slid over her hips and hugged her curves. For a moment, she stood before the mirror admiring her reflection, no longer feeling fifty but a frisky thirty-five.

When she stepped into the living room to model, she turned slowly from side to side.

He whistled soft and low. "Now, that dress is worth

a million dollars."

Heat rushed to Darcy's face.

"Let me get dressed, and we'll take a picture for Betty."

In the bedroom, she grabbed her cosmetic case. With trembling hands, she dabbed her nose with blotting tissue before freshening her lipstick. She stepped back from the mirror to examine her work. Smiling, she checked her teeth for smudges. Perfect.

Within minutes, he stepped out of the bathroom looking more dapper than he had the night of the Gala. He wrapped his arm around Darcy's waist and tugged her close. With his other arm outstretched, he took a selfie and sent it to Betty.

Moments later, Betty sent a text message.

Wow! You guys make a cute couple!

Too bad we're just pretending, Darcy thought.

Chapter 16

Arriving at the church a half hour before the ceremony, Darcy stepped out of the taxi into the slightly warmer and drier southern California air, clutching her purse in one hand and Victor's arm with the other. The air smelled like perfume and smog, an elixir of the rich and shameless. Skinny palm trees flanked the ancient cathedral, their leaves fanning the spires.

After climbing the dozen stone steps, they entered a hallow room full of stain glass windows refracting the afternoon light into jewel-tones.

She gasped, marveling at the majestic space. As she recalled her own wedding, a pinch of resentment hurt her chest. Her parents' backyard seemed so paltry next to the domed ceiling set with stained glass depicting God surrounded by several angels in a cloudless, cerulean blue sky. The altar dripped with lavish bouquets of roses and gardenias, the fragrant scent overpowering the dusty air. She remembered how her eyes itched from the freshly mown lawn, threatening to ruin her mascara.

Taking a seat on the groom's side, she searched for Joyce who was part of the wedding party. Instead, she found Nathan standing tall beside the altar, his hands clasped in front of his thighs, a bemused smile playing at the corners of his lips. She shuddered, hoping he had not noticed her. A pang of longing for the past squeezed her. When had he looked so devilishly handsome?

"Are you all right?" Victor scrunched his face.

"I'm jealous." She fanned her cheeks with a nervous hand. "They spent a fortune."

He squeezed her arm. "The more they spend, the quicker they divorce."

A slight smile raised her lips. How did he know what to say to cheer her heart? she wondered.

From a balcony, a choir of men and women dressed in white robes rose.

The conductor flicked his wrist.

The organist played the "Bridal Chorus."

A bevy of ethereal voices echoed the tune until the whole cathedral hummed.

They sound like heaven's blessing, she thought. At her wedding, she was stuck with a lousy record that skipped every few chords. She opened her purse and clenched a tissue.

Twelve women wearing either blue or gold dresses wove their arms with twelve men dressed in black tuxedos with matching blue or gold bow ties. They synchronized their steps to the beat of the music, their faces plastered with tight smiles.

At the very end, Joyce linked arms with Tyler. The two sashayed up the aisle, sporting their best grins.

"She's unhappy." Darcy touched Victor's elbow. "When she's happy, her smile is crooked."

He squinted at the couple without saying a word.

The organist belted out the "Bridal Chorus" in high octane volume.

The guests rose.

Darcy strained to see over the heads and shoulders

of the other guests as Tanya stepped out with her father. She widened her eyes at Tanya's gorgeous, strapless white gown with a heart-shaped neckline and tulip-shaped skirt. With her palms sweaty with envy, she felt her heart knock against her ribs. Leaning toward Victor, she hissed. "Who spends their life's savings on a wedding dress?"

Victor shrugged. "The same people who file for divorce six months later."

At the altar when Tanya's father lifted the veil to kiss her cheek, she beamed with her perfectly made-up face.

Darcy sat and rearranged her skirts, a knot of anger seizing her chest. Averting her gaze, she stared at the crucifix, unable to witness her ex-husband's expectant gaze at his soon-to-be wife.

"Are you okay?" Victor clutched her hand.

She shrugged, dabbing the corners of her eyes with the tissue. "I'm not sad Nathan never loved me like he loves Tanya. I'm sad because no one will ever love me enough to spend the type of money he's spent on her."

Wrapping an arm around her shoulders, he tugged her close. "One day is not a lifetime."

Feeling his hot breath and soft lips against her ear, she shivered.

With his other hand, he cupped her fingers. "They'll never afford a dream home with what they've spent on this wedding."

Smiling, she leaned closer. "*I* can't afford a dream home."

"Maybe someday the man of your dreams will." He winked, releasing her hand.

A flash of hope zipped through her. Someday, she

thought. Settling against the pew, she silently knotted her hands in her lap. As she watched her ex-husband pledge his undying love to the woman who stole him from her years ago, Darcy wished Victor was more than her pretend date. She wanted their relationship to be real, as real as the forever kiss of the bride and groom beneath the heavenly gaze of the stained-glass dome.

****

The Imperial Ballroom of the Empire Luxury Estates opened to a balcony with views of Los Angeles. Against the setting sun, the glittering blue and silver of the Pacific Ocean dazzled to the west, and to the east, a layer of smog draped over the shoulders of the San Gabriel Mountains. Skyscrapers lifted their steel gaze above the arteries of highways bleeding through neighborhoods of red Spanish-tiled roofs, stately palm trees, and rectangular swimming pools. The beauty of the overpopulated, self-centered metropolis always took away Darcy's breath, leaving her brokenhearted.

Nathan and Tanya stood at the foot of a marble fountain, greeting guests during the wedding reception.

Victor nudged Darcy. "They look like dolls."

Darcy winced. She hated how Nathan hadn't aged and neither had his beautiful bride. Their Malibu tans glowed against their beach-blond hair and whitened smiles. "He's still body building," she whispered.

"How can you tell?"

"Just look at the way his biceps tug against the sleeves of his tux."

He sipped from a glass of sparkling water and nodded. "You're very observant."

"I remember his body." At the distant memory of his strong arms around her waist, she smiled.

Victor frowned. "I've been in a long-term relationship, and I wouldn't remember my ex-girlfriend's arms if you pointed them out in a lineup."

Laughing, she wished she had a glass of wine to take off the edge from the suffering.

"Okay, time to introduce me." He offered his arm.

They waited behind another couple who kept leaning together and whispering.

"I feel so awkward." She wrung her hands.

"Don't be." He kissed her forehead. "We're having fun pretending to be a couple."

When he noticed Darcy, Nathan widened his gaze. "Well, well, well, I'm impressed. You actually showed up." He glanced at Victor and stepped back a foot. "I see you bought an escort. How much did he cost?"

Curling her fists, she flushed. "Don't insult my boyfriend, Victor Costello."

Victor shook Nathan's hand.

"Who do you play on TV?" Nathan asked.

"I'm not an actor. I practice law in Northern California. I protect and defend families torn apart by divorce."

Nathan yanked away his hand. "Ah, the divorce attorney and the divorce planner. Two predators feeding off poor victims of love went wrong." He sneered. "Business must be booming."

The bride flounced forward, throwing her arms around Victor for a hug. "I'm Tanya."

Victor untangled her arms from around his neck and stepped aside. "Nice to meet you. I heard you were the nanny at one time."

"I'm officially the stepmom now." She grinned and nodded toward Darcy. "Nice to see you again."

Darcy snarled, extending her hand. How dare she make a move on my current date, she thought.

Tanya sidled away from Darcy and ogled Victor. "You're very young."

Victor turned to Darcy and planted a kiss on her lips. "She keeps me feeling younger than I am. Don't you, sweetheart?"

The moisture of the kiss tingled Darcy's lips. She tilted her head toward Victor and smiled. "Playful, isn't he?"

Tanya did not respond to Darcy's comment and just stared at Victor.

A bristle of annoyance and frustration rippled up her spine. She touched Victor's lapel, eager to extract them from this rude and humiliating experience. "We should find our table and introduce you to the rest of the guests."

Victor laced his fingers through Darcy's hand. "Congratulations." He nodded to Tanya and Nathan. "We hope you have a long and happy marriage."

Tanya's gaze followed Victor.

Nathan tugged Tanya by the hand and redirected her attention to the next couple who wanted to congratulate them.

As soon as they strode far enough away, Victor exhaled. "No wonder you didn't want to come. That ex-husband is a jerk. His wife isn't any better." He shuddered. "I feel violated by the way she mauled me with her gaze."

Darcy sighed. "I'm sorry I didn't warn you about the shallowness of LA. Everyone only cares about your looks, your income, the neighborhood where you live, what you drive, and where you vacation. We paid our respects. We can eat and leave before they cut the cake, if you want."

"No, I want to stay to the bitter end and torture them." He narrowed his gaze and clasped his hands. "No one treats me like eye candy. And no one treats you like an over-the-hill hag. I'm a smart man. And you're a beautiful woman. No reason exists why we shouldn't be together."

She wiped sweaty palms on her dress. "But we're not together."

"Nobody knows we're not a couple. Our job is to make them believe the unbelievable." He patted his breast pocket. "We have to up our game. Lengthen the time of our relationship from three months to three years when people ask. And we're not just a couple. We're living together. In the Tuscany villa you wanted to own. I bought it for you as a promise gift."

"No way." Frowning, she shook her head. "I'm not outright lying to these people."

He pouted. "Why not?"

"They might come up to Sonoma County and visit. Then what will we do? Rent Gary's house for the day?"

He opened his arms. "Let's up the passion between us. Make them swoon with jealousy. Especially your ex-husband's wife."

With the thought, she melted. "Okay, we can do that."

"Let's practice." He drew her close and placed his lips on her mouth. His kisses started tentatively and grew more eager. Parting his lips, he slipped his tongue into her mouth.

She wrapped her arms around his neck and leaned her curves into his tight body, braiding her fingers through his thick hair. She closed her eyes, forgetting everything until someone called her name. Untangling her body from his, she stepped back to search for the caller.

As she darted across the room, Joyce waved. "Mom, was that you kissing your date?" She wore a beautiful midnight blue gown which contrasted with her pale skin and blond hair.

"Yes." She tugged him close. "This is my boyfriend, Victor Costello."

"Boyfriend?" Joyce widened her eyes. "I thought you both just started dating."

"Your mother didn't want to alarm you about the seriousness of our relationship." He winked. "We're inseparable."

Joyce crossed her arms under her chest. "That's not all my mom neglected to tell me. She didn't mention you were younger."

She's just as rude as everyone else here, she thought. Embarrassment flushed her face. "He's not that young."

He stood straighter and shook Joyce's hand. "I'm thirty-seven."

"I'm twenty-eight," Joyce said. "You're only nine years older than me. You could be my brother, and not my father."

"Thank goodness, he's neither one," Darcy said. Oh, couldn't they talk about something else? Who cared if he was thirty-seven or forty-seven or fifty-seven?

Tyler emerged from the crowd and approached. Recognition sparkled in his eyes. "Vic! It *is* you."

For a moment, Victor frowned before he

brightened. "Ty Gustafson, the long jump giant."

"That's right. Go Spartans!"

They embraced and patted each other's backs.

Darcy clasped her hands over her chest. What else did she not know about him which she should know as his girlfriend? "I thought you said you attended Stanford Law School."

"I did," Victor said, "but I earned my bachelor's degree from San Jose State."

Joyce shook her head. "You guys know each other?"

"We're like long-lost brothers." Tyler wrapped an arm around Victor's shoulders.

"Why don't we go to the bar and catch up?" Victor asked.

"Now you're talking," Tyler said.

"Wait." Joyce stepped between them. "Tyler, you said you gave up drinking."

"I—I—have," he stammered. "Vic and I will get iced teas. Do you want anything?"

"No, thank you." Joyce stepped aside.

What did she expect? Darcy felt her smile topple into a frown. For Victor to stay by her side and tell Tyler they could catch up some other time? She smoothed her hands over her dress. Of course, she did.

"Mom, your boyfriend's not good for my fiancé." Joyce crossed her arms over her chest and frowned.

Darcy touched her daughter's elbow. They walked away from the crowd and stood next to the goldenrod wallpapered wall. Across the room, a pianist played. Servers wove in and out of the guests, offering appetizers. "Tyler's his own man. He can make his own decisions. Victor won't influence him."

Joyce snickered. "That's easy for you to say. You're dating a guy who needs a mother."

Would someone guess the truth? She stiffened her shoulders. "Victor's an old soul with great fashion sense. He insisted I wear this dress instead of the gold one. He didn't want me looking like a disco dancer."

She pinched her eyebrows and lifted her arms. "A disco what?"

"Exactly." Darcy nodded.

Staring at her mother, she grabbed her hand and squeezed. "I'm sorry about what happened last week. I think I overreacted when I learned I lost my wedding venue. I shouldn't have lashed out the way I did. Can you please forgive me?"

Tenderness flooded her chest. She opened her arms. "Of course, I forgive you." She pulled her daughter into an embrace. "I just wanted a little respect."

Joyce sniffed. "I'll try harder to be more respectful."

"Good." Darcy smiled. "Now, I have some ideas for a new venue. The Grand Oak Plaza in Rohnert Park has a wonderful ballroom for the reception. Or we can reserve space at Foxtail Golf Club."

"Dad suggested we move the venue to LA." Joyce glanced around the room. "Maybe even this place."

She bit her lower lip and shrugged. "Okay, but if that's your decision then I'm soliciting help from my friend, Gloria, who lives and works as a wedding planner in southern California. She can negotiate better prices than I can."

Lifting her arms, Joyce widened her eyes. "I don't want anyone else helping me." She pointed. "Just you."

She narrowed her gaze. "You're still stubborn."

Tilting her head, Joyce shook her finger. "But I'm not disrespectful."

Darcy hugged her daughter. "I'm so happy to see you again."

Joyce squeezed her mom. "Me, too."

Darcy wondered how long their happiness would last.

****

Twenty minutes later, Tyler and Victor whooped and hollered as they loped into the ballroom like dogs off their leashes. Darcy linked arms and led Victor aside. "You've been drinking something stronger than iced tea."

"Don't tell Joyce, but we both had Long Islands." Victor snickered, slumping his shoulders. "So, technically, he didn't lie."

"Hmmm...I can see why my daughter thinks you're a bad influence." She placed her hands akimbo. "As for me, I'm just disappointed you didn't bring me a gin martini."

"I didn't want you to get in trouble with your daughter," he said. "But I can bring you a Long Island on my next trip."

"Looks like you and Tyler won't be making another trip." She pointed across the room. "They've taken seats at the head table."

"Let's mingle." He gestured around the room. "I want to impress everyone."

Arm in arm, Darcy and Victor strolled around the ballroom. Each time Darcy introduced Victor she received the same response. "He's so young!" She cringed, the words grating like nails against a chalkboard. No one seemed immune to the reaction, including Joyce's first grade teacher.

"The age difference is preposterous," Ms. Steele said. "He's young enough to be your son."

"I have great genetics." He winked. "I'm closer to forty than I look."

Ms. Steele harrumphed. "You can maul any cougar in this room."

Without saying a word, Darcy tightened her smile.

Victor brought Ms. Steele's hand to his lips.

Ms. Steele's face flushed as pink as her dress. "You're too young to be a gentleman."

Releasing her hand, he smiled. "My motto is never too young and always a gentleman."

How overplayed. She shuddered. Oh, how she wished she'd stayed home. She tugged on Victor's sleeve. Stepping away from the crowd, she frowned. "We should leave."

He tucked her hand in the crook of his arm. "Let's have a seat. They're serving dinner. Then we'll leave."

She traipsed after Victor to their assigned seating.

Three other couples occupied their table: John, an engineering friend of Nathan's, and his wife, Melissa; Georgia, a stylist friend of Tanya's, and her husband, Nick; and Mark and Cathy, Joyce's childhood friends, who married last summer.

"It's nice to finally meet my girlfriend's family and friends." Victor nodded and smiled.

John, a hefty older man with a gray beard, set down his iced water and gave Victor the once-over. "You're not bad," he said. "Darcy always had a thing for good-looking men like Nathan."

How dare he compare Victor to Nathan! Wringing

the napkin in her lap, Darcy squirmed. "Nathan was an inventor. He thought."

Victor curled a hand over her fist. "I'm a thinker and not a looker."

Georgia, a reedy woman with a coif of complicated looking hair, giggled. "You only look like you think."

"See?" John chuckled. "People don't change."

Victor tensed his jaw.

Forcing a smile, Darcy leaned forward. "Victor's law firm nominated him for partner, but he's starting his own business."

"Really?" John crossed both arms over his chest. "The whole self-employment gig is so overrated. Look what it got Nathan. Years of spousal support instead."

Oh, really? The comparisons continued. Darcy needed to think quickly and slay the man in his tracks. She arched an eyebrow. "If Nathan had been successful, he would have paid me." She stroked Victor's upper arm. "My boyfriend is the most celebrated divorce attorney in Sonoma County. If we break up, I'll receive palimony."

Smiling, Victor patted her hand. "Darcy's right. I owe her everything. She's so supportive she convinced me to recruit top talent and pay them accordingly."

"But think of all the overhead." Georgia speared a tomato in her salad. "That's why I'm mobile. I bring my clothes, shoes, and hair products to the client. The process saves me tons in rent. The only downside to working on location is if I forget something. But that's what assistants are for—stocking your car with the things you keep forgetting so you never forget them anymore."

Mark, a stocky man with round glasses, picked up

a water pitcher and nodded toward Victor. "Didn't you earn your degree online?"

Frowning, Darcy extended her glass so Mark could refill the water and floating lemons. "Who gave you wrong information?"

Mark did not reply. He stared at Victor.

"I graduated *magna cum laude* from Stanford." Victor straightened his tie and tugged his lips into a line.

John leaned back in his chair and wrapped an arm around his wife's plump shoulders. "Don't worry, honey, that's just a fancy phrase for someone who wants praise."

Darcy swiveled her gaze toward the head table, wondering if Nathan organized the seating arrangements specifically to humiliate her and her date.

"Ah, you know Latin." Victor raised his glass for a toast. "*Barba tenus sapientes.*"

John lifted his eyebrows and glanced around the crowded room.

Darcy placed the napkin over her mouth to hide a snicker. Truly, John was as wise as his beard, which wasn't wise at all.

Finding a server, John grabbed a basket of bread and buttered a roll. "Well, Victor, you may know languages, but you didn't excel in math, or you would have picked a younger girlfriend who could provide you with a family."

Lowering her napkin, Darcy clenched her jaw. Older women don't count in LA, she thought. "Victor doesn't want children." She picked through the limp lettuce smelling of vinegar on her plate. "He wants to spend the rest of his life traveling the world with me."

Victor smiled and grabbed Darcy's hand, lifting it to his lips for a kiss.

Darcy returned his smile. When she rescued him with the tiny white lie, she enjoyed how her whole body pulsed with satisfaction.

"But Darcy can't afford to take him anywhere," Cathy, another waif with dyed blond hair, said. "Joyce told us you're living in someone's living room, because you're too poor to afford an apartment."

A jolt of betrayal froze her spine. How dare her daughter divulge private details? She narrowed her gaze. "I'm housesitting for friends."

Mark shook his head. "My wife is right. Joyce said you make so little you don't have to pay taxes."

"That's not true." What information didn't Joyce tell these people? She straightened her spine. "She doesn't know how much I make since I fired her from preparing my tax returns."

A collective gasp traveled around the table.

"She divorced her husband and fired her daughter." Mark pointed to Victor. "I bet this guy doesn't last through the night."

Victor placed an arm around the back of Darcy's chair. "We're more serious about each other than you think we are."

Georgia giggled.

Covering his mouth with a napkin, Mark stifled a laugh.

John chuckled.

Cathy tittered.

Folding their hands in their laps, Nick, a gangly man, and Melissa, an overweight woman, remained quiet.

"Nathan's lucky he got rid of you when he did," John said. "I feel sorry for this poor sucker." He pointed to Victor.

Darcy held her breath and tightened her grip on the fork. Anger and shame rained on the dream she still harbored of gaining Joyce's love and acceptance. Was her daughter nothing but a spitting image of her father? Had she been so absent from her life, Joyce didn't learn any respect or discretion? Oh, why couldn't she have a relationship with her daughter like Gary had with his children? She should have never agreed to be Joyce's wedding planner. Lifting her chin, she relaxed her grip on the fork. She should only have agreed to represent her during a divorce.

Keeping his mouth shut, Victor twitched an eyebrow.

A quick glance confirmed the look of defeat on his face. Darcy needed to say something to restore their dignity. She tapped her glass with her fork. "Listen. Victor's a gentleman. He's not accustomed to the backbiting bitterness of LA." She glanced around at each person, meeting their gaze. "I'm so glad I found him. He doesn't judge me by my tax return or my age. He cares about the goodness in my heart, which no amount of money can buy. I love him more than I've loved anyone in my whole life."

Silence echoed around the table.

All gazes with arched eyebrows settled on them.

Flushed from the conversation and desperate to rectify things, Darcy turned toward Victor and kissed him until her heartbeat thudded against her dress.

Victor caressed her hair away from her forehead and cupped her cheek with a hand as his lips found hers again and again. When they parted, he gazed at her.

Darcy had never seen his eyes darker, richer, or more soulful.

He nuzzled her ear. "Thank you," he whispered.

A ray of unconditional love warmed her body. Darcy squeezed his hand. "You're welcome."

A few moments later, the servers nudged between the guests, clearing the salad and dinner roll plates and serving the main course.

Darcy nibbled at the roasted garlic chicken, buttery mashed potatoes, and barely steamed baby carrots on her plate, listening to the speeches given by the guests at the head table. After the initial rush of victory, she grew a little deflated, knowing she fabricated a story about a romance with Victor which did not exist. She sipped her water, wishing for a gin martini with two olives.

At the end of the meal, Victor grabbed her hand. He placed their intertwined fingers on the table for the guests to see.

Nathan and Tanya waltzed on the parquet floor to an old song Darcy remembered hearing in their living room the day she packed her bags and left. She wished she had not come tonight. No one said any kind words to her or Victor. She wondered if Nathan and Joyce divulged private and misguided information to sabotage their evening or if their mindless chatter was meant to be harmless. Had she been gone so long from this superficial community to remember how shallow everyone was?

"The dance floor is open." The DJ lifted his arms. "Everybody dance."

"Would you like to dance?" Victor waved toward

the crowd of couples swaying to the music.

"I thought you didn't dance." Darcy narrowed her gaze.

"You told me to get a life outside of work, so I took a few lessons."

Darcy arched her eyebrows. She mellowed with the thought of him taking her advice. "Well, we wouldn't want to waste them, would we?"

Victor swung Darcy into a waltz. They glided around the other dancing couples with neither one of them stepping on each other's feet.

She closed her eyes, giddy with a rush of adrenaline. The last time she danced was at a New Year's Eve party hosted by the DJ she'd been dating. He kept stepping on her feet and apologizing. She had blisters on her toes for three weeks. Laughing at the memory, she tossed back her head. As she swept across the parquet floor in Victor's capable and caring arms, a thrill of pleasure tingled through her body.

The momentum of their dancing bodies felt like falling in love.

When the dance ended, Victor led Darcy toward the bank of windows looking out at the dark terrace. The twinkling lights of the city sparkled like diamonds. "I'm tired of the ugly gossip about us." Darcy turned away from the window. "I'm impressed you're putting up with it so well."

"That second act at the dinner table ended brilliantly." Victor clapped his hands. "We need a grand finale." He rubbed his hands together. "Something fabulous that everyone will talk about forever."

Darcy turned toward him and gazed into his dark eyes. "Like what?"

"Oh, you'll see." He smiled.

A flicker of panic zipped through her body. She was not like Victor, who preferred last second preparations. She needed time and space to process suggestions. "Shouldn't I be prepped?"

He glanced up and down the length of her body. A slow smile ignited on his face. "No, you'll be more dramatic if you're unprepared."

She tensed her body. "I don't feel comfortable not knowing what we're getting into." She refused to accept his outstretched hand. "We should stop the charade now while we're ahead."

"Don't worry." He curled his fingers over her wrist. "We can pull off this scene. You're a great actress."

A shaft of apprehension tightened her legs. She was not acting. A fresh wave of shame crashed through her. She cared for Victor.

He led her through the crowd of dancing couples to the foot of the stage.

Motioning to the DJ, Victor cupped his hands around his mouth and spoke into the DJ's ear.

An increasingly uneasy feeling tightened her stomach. She could not hear what they were saying. She hated being surprised in public.

The DJ nodded, took Victor's offered cash, and walked center stage. "Excuse me," the DJ spoke into the microphone. "We have a slight change of plans."

Victor led Darcy up onto the stage.

A spotlight shone on them.

She stood on wobbly legs, staring into the crowd, but the bright light made distinguishing any faces impossible.

Placing his hand in his interior breast pocket, he curled his fingers around something. Kneeling on one knee, he grabbed one of her hands.

As beads of sweat burst against the crown of her forehead, she swayed like a palm tree caught in a tropical storm.

With soft eyes, he held up a ring.

The diamond shone like a tiny star. Tightening her throat, she blinked back tears. This proposal wasn't happening. But then she remembered Victor's promise to give everyone something to talk about. They will talk about this event for years, she thought.

"My darling Darcy," he said, loud enough for the silenced crowd to hear. "Will you marry me?"

The spotlight glinted off the diamond, blinding her with its radiance. For a long moment, Darcy wondered if the crowd suspected the ruse. A rush of feelings flooded through her, from the anxiety of being found out to the bliss of being falsely wanted. Heart pounding, she held her breath.

Victor gazed up at her.

She could stare into those kind brown eyes forever. Releasing her breath, she smiled. "Yes, I'll marry you."

The crowd cheered.

The DJ resumed the music, playing a love song.

Victor slipped the ring on the third finger of her left hand.

The cold metal warmed against her skin. A flash of vindication zipped through her body. Listen to the gossip now. Darcy and Victor engaged!

Nathan shoved his way to the front of the crowd of guests who surrounded them and grabbed her hand. He studied the diamond with squinted gaze. "It's real."

Tanya threw her body at Victor and kissed his cheek.

He shoved her away and sidled next to Darcy.

"Of course, it's real." He pointed to the diamond. "My grandmother wore it."

"An antique." Tanya clasped both hands over her heart. "How romantic!"

Tyler jostled through the crowd and raised his hand. "Way to go, buddy!"

Grinning, Victor slapped his hand in a high five.

Breathless from racing across the room, Joyce panted. "I don't believe it! You swore you were never getting remarried."

Victor wrapped an arm around Darcy's waist and kissed the tip of her nose. "She changed her mind because she met the right guy."

"That's right." Darcy nodded. "The right guy can change everything." As soon as the adrenaline rush subsided, she wondered how long the magic would last.

Chapter 17

After the reception ended a little after midnight, Victor bought Darcy a double gin martini with two olives from the hotel's bar. "What fun!" He clicked his glass against hers. "I can't believe how everyone bought our engagement. What a fabulous final act."

Darcy twirled the ring on her finger. She marveled at how perfectly it fit. When Nathan proposed after Joyce's birth, the ring he bought had to be resized. Darcy often wondered if the ill-fitting ring served as an omen, foreshadowing how everything about their relationship didn't fit just right. "Why did you borrow your grandmother's ring as a prop?"

"The ring is mine." Victor waved at the bartender for another round. "My mother gave it to me after my grandmother died. I carry it on me all the time as a memento."

What if Victor's grandmother's wedding ring, which fit her perfectly, foreshadowed a perfect married life? The premonition shivered up her spine. Wiggling the ring off her finger, she placed the diamond on the counter. "Here you go."

He stared at the ring and shook his head. "Keep it."

A shock of disbelief sent her mouth agape. "I can't keep your family heirloom."

"That's why I gave you the ring. My grandmother would have liked you. You're kindred spirits and full of spunk." With an intent glimmer in his dark eyes, he slipped the ring back on her finger.

The bartender placed their drinks on tiny paper napkins.

He lifted his glass. "To us."

She refused to toast. "There is no 'us.' Eventually, we'll have to tell everyone the truth. We're not getting married."

"Not if we never see them again."

"But some of the guests are family. I will see them again." She took a long sip of her sharp, bitter martini. "What about Tyler? Won't he ask about your wedding plans the next time he sees you?"

He flicked his wrist and scoffed. "I didn't give him my number."

"That doesn't mean he won't find you. He is, after all, engaged to my daughter who happens to come up to visit on a regular basis since I'm planning her wedding." She shuddered, wishing she had never agreed to the arrangement.

He sipped his martini. "Don't worry. I work a lot. I won't be available."

"You'll be if you're invited as my guest to their wedding."

"That's next year." He waved a hand. "I have plenty of time to scheme my way out of telling the truth."

She bit her lower lip, her stomach churning with guilt and regret. "I don't think I can keep up a lie for a whole year."

"Don't worry about how long we have to lie. Let's just enjoy the victory tonight."

She twirled the ring on her finger. If she wore it,

people would ask about her engagement. "What am I suppose to say when people ask about us?"

"You're a great actress." He winked. "You'll figure out what to say."

But she was not a great actress, Darcy thought. She cared about him. Staring at the diamond on her left hand, she shuddered from a cold breeze sweeping through her body.

"Hey, buddy." Tyler loped up to the bar and slapped Victor's back. "I thought I'd find you here."

Darcy gazed at Tyler. Should she tell him the truth? For courage, she swallowed another sip of her drink.

Tyler sat next to Victor at the bar. "What are you guys having?"

"Gin martinis." Victor twirled the olives on the toothpick. "Care for one?"

Tyler shook his head. "I can't afford a hangover. Not with Joyce around."

"You're whipped." Victor winked.

"You're no better." Tyler gestured toward Darcy. "You're engaged to her mom."

"They're polar opposites," Victor said. "I got the cool woman who doesn't mind my juvenile streak."

"That's because she babies you."

"She *joins* me." He waved to the bartender. "One more before you close."

Wincing, she didn't appreciate the lively boy banter about her and her daughter's personalities. Was this conversation typical among engaged men? She tried to twist the ring loose, but it stuck beneath her knuckle.

"Nice ring," Tyler said. "Do you mind if I take a

closer look?"

Holding her breath to suppress guilt, she extended her arm.

Tyler took her fingers in the palm of his hand and squinted at the diamond's intricate white gold setting.

"It's Art Deco," Victor explained. "My grandfather bought it from Sawyer's Jewelers in downtown Santa Rosa. He saved for three months. Their marriage lasted thirty years."

"That's what Joyce would call a good investment," Tyler said. "So, when will you get married?"

"Actually, we're not." Darcy squirmed.

Bending close, Victor kissed her lips before he turned to Tyler. "She means we've not decided yet."

"No." How could he misconstrue everything she said to benefit his cause? She straightened her back. "I mean exactly what I said. This whole proposal—"

"Overwhelmed her," Victor interrupted. "She didn't expect me to propose. We never discussed marriage. But when every moment you spend with someone feels like the best moment of your life, you want to feel that way forever. That's why we're getting married next year on Valentine's Day in the backyard of our Tuscany villa." He shifted on the bar stool. "Which reminds me, we have to call our real estate agent to up our bid before our offer expires." He glanced at his watch then frowned. "It's too late to do it now, but we should leave so we can wake up early to place the call." He winked at Darcy.

The knot in her stomach tightened. What happened to telling the truth? "Actually, I'm thinking we should withdraw our bid. The home is overpriced. We don't need all that space."

Pinched eyebrows arched above his wide eyes. "But it's your dream home."

Tapping her nails against the martini glass, she narrowed her eyes. "Not all dreams come true."

"Ours do." Victor withdrew his wallet and tossed a hundred-dollar bill on the counter. "Let's call it a night."

Tyler patted Victor's back one last time. "I'm sure we'll see each other soon."

"Take care." Victor nodded. "Tell Joyce we wish her a good night."

Wrapping his arms around her shoulders, Tyler hugged Darcy. "Congratulations, Mom."

Darcy flinched. "Thanks."

"Well done." Victor took Darcy's hand.

"I wasn't acting." When would he realize she cared about him?

Pulling her close, he kissed her cheek. "Even better."

They walked out of the bar together and rode the elevator in silence.

As soon as they entered their suite, Darcy flicked on the lights. "What have you gotten us into?"

He pulled out the sofa bed and sat, removing his shoes and unloosening his tie. "You're making a big deal out of nothing."

Panic coursed through her veins. She lifted her arms. "Are you delusional? My daughter's fiancé thinks we're getting married next year in the backyard of our new home. How will I break the news we're not getting married and we're not buying a home?"

"It's late." He removed his jacket and unbuttoned his shirt. "Why don't you get some rest? We can brainstorm a solution on the way home."

She kicked off her heels. "I won't sleep. I want a resolution now."

He stripped off his shirt and his slacks. "I'm brushing my teeth and going to bed. You can stay up and stew if you'd like, but I won't join you." He nudged past her to the bathroom and shut the door.

Wow, he looks good. She admired the chiseled muscles in his stomach and legs. A fresh wave of anger crashed. Why pretend to be engaged when we can't even have sex? Sighing, she retreated to the bedroom and undressed. She slipped underneath the sheets and waited for Victor to finish in the bathroom. As soon as the door clicked open, she cornered him. "I want you to meet with my daughter and her fiancé to tell them the truth about us."

He glanced up and down the length of her body. "I didn't know you slept in sweats. I always thought you were a long T-shirt, no pants type of woman."

Clenching her fists, she stepped forward and growled. "This conversation isn't about me. It's about ending the lie."

He yawned. "I'm too tired to resolve anything tonight. Now go to sleep. We'll deal with this problem tomorrow." He turned off the light and slipped underneath the covers of the sofa bed.

For a long moment, she stood in the dark, waiting for her eyes to adjust.

As he drifted off to sleep, his breathing deepened.

She wriggled the ring from her finger and set it on the table beside the sofa bed. What happened to their magical night? Their plans to impress only ended in lies. How would she avoid the hurt and humiliation when everyone discovered the truth? She stared at the shape under the blanket a moment longer. Should she wake him? No, she should not. He would only rant and rave about his need for beauty sleep.

Padding into the bathroom, she freshened up. Afterward, she shut her bedroom door and lay awake in darkness. The events of the evening played over and over in her mind. She tossed and turned, unable to sleep. Oh, how would she get out of this mess?

****

Someone rustled her shoulder.

Darcy yanked the bedspread over her head and rolled over. Bright light penetrated the covers. The scent of coffee tickled her nose. Oh, how can I stay mad at a man who brings me coffee in bed? She peered over the sheet.

"Morning, darling." Victor perched on the edge of the bed and held a mug. "I brought you breakfast from downstairs. The coffee is hot. I suggest you drink it first."

Sitting, she rubbed her eyes. "What time do we have to leave?"

"Check out is noon. For what it's worth, it's ten-thirty." He handed her the mug of coffee and stood. "I'll be in the other room packing."

She drank the dark coffee swirled with cream and nibbled on the fruit and scones he placed on the night table. Sunlight glinted off the diamond on her finger. When had he slipped the ring back on her hand?

On the night table, her cell phone rang.

"Mom, Tyler said you guys are bidding on a Tuscany villa. I know your finances. I'm worried. Are you marrying Victor for the wrong reasons?"

197

Anger flamed her cheeks. "No, I'm not. And I didn't appreciate you insinuating to your guests that I am." Frustration throbbed in her temples. "Why did you share my personal information with your so-called friends? Didn't I teach you about privacy and respect, or are you nothing but a spitting image of your father?"

"I'm sorry. I said those things in confidence when I was angry with you. I promise I won't do it again."

The conciliatory tone in Joyce's voice softened the breathless anger pulsing through her. Should she tell her daughter the truth? "Actually, Victor and I are—"

"Tyler just showed me a picture of the house. I can't believe Victor placed an offer for one million. The house looks like it's worth twice the amount."

Darcy choked on her half-eaten scone. "How did Tyler get a picture?"

"Victor just sent it."

Mounting frustration knocked against her temples, the start of a headache. Swinging her legs over the bed, she marched into the other room.

Victor sat on the sofa, texting.

"I'll call you back." Narrowing her gaze, she pressed the button to end the call. "What picture did you send Tyler?"

"Oh, the one I took for the real estate agent I recommended to Gary." He glanced up, raising an eyebrow. "Why?"

She placed her hands on her hips and flared her nostrils. "My daughter called to ask if I am marrying you for your money."

He snickered. "Well, are you?"

"No, I'm not." She resisted the impulse of flinging her phone at his head. "We aren't getting married, remember? Last night you told me we would come up with a way to tell the truth."

He shrugged. "You don't need a plan to tell the truth. You just say it."

"Not when you're in the other room perpetuating the lie." Tossing up her arms, she plunked next to him. "So, what's our game plan?"

Folding his arms behind his head, he leaned back on the sofa. "I kind of like the idea of us getting married. Feels good to have something other than work in my life."

"That's what hobbies are for." She narrowed her gaze. "Not fake weddings."

"Well, we can make it not a fake wedding, if you'd like."

A flutter of hope dispelled the tension in her head. Sinking back against the cushions, she cupped her mouth with a hand. Why shouldn't she marry him? She loved his good looks, good smarts, and good sense of humor. Too bad he also behaved as out of control as a toddler with a big wallet. Then again, she could not risk getting hurt. She had to end this charade. Now. Dropping her hand, she leaned forward. "Why endure marriage?"

"For the fun," he said.

"Fun?" She lifted her eyebrows. No one she knew considered marriage "fun."

Slapping his thighs, he sighed. "All right, let's compromise." He leaned forward and clasped his hands between his knees. "Here's our game plan. We keep up the lie for a few months then we have a huge fight and end our relationship. You don't have to get married again, and I have some fun pretending to be engaged.

Okay?"

What a stupid plan, she thought. "I'll be humiliated. I'd rather just tell the truth now before we both get hurt."

"No one will get hurt." He touched her shoulder. "We're just playing."

"Playing with everyone and their emotions." She swept her arms across the room.

"My plan is perfect." He tilted his chin and smiled. "Everyone thinks our relationship is real. When we break up, they'll believe our relationship is over. No one will know we've been lying."

"You'll know, and I'll know." She waved a hand back and forth between them.

"Please, pretend…for me." Clasping his hands, he pleaded.

If she agreed to conspire with him, would her pillar of reality crumble beneath the weight of the fantasy? "I can't." Folding her into his arms, he melted her body with a kiss.

"Have I changed your mind?"

A flash of hormones flooded her senses. "Will you kiss me every day?"

He curled his lips into a smile. "As long as we're pretending to be a couple, I promise."

Resistance melted against lust. "Okay, you win." She found his lips again. A niggling doubt overshadowed the pleasure. When would he tire of the playful seduction and end the relationship? As she touched the rough stubble on his cheeks, she pressed her soft body against his firm muscles. Oh, why couldn't she escape her fears and marry him for real?

Chapter 18

On Monday morning, Betty and Darcy sat at their favorite table at Katie's Koffee where a Thanksgiving scene had been painted on the window overlooking the main street.

Patrons jostled for a spot at the cream and sugar counter.

As she wiped down an empty table with a damp rag, a barista hummed along with the song playing on the speakers.

Betty sipped her bittersweet mocha. Cradling the phone with one hand, she scrolled through messages. "Did you enjoy the wedding?"

"Yes," Darcy lied. Worrying about the fake engagement, she had not slept much the previous two nights. Only Victor's supple lips and curious tongue could keep her reservations in check. If only he could kiss her forever, she would forget every problem she had. But the kisses eventually ended, and reality settled like a blanket of snow over her thoughts.

Betty glanced up before returning her attention to her phone. "I want details."

Cupping her mug of cappuccino, she warmed her face with the pungent scent of coffee. She did not hide the ring on the third finger of her left hand, but no one looked at her long enough to notice. "We enjoyed the typical LA wedding bash—overpriced food and plenty of dancing."

"How did Victor behave as your date?"

"The perfect gentleman." A brooding smile lingered on her face. If only she could confess to everything, then maybe she wouldn't feel so conflicted about her decision to lie just so she could indulge in her romantic fantasy of making out with a younger man.

Betty set aside her phone and focused her gaze. "What else can you tell me?"

An uneasy silence thickened the air. The phony engagement threatened to muddle her otherwise good judgment. Setting her mug on the table, she bounced her knee. "Umm, I had one little incident."

Gasping, Betty pointed at Darcy's hand. "Are you wearing an engagement ring?"

She clenched her stomach. How should she answer? She had never lied to Betty.

Narrowing her gaze, she shook her finger. "I knew something special existed between you two. That's why you kept telling me not to worry about Victor making partner. You probably asked him to step aside, and he did it just for you." Betty pointed at Darcy's chest. "Now, I know why you weren't nervous about bringing him as your date, because you probably knew he planned to propose in front of everyone. I just can't believe you kept it a secret."

She placed a hand over her heart. "I didn't know about the proposal."

Gasping, she scrunched her forehead. "You mean you were surprised?"

"I'm still shocked."

"So he waited to propose until after the reception, and away from everyone?"

"No." Shaking her head, she recalled how he knelt on one knee and held up the ring like a tiny star.

"So I *am* right." Taking a sip of her mocha, she stared off in the distance for a long moment. "I knew you loved him since the Gala. I guess fear kept you from saying anything because I would have told you he's too young."

Thoughts of the wedding reception drifted into Darcy's mind. Everyone speculated she couldn't land a young, successful man because of her age and financial status. Humiliation shuddered through her body. How could she tell Betty the truth when Betty thought no better of her than the so-called friends and family who derided her all night?

Betty grasped Darcy's hand. "Oh, my God, I can't believe you're getting married." The diamond glittered beneath the fluorescent lights. "The ring is so beautiful. I've never seen anything like it. Did he have it custom made?"

Darcy shrugged, deciding to drop her efforts at truth telling and go along with the lie. "Sawyer's Jewelers. The ring came from Victor's grandmother. She gave it to his mother who gave it to him."

"And he gave it to you." Betty smiled. "Oh, how romantic. A family heirloom." Releasing her hand, she sighed. "I should have suspected things were serious when you told me you'd been having lunch together, especially since you hardly ever date and Victor's not exactly the most social type."

She sipped her lukewarm cappuccino. "We kept our relationship a secret because we work together." The lies slipped off her tongue much easier than the truth. She didn't have to say much, but only confirm what Betty thought she might know.

"I understand." She nodded. "But I'm still surprised. I mean, you always said you never wanted to remarry. What made you change your mind?"

She remembered the adrenaline rush through her body once she accepted the proposal. The hugs and congratulations from the crowd wrapped around her like a new sweater. Nathan's quiet surprise and Tanya's obvious envy crowned the evening. Plus the shocking depth of the sweetness of Victor's kiss shattered her resistance to pretending to be his fiancée. The romance lingered long after the evening ended. "He told me dreams come true for those who believe."

Betty laughed. "It sounds like he sold you on the fairytale."

"Aren't you and Chuck living happily-ever-after?"

She shrugged. "We take two steps forward and one step back. Chuck is talking about vacationing abroad, and I'm talking about increasing our savings. He thinks I'll work long enough so he can enjoy a luxurious retirement, and I want to retire early to enjoy it with him. But the reality is we can't afford to travel right now, and I have to continue working. The situation is frustrating." As she touched Darcy's arm, she pouted. "I just don't want you to regret getting remarried. If you're having a midlife crisis, then you should just enjoy the affair without the commitment."

Hurt staggered through her. How shallow to have an affair. Lifting her eyebrows, she withdrew her arm. "Do you think I'm having a midlife crisis?"

"I don't know." Betty shrugged. "It's just not like you to plunge headfirst into anything. I don't want you to get hurt."

She bit her lower lip. Would Betty host a break-up party after her imaginary romance with Victor ended? A tsunami of sadness drowned her. "I have to go." With the sudden urge to see Victor, she stood. She needed to know if he sold his colleagues on their engagement, or if he fumbled for an excuse to back out now before their world changed forever.

Slinging her purse over her shoulder, she hugged Betty one last time before striding out the door. The cool autumn air slapped her cheeks, as if reprimanding her for not telling the truth, but Darcy didn't care. She enjoyed the play acting. She craved kissing Victor's coffee-flavored lips and smelling his musky cologne. She wanted to feel the rush of longing zip through her body from her scalp to her toes. But, most of all, she needed to melt her body against his and feel all of her doubts erase.

****

A line of people stood waiting to be helped in the reception area at Victor's office.

Darcy glanced at her watch every few seconds and shuffled from one foot to the next.

The receptionist glanced up and recognized her. "Go on in," she said. "I'll tell your fiancé you're here."

My fiancé, she thought. She beamed with pleasure. He'd told the whole office. Thanking the receptionist, she darted down the hallway and rapped her knuckles on the closed door. "It's Darcy."

"Come in, darling," Victor said.

Oh, goodness, she thought. He must have company. A trickle of dread stopped her from proceeding. She wanted to talk to him alone. Opening the door, she stepped into the small cozy room decorated with Tiffany lamps, leather chairs, and mahogany bookcases. The air smelled like old paper.

An elderly gentleman in a sharp suit standing next to Victor closed a manila folder and extended his hand. "I'm Albert Rollins, partner."

"Darcy Madison." She shook his hand.

"A pleasure to meet you." Albert smiled, glancing up and down the length of her body. "Victor's lucky to have such an attractive fiancée. Congratulations!"

Darcy flashed a tight smile. If this charade lasted a few months, how many people would they deceive along the way?

Victor winked. "Have a seat, darling. We're just finishing."

Albert cleared his throat. "We can meet after you take the future Mrs. Costello out to lunch." He turned to Darcy. "I assume you'll be taking his name."

Nervousness heated her skin. "Why, umm, of course, why wouldn't I?" she stammered.

"Actually, we've decided to take each other's names to represent the equality of our partnership." Victor picked up his name plate and pointed to the space between Victor and Costello. "Our new last name will be Madison-Costello."

"Victor Madison-Costello." Albert nodded. "The name has a nice ring."

A rush of delight at the proposal flooded through her. During her marriage to Nathan, she abandoned her maiden name and taken his without question. She believed it necessary to not confuse her child about whether or not her father and mother were married. She never thought to ask Nathan to hyphenate both of their last names to create a new unified identity. But Victor had. *Darcy Madison-Costello*. How wonderful the name sounded. Unfortunately, this entire exchange perpetuated the myth of a marriage that would never happen, and her elation deflated like air from a balloon.

"She looks a little piqued," Albert said. "Maybe you should both leave for lunch."

"Right." Placing the name plate on the desk, Victor grabbed his jacket. "What do you say, darling? Shall we dine at our usual spot?"

Narrowing her gaze, she wanted to hug and punch him for embroiling them in this charade. "Whatever you say, Mr. Madison-Costello."

****

"We have to stop this play acting now," Darcy said, once she and Victor settled in a booth at the café across the street. "I've already lied to Betty. Now, everyone at your office believes we're engaged. This little white lie is getting out of hand." She clenched her fists. "I think we should break up now."

"Whoa-whoa-whoa." He moved his hands up and down. "Let's not make any decisions on an empty stomach."

She growled. "I'm too upset to eat."

Λ server arrived to take their order.

Consulting the menu, he pointed. "The special for me and a tuna salad sandwich with extra pickles for my fiancée."

Eyes narrowed, she swatted his arm.

He flinched.

The server peered at Darcy's hand. "That's a beautiful ring. May I see it?"

A smile tugged on the corners of his mouth.

Darcy lifted her hand from his arm, even though

she wanted to swat him until he screamed, "Okay, we're not engaged!"

The server cupped Darcy's fingers and lifted her hand to examine the diamond. She exhaled and squeezed her fingers. "I swear it's something a princess would wear."

Darcy agreed. The ornate-but-not-gaudy, old-but-not-old-fashioned, large-enough-to-dazzle, but small-enough-not-to-overwhelm ring sparkled with clarity and brilliance on her finger. "It was his grandmother's wedding ring."

"Oh, how special." The server released her hand. "Congratulations! You both must be so happy. Please order dessert. It's on the house."

He broadened his smile. "We'll have the chocolate mousse."

The server grabbed their menus and twirled toward the kitchen with a skip in her step.

"See." He pointed to the departing server. "Our little game is making other people happy."

"That's because we're perpetuating a myth about the fairytale marriage." She dismissively waved her hand. "We don't even know each other well."

He frowned, scooting closer to the table. "I know you better than you think. Your favorite color is blue. You hate Valentine's Day but love Easter. You drink coffee, not soda. Your adult beverage of choice is a gin martini with two olives. Two olives so they won't get lonely—your words, not mine. And you tolerate reading literature with a boring book club because it keeps you busy at nights and occupies your Friday evenings."

She sighed. "Okay, you know a little bit about me.

But I know nothing about you other than you prefer work over everything else."

Raising his hand, he curled each finger toward his palm to mark off the item as he spoke. "My favorite color is red. I like Thanksgiving, but not Christmas. I don't have a favorite drink. I have no hobbies. And I am still mad you almost tricked me into joining your book club."

"That's not enough." Darcy raised her eyebrows. He had no signature drink. She assumed he loved gin martinis as much as she did.

"Okay. Let's get personal." Victor crossed his arms on the table and bowed his head. "My father died after my thirteenth birthday. My mother, who is Italian, and my paternal grandmother, who is Irish, raised me. She's the one who left me the ring you're wearing. I have a sister, but I haven't seen her since she moved to Texas ten years ago after I handled her divorce. No nieces, nephews, or any children I might have fathered. I had one serious relationship at seventeen, but she wanted to go all the way, and I wanted to remain a virgin." He tugged his lips into a line. "I practiced Catholicism back then."

"What do you practice now?"

He shrugged. "Nothing. I don't believe in anything anymore."

At the gravity of the statement, she nodded. "That's how I feel, too. Even if something greater exists, I see no point in believing because I'll only be disappointed."

The server delivered their sandwiches. "Enjoy!"

After they finished eating, Victor took Darcy's hand. "How do you feel now about playing up the engagement a little bit longer?"

She stared at their entwined fingers, braiding comfort and security into her life. Their relationship buoyed her spirits.

While Victor spoon-fed her the sickly sweet chocolate mousse, the other patrons sitting close by stole glances.

Even before marriage, Nathan never spoon-fed her anything. Victor's romantic tenderness softened her resistance. Keeping up the charade gave her the opportunity to finally be the woman other women envied. If Victor and Darcy broke up, all of the magic would disappear. She would return to being Darcy, a middle-aged divorced woman—not the future Mrs. Madison-Costello, luckiest woman in the world. She squeezed his fingers. "Okay, we'll keep up the lie just a little bit longer."

Raising her hand to his lips, he kissed each finger.

Lightning bolts of lust charged through her body.

"This pretending to be engaged is the most fun I've had in a long time," he said.

Me too, she thought. Too much fun.

She shuddered. Oh, what will I do when the charade ends?

Chapter 19

Two weeks later, Darcy sat cross-legged on her bed on a Saturday afternoon, folding her laundry, when her phone rang. She crawled over the bedspread, grabbed her phone from the night stand, and glanced at the caller ID identifying her daughter.

"Mom, Tyler and I would like to invite you and Victor to Thanksgiving," Joyce said. "You can see the house we bought in Marin, and we can talk more about a new wedding venue. We have some ideas to share."

Darcy sat straight and placed her bare feet on the cool hardwood floor. "I thought you weren't planning on living with Tyler until after the wedding."

"Tyler isn't living in the house," Joyce explained. "He's keeping his apartment in the city until after the honeymoon."

"But aren't you lonely living alone in a big house?"

"It's temporary," Joyce said. "We couldn't pass on the price, so we bought now. We have plenty of room for you and Victor to spend the night, if you'd like. In fact, Tyler hoped to share a room with Victor, so you and I could share a room. Like we did when you were living in the apartment before you bought the townhome, remember?"

Darcy groaned. Sharing a bed with her daughter who kicked didn't sound like the ideal way to spend the holiday. But at least, she wouldn't have to worry about whether or not Sam and Linda entertained any guests. She could give up her room for the long weekend and hang out with her daughter. They could storm the shops on Black Friday and eat lunch at a trendy new restaurant while Victor stayed at the house and watched football with Tyler and drank until the truth blurted out. A knot tightened her stomach. The charade became too uncomfortable to continue. "Umm…thanks, sweetheart, but I'll have to check with Victor to see what his plans are."

"Tyler already did, and Victor said we needed to check with you."

She tightened her grip on the phone. "Oh?"

"Yeah, he said you make all the major decisions."

"He did?" When had anyone in her personal life let her make all the major decisions?

"Yeah, so will you guys be there? You can bring your green bean casserole, and Victor said he can bake a pumpkin pie."

"He can?" Saliva filled her mouth when she thought of his pies tasting as wonderful as Gary's omelets.

She exhaled. "Mom, stop pretending you don't know what I'm talking about. He's your fiancé."

She didn't know what she was talking about, Darcy thought, and he was not her fiancé.

"So, are you guys coming or not?"

Somehow being the one to decide whether or not they would go pretend to be an engaged couple at her daughter's house on Thanksgiving didn't seem fair. At least, he could have warned her about his conversation with Tyler before Joyce called. That way, they could have come up with a plan together. But he chose to leave her in a lurch to fumble through this situation alone.

She rubbed her bare feet against the cold floor. What should she do? If she declined the invitation, she would have to make up a story about visiting Texas to meet Victor's family, and then she would have to feign knowledge of a place she had never been when Joyce called to ask questions and invite her and Victor to their house for Christmas. The knot in her stomach loosened into nausea. If she accepted the invitation, she could break up with Victor before Christmas. A strange calm descended, and for the first time in weeks, her stomach settled.

****

The following Monday, Darcy met Gary at his house while the children attended preschool.

Gary and his soon-to-be ex-wife hired a real estate agent over the weekend to list the property for sale. "We already have a preliminary offer, but one million is too low," he said. "That's why the real estate agent suggested we hire a staging expert who will arrive in the next hour."

The staging expert would suggest what to keep and what to place in storage before the first open house the following weekend. Darcy sat with Gary on the kitchen barstools, reviewing the listing agreement and the staging contract. The room still smelled of butter and warm toast. She placed a hand on her growling stomach. She skipped her breakfast date with Betty to make the appointment. Would asking him to cook her something be uncouth? He cooked so well.

Without a word, Gary stood and strode over to the refrigerator. "I'm out of eggs. Care for a homemade waffle?"

"You read my mind."

He flashed a smile. "Old habit. I'd hear my wife's stomach before her voice when she walked into the room, and I knew I needed to feed the beast." He blushed. "I'm not referring to you as a beast. I just meant I could tell you were hungry." He toasted the waffle, poured on a splash of agave syrup, and placed the plate before her with a fork and napkin and a mug of coffee.

For a long moment, she gazed at the sugary-smelling food, her mouth watering. What woman in her right mind would give up a guy like Gary to be alone with her work in a different city?

He sat beside her and stirred some cream into his second cup of coffee. "Am I doing the right thing by agreeing to sell the house?"

Swallowing the sweet, gooey, melt-in-your-mouth goodness, she nodded. "Moving forward with a new life is easier when you're in a different location. You encounter no memories, just create fresh experiences. Sometimes, selling the family home is harder on the children because they lose a familiar environment. They might be teary-eyed or restless or stoic or rebellious, depending on their temperament. But if they have a good psychologist to help them through the transition, selling the house is easier."

He stared at a spot on the granite counter. "Did you sell the family home when you divorced?"

She sopped up the sticky agave syrup with a piece of doughy waffle. "I moved out, but my daughter stayed in the home we shared with her father and the nanny. They carried on without me." The same old ache tickled her nose. She staunched the ensuing tears by pressing the back of her hand against her nostrils. "My new surroundings made it easier to accept the new circumstances." She shrugged. "I don't know how my daughter or her father managed living in the same space as before the divorce. We never discussed the situation."

He shifted his gaze, wrinkling his brow. "Are you?" He pointed to the ring.

Tucking her left hand into her lap, she shook her head. "It's not what you think."

He rubbed his eyes with his fists then pointed to her clenched hand. "How can you get remarried when you know how marriage ends?"

To loosen the tightness in her throat, she swallowed. "Marriage doesn't always end in divorce."

"Sixty percent of second marriages do." He gaped, wagging his head from side to side. "That's ten percent more than first marriages."

Be wise, she thought. Be clever. "My best friend is working on her second marriage. They've been together for fifteen years. That's longer than both your and my marriages."

Frowning, he gathered the papers on the counter. "I don't know why you're taking an unnecessary risk. Be safe and just live with the man for the rest of your life." He shook his head and pointed left then right. "You have your things. He has his things. Nothing is co-mingled. If you get angry, you move out. End of story. Out of all the people in the world, you should know better."

Clenching her hands in her lap, she longed to tell Gary the truth, but she couldn't. What if he told his friends who told their friends who told a client of Victor's who told the office staff, and then what? They would lose their credibility.

"I do know better." A pounding heartbeat grew loud in her ears. "That's why I am marrying a divorce attorney. We have a prenuptial agreement in which we agree not to co-mingle any funds. He's keeping his house vested in his name. I am keeping my daughter as the beneficiary on my retirement accounts. We are not opening a joint checking account. We are not investing in anything together. We are entering into this marriage separately together. If it ends, we leave with everything that's ours. Nothing is shared."

Gaping, he spread his arms wide. Papers scattered on the floor. Bending, he scooped them with fumbling hands. "Why even bother getting married?"

"Oh my, the rewards are endless." Lifting her hand, she ticked off each item on her fingers. "First, you gain respectability. How many people want a president with a shack-up girlfriend or boyfriend? What would you call the person? The First Girlfriend or the First Boyfriend, rather than the First Lady or the First Gentleman? How stable does our country look if the couple running it isn't committed to each other? Marriage is not important if you're working minimum wage and living in a crappy apartment in the worst part of town, but it's essential if you want to be promoted." How convincing I sound, she thought.

"Second, your taxes are lower in spite of what they say about the marriage penalty tax. Third, if your spouse gets hospitalized, you have next-of-kin rights, even if you don't have a medical power of attorney. Fourth, if someone dies, the other person gets Social

Security death benefits. Fifth, you don't have to worry about paying estate taxes, because no taxes are due if your spouse dies and doesn't have a will or trust. Everything goes to the surviving spouse tax free and hassle free." She took a breath and arched her eyebrows. "Do I need to continue?"

He shuddered. "You make marriage sound like another business decision."

Through clenched teeth, she growled. "Love has nothing to do with marriage unless you're poor. Only poor people can afford to marry for love."

Setting the papers in a neat stack on the counter, he sank onto a barstool and hung his head. "That's so dark and cynical."

She pounded a fist on the counter. "It's the truth."

"So, this marriage you're entering into is a business decision you and your divorce attorney decided on because you'll both benefit professionally, right?"

She nodded. She didn't want to sound so cold, but she didn't know how else to justify her position.

"If that's the case, I should start looking for a sugar mama again, right?" With wide eyes, he searched her face.

Oh, no, she had talked too much. She held her breath. She didn't want Gary to make a stupid decision, because she pretended to be a happily engaged woman. "I think you should join a support group for divorcing spouses. You can mingle, share your experiences, and grieve the loss of your marriages together."

Pointing, he nodded. "Like you did?"

"No, but it's what I should have done." She sighed, shaking her head. "I spent all my time working. I didn't even see my daughter much, only every other weekend, and the lack broke my heart."

"But you guys are close now, right?"

Darcy shrugged. "Not like you are with your children." Tears misted her eyes. She and Joyce spent more time together since Joyce's engagement, but they never joked around like Gary and his children. Although she could not rewind the clock, she wished to establish a better footing in her daughter's life, kinder and less contentious, so she might become a closer, more playful grandmother, if Joyce decided to have children.

"I sacrifice a lot for my relationship with my children." He patted her shoulder. "You're a good person. Your daughter is a grown woman. I have faith you both will find something that works."

The doorbell rang.

The staging expert had arrived. Darcy stood, slung her purse over her shoulder, and placed her dishes in the kitchen sink. "Thank you for breakfast. Shall I come by next week? Same time?"

At the front door, he stopped and turned. "I know it's none of my business, but I don't see why you're getting married if you don't love the guy."

"You're a romantic." She smiled.

"No, I'm not. But I don't think I would have married my wife as a business decision. I wanted to share my life because I enjoyed her company. I wanted to build a life together, co-mingling everything, even though doing so makes no sense from what you've just shared." Tears clouded his eyes. "I'm just scared you're making the wrong decision. If you want a business partnership, that's fine. Work something out that way." He shook his head. "But to get married just because it's the right thing to do professionally won't work in the long run if no love is involved."

"I think Tina Turner nailed the essence of a good marriage." Lifting her chin, she straightened her spine. "Love has nothing to do with it."

Chapter 20

Three hours later, Darcy stepped into the warmth of the café and searched for Victor.

He sat in a booth toward the back of the café, reading a newsletter.

She wound her way around tables, dodging servers with their arms laden with plates. Patrons chattered, and silverware clicked. Tugging off her gloves, she rubbed her palms together. "Brr...it's cold outside." She shimmied out of her wool coat and slid into the booth. A steaming cup of herbal tea greeted her. "Thanks for ordering."

"No problem. I know you're cutting back on caffeine, so I ordered you orange and passion fruit tea. You can never have too much passion." He winked. "I also ordered you pumpkin soup with half of a turkey sandwich." After folding the newsletter, he tucked it into his briefcase. "I have an appointment at one o'clock, and I couldn't risk waiting any longer."

"I'm not late, am I?"

"No, you're not. But the server stopped by, and I ordered not knowing when she might come by again. I hope you don't mind."

"Of course, I don't." She warmed her face against the steam from the fragrant floral-smelling tea. "I had a weird meeting with Gary. He saw my ring and went a little nutty. He thought he could convince me not to marry you."

Victor frowned. "You told him you were marrying me?"

"No, I never mentioned your name."

"What did you tell him?"

She fluffed the napkin like a matador before placing it on her lap. "My engagement to a divorce attorney originated as a business decision."

He smacked his forehead with the palm of his hand. "Don't you know men?"

She shrugged. "I thought phrasing marriage in terms of business would make sense to a man."

"Wrong." He wagged his head from side to side. "You'll come off as some money-grubbing gold digger who's insecure. Men are romantics. Think Hans Christian Anderson and the Grimm Brothers. Men invented happily-ever-after." Folding his arms on the table, he leaned forward. "You should have told Gary you were marrying for love."

Tossing back her head, she groaned. "I would have never thought of that excuse. You guys are always the ones dragging your feet in the relationship. You take the easy way out. You never do any of the heavy lifting. You make us women think we're wasting our time waiting around for you to figure out whether or not you love us enough to put a ring on it."

"I did." He pointed to her finger. "I didn't take long at all."

"*This* engagement is a joke." She held up her hand. "And it better end at Thanksgiving dinner or we'll end up celebrating Christmas together."

A slow smile spread across his face. "Spending Christmas together wouldn't be so bad, would it?"

And torture me longer with your perfection? She grumbled underneath her breath.

The server delivered their soups and sandwiches.

He took a bite of his roast beef sandwich and chewed. He lifted his eyebrows. "I put in a very low offer on Gary's house, but the real estate agent refused to present it. I think I can qualify for a bigger loan, but I'll need twenty percent down. How much money do you have?"

The cup slipped from her hand and clattered against the saucer. "You're the one who wrote a low-ball offer? Does Gary know it's from you?"

"No one knows." He shrugged. "The broker will only present offers starting at two million dollars."

Who had that type of money? Of course, she didn't. "I'm not buying a home with you."

"It's for us." He waved a hand between them. "We can sell it later. Right now, the place would be the perfect stage for the final act of our play."

"No, no, no." She mopped up the tiny spill with a napkin. "You said the final act ended with the proposal at the wedding. Now, look at us." She motioned between them. "We've started a whole new play."

Sitting back, he crossed his arms over his chest. "You're being unreasonable, Darcy. Where will the guests stay during Christmas?"

"We'll be broken up by then." She pressed her lips together. "We're breaking up on Thanksgiving. At my daughter's house. Thanks to your little chat with Tyler."

"That's too soon." He stirred his chunky vegetable soup. "You agreed we could have fun until a little after New Year's. I've always wanted to go to Las Vegas and live it up on that special night. We could see *Cirque du Soleil.* Do you know they have an erotic version?"

She squirmed. She didn't want to see an erotic show with Victor unless he promised to spend the rest of the night making love, which she doubted. Their faux love affair never escalated beyond kisses, which had become few and far between over the past weeks. Her idea of fun did not include pretending to be a couple without sex. "I'm afraid you'll have to go with someone else."

He dabbed his lips with a napkin. "Will you at least be my date for the partnership dinner next Friday night?"

She finished chewing her dry turkey sandwich and swallowed. Then she lifted her cup of tea. "I have my Books and Booze Club on Friday nights."

"It won't hurt to miss a week."

Narrowing her eyes, she tapped her foot beneath the table. "Why don't you go alone?"

"Because attending the biggest company event of the year without my fiancée will appear very odd." He crossed his arms over his chest. "Besides, your best friend is getting recognized."

"I know. I'm always her date when Chuck's not around."

"Please, be my date."

"I can't. I'm busy." She flashed a warning glance. "Men expect women to make all the sacrifices in the relationship. Never have you offered or accepted a compromise."

Leaning forward, he unfolded his arms. "What compromise are you proposing?"

Friendship is reciprocal, she thought. He'll never reciprocate. "If I attend the partnership dinner with you next week, you attend my Books and Booze Club this week."

He widened his gaze. "I don't even know what you guys are reading."

Removing a battered paperback from her purse, she slid it across the table. "*Wuthering Heights*."

"I prefer *Pride and Prejudice*."

Was he serious? He sounded like he actually read the book. "You missed out. We read that book last week."

Frowning, he flipped through the pages. "This book is massive. How can I finish reading this assignment?"

"You have until Friday." She pointed to the calendar on her phone. "Our meeting starts at seven. I'll pick you up at six-thirty, in case you want to drink more than you want to discuss books."

As if taking an oath, he placed his hand on the book. "Okay, I accept the compromise."

She smiled widely, pleased with the arrangement before she realized she faced another round of pretending.

****

On Friday evening, Darcy held Victor's hand as they wove through the crowd at Ophelia's Bar and Steakhouse to the special events room where her book club met. The room smelled of old books, new carpet, vinegar dressing, and spicy chicken wings.

Charlotte lifted her head and gawked before closing her mouth and waving for Darcy to sit by her side. "Who's your friend?" she whispered.

"This is my fiancé, Victor." She decided for the sake of convenience to keep up with the lie so she wouldn't have to remember who she'd told about the engagement.

Charlotte shook Victor's hand. "Welcome to our Books and Booze Club. I hope you read the assignment."

Victor set his copy of *Wuthering Heights* on the table. "I just finished this afternoon while waiting for a judge to decide a case. This book must have the most depressing ending ever written."

"It's also considered one of the most romantic novels ever written." Charlotte touched the book cover and sighed.

He scoffed. "How can the story be romantic when love is blocked by societal standards and almost everyone dies without achieving their potential?"

"You're quoting Maslow." Darcy scrunched her face.

"Maslow didn't write novels." Charlotte frowned.

"He should have." Victor glanced around the room.

A server arrived to take their orders.

Charlotte ordered a bottle of the house chardonnay for the group and a side of cheese and crackers.

Victor ordered a beer.

One night without booze was worth one night with Victor, Darcy thought. She ordered water with no ice.

"What about your gin martini with two olives?" Victor wrinkled his forehead.

"I'm driving." She jangled her keys. "I'm sure you'll switch to hard liquor before the end of the night."

The rest of the group arrived.

Barry shook Victor's hand and offered to share a platter of wings.

Victor declined.

Anita could not keep her eyes or hands off of him. She pinched his butt on his way to the bathroom.

"That's my fiancé you're mauling." Darcy slapped Anita's wrist.

"How crude!" Charlotte echoed.

Victor countered each invasive touch by kissing Darcy.

Dizziness invaded her head from a lack of oxygen from the prolonged kissing. If letting those women taunt him led to more opportunities to be kissed, she would ignore the uncomfortable sexual innuendos and soak up the affection.

Lucas kept tugging his pony tail while he talked. "Heathcliff should have insisted on marrying Catherine."

"Poor orphan boys don't have the right to marry ladies." Eric rapped his knuckles against the table. "Didn't you read *Oliver Twist*?"

Barry chuckled. "See what happens when they don't end the story where it should end? If the story ended when Catherine dies, then we wouldn't have to endure the legacy of their children attempting to make things right the second time around."

"Marriage is harder the third time around." Victor waved to the server and ordered a shot of tequila. "I know my grandmother missed out on the love of her life. Not the grandmother whose ring Darcy wears, but my other grandmother who married a man out of convenience. My mother married well and loved my father with all of her heart, but he died and left her a widow at forty-three."

Darcy hunched her shoulders. Married out of convenience, she thought. Wasn't that sentiment similar to what she shared with Gary about her own supposed engagement? She placed a hand on Victor's forearm. "Not to make light of your comments, dear, but we need to focus on the book, not your personal life."

Covering her hand with his, he frowned. "Catherine and Heathcliff were doomed. The universe hates happy lovers. Like Romeo and Juliet."

She leaned closer, narrowing her gaze. "We've already discussed that play." Turning toward the others, she forced a smile. "I'm sorry he's straying."

Barry raised his eyebrows and folded his burly arms on the table. "This is one reason why we normally don't allow guests."

Heat penetrated her cheeks. "Maybe we should go." Shaking off Victor's hand, she placed a twenty dollar bill on the table and stood.

"Don't." Anita threw an arm around Victor's shoulders and leaned close.

Turning from Anita's cleavage, he rose and took Darcy's hand. "We should go."

Together, they marched through the special events room.

Although tempted to stop at the bar for a quick gin martini before hitting the road, she bustled out of the restaurant. How could he embarrass her? A cool breeze tickled the back of her neck, and she shivered. "I don't know what I was thinking bringing you here." Without the din of constant chatter, she heard the harsh tone of her voice and winced.

Dipping his head, he studied her. "I told you I didn't want to come."

Meeting his gaze, she nodded. "I know." A lump formed in her throat.

Wrapping his arms around her, he pulled her close. "We don't have to share the same interests to be a couple."

Warmth radiated from his body. Oh, how comforting he felt, she thought. She turned her head and rested her cheek against the roughness of his wool coat. Are we a couple? Closing her eyes, she swallowed. "I'm dreading the partnership dinner."

He rubbed her back and kissed her hair. "You'll do fine."

Oh, if only he knew how much she hated lying to her best friend.

Chapter 21

A week before Thanksgiving, Darcy's phone rang in the middle of the night. She groped for the phone to stop its insistent ring before it woke up her roommates. "Hello?" Muffled sobbing greeted her.

"It's me. Monica."

Turning on the light beside the bed, she squinted at the digital clock. Two o'clock in the morning. She had not heard from Monica since the divorce party months ago. "What's wrong?"

"I don't want to spend Thanksgiving alone," Monica cried. "I miss being a family. I miss the life I had before my divorce. You didn't tell me I would feel worse."

A rush of sympathy flooded Darcy's body. "You wouldn't have believed me." She leaned against the pillows. "You're still grieving, which is normal. I promise you'll feel better after you feel worse. Next Thanksgiving, you'll feel grateful."

Monica continued sobbing. "My family doesn't want me to visit. They say I'll go to hell for getting rid of my husband."

Rubbing her forehead, she sighed. Most of her clients, even the ones who initiated the divorce, often called for consolation on significant days when loving memories surfaced. "Why don't we meet tomorrow for lunch, around twelve-thirty, at Jasper's? It's only five

229

minutes from where you work."

Monica's sobs muffled into hiccups. "Okay," she mumbled.

"Now, try to get some sleep." She fluffed her pillow. "Close your eyes and think of butterflies." When Joyce woke up from a nightmare as a child, Darcy always told her to think of butterflies.

"Why butterflies?"

"Because they're light and beautiful." A sweet smile creased her face. "Best of all, they snatch your troubles and float away with them." Oh, how Darcy wished she was always surrounded by butterflies.

****

At twelve-thirty-five, Darcy took a seat at the bar in Jasper's. She spread her napkin across her lap and ordered a gin martini with two olives and an extra basket of bread and butter for her soon-to-arrive guest. The dimly lit room smelled of furniture polish and sour beer.

"I'm sorry I'm late." Monica flounced over to the bar with her wild black hair falling over her face. Her emerald green dress suit looked crinkled and her black leather heels appeared scuffed. She hopped up on the bar stool, broke off a hunk of sourdough bread, and slathered it with salted butter. "I'm starving. I can't afford to eat lunch. All my money goes to rent and utilities. I'm lucky enough to qualify for food stamps, so my son doesn't starve."

Darcy placed a hand on Monica's wrist. "I understand."

She widened her eyes and placed a hand over her mouth. "Oh my god! You're engaged!"

Darcy jerked away her hand and tucked it into her

lap. "It's not what you think."

"Of course, it is! You're leaving the ranks of the divorced to be married again." She leaned closer and narrowed her eyes. "Who is he? And how did he convince you to abandon your vow of being a spinster?"

She bowed her head. Should she tell Monica the truth? Hammering heartbeats thundered in her chest. She would have to confess eventually. Why not now? Wiping her sweaty palms in the napkin, she took a deep breath. "I'm not engaged. We put on an act at my ex-husband's wedding to convince the guests I'm not too old to snag a thirty-something male."

Monica gulped and seized another piece of bread. "Who is he?"

Darcy took a sip of her dry martini and gazed off into the distance. When she thought of Victor, she smiled. "He's a divorce attorney."

"Which one?"

She jittered her leg against the bar stool. Maybe she shouldn't have confessed her secret. "Doesn't matter. We're not getting married."

"Then tell me."

Lifting her head, she met Monica's gaze. Should she trust her? After all, Monica's professional ambition and personal love for her disabled son paralleled Darcy's younger, more innocent self. How could she not trust her? She bowed her head. "His name is Victor Costello," she whispered.

Monica gasped. "The hunk from Legal Aid? The one with those killer brown eyes?"

Darcy twitched with regret. I'm so stupid, she thought. Monica might tell someone they both knew and then the truth would be exposed—Victor and Darcy were liars. "You know him?"

"I met him when I signed my final paperwork." Monica shredded her bread into tiny pieces and stared across the room. "I wished I hadn't finished my divorce yet, because I would have requested to work with him." She licked her lips. "He's hot."

Oh, yes, I agree, she thought. She swirled the dregs in her martini glass and briefly considered ordering a second, but decided to switch to water. An idea blossomed, captivating her with its ripe potential to solve her fake engagement problem. "Maybe I should introduce you to Victor. You both might hit it off."

"Would you?" A light beamed from her face.

"Sure, why not?" Smiling, she sipped her water. If Victor and Monica became a real couple, then Victor would have fun, and Darcy would be free again. She would only miss his incredible kisses, but no kiss was worth remarriage.

Monica pointed to Darcy's hand. "If you're not engaged, then why are you wearing a ring?"

"Because everyone thinks we're a real couple." She pulled Monica closer. "I expect you to keep our little secret. Victor and I will break up sometime before the wedding. No one is supposed to suspect we've been playing a ruse, okay? Not even you."

Monica wrinkled her forehead. "When are you guys breaking up?"

Darcy crossed her fingers. "I'm hoping for Thanksgiving."

Selecting another piece of bread, Monica spread a layer of butter. "If I were you, I wouldn't break off anything, act or no act."

"You want to get remarried someday?" She squared her shoulders.

Chewing, Monica nodded. "Mmm-hmm."

"Why?" No man could appreciate a young, smart, ambitious woman with a huge heart of love, so why would Monica waste her potential on a man?

"I want to belong to someone."

She laughed, raising her arms in defense. "We're living in America and not a foreign country where women are considered chattel." She pointed at Monica's chest. "You belong to yourself."

Monica sighed. "I mean belong in a metaphysical sense."

Soul mates, she thought. Oh, why had she offered up Victor like a door prize? They had a connection, whether or not they were pretending to be a couple.

Monica ordered a glass of water and a bowl of tomato soup. While she waited, she twirled the napkin in her lap and snuck glances. "Victor is amazing. Everyone says he's the best divorce attorney in Sonoma County. He's also easy on the eyes. I could stare at him all day. I can't believe you offered to introduce us." She tilted her head and stared across the room. Widening her gaze, she turned toward Darcy. "What's wrong with him?"

"What do you mean?"

"Something has to be wrong with him, if you're willing to give him up."

"Nothing is wrong with him." Darcy twirled the stem of her glass. "It's me. I don't want to settle down with anyone anytime." She breathed in the savory smell of Monica's tomato soup. She reached for a piece of bread, skipping the butter.

Monica clasped her hands against her chest. "I'm so lucky. You're the most generous woman in the world."

Too generous, she thought.

****

Darcy cringed at the party decorations for the partnership dinner held in one of the smaller ballrooms of the Hyatt Vineyard Creek Inn. "The room looks like a senior prom, not a promotion dinner." She pointed to the black and gold confetti glittering on the white tablecloths. A single podium stood at the front of the room. Hotel-style catering complimented the corporate-style introductions. No open bar. Only cheap, sour-tasting wine served with dry tri-tip and overcooked chicken breasts. She wished someone consulted her for the event. Planning a dinner to remember, she would have selected a more intimate venue with warmer colors and richer foods.

Before dessert, Albert announced Betty as the firm's newest partner.

Betty smiled at everyone at her table before she turned to her husband to accept his congratulatory kiss. She wobbled on her heels toward the podium and hugged Albert who presented her with a plaque for her office announcing her new status with the firm. Brushing the bangs out of her eyes, she leaned closer to the microphone. "I'd like to thank a few key people for their support over the years. Most of all, I'd like to thank my husband, Chuck, who has endured my long hours away from home."

She waved at her smiling husband sitting at the table. "Next, I'd like to thank the existing partners, Albert and Ralph, for awarding me this honor. Lastly,

I'd like to thank my best friend, Darcy, for her patient listening, and her fiancé, Victor, who almost beat me out of this honor." She clasped the plaque against her chest and beamed. "I'm so happy they're getting married. I wish them both as much happiness as I've had with Chuck over the years." She lifted her plaque and smiled. "And as much happiness as I hope to have in my new role with the firm. Thank you!"

Oh, how sweet, Darcy thought. Tenderness spread like rays of sunshine through her body. In the midst of the applause, she jerked around her head to meet Victor's gaze.

He smiled and took her hand.

Although warmed by his skin, coolness surfaced. How could she enjoy his company without plunging farther into the abyss of romantic love? What better way to terminate their false romance than to introduce a new third party who would replace her? Before she lost her courage, she leaned over forcing her voice low. "I have someone who wants to meet you."

He raised his eyebrows and glanced around the room. "Where is he?"

"The person is a she, and she's not here," she whispered. "Her name's Monica. She saw you at Legal Aid and thinks you're hot."

He widened his gaze. Scooting back his chair, he motioned for her to step away from the table. "What makes you think I want to meet her?"

She sidled close and sighed. "Because you're single."

He grabbed her elbow and steered her toward the far corner of the room away from doors and entrances. "I'm with you, remember?"

"But she knows we're not engaged."

A flicker glinted in his dark eyes. "You *told* her the truth?"

She flinched, involuntarily taking a step back. She turned up open palms. "The truth had to come out some time or other. Why not with Monica? She wants to date you. A romance with her would be a good transition."

Victor smacked his forehead. "She might tell someone. Our credibility would be over."

"She won't tell anyone. She knows we will announce our breakup at Thanksgiving. Then you both can wait a couple of weeks before you go on your first date. I'll even set it up, so you only have to show up. If things work out, she can replace me at the New Year's Eve bash in Las Vegas." Shrugging, she lifted her upturned palms. "Who knows? Monica's interest in you might be the perfect solution for all of us."

"No way." With widened eyes, he shook his head. "I'm not going, and you can't make me." He folded his arms over his chest. "We're not breaking up on Thanksgiving, either. Remember, we agreed it would be after New Year's but before Valentine's Day so we can dodge the bullet, as they say."

Betty wandered over.

As servers collected empty plates, the clatter of silverware against china echoed from the center of the room. Subdued laughter from the guests floated like bubbles.

"Is everything okay?"

Narrowing his gaze, Victor grabbed Darcy's hand and squeezed too hard. He strained his face with a tight smile. "We're sorry, but Darcy and I should be going. We have an early day tomorrow."

Betty flashed a smile. "What do you guys have planned?"

"We're hiking in Annadel then heading into the city for lunch," he said.

Another lie, she thought, although the plan sounded delightful. She glanced at their table. "They're serving dessert. Don't you want some cheesecake?"

Chuckling, Victor patted Darcy's tummy. "We need to keep down our weight if we'll fit into our wedding dress."

"You already have your wedding dress?" Betty widened her stance. "You told me we were shopping together."

How many lies could he tell in one night? She swatted Victor's hand away from her body. "I *don't* have a wedding dress."

"Of course she does." He lifted his chin. "She's wearing my mother's dress."

How dare he plan the imaginary wedding? Glowering, she widened her stance. "I'm not wearing that dress." She recalled the photo of his mother in his living room. She wore a modest slip-like dress without embellishments. "The dress won't fit, because she's shorter than me."

Removing his wallet, he showed Betty a picture of his parents' wedding. "See, I'm a little taller than my father. Don't you think Darcy's about my mother's size?"

Betty grabbed the wallet and shared the picture with Darcy. "I think your mom is a little short and a lot less curvy. Plus the dress is too plain and angular. Darcy needs a more flattering cut." She handed back the wallet. "Don't you want your wife to look her best on your wedding day?"

He sighed. "My grandmother wore the same dress. I hoped to keep the tradition going."

"Well, if that's the case then we need to bring the dress to a seamstress to see if we can alter it."

Darcy shuddered. What an old and ugly dress! The gown was worse than her mother's dress which Darcy wore to her first wedding. At the time, she was too poor to buy the wedding dress of her dreams—a beaded lace bodice with a voluminous tulle skirt which ended in a three-foot train. Angry tears threatened. "I'm *not* wearing that dress."

"Why don't we go shopping when you get back from the city tomorrow?" Betty suggested. "Chuck and I have no plans. You guys could get together and watch college football while Darcy and I go browse the bridal boutiques, okay?"

"That plan won't work." Darcy shot a pleading look at Victor. "We'll get back too late."

"Oh, let's cancel our plans." He waved a hand. "We can go to the city next weekend. Chuck and I will barbecue lunch, and you girls can leave to shop when the game starts. How does that idea sound?"

Betty clapped her hands. "Oh, how perfect!"

Holding her breath, she clenched and unclenched her fists at her sides. Why buy a dress she would never wear?

"I can't afford to go shopping." She gazed at Victor, hoping he would understand the deeper meaning beyond the words.

He removed his credit card and tucked it into her hand. A grin bloomed on his face. "Oh, yes, you can."

Darcy stared at the credit card, a gleaming

talisman, taunting her to keep the charade going even as she fell harder into the snares of the fantasy. Glancing up, she caught Betty's beaming smile. Disappointment sank into the pit of her stomach. She couldn't disappoint her best friend. Turning to Victor, she forced a tight smile. "Thanks, sweetheart."

He smiled, leaning forward to kiss her cheek. "No problem, darling. What's mine is yours."

She sighed, wondering how long she could stare at a never-worn wedding gown in her closet before guilt and sadness tore through her heart.

Chapter 22

The bridal showcase room smelled marshmallow sweet. Dozens of mannequins modeled frothy white wedding gowns. Racks and racks of dresses hung from displays. As she strolled across the plush carpet, Darcy floated like a little girl into a magical world of make believe.

"I'm so excited." Betty gravitated toward the gemstone bridesmaid's dresses. "What are your theme colors? Blue and—"

"Red." Darcy remembered Victor's favorite color.

Betty selected a ruby red sheath, which graced her ankles. "What do you think?"

Touching the red satin fabric, she smiled. "Try it on."

"Welcome to Wedding Dreams Come True. I see you've found a bridesmaid's dress." A young salesclerk greeted them.

"Yes, I have." Betty hugged the dress to her chest. "I'd like to try on this dress. My friend, here, needs a wedding gown."

The salesclerk led Betty to a fitting room and returned to Darcy. She gave her a critical onceover. "The perfect wedding dress starts with a few questions." She puckered her lips and tapped her chin. "I'll need to know if this wedding is your first or subsequent marriage."

"It's my second."

The clerk sauntered over to a rack of pastel-colored dresses and selected a tea-length gown. "Try on this one."

The dress looked like something the mother of the bride would wear. She furrowed her brow. "I want to wear white."

The clerk waved a hand over the satin skirt. "We need to focus on the softer pastels. White is tacky the second time around. After all, you're not a virgin."

"Neither are most first brides." Tightening her face, she forced a laugh.

The salesclerk hung the pastel dress back on the rack and stalked down another aisle. "Are you having an indoor or an outdoor wedding?"

"I don't know," Darcy stammered. Victor had asked her to part with four hundred thousand dollars in her 401k as a down payment on Gary's home with the promise of replenishing her 401k as soon as he secured funds from his own investments. When she told him she only had forty thousand dollars saved from the years she worked as an event planner for a big Los Angeles firm, he said he would find a way to buy the house without her financial assistance.

The salesclerk snickered. "Maybe you should come back when you have more information."

Inhaling a long breath, she narrowed her gaze. Don't snap, she thought. Remain professional. No need to stoop to her level.

Betty stepped out of the dressing room and modeled the ruby red dress. "What do you think?"

The style emphasized her tiny waist. "It's perfect."

"Okay, I'll get it." Betty twirled before the mirror

and flashed a smile.

Oh, great, Darcy thought. She's spending money on a dress she'll never wear. "Umm, on second thought, why don't you just put it on hold? We have other boutiques to try."

Betty shook her head. "I like this dress. I'm buying it."

The salesclerk turned toward Darcy. "I have the perfect dress to match your bridesmaid." She marched down an aisle crammed with white dresses covered in plastic. "Here's something you might like." She withdrew a tea-length gown in a pale cream color. "It's simple and elegant for a more mature woman entering her second marriage."

"I'm not wearing that dress." She frowned. "I want a white, floor-length gown with a train."

"The traditional look is not good for second weddings." The salesclerk frowned. "Pulling off a big ball gown is hard when you're over forty."

"I might as well wear something out of my own closet then." Sighing, she turned to leave.

"Just show her something else." Betty clasped her hands.

The salesclerk sauntered down the aisle, yanked out a random white dress here and there.

Darcy trailed behind, shaking her head. "No, no, no." She waved aside each dress, not wanting an A-line, a mermaid, or a trumpet skirt. Tears thickened in her throat.

The salesclerk shoved a blush-colored dress back on the rack.

A flash of rhinestones caught Darcy's attention. She slipped a hand between the dresses and plucked a gown with a beaded bodice and a flounced skirt with a modest train. "May I try on this dress?"

The salesclerk wrinkled her forehead. "The dress is too young for you."

Darcy stepped back, as if she had been slapped. Her whole body trembled with anger. How dare the salesclerk insult a customer? "C'mon, Betty, let's shop where customers are shown respect." She shoved the dress back on the rack and stomped outside.

Betty darted after her. "Wait for me. I have to first pay for this dress."

Darcy unlocked her car door and sat inside, staring out the window for a couple of minutes. The entire shopping experience replayed in her mind like a rerun no one wanted to watch. She cringed with humiliation when she remembered the salesclerk's reprimands. No traditional white gowns for middle-aged brides. Just tacky tea-length dresses in cream or blush colors. Pouting, she started the engine.

A few moments later, Betty rushed out of the store, clinging to the red bridesmaid's dress covered in plastic. She opened the passenger's door and slid inside, folding the dress into her lap.

"I can't believe you bought the dress." Darcy arched an eyebrow. "Especially after the way the clerk treated me."

"My dress has nothing to do with how you were treated." Betty caressed the fabric beneath the plastic cover.

Darcy backed out of the parking spot and drove down the main street. To steady herself, she took a few deep breaths. "After this experience, I realize it's much worse being a middle-aged bride than I thought. You get no respect." Tears pricked her eyes.

Betty patted Darcy's knee. "Relax. We'll go to Brides and Maids. I'm sure someone will help us."

Merging onto the freeway into Saturday afternoon traffic, she shuddered. How much longer would the charade continue? Already, Betty spent her hard-earned money on a fabulous dress she would never wear. Now, they traveled to another bridal store to shop for a wedding gown which Darcy would never wear. Who cared if Darcy and Victor agreed to break up on Thanksgiving? The engagement needed to end now before things escalated even more out of control. Tightening her grip on the steering wheel for strength, she stared straight ahead. "I'm not getting married." Finally, she told her best friend the truth.

"Everyone gets cold feet." Betty lifted her arms, palms up. "I almost didn't marry Chuck, but my future mother-in-law took me aside and explained the reason for second marriages. People learn and grow from the mistakes they made the first time, and they're more determined than ever to make things work the second time." She pointed to a road sign. "Take the next exit."

Darcy veered off the freeway. Why didn't Betty believe her? What else did she need to say? Pressure and frustration built behind her eyes. She lied about being engaged, because she got caught up in the fantasy of being a middle-aged bride. A tear dribbled down her cheek. She wished she could have told Victor, "No," when he proposed. She wished she could have told Joyce she didn't want to plan her wedding. She wished she could have told her ex-husband she didn't want to pay for a nanny.

Wiping her moist cheek with the back of her hand,

she shivered. At least she walked out of the store when the salesclerk insulted her. She told Betty the truth about not getting married, even though her friend didn't listen. At the next light, she circled back onto the freeway and drove south in the direction of Betty's house.

"Where are we going?" Betty glanced out the window at her surroundings.

"I'm taking you home." Why continue the charade by visiting another bridal boutique? She gripped the steering wheel tighter.

Betty pursed her lips. "Are you mad at me for suggesting we go someplace else to shop?"

"No, I'm mad because you didn't hear what I had to say." She tensed her jaw until her teeth hurt. "I'm—not—getting—married."

"Of course, you are." Betty patted her shoulder. "You're just angry things aren't going your way, and you're taking out your anger on me. That's what people who are close to each other do sometimes because it's safer than keeping things bottled inside."

Darcy pressed her foot on the accelerator and switched to the fast lane.

"Slow down and get off on the next exit." Betty pointed to a street sign. "We'll find you a dress. Things aren't as bad as they seem."

"You sound like a psychologist rather than a lawyer."

"Chuck and I are still seeing a marriage and family therapist once a month. When we first started going, I dreaded it. Now, I look forward to the appointments. Things work better between us when we go check in with someone else. A neutral third party holds us more accountable for the changes we promised to make for one another. Maybe you and Victor should consider pre-marital counseling."

Darcy groaned. She sped across two lanes of traffic to the exit and drove into the nearest parking lot. She wanted to turn off her engine, face her friend, and explain in tiny, painful details the whole shenanigan from start to finish.

"Oh my God, look at the woman leaving the store." Betty pointed.

Darcy swiveled for a look.

A gray-haired woman carried a white wedding gown out of a boutique. The dress almost touched the pavement. The woman carrying the dress looked well over sixty.

"The dress must be for her granddaughter." Darcy sighed.

"I'll bet you fifty dollars it's for her." Betty opened her wallet and shook two twenties and a ten.

Hope tingled beneath her skin. What if Betty was right? Sliding into a parking spot, Darcy turned off the engine and stumbled out of the car, almost tripping with excitement. Beads of sweat dampened her palms.

Betty opened the car door and ran after the older woman. "Excuse me!" she yelled. "Excuse me, ma'am! Is that dress for you? Or did you pick it up for someone else?"

The older woman stopped and glanced over her shoulder. "Who wants to know?"

Betty pointed to Darcy who stood beside her. "My friend here is engaged, and she's having problems getting a traditional dress. Everyone says she's too old."

Darcy nudged Betty in the ribs. "Not everyone.

Just one salesclerk."

The older woman showed them the dress. "It's for my third wedding to the best man I've ever met. My first husband left me for a younger woman. My second husband died too early for me to enjoy him. I'm hoping the third husband will last."

Darcy stared with a slack jaw at the white taffeta gown with a six-foot train tied high in the back to keep it from dangling out of the plastic bag. She clasped her hands against her rapidly beating heart. If the older woman could find a long white dress, why couldn't she?

"C'mon." Smiling, Betty grabbed Darcy's hand. "Let's find the perfect wedding dress."

Once she stepped inside the bridal store, Darcy forgot her resolution to explain the truth. Beautiful gowns hung from golden hangers on one side of the room. Mirrors lined the opposite wall. A bank of dressing rooms covered the back of the store.

As the door swung closed, a tiny bell chimed. A woman with a coif of blonde hair smiled, glancing from Darcy to Betty. "Which one of you is the lucky bride?"

"She is." Betty pointed to Darcy.

The woman opened her arms and hugged her. "Congratulations! I'm Edith, and I'm the owner. I enjoy helping people find a dress which speaks to them. Do you know what you want?"

After a moment of hesitation, Darcy explained the dress she wanted as a young woman.

Edith listened and nodded before disappearing behind a white curtain and returning with the exact gown Darcy described. "Go ahead and undress." She guided her into a fitting room. "If you need help with the zipper, let me know. I'll be just outside."

Stripping out of her sweater and jeans, she fumbled with the zipper and the netting in the tulle skirt. Stepping into the dress, she wiggled the material up her waist and over her breasts. As she zipped it up the back, the bodice hugged her curves. The skirt flowed against her hips and kissed the floor. She twirled and glanced at the back of the dress in the mirror. The three-foot train swirled like a tiny white puddle. Pleasure tingled throughout her body, and a quick smile lifted her face. Parting the dressing room curtains, she stepped into the showroom.

Betty covered her mouth and gasped. "Oh my God, you look like a princess."

Edith smiled. "You'll make one lucky man proud to call you his bride."

Darcy spun, tugging along the train. She gazed at herself in the mirrors surrounding the showroom. A glow of happiness radiated from her. Finding the perfect dress on the first try must be a sign. "I'll take it!" She clasped her hands to her chest.

After changing into her clothes, she stood at the register, sweat beading against her forehead. How could she buy a dress she would never wear even if Victor paid?

"With tax, the dress costs four thousand fifty-two dollars and eleven cents." Edith held out her hand for payment.

Darcy refused to open her wallet.

"What's wrong?" Betty asked.

Tears filled her eyes. "I can't buy the dress."

Betty hugged her. "Yes, you can. Your future husband's paying. He expects you to come back with a dress."

Shaking her head, she couldn't stop the tears spilling down her cheeks. "You don't understand," she sobbed.

Edith touched her hand. "I understand the amount is more than you want to spend, but it's worth the investment."

"I'm not crying about the dress." Darcy snuffled. "I'm upset about the engagement. It isn't—"

"Is your phone ringing?" Betty pointed to Darcy's purse.

A dance melody played somewhere inside Darcy's purse. She plunged her hand into a pocket and grabbed the phone.

"Have you found anything?" Victor asked.

Darcy wiped her eyes with the back of her hand. Just hearing his strong, reassuring voice steadied her emotions. "Yes, I did."

"Send me a picture," he said.

Again, she started sobbing. "I can't," she mumbled. Turning from the register, she walked toward the back of the showroom. "I can't wait any longer to end this masquerade. We have to break up now."

"Not today," he said. "We'll break up on Thanksgiving. That's not too far away, okay?"

She rubbed her nose and sniffled. "No, I want to end this game now."

"Darling, you're emotional," he said. "I respect you more than you know. I'm not breaking up with you over the phone. When we break up, I want to see you, touch you, and reassure you everything will be all right. Okay? Can you wait until then?"

The tone of his voice steadied her. The shakiness in

her arms disappeared. "I guess I'll have to wait."

"Now, please send me a picture of you in the dress."

"Why?" She didn't understand why anyone would want to see a fake bride in a real wedding gown.

"Because I'm here and you're there," he said. "I'm missing all the excitement."

The disappointment in his voice startled her. She arched her eyebrows. "Shopping is exciting?"

"Anything with you is exciting. Please, humor me and send me a picture."

Ending the call, she returned to the register. "My fiancé wants a picture of me in the dress before I buy it."

"No way." With furrowed brow, Betty shook her head. "For the groom to see the bride in her dress before the wedding is bad luck."

Hmm…maybe she could get out of buying the dress, after all. She slung her purse over her shoulder and stalked to the door.

"Where are you going?" Betty asked. "You need to pay for your dress."

"Victor's not buying until he sees me in the gown."

Edith suggested they send Victor a picture of the dress modeled by a woman in the vendor's catalogue she carried for the store.

"No mannequins and no models." Darcy lifted her chin and placed a hand on her hip. "Only me."

Betty sighed. "I guess we'll have to cross our fingers and ignore the old wives' tale."

Edith guided Darcy back into a fitting room and helped her into the dress. "Your hair would look wonderful down against your shoulders." She touched the ends of Darcy's hair. "It's such a rich color. Where do you have it done?"

"I do it myself." Darcy smiled.

"Are you a hairdresser?"

"No, I'm a divorce planner."

"No wonder you're so upset." Edith met her gaze in the mirror. "This experience must be hard after seeing so many broken marriages day after day. What does your fiancé do?"

"He's a divorce attorney." She gestured toward the showroom. "Betty introduced us."

"Ah, so she's the one responsible for transforming both your lives."

"Transforming is a great word to describe our relationship." Darcy smiled. "Victor says I bring a lot of fun into his life."

"Of course you do, dear." Edith smiled at Darcy's reflection. "You're fun and hopeful."

Darcy admired the woman reflected in the mirror. Tears again filled her eyes. "This wedding isn't real," she whispered. If I keep saying the phrase aloud, she thought, then maybe I'll believe it.

Edith squeezed her shoulders. "I understand you must be overwhelmed with all the planning, but your feelings are very real. You deserve happiness. Now, take a deep breath and relax. Let's go out there and show your future husband what he has to look forward to, okay?"

Darcy stepped into the showroom and stood on the podium by the wall of mirrors.

Betty took several pictures from different angles and sent the best to Victor.

By the time Darcy changed back into her clothes,

her phone rang.

"I like it," Victor said. "How much is it?"

"Over four thousand dollars."

He whistled. "That's a bit much, isn't it?"

"Yes, all of this pretending has been a bit much." She stepped away from Edith and Betty. "I can't wait until Thanksgiving. I need to say something now."

"Calm down," Victor said. "Thanksgiving is less than a week away. You can wait until then. Just don't buy the dress. Leave the store. And please promise me you won't tell Betty anything until we've discussed how we will inform people about our broken engagement, okay?"

She agreed. Ending the call, she returned to Betty and Edith. "Victor said the dress costs too much. He wants me to keep looking."

"But this gown *is* the one." Pinching her eyebrows together, Betty picked up her phone and scrolled through her contacts. "Maybe I should talk to him."

"No, please, let's just go." Darcy turned to Edith and smiled. "Thank you for all of your help, but I won't be buying the dress after all."

Edith braced her hands on the counter. "I understand your concern about the price, but I guarantee you won't find the same quality anywhere else."

Darcy stared at the beaded bodice and the flouncy tulle skirt. She would have paid double the price for the dress, because the gown represented the love she always envisioned would be hers.

Edith hung the dress on the rack behind her. "I'll put it on hold for you for one week, in case you change your mind."

Tears clung to her lashes. "That gesture won't be necessary."

"I've been in this business for thirty years. Miracles happen all the time." Edith removed a white tag and clicked a pen. "May I have your contact details?"

After she relayed the information, Darcy clutched her hands and turned away, thinking of the wedding that would never be. Oh, what miracle would get her out of this mess?

Chapter 23

As soon as they parked in Betty's driveway, Betty released her seatbelt and dashed out of the car.

"Why are you in a hurry?" Darcy ran across the grass.

"He's not getting away with it." Betty fumbled with the lock on the front door and darted inside, heels clip-clopping against the hardwood floors. "Victor!"

A flash of fear whipped through her body. Darcy dashed into the house and slammed the front door with her heartbeat racing faster than her feet traveled. "Don't talk about the dress," she ordered.

Betty ran through the maze of hallways until she entered the family room where Chuck and Victor sat on the couch in front of the big screen TV watching the last few minutes of the football game.

Chuck turned and flashed a smile at his wife.

Betty jostled in front of the TV and pointed her finger. "How could you refuse to let Darcy buy the dress of her dreams?"

Victor swallowed then glanced over at Chuck.

Betty strode back and forth in front of the TV. "Every woman has a list of must-haves on her wedding day. The perfect dress is a must-have. If you love her, you'll buy her that dress."

Lurching for her friend's arm, Darcy intervened. "Betty, he doesn't have to buy me anything. I'm not a little girl. I'm a grown woman, and if I want the dress, I'll buy it with my own money."

Betty shook her head. "You can't afford the dress. He can. You're not responsible for buying the dress. He is."

Chuck stood and wrapped his tattooed arms around Betty's waist. He folded her against his chest and kissed the top of her head. "Okay, muffin, that's enough. No one's on trial. Let these lovebirds work out those details for themselves, okay?" He held her by the shoulders and gazed into her eyes.

"I just want things to be perfect for Darcy." Betty sniffled. "She's been through a lot. I don't want her to start out her new life with disappointment over how the wedding goes."

Chuck steered his wife into the kitchen. "We'll be back in a few minutes. Darcy, may I get you a drink?"

What a great husband, she thought. He rescues everyone. Exhaling, Darcy sank into the couch beside Victor. "No, thank you."

After they left, Victor placed his hand on her knee. "I didn't know you girls get so emotional over a wedding dress."

"It's symbolic." She thought of her mother's wedding gown and how it symbolized the imposition of her mother's ideals on a marriage Darcy wanted under different terms and conditions. Her thoughts drifted back to the wedding dress Edith placed on hold and how it symbolized another chance to live out her original dreams of a marriage based on equality.

Victor patted her knee twice before removing his hand. "I understand why you want this engagement to be over. It's not fun anymore."

Concern softened his brown eyes. She exhaled with relief and relaxed her shoulders.

"I'm sorry you had to go through that experience with Betty." He sighed. "If I had known, I wouldn't have sent you out shopping."

Darcy swallowed the tightness in her throat. He cared. He understood. He apologized. All three things had been missing from her first marriage. "I'm sorry, too." She grasped his hand. "I shouldn't have allowed Betty to scold you in front of her husband. How embarrassing."

"Not as embarrassing as losing in court." He squeezed her fingers.

She widened her gaze. "You've lost to Betty?"

A stern line tugged his lips. "More times than I'd like to admit."

She laughed.

"What's so funny?" Frowning, he shifted against the sofa cushions.

She gazed at his furrowed brow, his tense shoulders, and his clenched fists. "You are funny. You care more about what people think of you at work than you care about what people think of you outside of work."

"What's wrong with that attitude?"

"Nothing." Leaning over, she kissed his nose. In some ways, he reminded her of an adorable puppy full of easy-going naiveté. In other ways, he reminded her of a tough, relentless pit bull with his refusal to surrender. She liked how he balanced those pieces of himself, never giving into one side or the other, but walking the tightrope between them.

Victor's hands cupped her face, and he planted a

long kiss on her lips.

Lust swept through her body from her head to her feet.

"Even when things aren't fun anymore, I still enjoy your company." With a finger, he traced her jaw. "We'll have to find a way to keep the connection after we announce our breakup."

With the thought of losing him, she shivered. "Keeping in touch after a breakup is hard."

He kissed her lips once more. "We'll find a way," he promised.

Fear stiffened her body. "What if we can't?" She searched his face for hope.

"We have to." He slipped his tongue into her mouth.

She closed her eyes, wrapped her arms around his neck, and collapsed into the kiss, shoving aside her doubts.

****

While she drove to meet Betty at Katie's Koffee on Monday morning, Darcy heard her phone trill. She waited until she parked before listening to the voice mail. Joyce sounded breathless and angry.

"You need to tell Victor to stop giving Tyler bad advice," Joyce said. "This morning, as I'm getting ready for work, Tyler says he's changed the venue for his bachelor party from a golf weekend in Palm Springs to a weekend in Las Vegas, because that's where Victor is having his bachelor party." She gulped back a sob. "Mom, you better make things right, or I'll never talk to you again."

When would her daughter learn ultimatums led to alienation, not closeness, and disrespect led to resistance, not cooperation? Darcy leaned her forehead on the steering wheel and listened to the voice mail once again. Maybe she should call Victor and find out his version of the story. She bit her lower lip. If she waited, Joyce might call her father to complain about Darcy being a terrible mother engaged to a juvenile man who always redirected Tyler's otherwise-good judgment. Darcy cringed from the imagined humiliation. Instead, she called Joyce.

Joyce picked up on the second ring. "How could you, Mom?"

"That's the wrong tone to use when you speak with me." She bristled. "No one told me anything about either bachelor party."

"Really, Mom?" Joyce sighed. "They want to go party big-time—booze, strip clubs, gambling. All the vices Dad taught me to avoid."

Darcy snickered. "Not everyone is as *virtuous* as your father."

"Stop being condescending."

She clenched her teeth. "I'm being sarcastic."

"You're being mean, and I don't like it. Dad told me to talk to you so you can talk to Victor so he can talk to Tyler and make him change his mind before plane tickets are bought and hotel rooms are booked."

She exhaled. Of course, Joyce had already spoken to her father. Why would she bother to call her mother first? "I'll talk to Victor, but I can't guarantee your fiancé will change his mind."

"He has to," Joyce said, "or no wedding whatsoever will occur. Got it?"

Look how spoiled Nathan and Tanya raised Joyce. Darcy gritted her teeth. "No one *has* to do anything, especially when you refuse to show anyone an ounce of respect. I'm your mother, not your errand girl. Tyler is a grown man. He can make up his own mind. If he wants to party in Vegas, he'll party in Vegas. Neither you nor Victor can change his mind."

Silence strangled the tension.

"I'm sorry, Mom. I'm just in the habit of telling people what to do."

"Well, you better learn a new habit and let people decide for themselves what actions they want to take, or you'll end up bitter and alone."

Joyce sobbed.

Darcy grimaced. She hated hearing her daughter's pain. An image of eight-year-old Joyce standing in the hallway in her nightgown with tears streaking her cheeks flashed in her mind. *How can you leave us? Don't you love me anymore?* Darcy knelt, her heart breaking, as she gathered her daughter into her arms and stroked her hair. *I love you forever. Daddy has found someone to replace me, but no one can replace you.* When she left, she never imagined she would one day battle against the little girl she failed to raise into a grateful, respectful young woman. Was she too late to change the dynamics of their relationship? Maybe she should relent a little and help out. Glancing at the calendar she kept in her purse, she noticed Victor had a mediation meeting with Gary in the afternoon. Maybe she could accompany them. "Don't worry about the bachelor party. I'll talk to Victor this afternoon. We'll straighten out things, okay?"

"Thanks, Mom." She sniffled. "I appreciate your help."

Did she? Darcy wondered. Oh, when would she

learn to stop trying with her daughter and just let the relationship go?

****

When she pulled open the door and stepped inside, Darcy noticed Gary striding back and forth across the reception area of the mediation office.

He glanced up with wide eyes as soon as the bell on the door jangled. "I thought you didn't show up to mediations."

She offered a sweet smile. "I'm here for extra support in case you need it. Why don't we sit and practice deep breathing while we wait for Victor." She gestured to the office chairs against the wall.

"No, thanks, I prefer walking."

While waiting for Victor to arrive, Darcy sat in the nearest chair and grabbed a battered tabloid magazine. Earlier, she sent Victor a text alerting him she would be here for Gary's moral support.

A couple of minutes later, Victor strode into the office and signed in with the receptionist. "Are the other party and her attorney here yet?"

"No." She waited for Victor to sit. He wore a smart suit with a splash of woodsy cologne that made her pulse race. Leaning close, she whispered, "Joyce called. She's upset over something you said to Tyler which caused him to move his bachelor party from Palm Springs to Las Vegas. She asked me to talk to you to get him to change his mind. Can you call Tyler between appointments today?"

He sat back and shook his head. "I told him I'm having my bachelor party in Las Vegas. I didn't know he changed his mind about Palm Springs."

She rolled up the magazine. "Why did you tell him

about a bachelor's party?"

"He asked me before the bridal dress fiasco." He removed a case file from his briefcase. "I thought why not live large and dream big when it will be over before Valentine's Day."

She tightened her grip on the magazine. "Have you spoken to him since then?"

Grabbing the papers in his lap, he glanced up at the ceiling. "He called last night to ask for advice on how to talk to Joyce. He thought I might have some good ideas since I always convince you to give me what I want."

She swatted his thigh with the magazine. "That's when you should have told him you weren't having a bachelor's party in Las Vegas."

Gary glanced over at them and stopped pacing. With wide eyes, he gaped and pointed. "You're the divorce attorney she's engaged to, aren't you?"

"Well, uh…" Stammering, Victor shuffled the papers in his lap.

"Yes, he's my fiancé." She placed a hand on his knee. If Victor deepened the conflict with her family by continuing the charade, then she would play along and create conflict in his professional life.

Flinching, he swiped her hand off his leg. "Our relationship is not what it looks like—"

"Of course, it's not." Gary lifted his arms and glowered. "She already told me how you two are marrying because it's a solid business decision. I told her to not marry you. She'll be sorry in five years, because she doesn't love you. Love counts for a lot, you know."

The door swung open, and Darcy swiveled.

Kathleen entered on the arm of her attorney. Her helmet of jet black hair hugged her cosmetically enhanced face. Her young, handsome attorney sported wavy blond hair, hazel eyes, and dimples. Darcy recognized him as Rick Lucky, a highly powered, highly paid, and annoyingly prideful divorce attorney.

Gary narrowed his gaze at them.

The mediator, an older woman with frizzy gray hair and a crooked smile, hobbled out of the conference room. "Are we ready?"

Rick cracked his knuckles. "We're ready whenever you are."

Darcy didn't recognize the mediator but trusted the woman was someone Victor and Rick had agreed upon. She stood and hugged Gary. "I know you're nervous, but you'll be okay. Just remember to breathe and let Victor do the talking."

Gary inhaled to the count of three and exhaled to the count of four.

Victor slipped the papers into his briefcase and stood. He hardened his eyes into pellets and twitched his jaw muscles. "Are we ready?"

Gary and Darcy nodded.

All five of them followed the mediator into the conference room.

Darcy poured three glasses of water from the pitcher on the table. She handed one to Gary and another to Victor. She sipped from the third glass before taking a seat on the other side of Gary.

The mediator placed a legal pad on the table and started scribbling. "The hot topics for today are spousal support and child support. If we get through those before the two hours are up, then we'll move on to the assets and liabilities."

Gary trembled.

Darcy placed a hand on his forearm. "You will be okay. You're entitled to as much support as you can get."

The mediator placed a pair of glasses on the bridge of her nose and read off the statements both parties prepared. "Kathleen wants to pay five years of spousal support, but Gary wants more." The mediator glanced above her glasses. "How long were you two married?"

"Ten years and ten months." Victor tapped a pen against a sheet of paper. "Gary is entitled to spousal support for life."

"That's not true." Rick almost rose from his seat. "He's entitled to limited support after he transitions back into the workforce."

"Gary has never worked outside of the home." Victor folded his hands. "He championed his wife's career by sacrificing his own ambitions. He had an opportunity to go to France to study with a Cordon Bleu chef, but he put his life on hold to cater to Kathleen and the children."

"He can cook, which means he can hold a job." Rick stood. "Kathleen cannot be expected to financially support him forever, especially if she remarries and has other children."

Gary gasped. "Are you pregnant?"

Shaking her head, she narrowed her gaze. "I am not pregnant. I'm involved with a man who has children who I might or might not adopt."

"And if she has more children to support, the amount of money she can give will be affected." Rick sat, perched on the edge of the chair.

The mediator jotted more notes. "Okay, so we'll leave open the terms of spousal support. What about the children?"

"My client wants fifty-fifty legal and physical custody." Rick raised his hand.

The mediator glanced at Victor. "Is that proposition agreeable with your client?"

Victor tapped his sheet of paper. "No. Gary has been the full-time parent since the children were born. He wants one hundred percent legal and physical custody."

"Outrageous!" Rick slapped the table. "She's the mother!"

"And he's the father." Victor hardened his face and pointed to Gary.

Darcy hunched beside Gary and remembered her own mediation twenty years ago. She sat opposite Nathan, arguing with the mediator about how she supported him so he could stay home and be a full-time parent and how her career didn't mean she forfeited the right to be with her daughter fifty percent of the time. She left each session exhausted and lonely, both eager to find a quick resolution and to battle for however long needed to ensure she received partial custody of her daughter. Now, she glanced at Kathleen who sat beside her attorney, clutching a tissue in her manicured hand.

"Kathleen deserves at least fifty percent legal and physical custody," Rick said.

"I disagree." Victor gestured across the table. "Kathleen has only seen the children twice since the separation six months ago. Since she lives over two hours away, her time with the children will unlikely increase once the divorce becomes final."

Darcy tensed her shoulders, torn between her loyalty to Gary and her empathy for Kathleen.

The mediator nodded. "Distance is a problem if the children reside with their father."

Don't take her rights away, Darcy thought. She deserves time to parent.

"Force him to sell the house and move closer to their mother." Rick raised his arms. "The kids aren't in school. They can live anywhere."

"Ah, but they do attend preschool three hours a day, five days a week." Victor folded his hands on the table. "Gary has been making the decisions for them without Kathleen's advice since she refuses to return his calls. That's why Gary would like full legal and physical custody with visitation rights for Kathleen every other weekend."

Turning, Darcy glared at Victor. How could he advocate for visitation rights? Didn't he understand how much pain Kathleen already suffered?

"Why not just split it ninety-ten?" Rick leaned back against the chair and pursed his lips.

Darcy raised her hand. "That's reasonable."

"No one asked for your opinion." Victor leaned across the table and narrowed his gaze. "Gary doesn't want to be obligated to drop off his children every other weekend in San Jose with Kathleen and whoever she's entertaining at the time. He wants scheduled visitation at the family home in Petaluma."

She's going to lose her children. Tears rushed, and Darcy bowed her head.

Rick crossed his arms over his chest. "That proposal will interfere with Kathleen's work schedule."

"And fifty percent custody won't?" Victor slapped

the table with an open palm.

She can manage, if she wants to, Darcy thought. If I had fifty percent custody, I would have made it work.

"Depends." Rick waved his arms wide. "Kathleen wants to work around her special events and overtime, but when her schedule allows, she can take extended absences."

Victor shut his notebook. "He's not budging on the full legal and physical custody."

"If we can't agree, then we'll go to court." Rick clenched his fists.

The mediator raised her hand. "I think you attorneys should leave the room for a half hour while I talk to the clients alone."

Darcy stood on trembling legs.

Gary grabbed her arm, widening his eyes. "Don't go," he pleaded. "She'll eat me alive."

"My presence will only hurt you." Didn't he know as a mother she would only advocate for Kathleen? Hoping to be excused, she glanced at the mediator. "Shall I also leave?"

The mediator nodded.

"You'll be fine." Darcy patted Gary's arm. "Remember, you're strong. You take care of your children. Therefore, you can take care of yourself."

"We'll be right outside." Victor pointed to the door. "Whatever you both agree to, I have to review and sign before the agreement becomes final, okay?"

Rick stepped outside the building to make a phone call.

Victor and Darcy sat in the waiting room. The silence stretched between them.

Darcy squirmed. For months, she witnessed Gary's

distress, but today, she observed Kathleen's determination through her attorney to regain some traction in her children's lives. Tears threatened, and she squeezed her eyes shut, willing them away. In a divorce, everyone lost.

"Are you all right?" He touched her arm.

She blinked open her eyes. Concern creased his forehead. His fingers warmed against the sleeve of her jacket. "I don't know why I'm a little shaken." She tugged her jacket close against her breasts. "I've seen a thousand divorces. You'd think I'd be immune by now."

Nodding, he squeezed her arm. "You care about Gary but you identify with Kathleen. I understand that's why you're distressed. How two people can be against each other without one of them being the villain doesn't make sense."

She gulped. "I was the villain in my divorce."

"That's why you try too hard to please your daughter at the expense of your own happiness," he said.

Oh, why did Victor always have to be right concerning Joyce?

"Don't worry." He released her arm. "I'm sorry I snapped at you during mediation. I just don't want you jeopardizing Gary's case."

The walls of the room suddenly felt too close. Tightness clogged her throat. "Don't you understand how hard not seeing your children is?"

"Relax." The lines around his mouth softened. "I'm fierce, but I'm not heartless. I won't keep Kathleen from seeing her children no matter how the custody arrangement works out." He bowed his head. "I also apologize for what I said to Tyler. I'll call him tonight and let him know I'm not having a bachelor's party out of respect for you. Hopefully, he'll get the hint and abide by Joyce's wishes."

"Apology accepted." She sighed, and something deep inside melted. "I'm sorry for making a scene in front of Gary and for speaking up during mediation when I should have remained quiet. I know to be personally attacked in public hurts your professional credibility, and I know I have no right to verbalize an opinion when I don't practice law."

He rolled up a magazine and swatted her arm. "Just wait 'til I get you alone."

"What will you do to me?" She lifted her chin.

He lowered the magazine, leaned over, and pecked her lips.

A wave of love swept over her. How could forgiveness deepen her feelings? A flicker of lust ignited in her belly. Oh, why did make up kisses always burn hotter?

Chapter 24

When she joined her roommates for breakfast on Thanksgiving, Darcy suspected something amiss.

Sam lowered his head and poured the coffee, staring into the cup.

Linda, who loved to chatter, passed around the cream and sugar without saying a word.

In spite of the tight knot in her stomach, Darcy sipped her coffee.

Sam sat beside her and cupped his hands around his coffee mug, staring into the swirls of cream. "I'm sorry to have to ask at the last minute, but our daughter has decided to come home for Thanksgiving. She'll be staying until Sunday night. Can you make other arrangements? We'd hate to ask her to sleep on the couch."

Darcy shuddered. Where would she go for the next four days?

Linda held out a plate of blueberry muffins. "Aren't you visiting your daughter for Thanksgiving? Maybe you could ask her if you could stay the weekend."

"I'll call her." Although Darcy declined the invitation to stay the night when invited to Thanksgiving, she hoped her daughter might be thrilled by the change in plans. After all, a breakup with Victor justified an all-girls' weekend of junk food and chick flicks. But knowing Joyce, the weekend would probably end in a spa day and juice cleanse. Either way, spending time with Joyce would be better than spending the holiday weekend alone.

Darcy picked up her coffee mug, strode into her bedroom, and shut the door. Sitting on the edge of her bed, she called her daughter.

Joyce answered on the second ring. "Is anything wrong?"

"Nothing's wrong. Just a change of plans." She gripped the phone tighter. "You see, my landlords' daughter is spending the holidays here, and they asked me to vacate my room until Sunday night. Is it okay if I stay with you?"

"Well, of course," Joyce said. "You can share the downstairs with me and Tanya."

Why was Tanya coming to Thanksgiving? She flinched. "I thought only Victor and I were invited."

"Why does it matter?" Joyce asked. "We're all family."

"No, we're not." Darcy ran her fingers through her hair, wondering how her daughter kept forgetting she didn't get along with Nathan or Tanya. "I wish you would have said you invited them."

Joyce sighed. "If I told you, then you wouldn't come."

"You're right, I wouldn't." She gazed up at the ceiling and shook her head. After she broke up with Victor, she could not face her ex-husband and his new wife. The painful humiliation would crush any remaining dignity.

"Mom, you need to go to therapy to get over your hostility toward Tanya."

"No, I don't. You, my dear, need to stop replacing me with that woman! I'm the one who gave birth to you and not her."

"She raised me after you moved out," Joyce said. "She's been more of a mom to me than you have."

Tears clotted her throat. She gulped. "If that's how you feel, then neither Victor nor I should show up today."

"Don't be silly. You're still my mom," Joyce said. "I'm getting married, and I'm having children. I want my children to know both my parents and my stepparents."

"I can't." With each breath, she thought with resentment how she much she hated Tanya for entering their lives and how much she blamed Joyce for her devotion toward the woman who divided their family. "I can't be their friends."

"You don't have to," Joyce said. "When you see them, I just need you to be civil. You and Victor don't have to spend the night."

"But Victor isn't—"

"I'm sorry, Mom, but I have to go. See you in a few hours."

Click. With her heart hammering in her chest, Darcy speed-dialed Victor.

"Hello?"

"I need your help," she stammered. "Sam and Linda have their daughter staying in my room until Sunday night, and Joyce is entertaining her father and his new wife through the weekend. I don't have any place to stay."

"Your ex-husband and his wife will be at Thanksgiving dinner?"

"Yes, and they're staying the entire weekend."

"Well, that fact sure complicates things."

"I know." She grabbed a fistful of bedspread. "After we break up, I can't face them for three more days."

"We can't break up now," Victor said. "At least, we can't break up tonight. They are the entire reason why we're together in the first place. If we break up, they will gloat with their victory over our misery. The entire evening will be unbearable."

"What will we do?" Adrenaline spiked, and her hands trembled.

He expelled a long breath. "We will put on a brave face and pretend one last time we are an engaged couple. Then after this weekend, you call Joyce and tell her the engagement has been canceled because we had a big blowout fight, and you decided it is best if we go our separate ways. We intend to remain professional colleagues. Okay?"

"Okay." Finally, he agreed to end the madness of the charade. She placed a hand on her chest, waiting for the rapid heartbeat to subside. "But where will I spend the rest of the weekend?"

"With me, of course. You can stay as long or as little as you like. How does that idea sound?"

She bit her lower lip. For all of their flirting and kissing, Darcy and Victor had never taken their physical relationship any farther. How could she cope with her attraction in such close, intimate quarters for several days?

"Staying here won't be so bad. You'll have your own bedroom and your own bathroom. I'll leave you alone. Or you can spend the weekend watching old black-and-white movies with me. I have quite the collection. *Casablanca* is my favorite."

He made the thought of spending the weekend with him sound so simple. "Okay." She loosened her grip around the phone. "I'll stay with you."

What could possibly go wrong?

****

Later that afternoon, Victor drove down the wet highway toward Marin County.

Darcy sat beside him, staring out the window, wondering what to say to her daughter next week when she announced her breakup with Victor.

Smells of pumpkin pie and green bean casserole wafted through the car. They packed the food in the backseat along with two bottles of merlot, one for Darcy and one for Victor, to help ease them through the night.

Stop-and-go traffic clogged the drive to Kentfield.

Victor turned on the news.

The announcer said to expect more showers starting tonight and escalating through the weekend with a possible flood alert for Sonoma and Marin counties.

"We'll need to leave before it starts raining." Darcy pointed toward the sky. "We don't want the highway between Sonoma County and Marin County to close."

"Don't worry." Victor turned on the indicator and glided into the fast lane. "We're eating early."

"How do you know?"

Turning his head, he winked. "Tyler tells me everything."

Glancing out the window, she grimaced. Her own daughter neglected to tell her Nathan and Tanya would be staying Thanksgiving weekend, but Tyler told Victor the entire schedule for the night. How unfair!

An hour later, they turned off the freeway and drove down a narrow, two-lane road until they arrived at a private driveway leading up a hill. The paved road widened into a spacious clearing where a large, two-story, brown-shingled house nestled amidst a grove of redwood trees.

Victor parked the car in the driveway and opened Darcy's door.

"It smells like rain will fall again." She inhaled the moist, fresh air.

"Look at the view." He pointed to the Golden Gate Bridge through a thin layer of fog.

With her hands on her hips, she marveled at the panorama of the valley. Whether she married or not, she never could afford anything this spectacular. Even if Joyce paid for her own education, Darcy wouldn't have the four million dollars purchase price. A surge of pride swelled her chest, knowing her daughter and her fiancé could afford such luxury, from the infinity pool to the acres of hilltop privacy. She carried the green bean casserole, followed Victor up the stairs to the wraparound porch, and rang the doorbell.

"Happy Thanksgiving!" Joyce flung open the door and invited them inside a wide foyer. She had cropped her blond hair to just below her sharp chin which softened her prominent cheekbones. Bracelets dangled from her narrow wrists. She wore a baggy white angora sweater, tight black leggings, and white ballet flats.

With one arm, Darcy hugged her daughter, who smelled of fresh apples.

Joyce took the casserole from Darcy and frowned

at the grocery bags in Victor's hand. "I hope you didn't bring more than we asked you to."

"Just pumpkin pie and a couple of bottles of wine."

She pinched her eyebrows together and broadened her stance. "We don't drink."

Victor lifted the bags. "We do."

With pursed lips, Joyce shook her head. "I wish you both would take better care of your bodies. You won't be young forever. And, quite honestly, I do not want to take care of either of you."

Victor snapped his fingers back and forth.

Watching him mimic someone talking, Darcy suppressed a giggle.

They followed Joyce down a small flight of stairs into the gourmet, stainless-steel kitchen with an island as large as Sam and Linda's living room.

"Tyler and Dad are watching the game in the entertainment room upstairs." Joyce set the casserole on the marble counter. "The tofu turkey will be ready in a half hour. Would either of you care for some carrots and humus?"

"I'm fine." Victor placed the bottles and the pie beside the casserole. "I'll go upstairs to chat with the guys." He glanced from Joyce to Darcy. "Is that plan all right with you, darling?" He pecked her cheek.

Darcy nodded and returned the kiss. Although she didn't want to be alone with Tanya and Joyce, she didn't want to look clingy. "Have fun."

He winked and strode away.

Joyce led Darcy to the family room with its wide windows overlooking Mount Tamalpais. They stepped down the hardwood stairs into a white cloud of carpet. Two leather sofas faced a pair of built-in bookcases full of art, books, and sculptures. Soft yellow tea lights filled every counter space.

Everything glowed, even Tanya. She sat with her feet tucked under her hips on the leather sofa. Her blonde hair cascaded over her bronze skin and golden sweater dress. She held a magazine open on her lap and patted the seat. "Come see this dress, Joycie."

Joyce grabbed her mother's hand. "Tanya and I are looking through bridal magazines. I've decided to get a new dress after seeing the one you're wearing."

Darcy felt her stomach drop. She stopped in mid-stride and clutched her daughter's hand tighter. "What dress?"

"You know, the picture of the gown Victor sent to Tyler."

Blood rushed through Darcy's veins. "I don't understand."

"Here, I'll show you." Joyce tugged free her hand and snatched her phone off the coffee table. "This one."

The photo Betty snapped of Darcy in the wedding dress of her dreams glowed on her daughter's phone.

Panic rushed into Darcy's throat. "When did you get that picture?"

Joyce frowned. "Last Monday."

That information couldn't be right, Darcy thought. She shopped with Betty on Saturday. "What time did Victor send this picture?"

Joyce bit her lower lip. "I had just left Tyler's apartment to come here so it must have been between five and seven. He sent this photo and one of him in one of those uniforms the guards at Buckingham Palace wear minus the ridiculous hat." She scrolled through the pictures and extended her phone. "Here."

As she studied the photograph of Victor wearing a scarlet tunic with gold piping along the shoulders, a white belt, and black slacks, she clenched her jaw. Victor looked more like a prince than a soldier. She pressed the "More Information" button on the screen. The date and time stamp read Monday at six p.m. "I don't believe it," she whispered. Victor sent those pictures two days after they agreed to end the charade. A patter of footsteps distracted her from her thoughts, and she glanced up just as Victor stepped into the family room.

"What are you lovely ladies discussing?" Smiling, Victor scanned the room.

Tanya uncurled her legs. "Aren't you excited about the double wedding?"

With wide eyes, he glanced from Tanya to Darcy.

"What double wedding?" Darcy placed a hand on her churning gut. She spun and narrowed her gaze.

Tanya clasped a hand over her mouth. "Oopsie! I'm sorry. I thought Joycie had already asked you."

"Joyce never tells me anything until after she tells you." A knocking heartbeat rattled against Darcy's ribs. She cocked her head to the side and placed her hands on her hips.

"That's because we're as close as sisters, right?" Smiling, Tanya stood and wrapped an arm around Joyce's shoulders.

Joyce bounced her gaze back and forth between Tanya and her mother.

Tightness constricted Darcy's chest. She turned to Victor. "What do you know about a double wedding?"

Tyler entered the room. "Don't blame him, Mom. Joyce said she missed your play dates, so I suggested she come up with an adult version."

"Tyler's right." Joyce wriggled out of Tanya's embrace and retrieved her phone from her mother. "So, what do you say about a double wedding on Valentine's Day in the backyard of your new home?"

Valentine's Day? New home? Darcy clutched her head, willing the tea lights to stop fluttering around the room like fireflies. She sank onto the sofa and closed her eyes. The lights disappeared, but her head throbbed like a beating drum. How could Victor let her daughter plan a wedding for a venue which didn't exist?

"Brilliant, Joyce." As Nathan entered the room, he clapped his hands. "You were always the smartest of us three."

"I think it's a great idea." Victor flashed a smile, nodding.

Darcy rubbed her face with the palms of her hands. "The idea is terrible." She lifted her head and directed her gaze at Victor. "Just like the photos of the wedding dress and the Prince Charming tuxedo you sent them."

Victor raised his eyebrows, but he didn't say a word.

"Listen." Darcy glanced at every face in the room.

From the kitchen, a timer buzzed.

Joyce darted up the stairs. "The tofu turkey's done."

Tanya hustled after her. "I'll help you set the table." She glanced at Darcy. "Want to help with the silverware or glasses?"

Standing, Darcy shook her head. "I had something very important to say and everyone except you took off."

"Oh, Darcy, don't be so dramatic." Nathan scoffed.

"It's Thanksgiving. All this wedding talk can wait 'til later."

Darcy gazed at her ex-husband's arrogant face. "I understand you guys are close, closer than she is with me, but for you both to plan everything and then tell me is not fair."

"I had nothing to do with the double wedding idea." Nathan lifted empty palms. "You might blame Joyce. So, don't play the victimized ex-wife card and blame me."

Darcy glanced around the room. Everyone else had left, even Victor. She stood alone with her ex-husband, the man who failed to live up to her expectations. Why was she still trying to impress him? "I'm not blaming you. I just wanted to tell everyone the truth."

"About how I'm a bad ex-husband and father?"

She shifted her weight to one foot. "This conversation isn't about you."

"Then what is it about?"

"Me." Darcy pointed to her chest. "I made a terrible mistake to impress you. I'll never meet your expectations just like you could never meet mine."

"So, we're even." Nathan folded his arms over his chest.

"Not really." Darcy thought of her false engagement. "I still have to fix my terrible mistake."

Joyce entered the room carrying a dish towel. "Dinner's ready."

"What mistake?" Nathan asked.

Joyce stood between her parents. "What's happening?"

Darcy glanced at her daughter. She had the same look in her eyes she had as an eight-year-old when

Darcy and Nathan argued in the family room about their impending divorce. The old heartache stabbed her chest. She never wanted anyone feeling heartbreak again, even if she had to keep up the lie. "Nothing." She nudged Joyce in the direction of the kitchen. "Let's go eat."

At the dining room table, Darcy took the seat at the end of the table next to Victor. She avoided his curious gaze and focused on her plate full of rubbery tofu turkey, fluffy mashed potatoes, creamy green bean casserole, and gluten-free bread rolls. "I thought we were serving ourselves."

"We are." Tanya pointed her fork across the table. "Victor served you."

Victor poured a glass of wine and handed it to Darcy. "Cheers."

She took the glass. After dessert, she could gather everyone into the family room and announce her decision not to marry Victor.

Joyce lifted her glass of sparkling water. "Happy Thanksgiving!"

"Happy Thanksgiving!" everyone echoed. Their glasses clicked.

With relief, Darcy took a long sip of tangy wine. Finally, she found a way out of this mess! In a matter of minutes, she would break up with Victor over a petty argument while everyone enjoyed dessert, and they would escape from the charade, happily separate again.

After dinner, everyone gathered in the family room to eat pumpkin pie.

Tanya and Nathan sat on the love seat.

Tyler and Joyce sat on the sofa with Victor and Darcy.

Setting her plate on the coffee table, Darcy turned toward Victor. For a moment, she glimpsed the contentment in his face, and knowing she planned to upset him created a pang of guilt. Steeling her spine, she took a deep breath for courage. "I didn't appreciate you buying our wedding outfits without consulting me."

Victor waved a hand. "You liked the dress."

"Even you agreed, we can't afford the price."

"Your matron of honor said if I love you, I would buy the dress no matter what the cost."

But you don't love me, do you? she thought. You're just pretending. "I don't care what she said." She pointed to her chest. "You're supposed to listen to me."

Joyce shifted on the sofa. "Why don't you both go into the other room if you're arguing?"

"We're not arguing." Darcy smoothed her skirt. "We're having a discussion."

"The conversation is not one the rest of us want to hear." Joyce waved toward the guests.

Darcy stood. She needed to accelerate this battle, so she could slaughter the engagement in front of everyone.

"Come, sit down." Victor tugged on her hand. "If you don't like the dress, we can take it back."

She resisted his hold. "What about your Prince Charming tuxedo?"

He winced. "I'm not returning that outfit. Even if you won't let me wear it to the wedding, I'll keep it for Halloween."

"You look great in that outfit." Tanya fluttered her eyelashes. "I wish Nathan would have worn something that creative."

A stab of jealousy pierced Darcy's chest. She pivoted to face Tanya. "Maybe you should have married Victor instead of Nathan."

Tanya blushed, raising her eyebrows and glancing at Nathan.

"It isn't too late." Darcy shook a fist. "You stole one man from me. You can steal another."

Victor stood and grabbed Darcy's hand. "No one can steal me away." He tugged her close for a kiss.

The passion of the kiss crinkled her scalp and buckled her knees. Clutching his shirt, she steeled herself against him to remain standing. What did she want to say?

Releasing her, Victor placed his hand on the small of her back and escorted her up the stairs. "I'll show Darcy the view from the balcony. We'll be right back." After climbing to the second story, he guided her down the hallway to the entertainment room. Opening the French doors, he stepped out onto the balcony.

She shivered in the cold, wet air.

He steered them underneath a canopy where they could still enjoy the view of the San Franciscan lights and stay dry. "I know what you're doing," he whispered. "But we agreed we cannot break up tonight."

With arms crossed over her chest, she swallowed. "My daughter believes all four of us are getting married on Valentine's Day in the backyard of a home we do not own. How could you trick her? She already suffered the loss of Paradise Ridge Winery. How dare you plunge her into more disappointment when she discovers the truth!"

Glancing away, he exhaled.

"I know how this situation happened." She broadened her stance. "You were talking to Tyler, one upping each other like you always do." Narrowing her gaze, she released her arms and clenched her hands into fists. "I bet you mentioned something about the house we were allegedly buying and how having everyone get married at the same time would be fun and how affordable the venue would be, right?"

Bowing his head, he stared at his feet.

"Now, my daughter wants to buy a new wedding dress for a new date at a new location which doesn't exist." She threw up her arms. "What am I supposed to do to fix this situation without us breaking up tonight?"

"You don't need to fix anything." He raised his face and lifted his hands, palms up. "I bought the house with the money I saved to start my own practice as a down payment."

She gasped. Why was he always so impulsive? "Without funds, you can't start your own firm, can you?"

"The house was more important." Moistness glistened in his eyes. He dropped his arms to his sides and lowered his voice. "I signed the purchase agreement last night, and we had an accepted offer this morning."

"We?" Stepping back, she pointed between them.

He stepped forward and wove their fingers together. "I thought about how much fun we were having. I didn't want the fun to end. After the dress fiasco, I realized I love you. I want to have fun with you for the rest of my life." He knelt on one knee. "I know the first time I asked, we were pretending for an audience, but right here, right now, I'm asking you for real. Will you marry me, Darcy Madison-Costello?"

She caught her breath in her throat. Marry him? For real? "I c-can't," she stammered.

"Why not?" A gust of wind pelted them with rain.

She tugged him to his feet.

They ducked inside.

As she closed the doors to the balcony, she swallowed the lump in her throat. "I don't want to get married. We're not a couple. We're a joke."

He touched her arm. "I didn't know my feelings for you would become real."

"Maybe they're not real." She glanced up from where his fingers warmed her skin and gazed into his dark eyes. "Maybe they're pretend feelings."

He puckered his lips in a kiss.

She turned away her head.

"Don't you love me?" He leaned closer.

She blushed. "I'm attracted to you."

"I thought your feelings went beyond the surface." He wagged his head from side to side. "I'm sorry I misread you."

With a churning stomach, she wiggled off the ring on the third finger of her left hand. She admired the starlight brilliance for one more moment before returning the ring.

Tears clouded his eyes as he waved his hand away. "Keep it."

"I can't." She held out her hand.

He glanced at the ring and swallowed. "We're breaking up for real, aren't we?"

Holding up the ring, she nodded.

"I guess we don't have to pretend anymore." He tucked the ring in his breast pocket.

"We still need to figure out how to break the news to everyone."

"Not tonight." He sniffed and rubbed his nose with a handkerchief. "I need some time to process this new reality."

Rain pounded on the roof like angry fists. "We should leave." She pointed to the rain streaked against the windows. "We don't want the Sonoma Marin line to close."

Downstairs, everyone else talked about Joyce's wedding dress options and discussed the new locale for the wedding.

Nathan stopped chattering and pivoted toward Darcy. Squinting, he examined the expression on her face. "What's wrong?"

"Nothing." She just broke up with a man who loved her the way she needed to be loved, but she was too scared to take a chance on love again.

"Let's go before the rain gets worse." Victor gestured toward the exit.

A wave of relief flooded through Darcy. She fluttered around the room, hugging everyone goodbye.

"You guys don't have to go." Joyce waved toward the hallway. "We have an extra bedroom."

Darcy didn't want to spend the night in the same bed with Victor knowing how he felt about her and how she didn't want to feel about him. "Thanks, but we'll pass this time." Darcy offered Tanya a hug. "I'm sorry I snapped at you earlier."

"What happened to your ring?" Tanya pointed to Darcy's left hand.

She stared at her finger. "Oh, I, uh…"

"I have it." Victor removed the ring from his breast

pocket. "I need to get it resized. It's loose since she's lost weight. Haven't you, darling?"

Everyone gazed up and down the length of Darcy's body. Since the October wedding, she had actually gained a few pounds.

"That's what's wrong." Nathan peered closely at Darcy's face. "You guys just broke up."

Silence echoed in the room.

Victor clasped his hands together and rocked back on his feet.

The pounding escalated in Darcy's head. She glanced around at the stunned and confused faces. "We never were together," she confessed. "We just pretended to get everyone off our backs."

"I don't believe it." Tyler stood. "Vic's a good man. He wouldn't lie to me."

"Unless he lied to himself." Darcy shrugged.

Victor broadened his stance. "I haven't lied to anyone."

"Then what's happening?" Joyce lifted her arms and stared at the ceiling.

Victor softened his gaze. "I love your mother, but she doesn't love me."

Tears filled Joyce's eyes. Her bottom lip trembled. "She doesn't love anyone."

"That's not true." Darcy moved toward her daughter. "I love you, sweetheart."

Joyce nudged aside her mother and sidled up to her father. "You couldn't love me, and you couldn't love Dad. I bet you don't even love yourself." She buried her face in her father's shirt and sobbed.

Nathan patted his daughter's back. "Look what you've done." He shook his finger at Darcy. "You've ruined Thanksgiving! And you've ruined Joyce's wedding."

"I didn't ruin anything." A stab of pain ripped through her chest. All her life she wanted only to protect and nurture her daughter, but every time she tried, she was thwarted until she felt she had no choice but to distance herself from the intimacy she craved. She lifted her chin. "I just told the truth."

Tanya glanced over at Victor. "You broke his heart." She strode over to him with outstretched arms.

Victor ducked away from her embrace. Grabbing Darcy's arm, he steered her toward the stairs. "We need to go. The storm's getting worse."

As she marched up the stairs and into the kitchen to retrieve the empty grocery bags, Darcy remembered all the meals during Joyce's childhood when she listened to her parents bicker. No wonder she was so thin. Who could eat when food became synonymous with unhappiness?

"Leave the extra bottle for Tyler." Victor pointed to the wine. "He can drink the wine when Joyce is not home."

"He'll never drink it." Darcy shook her head. Heaviness weighed against her shoulders. "She would notice and scold him."

Tyler followed them into the kitchen. "Joyce said I should walk you guys out to your car."

"Should we leave the extra bottle for you?" Victor pointed toward the wine.

For a long moment, Tyler glanced at the bottle then shrugged. "Sure. We can always use it for cooking."

At the front door, Darcy turned. "I'm sorry we deceived everyone."

Tyler shrugged his shoulders into a raincoat and unlocked the front door. "I'm just a little stunned. You guys make such a great couple. You never fight like Joyce and me. You always agree on everything that matters."

Heat flushed her cheeks. "We're great actors."

"You sure fooled me." With downcast eyes, he shook his head. "I thought you guys were real."

Victor opened the car's passenger door, waiting for Darcy.

Raindrops pelted her forehead and dripped from the tip of her nose. "Please, tell Joyce I'm sorry, and I love her." Darcy hugged Tyler.

Tyler squeezed her tightly before he released her. "I'll tell her, but I don't think she'll listen."

A gust of rain blew between them.

Shoving his hands into his pockets, Tyler shuddered. "Our relationship is different than yours is with Victor. She never listens to me."

"Why are you marrying her?" Darcy always recognized the uneven balance in their relationship but believed the dynamics worked until now. She pinched together her eyebrows.

Tyler shrugged. "Because I love her?"

Darcy broadened her stance. "You say you love her like you're questioning your own feelings."

The moonlit brilliance illuminated his blue eyes. "Maybe I am."

Another blast of rain bombarded them.

"C'mon, the weather's getting worse." Victor ushered Darcy into the car and shut the door. He patted Tyler's shoulder once before he slipped into the driver's seat and started the engine.

As the car backed out of the driveway, Darcy waved to Tyler. He stood on the porch looking as lost as she felt. Leaning back her head against the seat, she closed her eyes. The throbbing between her temples would not stop. She hoped she hadn't ruined her daughter's life.

Chapter 25

Darcy sat in the warm car while Victor drove. The windshield wipers slapped against the glass. Victor loved her. He wanted to marry her. But did she love him? Did she want to marry him? The real answers to these real questions troubled her. She turned away her head, staring out the passenger's window at the passing traffic. How could a little attraction and a little white lie escalate until love and marriage loomed large around her?

Victor gripped the steering wheel until his knuckles glowed. "Why don't you love me?"

The rain zigzagging the glass matched the tears streaking her cheeks. "I already said I'm very attracted."

"Do you love me?"

Turning toward him, she narrowed her gaze. "You sound like a woman."

"And you sound like a man." He slapped the steering wheel. "Why don't you love me?"

Sniffing, she turned her head toward the window. "Why does love have to lead to marriage?"

"What you're really asking is, why does marriage have to end in divorce?" He switched lanes and sped up. "Marriage does not have to end. Some of my clients whom I wrote prenuptial agreements for return to celebrate their wedding anniversaries with me. They say the prenuptial agreement was like signing an employment contract, knowing the terms and conditions up front so nothing is unexpected."

"Even people with pre-nups divorce." Closing her eyes, she groaned. "I lived in LA, remember? Land of the wed and divorce routine. That's why my business boomed down there, and I could support two households *and* save for retirement."

"You shouldn't have paid for Joyce's graduate school." He shook his head. "Then you would have bought a home."

"Why should I buy a home, when you've already bought one?"

"I couldn't pass up a good deal." He slowed the car to let a truck pass. "I bought it for two million. Clean pest inspection, clean home inspection, and a three-week close so we can move in before Christmas."

Discontent churned her stomach. "You just assumed I would move in with you when we weren't even a couple."

He shrugged. "I thought I'd change your mind."

She laughed. "You *are* a woman."

Flinching, he gripped the steering wheel tighter. "You're worse than a man. Men compromise."

"Couples compromise." She shook her finger. "Most men say what they mean and mean what they say. I told you upfront I didn't want to get married."

He glared at her sideways. "Why did you say yes when I proposed?"

She glowered. "I thought we were acting."

For a long while, he drove in silence. "What will become of us?"

"You'll tell your co-workers, and I'll have to tell

my clients we're no longer a couple." She ignored her fears of how people would respond, choosing to stay focused on an action plan. "If we tell them the truth, then we can still be friends. We'll just have to live with the humiliation of being liars who pretended to be engaged to prevent me from looking like a fool at my ex-husband's wedding. But if we keep up with our lie, then we'll have to stop seeing each other except for business."

A twitch tightened his cheek. "I can't live with those options."

"And I can't marry you." She bit her trembling lower lip, staunching the thoughts of arriving at their Tuscany home and seeing his shoes beside the front door, his keys in the bowl in the foyer, and his jacket hung beside her dress in a shared master bedroom closet.

He straightened his shoulders and glanced at her. "Why not?"

"I already lived through one divorce. I don't want to live through another. I don't want to get hurt."

"How have I hurt you?" he asked.

"You lied to me about how you felt."

"I never told you how I felt."

She raised her empty palms. "That's lying by omission."

He switched lanes. "I can't believe I read you wrong. I can't believe I bought the house."

She glanced at his silhouette. "Can't you get out of the transaction?"

He sighed. "I can, but I will lose my four-hundred-thousand-dollar deposit."

She gasped. "What about the loan contingency?"

"I removed it. The appraisal just needs to be reassigned from the seller to the bank before the loan can close."

She grunted. "Why didn't you talk to me first before buying a house?"

"I wanted to surprise you." He swallowed and glanced at her. "I wanted to see the look on your face when I handed you the keys to your dream home."

Oh, why did he have to look like he worshipped the ground she walked on? She cupped her face in her hands. "There has to be a way out of buying the house."

"There is. The solution just costs my sizable down payment."

Lifting her head, she surveyed the surroundings. "I don't want to spend the night with you. Rohnert Park has hotels. Maybe one will have a vacancy."

"I doubt it. The hotels are by the casino." He frowned. "Do you know how many lonely people gamble during the holidays?"

"Maybe they're locals who have a house or an apartment they can go back to." She tried to remain hopeful.

He pointed to the tour bus driving beside them on the freeway. "I doubt those tourists will return home tonight."

"Let's just try."

"Why don't you call first?"

Taking out her cell phone, she pulled up a search and dialed the number of a local hotel. "Do you have a room for one? I don't care if it's smoking or non-smoking. I just need a place to stay for tonight." While she waited for the clerk to check room availability, she held her breath. "No, you don't? Are you sure? Okay.

Thank you. Good night."

"Looks like you're coming home with me." He glanced into the rearview mirror. "You can stay in the spare bedroom."

"I don't want to spend the night with you." She didn't want to marry him, but she still felt physically attracted. She feared being alone with him without an excuse to leave and somehow ending up in a compromising position in which he might confuse her fascination with his youthful body for true love.

"Where else will you go?" He adjusted the windshield wipers.

She sighed. "A homeless shelter."

"No, I won't allow you to stay at a homeless shelter. I'm doing the right thing, and that's letting you spend the night at my place, even though we just broke up."

She pinched together her eyebrows and shook her fists. "We didn't *really* break up. We weren't even *really* together."

"Then why are you *really* crying?"

She wiped her cheeks with the back of her hand. Everything she had been living for had drained away. The loss swept over her, and fresh tears pierced her eyes. "I don't know why breaking up with you feels real."

"Because it *is* real." Lifting one hand off the steering wheel, he waved between them. "Everything is real. You and me. Us. We're *real*. I see the way you look at me. I watched how you defended me at the wedding reception and at Betty's house in front of her husband. You can't tell me you don't have any feelings for me or the feelings you do have are not real."

She knew he was right, but she didn't want to agree. Fatigue overwhelmed her body. "Drop me off at my home."

When Sam opened the front door, he leaned his body against the doorjamb, blocking the entrance to the house. "We told you already you can't stay."

Tension knotted Darcy's shoulders. Oh, why couldn't he show a bit of compassion? She squeezed by him and set her overnight bag inside the foyer. "I broke up with my fiancé, and my daughter hates me. Just give me a couple of minutes to make a few phone calls, and then I'll be gone until Sunday night."

Sam followed her down the hallway. "Well, since you're here…"

Darcy stopped and glanced over her shoulder.

"Why don't you come into the kitchen and have a cup of coffee? We can discuss a few things I thought would have to wait until Monday."

The bottom of her stomach fell. Oh, no, she thought. Now what? She knocked on her bedroom door.

"Come in," a female voice said.

Darcy opened the door and peered at Sam and Linda's twenty-one-year-old daughter. She had Sam's full head of soft brown curls and Linda's trim body. She wore a pair of baggy, unattractive sweats as she sat cross-legged on Darcy's bed, flipping through the sales ads with an absentminded expression on her otherwise preoccupied face.

"You must be Darcy." The girl extended her arm. "I'm Noreen."

"Nice to meet you, Noreen." Darcy shook her limp hand. "May I ask a small favor? I need to make a few phone calls to find someplace to stay until Monday night. And I wanted a bit of privacy. Do you think you can leave the room for five minutes?"

Noreen studied her face. "You don't look fifty."

She blushed. What else had her parents told her?

"You look more like forty." Noreen's gaze scanned Darcy's body. "And you don't look like a loser."

"I'm not a loser." Darcy shook her fist and steadied her voice. "I'm a business owner."

She widened her eyes. "My parents say you can't afford to live anywhere else. If that's not the definition of a loser, then what is?"

Inhaling, she straightened her spine. "A loser is someone who doesn't try. Someone who lacks drive and ambition. Someone who would rather take the easy way out than the hard way through. Trying doesn't mean the person is guaranteed success, because some people, no matter what they do, fail. A successful person accepts failure, and most importantly, has the courage to take a risk and try something different."

Tears sprung into Noreen's eyes.

Darcy took a step back, her heartbeat racing. Oh, no, I upset someone else's daughter now, she thought.

Noreen reached out and tugged Darcy's hand until she sat beside her on the bed.

Darcy patted Noreen's back. "I didn't mean to upset you."

"You didn't," Noreen mumbled. "My parents did. They said if I take a year off college to have this baby, I'll never go back and finish my education. I'll be a loser, just like you, living in a rented room in someone else's house after my kid is grown because I never finished school." She hiccupped and shrugged away, wiping snot on the back of her hand. "They want me to kill my baby."

Darcy held her breath. When she confessed to her parents she was pregnant, they never suggested abortion as a solution. She handed Noreen a tissue from the nightstand. "I had a child young, and I married her father. I didn't have the same resistance your parents are giving to you." She gazed into Noreen's eyes and nodded. "Yes, I finished my degree, but I never returned to get my master's or doctorate. Instead, I worked. For a long time, I made very good money, but I lost my family in an ugly divorce." She glanced away. "When I moved here, I thought I could start over and buy a vineyard and retire in luxury. But the market is different here than in LA."

Swallowing, Darcy straightened her spine. "The prospect of seeing more of my daughter who lives in Marin kept my dream alive. If I had stayed in LA, I would be living in a house I own. But I took a chance on a dream." She squeezed Noreen's shoulder. "So what if the dream failed? One failure does not condemn a person as a loser. I am a remarkable human being for committing to something I wanted more than anything in the world." She sighed. "I'm not saying if you have the baby, you'll magically finish school, get a great job, and live an easy life. What I am saying is it's more important to follow your heart than to follow your parents' advice. They mean well, but they are living their own lives, and not yours."

Noreen sobbed. "I don't know if I can be a single mom."

"Trust me, if you have the baby, you won't be alone. You'll find friends you haven't met yet and opportunities you can't imagine now. I'm a divorce planner. I see relationships fail every day. My job is to help people navigate the end of their lives together. I know you can make it as a single parent. Again, I'm not saying the task will be easy. I'm saying single parenting might be much more pleasant than being wed to someone who is marrying you because you're having a child together. You deserve someone who wants to be with you because he loves you, and not because he's doing the right thing by marrying you so the child has a family. Okay?"

Noreen nodded.

Darcy hugged her one more time before she strode toward the kitchen. The turkey carcass sat next to the kitchen sink. The scent of Thanksgiving lingered in the air.

Sam and Linda sat at the breakfast bar. As soon as they noticed her, Sam stood, poured Darcy a cup of coffee, and offered her the seat between them.

The bitter coffee warmed her. Darcy studied their faces. They both looked grave and ashen with mourning. As a mother, she knew their dreams for their daughter had died. "I think I know what you're talking about." She gripped her coffee mug like a life preserver, the only solid remnant in her crumbling life. "You need me to move."

Sam shrugged. "If she stays in college then you have another year."

Linda shuddered. "I don't want a baby in our house. They cry and scream and poop all the time. That's why we stopped with one kid."

"Everything is always temporary." Darcy waved the mug.

"No, it's not." Sam widened his eyes. "If she has

this baby, the child will be with us forever."

"True." Darcy nodded. "But the baby won't remain a child. Your daughter will one day move out and have her own life. She just needs your support right now while she goes through this transition."

"You think she'll have the baby? Because I warned her parenthood wouldn't be easy." Linda narrowed her eyes and shook her finger. "Is that what you told her?"

"No, I did not tell her being a single parent was easy. I told her the truth. The same truth I would tell my own daughter if she became pregnant without being married."

"But your daughter isn't pregnant." Linda frowned. "She learned from your mistakes."

"And you and Sam never made any, did you?" Darcy clutched her mug and stared at her hands. Her finger felt naked without the ring. Relief from not having to pretend overwhelmed the sadness from losing the false engagement. "I admit my life hasn't been perfect. I'm divorced. I didn't raise my daughter; my ex-husband and his new wife did. I sold my home and moved here, thinking I could start over, and I failed. But my predicament doesn't mean I'm a loser any more than it means your daughter will be a loser if she decides to have and raise this baby she seems to want more than anything in the world. Her situation just means she's a dreamer with a dream bigger than all of us." Darcy stood and set her empty mug in the kitchen sink. "When do you want me to move out?"

Sam and Linda both stared at the counter.

"If she keeps the baby," Sam said, "then she'll be moving back at the end of the semester around Christmas time."

Less than four weeks, she thought. How difficult to find a place to rent around the holidays. Sighing, she straightened her shoulders. "I'll be out before then."

"Where will you go?" Linda asked.

Darcy thought about the possibilities. Right now, she had none. Her daughter and her future son-in-law refused to speak with her. She had just broken up with Victor who, at this moment, she never wanted to see again. And all the hotels she had called had no vacancies. "I'll sleep in my car, if I have to."

"An ordinance exists against that action." Sam shook his head.

"I need to make a few phone calls." Darcy slipped into the living room, sank down on the sofa, and dialed Betty's number. After five rings, the call rolled over to voice mail. Darcy left a message. Then she called every member of her Books and Booze Club, leaving a message each time. After several minutes, her phone rang.

"What's wrong?" Betty asked. "You sounded urgent."

"Are you and Chuck in town?" Darcy crossed her fingers.

"Yes, we're at Chuck's brother's house." The sounds of Christmas carols filled the background. "Are you okay?"

"I'm fine. I just need a place to stay tonight, but if you're not home, I'll call someone else."

"Why aren't you with Victor?"

Darcy rubbed her forehead. She didn't want to tell Betty the truth over the phone.

"Oh, no." Betty sighed. "Did you guys have a fight? Don't worry. We'll be home in an hour. Can you meet us then?"

She relaxed her shoulders. She had a place to spend the night. That's all she needed right now. "Yes, I can meet you in an hour. Tell Chuck thank you."

"You can tell him yourself when you see him," Betty said.

Relieved, Darcy ended the call. Oh, how quickly everything changed. A shudder rippled across her shoulders, and her jaw tightened. How would Betty and Chuck react to her news?

Chapter 26

Darcy sat with her legs tucked under her hips on the leather sofa in Chuck and Betty's living room. The scent of a vanilla candle burned on the coffee table. The flickering light illuminated the family photographs on the cream-colored walls. In the background, Christmas carols played.

"So, tell us what happened." Betty handed Darcy a mug of eggnog and sat beside her.

Chuck knelt in front of the fireplace to fix the gas starter, so they could complete the idyllic holiday setting. "Do you want me to leave? I can go into the kitchen."

"No, you can stay." Darcy waved for him to take a seat. "Getting another man's point-of-view might be refreshing."

Chuck nodded and returned his attention to the gas starter.

Darcy began with her breakup with Victor and wound her way backward to the engagement deception. The longer she spoke, the wider Betty's gaze grew.

Chuck abandoned his project and leaned back in the recliner across from them. As he listened, he kept nodding.

"Then to make matters worse, I have to move out of my rented room by mid-December." Darcy raised her arms. "Sam and Linda's daughter is pregnant and taking off a year from school to have the baby. She's moving back home."

Chuck whistled long and low. "That's an awful lot to happen in a few hours."

Frowning, Betty shook her head. "I can't believe you lied to me."

"I'm sorry." Darcy's stomach twisted, and she glanced away.

Betty set her empty mug on the coffee table. "I get why you did it, but I don't get why you continued with the charade once you got home."

Darcy stared at her bare hands. She bit her lower lip and steadied her voice. "I told the truth, but you didn't believe me."

"I thought you had cold feet." Betty widened her eyes and lifted her hands. "I didn't think you were lying."

Darcy closed her eyes. "Every time I attempted to stop the farce, something interfered to make continuing easier." Remembering Victor's kisses, she opened her eyes and smiled. "I enjoyed being wanted, even if the feeling was pretend."

Chuck leaned forward and clasped his hands between his knees. "But you *are* wanted. He said he loves you."

Darcy gazed at the third finger of her left hand and frowned. She didn't want to admit the start of having real feelings for Victor, and the fear of getting hurt forced her to let him go.

"Do you love him?" Chuck asked.

Inhaling, Darcy thought about Victor pestering her in the car. Do you love me? Why can't you love me? Always about the love she couldn't admit to feeling.

She swallowed over a lump in her throat. "No, I don't," she lied.

"You made the right choice." Chuck smiled and nodded.

Darcy burst into tears. Why did her decision feel like the wrong selection?

"Don't cry." Betty wrapped her arms around Darcy's shoulders and hugged her close. "The lying is over."

Why did Darcy feel like the lying had just begun?

****

On Sunday morning, Darcy sat alone in the Barnes' living room while Chuck and Betty Christmas shopped. They wouldn't be home for a couple of hours. Darcy drank two cups of coffee, ate half a package of Danishes, and finished reading the book of the week, *Watership Down*.

Her phone rang. Darcy stared at it for a long moment.

Joyce's phone number flashed on the caller ID.

Should she pick it up? Or let it go to voicemail? Darcy grabbed the phone. "Hello?"

"Mom," Joyce sobbed, "when Tyler left to drop off Dad and Tanya at the airport, he said he needed space to figure out things. I asked him what about, and he said his feelings for me. What's going on? Has Victor been talking to him again?"

Darcy stiffened, recalling her conversation with Tyler and her fear she might have ruined her daughter's life. Now, Tyler refused to talk to Joyce, and Joyce insisted on blaming someone. Of course, Darcy would never admit her guilt to Joyce. "I don't know if Victor and Tyler have spoken."

"Why is he reconsidering his feelings for me?"

"I don't know." Darcy shrugged. "Maybe the stress from planning the wedding is the reason. I've watched you over these last couple of months, and I've noticed you don't always treat Tyler with the respect he deserves." She braced her shoulders, waiting for Joyce's backlash against her advice. When she didn't hear anything, she softened against the sofa cushions. "Sometimes, you treat him like he's your child and not your partner. Maybe that's why he doesn't feel the same way he used to."

"Are you saying he's fallen out of love with me?"

She winced, hearing the hurt in her daughter's voice. Leaning forward, she wished she could wrap her arms around her daughter and hug her until the pain disappeared. "No, I'm saying he needs to be alone for a little while to sort out how he does feel about you."

"But how can we plan a wedding if we're not communicating because he needs his space?"

"Put the wedding on hold. You don't even have a place to get married anymore." She cupped her forehead, knowing she spoke rationally about the decision. "I've asked Victor to stop with the purchase of the house."

Joyce sobbed louder. "I wish you had never broken up with Victor. Whatever Victor does, Tyler has to do."

"Their need to mimic each other's actions is ridiculously juvenile if it's true." Why did her daughter always have to blame someone other than herself? "My advice is to give Tyler as much space as he needs. No phone calls, no text messages, and no surprise visits. No communication until he's ready, understand?"

"Is that what you did with Dad when you weren't

getting along?"

The sharp tone of her daughter's voice startled her. She thought back to their fights, how they never respected each other's boundaries or opinions. Tears blurred her vision. "No, but I should have given him space. We might have saved the marriage." She choked. "If we had stayed a family, I might have a better relationship with you."

Joyce gasped. "Oh, Mom, I'm sorry."

The softness in Joyce's voice soothed Darcy's jagged breathing. She closed her eyes, wishing she could go back in time and change everything to have the intimacy she craved with her daughter.

****

On Monday, Betty and Darcy sat toward the back of Katie's Koffee, sipping gingerbread lattes and eating cinnamon scones.

Betty pinched her face. "I'm not as forgiving as Chucky." She wagged a finger. "If I had my way, I wouldn't let you stay another night, let alone for however long you'll need to find a new place."

Darcy sighed. "I apologized for lying. What else can I do?"

Betty pursed her lips. "To earn back someone's trust takes a long time. Sometimes, it's impossible."

Swallowing, Darcy brushed the crumbs off her skirt. "What if I had told you the truth from the very beginning? Would it have made a difference?"

Betty tilted her head to the side. "I don't think I would have believed the truth. You and Victor have a lot in common with your work ethic and your professional reputation. When I see you together, the age difference doesn't matter. You can't fake the synchronicity."

Of course, they appeared perfect together, because they were ideal for each other. Darcy stared into her coffee mug. "Victor said I was a good actress, but most of the time, I wasn't acting."

Betty sighed. "Does that mean you have feelings for him?"

Cupping the mug, she inhaled the spicy scent, steam rising and moistening her face. Sipping a mouthful of foam, she thought about her feelings for Victor. The way she anticipated their time together, the banter they shared, and the kindness and insight he offered. She grimaced. The irritation she felt at his competitiveness with Tyler, his obsession with work, and his impulsive nature which always kept her guessing. She set down her mug. Why did she struggle with the truth? "I don't know."

Betty bowed her head. "I feel bad for Victor." She glanced up and met Darcy's gaze. "Why did you hurt him?"

Biting her lower lip, she glanced away. Had she hurt him? A cold sensation swept through her, and she shuddered. Of course, she hurt him. And she would probably do it again.

"I'm not looking forward to work today." Betty stood and brushed the crumbs from her skirt. "I hate the fallout after a breakup."

"Don't worry." Darcy gathered her belongings. "Nothing will affect his work. He's a professional. Like me." But would her professionalism crack under the weight of her unexpressed feelings?

Chapter 27

"We sold the house," Gary announced during his weekly meeting with Darcy.

From where she perched on the couch, she gazed around at the stainless steel pots and pans hanging over the stove to the children's coloring books on the family room coffee table to the empty patio and harvested vineyards outside. An ache all out of proportion gripped her. Gary no longer owned this fantasy house. She wanted to ask about the new owner, but a fearful tightness squeezed her throat.

Gary sat beside her on the couch. "We sold it right before the Thanksgiving weekend for the full asking price. The kids and I have to move out before Christmas."

"Congratulations!" Pain knotted her chest. She forced a smile. Their weekly visits would no longer take place in the comfort of the kitchen with the aroma of bacon, eggs, and coffee swirling in the warm air.

"Thanks." He clasped his hands and gazed into her eyes. "I remembered something you said about how creating new memories with the kids in a new home would be easier. I hope that's true."

Darcy studied him closely. His eyes were no longer red-rimmed and puffy from crying. His round face glowed with a healthy color. "You look happier."

"I *am* happier." Gary smiled. "I met someone."

"You did?" She widened her gaze.

He shifted against the cushions. "My ex had the kids for Thanksgiving weekend, so I helped out at the soup kitchen. I volunteered with a single mom who has been divorced for six years. We struck up a conversation that's still going." He plucked his phone from his breast pocket to glance at an incoming text message. As he tapped a response, a smile creased his face. Afterward, he slipped the phone back into his pocket. "She's incredible." Peacefulness emanated from his body. "I know it's too soon, but I wouldn't be surprised if I'm in love."

Love. How could he say that word about a woman he had met only a few days ago? "I'm happy for you." When she thought about Gary no longer suffering from depression, calm settled over her. For a second, she thought about warning him about how the experts advised against dating anyone the first couple of years after a divorce, but she chose to remain quiet. Why ruin his happiness? Let him enjoy the bliss of new love for however long the feeling might last. She bit her lower lip and thought of Victor loving her. Another swell of emotion rose within her chest. Oh, how she wished she had the courage to tell him she loved him, too.

****

On Friday night, Darcy arrived early for her Books and Booze Club. She ordered a bottle of champagne and offered a toast to start off the night. "I'm not getting married."

Anita drew together her eyebrows and lowered her glass of champagne. "Why is that breakup a reason to celebrate?"

When she heard Anita's words, she tensed her

lower back. Why celebrate the end of anything? Because endings marked milestones as much as beginnings, she always told people. She often battled objections from others when she planned Freedom Parties. Some restaurants refused to serve a cake decorated with "Happy Divorce" although they had no problems serving one decorated with "Happy Anniversary." The discrimination she faced could be disheartening, but Darcy refused to let it stop her tonight. She needed closure from the amorous feelings she squelched whenever she heard Victor's name or recalled a moment they had spent together. She lifted higher her glass of champagne. "I'm celebrating my decision to not get married again. Here's a toast to freedom!"

Eric shook his head, gazing at his untouched glass on the table. "You'll regret your decision someday. I performed thousands of weddings for couples during my thirty years as an Elvis impersonator, and not one of them returned to say they regretted getting married unless, of course, they said their vows drunk."

"Well, Victor switched from beer to tequila." Barry waved to the empty wine glasses on the table. "So, Darcy made the right decision to let him go."

Lucas drained his glass before crossing his arms on the table. "I could tell he didn't want to be here. He's not a very artistic person. I'm sure we started boring him to death."

Smiling, Anita lifted her glass. "Here, here, a toast to the poor bastard who Darcy abandoned." She gulped the champagne and refilled her glass. "Please tell me you didn't erase his number from your phone. I'd like to call him and offer my condolences."

A stab of jealousy pierced her, and she narrowed her gaze. "No, I'm not subjecting him to any more humiliation." She swallowed the last mouthful of champagne and ordered her signature martini.

"I'm sure he'll be trolling around the Internet by Christmas." Barry chuckled.

"Or sooner." Lucas refilled his glass of champagne. "A guy like that needs company in order to feel secure."

"I could help him." Anita waved across the table. "Just give me his phone number."

Charlotte lifted her paperback and cleared her throat. "When will we discuss this week's book instead of Darcy's love life?"

Barry cocked an eyebrow high and flipped through the pages of *A Christmas Carol*. "We could frame our discussion around Darcy's ghost of marriage past and the ghost of broken engagement present and the ghost of singlehood future."

Lucas snickered.

Eric cupped his head with both hands.

Anita mumbled something about how she could save Victor.

Charlotte wrapped an arm around Darcy's shoulders. "You shouldn't have allowed your fiancé to tag along a couple of weeks ago. I think going forward all guest members need to be screened for suitability and longevity."

Darcy shrugged away from Charlotte and glowered at the book club members gathered around the table. "I can't undo what's already been done."

"I agree with you." Barry shook his head. "No guests in the future."

"Who decides what's suitable?" Eric glanced around the table. "Because sometimes I think everyone here is unsuitable for me."

"We need to have an interview process and a vote." Charlotte raised a hand.

"I vote for no voting." Lucas waved his hands back and forth across his body. "It wastes what little time we already have."

A bristle of annoyance snaked across her shoulders. Darcy pushed back her chair and stood. "I'm sorry I broached the subject, but my daughter blames me for all the drama since I initiated the breakup on Thanksgiving in front of everyone, including her fiancé who's not sure whether or not he loves her anymore. Sometimes, I wonder how I got into this mess in the first place."

Barry stared at the opened book. "The ghost of marriage past is supposed to show Darcy where she failed in her first marriage."

"I know." Lucas raised his hand. "You didn't follow your artistic sensibilities the first time around and instead chose a logical man who would make reasonable choices with you."

Darcy winced. Yes, Nathan was logical enough to conduct experiments in the garage, but he never reasoned through any of their decisions together.

"That's incorrect." Anita swayed in her seat. "She married for love the first time around, and the selfish bastard broke her heart."

As Darcy remembered finding Tanya in Nathan's arms one day after work, a stab of pain pierced her chest.

"I disagree." Charlotte lifted her chin. "Darcy's a

tough woman with a career and a vision. She married because she got pregnant and wanted to raise the child with the father. If she had not given into tradition, she would have made a marvelous single parent with a fabulous daughter."

The bottom fell from her stomach, and Darcy thought of Noreen, alone and pregnant with parents advocating for an abortion. She waved her hand, silencing everyone. "You're all right, and you're all wrong." She glanced around the table. "I married for love, that's true, but I didn't realize my continual love could not prevent my husband's love for someone else. I married an idealistic man who fulfilled my romantic visions, but he had no practical bone in his body and never earned much money throughout his life. Being pregnant influenced my decision to marry, but I don't think I would have made a better parent if I had remained single, since I ended up working full-time to support the family I divorced. Plus, my relationship with my daughter to this day is almost non-existent."

Everyone around the table clapped.

Exhausted, Darcy slumped into her seat.

"Act Two," Barry said, "the ghost of broken engagement present."

Charlotte raised her glass. "Darcy broke up with her fiancé because she's a self-righteous feminist."

Darcy widened her eyes. I broke up with him because I'm afraid of love, she thought.

"No, she didn't." Eric shook his head. "He broke up with her because she's not romantic."

She grimaced. Maybe she didn't indulge every one of Victor's fantasies, but she played along, didn't she?

Anita waved the empty bottle of champagne.

"They were sexually incompatible."

Heat rushed to her face. Darcy bowed her head. She didn't want to admit she couldn't handle the fact Victor loved her. Everyone at the table stared, waiting for her to speak. "I don't even know what a self-righteous feminist is, so how can I be one? My fiancé broke up with me because I refused to marry him." She turned toward Anita. "We never had a chance to discover whether or not we were sexually compatible."

Anita bristled. "Well, dear, that tidbit explains everything. You're frigid."

Narrowing her gaze, Darcy leaned closer. "I'm not frigid. I'm careful. Getting intimate too soon always ruins romantic relationships."

Charlotte nudged forward. "Why didn't you want to marry him?"

Tears clotted her throat. She gulped a mouthful of water, trying to ease the pain churning in her stomach. "Because I made a promise to myself I would remain single."

"Even if you found someone to love?" Eric opened his arms.

I never expected to find someone to love, she thought.

"People with unrealistic expectations never find love satisfying." Lucas gazed off into the distance.

Darcy twisted the napkin in her lap. "I never told Victor how I felt even when he asked."

"Why not?" Charlotte widened her eyes.

"Because," Darcy stared at the napkin in her lap, "because I didn't want to marry him."

"What's so bad about getting married?" Eric wrinkled his forehead.

Darcy glanced up, sitting straight and strong. "The divorce."

"Not everyone divorces." Barry set aside his book and leaned back against the chair.

"Everyone here is not married." Darcy swept her gaze around the table and counted five single people. "So, I don't understand how any of you can pass judgment."

"I married my soul mate." Pouting, Eric twisted the napkin. "She died in an auto accident three years after we were married. I left town and became an Elvis impersonator for weddings. I wanted to see the beginning all over again because of the happiness. But if I think about my choice too hard, I know the real reason I worked in Vegas for so long is because I didn't want to face the end." He paused, holding back a sob. "I hurt too much losing the one person I thought I would be with forever. Each morning, I woke up wondering how I could be alive when my beautiful bride had been taken from me." He blew his nose into the napkin.

That's how I feel, Darcy thought. Shattered inside.

Charlotte sipped from her glass of wine. "My parents had a love like that. They were together for thirty-three years before my dad died. I never witnessed them fight. They were always affectionate with each other."

Even when we fought, we always made up, Darcy thought, remembering Victor's kisses.

"Love is harder the longer you're together." Lucas fiddled with his fork. "My last girlfriend only lasted a few months, but the one before lasted five years. We lived through a lot of stuff together—her mother's cancer, my father's heart attack, adopting a puppy, applying for graduate school, getting laid off of work, and losing our rental. We fought over our differences, but we pulled through each time until we couldn't do it any longer."

"What happened?" Charlotte widened her eyes and leaned against the table.

"She found someone else." Lucas dropped the fork, which clattered against a glass of water. "Someone more financially stable."

Darcy flinched. Victor was financially stable. Why did she reject his love? Absorbing the tales of love and loss, she sipped her martini. "Victor and I got along well, even though we are opposites. His impulsive, romantic, imaginative nature contrasted with my organized, practical, realistic nature. But, somehow, we came across as very compatible."

"Maybe you were." Charlotte reached over and patted her hand.

Anita laughed. "You would have known either way if you had tried out the sex."

Barry waved for everyone's attention. "Now, for Act Three, and the grand finale of the night, we encounter the ghost of singlehood future."

The server delivered their orders of hot and spicy chicken wings, creamy spinach dip and crispy chips, fried mozzarella sticks, chicken quesadillas, and a pitcher of beer.

"Not to take away from our discussion..." Barry poured a mug with beer. "But dinner and drinks are on me tonight because I passed the bar exam. I'll be a practicing attorney at the beginning of the year."

"Congratulations!" Everyone lifted their beer mug for a toast.

"Now, back to the ghost of singlehood future." Barry waved his mug toward Darcy.

Lucas chewed a slice of cheesy quesadilla and wiped his salsa-stained mouth with a napkin. "I think Darcy regretfully dies in a studio apartment, and her body is found after she doesn't pay her monthly rent because no one calls to check up on her."

Coldness tensed her shoulders when she heard Lucas' prediction. Although she didn't necessarily want to get married, she didn't want to be alone either.

"That's sad." Charlotte gnawed on a saucy chicken wing. "She does have a daughter."

"Who she doesn't speak with on a regular basis." Lucas raised a finger toward the ceiling.

"That situation can change." Charlotte shifted in her seat. "Right, Darcy?"

Darcy sighed with disappointment. "Historically, Joyce won't check in with me unless she wants something."

"Bingo!" Eric raised his hands. "History is everything. Since you have a history of failed relationships, you'll be doomed to die miserable and alone. Even Elvis will leave the building first."

Darcy clutched her churning stomach. Just because she didn't believe in romantic relationships didn't mean she couldn't be surrounded by loving people. Like her former roommates, Sam and Linda, and her current roommates, Chuck and Betty. Even though, she knew, roommates suggested temporary living conditions, and not long-term commitments.

"I know." Anita waved her empty glass. "She moves into a retirement community and becomes slutty like me! I've had sex with almost every guy in the complex."

Eric hunched his shoulders and blushed.

Lucas raised his mug of beer and grinned. "*Et tu*, Brute?"

Anita gazed up at the ceiling. "Oh, please, I wouldn't touch that man if he was the last one living."

"Isn't that comment a little harsh?" Charlotte slapped Anita's wrist. "He's sitting right here. Can't you be polite?"

Barry gazed at the empty champagne bottle. "She's had too much to drink."

"Someone always has too much to drink." Lucas laughed. "That's why it's called a Books and Booze Club."

Exhausted from the conversation, Darcy motioned for everyone to be quiet. "I want to end this discussion now." She stood and surveyed the group. "Yes, I live with roommates, and I'm single. If I die, then my dead body won't be rotting in an apartment for a few weeks until the landlord collects the rent. Yes, I don't get along with my daughter, so I don't expect her to be notified first. No, I will not become slutty and have sex with everyone in my retirement community. Sex doesn't interest me as much as it interests most people."

"You're a frigid feminist," Anita scrunched her face and hissed. "No wonder Victor broke up with you."

"*I* broke up with him on Thanksgiving." Darcy didn't feel the need to confess to the entire scam of pretending to be engaged in the first place. She wanted out of this discussion, so she could find out the next book to read and whether or not they would take a hiatus until after the New Year.

"Well, I wouldn't have broken up with him without trying out the sex first." Anita peered beneath her reading glasses.

Rushing blood flamed Darcy's cheeks. She sat and buried her head in her arms. She always wondered how Victor would feel naked against her body. Now, she would never know.

Charlotte snickered. "Oh, really, Anita, you think after what Darcy said she cares about sex?"

"I would." Anita touched her chest. "Sex is everything. It's the meaning of life."

Lucas laughed.

Eric finished his beer. "I agree with Anita, except I think sex with love is the meaning of life. You've got to have the love part. Sex with just anyone is just sex."

Barry studied his paperback copy of *The Christmas Carol*. "How did we get from the ghosts of relationships to sex?"

"Every book we ever read involves sex from Anita's point of view," Lucas said. "Even when we read *Lord of the Flies*, she sexualized the pig brutality scene."

Darcy glanced up at the food-laden table. She hadn't touched anything other than the one glass of champagne and half of her extra dry martini. Grabbing a smoky barbecued chicken wing, she changed her mind about leaving early. No one waited for her at home. At least here, she could stay in the company of friends, eat a full meal, and continue talking until the last person in their group left. Then she'd be alone.

Chapter 28

On Monday night, Darcy sat at Betty's kitchen table to eat dinner. She had a long day with back-to-back client appointments, and she neglected to eat lunch. A deep ache throbbed between her temples, and a grumble erupted from her stomach.

"Go ahead and eat." Chuck set a platter of roasted, garlic-smelling chicken on the table beside the steamed broccoli and fluffy brown rice. "Betty's finishing with her last client. She'll join us when she's through."

Halfway through dinner, Betty pushed back the swinging door to the kitchen and tossed her purse and keys on the red-and-white tile counter. She squeezed Darcy's shoulder and kissed the top of Chuck's head on the way to her seat. The bracelets on her wrist jangled as she spooned rice onto her plate. "Guess what?"

"You won your case today." Chuck winked.

"Guess again." Betty glanced at Darcy.

She shrugged. Why was Betty playing a game? "You have a referral for me."

"Wrong again." Betty shifted her gaze from Darcy to Chuck. "Victor's dating someone."

The air knocked out of Darcy's lungs. She dropped her fork, which clattered against her plate. With trembling hands, she picked up her fork.

"That fast, huh?" Chuck spooned another helping of steamed broccoli onto his plate.

Blinking her burning eyes, Darcy glanced at the calendar on the refrigerator and mentally counted backwards. Three weeks.

"Maybe he needs someone to celebrate Christmas with." Turning toward Darcy, Betty frowned. "Are you okay?"

For the last three weeks, Darcy told everyone she felt fine. How much longer would she go on pretending? She glanced away to prevent Betty from seeing the mist in her eyes.

"I didn't think he would move on so quickly." Chuck tapped Darcy's wrist. "I believed he really cared about you."

Tears clotted her throat. If only she had the courage to tell Victor she loved him, then she wouldn't be sitting here with Chuck and Betty on a week night. She would be packing her belongings to move into a new home with her future husband. Swallowing, she found her voice. "I'm not okay." She turned toward Betty. "Do you know who she is?"

Betty stared at her half-eaten chicken breast. "No, but I did overhear him talking on the phone scheduling a date around her childcare."

She's younger, Darcy thought.

"Do you want me to ask him?" Betty raised her eyebrows and leaned closer.

She winced, hearing the pity in her friend's voice. "No, thank you." Of course, she wanted to know who replaced her in his heart, but she didn't want Victor to know she cared.

"When will you start dating?" Chuck lifted his eyebrows.

"I'm not." She straightened her spine. "I'm through

with men."

"Temporarily?"

She wanted to avoid the disappointment of failed expectations. "Forever."

****

The following morning, after the frost melted, Darcy drove to Gary's new townhome on the other side of town.

He answered the door wearing his "Dad Cooks Awesome" apron. Sweat gleamed on his bald head. He led Darcy into the tiny galley kitchen. "The kids are still sleeping."

Taking a warm muffin and a mug of sweet-smelling hot chocolate, she sat at the small dining room table in the breakfast nook.

Gary wiped his head and his hands on a dishtowel. From the other room, he retrieved a file folder and a checkbook. Sitting, he shared the paperwork first. "Here is the final Marital Settlement Agreement. Victor and I already signed. My ex and her attorney sign this week. Then I have to wait another six to eight weeks for the judge to sign and have the document recorded. I should be divorced as early as the first week of March."

"Congratulations!" She scanned the agreement. "I'm happy things worked out for you and the children."

He nodded. "That settlement is not all that's worked out for me. I have a girlfriend and a part-time job as a sous chef in Sonoma. I'm off antidepressants, but I'm keeping my therapist for monthly sessions until things settle a bit more. My ex-wife gets the kids every other weekend and every other holiday, but otherwise, they're with me." He opened his checkbook and started writing. "I couldn't have survived the divorce without you. I owe you more than I can ever repay you." He handed Darcy a check for five thousand dollars.

Pulse racing, Darcy gaped. "You've already paid for my services."

"Consider it a tip."

"A very generous tip." She shook the check like a fan. "I've never received this much money, not even from my Hollywood clients."

"Maybe that's because they take everything for granted."

After staring at the number for a long moment, she slid the check across the table. "Thank you, but I can't accept the gift."

"Yes, you can." Plucking the check off the table, he placed it in the palm of her hand. "At the very least, take the money and hire a therapist to talk about whatever's been bugging you. I'm not a professional, but you seem depressed ever since the holidays started."

Folding the check, she tucked it into her purse. "Thank you. I didn't think anyone noticed."

"I know it's none of my business, but does your mood have anything to do with that ring you haven't been wearing?" He pointed to her bare hand.

Biting her lower lip, she rubbed her finger. "What do you know?"

He folded his hands on the table. "Victor told me he asked you to marry him at your ex-husband's wedding to create a scene, and you said yes. When he asked you to marry him for real, you said no."

Glancing away, she blushed. A sinking feeling plunged in her stomach.

"During my marriage, I noticed everything." He raised his arms to create a circle. "I knew when my wife landed a big deal and when she lost one. I could tell who she talked to and what they said by the gestures she made as soon as she entered the room. As a very attentive husband, I learned to be a very observant man." He scooted his chair closer. "Talk to Victor and tell him how you feel."

She stared at her hands. "He's seeing someone else."

"Their relationship is not serious."

"How do you know?" She met his gaze.

"Because his face doesn't light up when he mentions her name like it did when I mentioned yours." Gary sighed. "Victor's a great attorney, but he has some growing up to do as a man. He reminds me of myself before I met my ex-wife. I came across as confident professionally, but a mess emotionally. Once I had children, I grew up. Ironically, my maturity ended my marriage. My ex expected me to stay the same. She didn't anticipate being with a person who changes with time and experience."

She expelled a sigh. "Even if I talk to Victor, what would I say? 'I didn't mean to fall in love with you' or 'I'm sorry we ever met'?"

"Say whatever's in your heart." Removing an envelope from his paperwork, he slid it across the table. "From Victor."

She tore open the envelope. A set of keys jangled on the table. Unfolding the note, she read:

Darling,

Please accept this gift.

I'm keeping the house until after Tyler and Joyce's

324

wedding.

In March, when the weather is better, I'll sell it. In the meantime, please move in.

Enjoy the dream for however long it lasts.

With all my heart,

Victor.

Tears filled her eyes, and her hands trembled. Words blurred around the edges. The depth of his love for her mirrored the solemn weight of the keys in the palm of her hand.

"He loves you." Gary tapped the note.

"But he's dating someone else."

"I told you their relationship is not serious."

Lifting her head, she widened her eyes. "Is that the explanation he gave?"

He shrugged. "He needs a distraction to stop thinking of you and the business he lost because of his stupidity, selfishness, and impulsiveness."

Victor hadn't thought beyond the moment. Otherwise, they would have never arrived here— pretending to be together for a little while and now truly apart. She furrowed her brow. "He said those words?"

"Not exactly." He laughed. "He said he bought my house under the assumption you both would get married when he should have used the money as a down payment on an office building so he can start his own law firm."

She shook her head. "He can buy the office building after he sells the house in March."

"Are you moving in?" He pointed to the keys in her hand.

"Should I?" A prickle of apprehension danced across her scalp. She glanced around the tiny kitchen in

Gary's townhome, recalling the lavish gourmet stove and copper pots hanging over the range in the Tuscany mansion. Warmth flooded her. She smiled, recalling the first time she sat at the breakfast bar watching the children play outside while Gary cooked. What would Betty say once she shared the news?

"I would." He smiled. "The jetted bathtub in the master suite is perfect for relaxing after a long day. A library with all those shelves is perfect for your books."

She narrowed her gaze. "How do you know I have books?"

"Victor said you belonged to a club."

A smile blossomed on her face. "Did he tell you what type of book club?"

"I left the bar in the entertainment room fully stocked."

A bolt of excitement raced up her spine. She imagined soaking in the jetted tub with a paperback novel and a gin martini. She deepened her smile. "When can I move in?"

"Whenever you want."

Twirling the keys in her hand, she envisioned stocking the shelves in the library with her books. The rest of the house would be void of furniture. A burst of sadness dampened her enthusiasm. How could she make the house a home without someone to share it with?

Chapter 29

The next morning, during their breakfast at Katie's Koffee, Darcy confided in Betty about Victor's offer to move into the Tuscany dream house.

"I think you should move." Smiling, Betty nodded. "Otherwise, the property will be vacant for three months."

Darcy fiddled with the keys. "What do you think Chuck will say?"

"Why don't you ask him?" Betty said. "He's joining us for breakfast."

A few minutes later, Chuck strolled into the coffee shop, scanning the room for them. He sat on a chair between the two women. "What should I order? A muffin or a scone?"

"Definitely, the muffin." Betty smiled.

Darcy lifted her paper cup. "And a cappuccino."

When Chuck returned with his bittersweet coffee and cinnamon-smelling muffin, Betty pointed to Darcy. "Guess who has some news to share?"

Darcy stared at the keys in her hands. "Victor bought the Tuscany home with the hobby vineyard I told you both about, and he gave the keys to a mutual client to give to me along with a note stating I could move into the home. He'll sell the house in the spring after my daughter's wedding." She glanced up to meet Chuck's gaze. "What should I do?"

"Is he moving in with you?" Chuck raised an eyebrow.

She shook her head. "He has a condo. The house he bought for the wedding is vacant. I can move into it if I'd like, or I could stay with both of you."

"Move in." Chuck pursed his lips. "Living in the house couldn't hurt."

"We'll miss you." Betty patted her friend's hand. "But you can visit anytime."

Darcy's heartbeat fluttered in her chest. She jangled the keys. "And you both can visit me."

****

Darcy had not heard from Joyce since she called the day relating Tyler wanted his space to figure out things. A month had passed. From experience, Darcy knew Joyce also needed her space. When Darcy separated from Nathan over twenty years ago, she called Joyce every night to wish her sweet dreams.

After a month of calling, Nathan refused to let Darcy talk to Joyce. "She's confused," he said. "She wonders why you aren't coming home. You should stick with seeing her every other weekend and leaving her alone the rest of the time."

At first, Darcy resisted. She continued calling every night, even when Nathan picked up her calls. Eventually, Darcy gave Joyce her space. Five years later, Joyce started calling her voluntarily once a week then twice a week then once a day. Over the years, whenever Darcy and Joyce suffered a disagreement, Darcy learned not to pester her daughter with phone calls, text messages, voice mails, or emails. No matter how many days, weeks, or months passed, she just waited until Joyce made contact.

Two nights before the move into Victor's house, Darcy's phone rang. She sat on the futon where she slept in Chuck and Betty's office. The caller ID showed Joyce's number. Darcy fumbled with the phone, anxious to hear what her daughter had to say.

"Mom, your advice worked," Joyce said. "I left Tyler alone, and he finally called me."

Darcy tucked the sheets around her waist. "What did he say?"

"He still loves me and wants to marry me, but only under his conditions."

When she heard the tension in Joyce's voice, Darcy leaned forward and tightened her shoulders. "What are his conditions?"

"He wants to start drinking beer and eating chicken wings with the guys once a week. He's almost forty, and he wants to act like he's twenty-one all over again. What's even worse is he says I need to relax more around him and not be so uptight about everything being perfect. He wants to live a little, and he said he couldn't relax with me." She sucked in a breath. "He says he'll call off the wedding if I don't agree to those conditions."

"Those conditions are not so bad. He's not asking to work long hours, have an open marriage, or start using illegal drugs. He just wants to hang out with his friends one night a week without his wife complaining."

"His conditions are terrible," Joyce sobbed. "I don't go out with my girlfriends. I don't drink or eat meat. Why should he?"

"Because he's a different person than you are." She shifted to get more comfortable. "Tell me about your initial impression of him when you first met."

Joyce hiccupped. "He drank socially, and he ate whatever he wanted. We both cut out alcohol and meat a year after we started dating."

"What else did you eliminate?"

Joyce sighed. "Well, we were both starting our careers so we worked a lot and didn't go out much. We stopped seeing our friends."

Good, Darcy thought. She figured out the problem and can't blame me this time. "You stopped having fun. What's the point of being together if you no longer have fun?"

Joyce sniffled. "You sound like Tyler. He said the relationship is not fun anymore."

"Well, if you want this marriage as much as you say you do, then you'll make the relationship enjoyable again."

"I don't know how."

A stab of pain seized her chest, and she held back a gasp. Had she neglected to teach her daughter how to find joy? She leaned against the cushions and tucked her feet under her hips. "Come here for Christmas, and I'll show you."

"I can't. I promised Dad and Tanya I'd see them."

"Then come this weekend and help me move."

"Whose house are you moving into now?"

"Victor's. He bought the home for us, for the wedding, and he's keeping it until the spring. You're welcome to stay as long as I'm welcome."

"Are you and Victor together again?"

Hope sounded in her daughter's voice. Darcy felt her heart stutter. "No, we're not." She stroked the soft sheet and imagined caressing Victor's arm. "He just doesn't want the house to go to waste."

The silence on the phone stretched between them.

"Okay," Joyce said. "I'll drive up this weekend."

Darcy ended the call and held the phone to her chest. More than anything, she wanted to heal their relationship, if the damage inflicted since her divorce wasn't too great.

****

The next day, Darcy strode into Jasper's a little before noon, searching for Monica, who invited her to lunch.

Monica sat at the dimly lit bar, sporting a new angled bob. A purple sweater dress hugged her curves. She gestured to the seat beside her. "I've taken the liberty of ordering you a gin martini with two olives."

Smells of garlic and onions stimulated her appetite. Slipping out of her wool coat, she hung it on the back of the chair. "What are we celebrating?"

"I asked him out." Monica arched an eyebrow.

Confused, Darcy frowned. "Who did you ask out?"

"Victor Costello." Monica grinned and squealed, wiggling in her seat.

The bottom of Darcy's stomach dropped. She took a sip of her drink, but she didn't touch the bread. Suddenly, she didn't feel hungry anymore.

Monica lifted her glass of champagne. "He said yes. Thanks to you, I'm no longer single. Cheers!"

With a trembling hand, Darcy touched her glass with Monica's. The hollow clink echoed a bit too loudly. She gulped her stark drink.

"He's such a great guy." Monica gushed. "He's so good with my son. I can't believe it. I wish I could be with him for Christmas, but he's visiting his mother and sister in Texas. My son throws tantrums when we fly, so I won't see him until we spend New Year's Eve together in Las Vegas."

"How romantic." She hoped she faked an upbeat voice to mask the shock and disappointment ricocheting through her body.

Monica clasped her hands to her chest. "I've never been happier. He's the best guy I've ever met. I still can't believe you two broke up."

She twirled the stem of her empty martini glass. "We were never together."

Monica arched an eyebrow. "Not according to Victor."

She blinked and stopped fiddling with her glass. "What did he say?"

Placing her hands on her chest, Monica glanced up at the ceiling. "You broke his heart."

"Stop with the melodrama. I didn't break his heart." Darcy propped an elbow on the counter and cupped her chin in a hand. "Most guys pine for their first girlfriend or a woman who's out of their league. I don't fit that description. Plus I didn't stay in his life for very long."

Monica shrugged. "Your loss is my gain." She ordered Darcy another gin martini. When it arrived, she lifted her champagne glass for another toast. "All I know is I'm never letting him go."

After another toast, Darcy sipped the martini. She relished the sharp taste, thankful she had no clients to see afterward. She wanted to be alone to mull over this fresh revelation and ruminate over the many what if's playing through her mind, haunting her with regrets she could do nothing about except struggle to let go.

Chapter 30

After Monica paid for lunch and returned to work, Darcy lingered at the bar, ordering one too many gin martinis and gazing at her bare left hand, wondering where she had gone wrong. After all, Victor didn't need space. When Darcy left, he discovered his need for someone younger, prettier, and warmer. No, Darcy had been the one who needed space, but space only increased her pride to the point where she became paralyzed with fear. She could not talk to Victor about anything, not even about the many clients they shared—which was why she sat alone on a Thursday afternoon, a week before Christmas, staring into an empty martini glass.

A little depressed and a lot tipsy, Darcy stumbled out of Jasper's into the late afternoon sunlight. The bright winter glare reflected off the parked cars and office buildings. Slipping her sunglasses over her nose, she hobbled down the street with her hands thrust into the pockets of her wool coat. When she moved into his house, she wrote a brief thank-you note, which she gave to Gary to give to Victor, much like children passing notes in class. Should she call Victor and tell him how she felt? What would she say?

Preoccupation forced her to stride past her car and across the street into the business district. At the following crosswalk, she glimpsed her reflection in the window of an office building. The lank hair and forlorn expression startled her. Had she ever looked or felt so hopeless? Not even when her marriage ended. Since the breakup on Thanksgiving, she felt she was missing something essential like an arm or a leg. Once in a magazine in a doctor's waiting room years ago, she remembered reading about ghost limbs. Victor felt like her ghost limb.

The light changed, and she continued walking for a few blocks. Another bright spot of sunshine reflected off the windows of a vacant office with a For Lease sign. She turned and cupped her hands against the window to study the space closer. The eight hundred square feet encompassed two rooms and a reception area facing the street. From the flyer taped to the inside of the window, she could afford the rent.

If Victor wanted to start his firm now instead of waiting until after the house sold, this location would be perfect. She smiled. Why not lease the space and surprise him like he had surprised her with the house? As she fumbled in her purse for her phone, blood rushed to her cheeks. She jabbed at the numbers and waited for someone to answer. "Yes, I'm interested in the office building you have for lease." She glanced up at the street signs. "It's the space on the corner of Fifth and E Streets." She crossed her fingers, hoping the space was still available, because she needed to win back his heart.

****

Darcy watched Chuck set the last box of books on the floor in the library of Victor's new house.

"Well, the books are moved." Chuck stood and shook the dust from his hands. "Betty and I need to

334

leave to get ready for her firm's holiday party."

"Thanks for your help." Darcy led him down the wide hallway to the kitchen where Betty, Charlotte, and Joyce unpacked pots, pans, and dishes purchased at the Dollar Store.

"Just think, Mom, if you hadn't canceled the wedding, then you'd have nice new plates and silverware."

Darcy winced, thinking of Victor. Joyce doesn't know I love him, she thought. "These items were the only things I couldn't rent." She waved toward the furniture. "Otherwise, I would have."

The front door swung open. Eric and Lance carried in a leather sofa. "Where do you want this sofa?" Eric asked.

"Over here, in the family room in front of the fireplace." She pointed to the spot.

The men maneuvered the sofa and set it down.

She glanced around the room. "Anything else?"

"Just the mattress," Eric said. "We have to return the truck by four. If you don't mind showing us where you want to place it, we'll setup the bed before we go."

"Of course." She led the men up a flight of stairs and down a long corridor to the master bedroom suite. "You can place the mattress against the wall."

"This room looks empty." Lance glanced around the massive space with a separate sitting area complete with a window seat.

Eric shook his head. "How many rooms does this place have?"

"Twelve." After walking through the home several times, she memorized the number. "Before today, I only knew about the great room, the kitchen, and the office. Now I know about the ballroom, the formal dining room, and the entertainment room." A thrill of pleasure zigzagged through her. She could indulge in a dream-come-true, if only for a little while.

"The house looks naked." Eric wrapped his arms around his chest and shivered.

Darcy bristled. "I'm thankful I could afford to rent the basics."

Lance swept an arm around the space. "Well, at least four of the rooms are unfurnished."

"They can stay unfurnished." The four rooms would have been Victor's office, a home gym, and two guest bedrooms for his mother's and sister's visits. Darcy spun to hide the shadow of sadness passing over her face. "I won't be living here long."

Lance followed her down the stairs and pointed to the formal dining room. "We should host the book club here one night. We could rent a ten-person table."

"I'm not renting any more furniture." She crossed both arms over her chest. "This minimal setup has already cost me a mint."

The two men bounded out the front doors to retrieve the mattress.

Darcy returned to the kitchen to hug Chuck and Betty good-bye.

"Shall we say hello to Victor from you?" Betty asked.

"No need to unless he says to say hello from him, then tell him I said hello. You can also let him know I've moved in and am enjoying paradise."

Betty squeezed her friend. "I promise I won't say anything if Monica is there."

"Good." Pain squeezed Darcy's chest, and she nodded. "I wouldn't want to create a scene."

"I just wish you were coming with us."

"I don't work at your firm, so I have no reason to attend." Darcy bit her lower lip to stop it from trembling.

Betty rubbed her back. "But if—"

Darcy stepped away. She didn't want to think about how she would be attending tonight's event if she hadn't broken up with Victor. The thought increased her sadness. "I know what you're saying, but I cannot be selfish and wish he was single." She rubbed her nose with the back of a hand. "He's happy."

Betty frowned. "How do you know?"

"Because Monica is happy."

After Chuck and Betty left, Charlotte cornered Darcy by the French doors leading to the flagstone patio and the hobby vineyard while Joyce carried the flattened cardboard boxes to the recycling bin in the garage. "I can't believe your ex-fiancé bought this house for you and is letting you live here rent free until he sells it next year. You'd think he would be the one moving in with his new girlfriend. At least, I would."

"He's not like the rest of us." The memory of his raffle ticket purchase brought a smile. "He's a little more generous."

"I want a boyfriend like him." Charlotte pouted.

"You can stand in line and claim him after Monica is done." Churning burned her stomach. Oh, how she wished she never revealed his identity to Monica.

"What about you?" Charlotte pointed to Darcy. "Don't you want him back?"

She tucked back her shoulders. "I'm realistic.

Relationships never work if people break up and get back together. Look at Brad and Angelina, Antonio Banderas and Melanie Griffith, Jennifer Aniston and Justin Theroux. I'm sure at least a dozen others have happened that I can't recall." She narrowed her gaze and shook a finger at Charlotte. "So don't tell me I should get back together with him."

Charlotte strolled into the kitchen and stacked plates in the cupboard. "Your daughter says you both weren't really together, so the relationship wouldn't be like the others who broke up and reconciled."

Darcy opened the silverware drawer and shoved the utensils into the slots. She couldn't believe her daughter revealed her secret to a Books and Booze Club member. "Stop listening to Joyce. She's a romantic like Victor."

Charlotte slammed the cupboard and placed her hands on her hips. "You're as cynical as your daughter says you are."

Joyce sauntered into the kitchen and frowned, glancing from one woman to the other. "What are you both talking about?"

"Your mom's biggest mistake." She pointed toward Darcy.

Joyce pursed her lips. "I don't appreciate you talking about Dad when he's not here."

"Not your father." Charlotte giggled, shaking her head. "It's Victor."

Joyce gaped. "You think Victor is my mom's biggest mistake?"

"Of course." Charlotte shrugged. "She should have married him."

For a long moment, Joyce studied the floor. "You

know, Charlotte, you're right. If she had married him, then I wouldn't be having problems with Tyler. We'd have a double wedding after all."

A bundle of nerves rattled Darcy's hands. She fumbled with linens, folding them into neat stacks which kept tumbling over on the kitchen counter. She didn't want to think or talk about Victor. "Charlotte, are you joining us for dinner?"

"I'd love to, but I have a date with Barry."

Darcy raised her eyebrows. "Barry from our book club?"

Charlotte blushed and nodded. "Don't tell the guys, or they'll be upset. Barry's planning a romantic dinner for me, and he needed the extra time to prep the food."

I never would have guessed, Darcy thought. They're nothing alike. She narrowed her gaze. "You said you wanted a boyfriend like Victor, but you're dating Barry. What gives?"

"I'm single." Charlotte wiggled ringless fingers. "I'm entitled to play the field. I can date whoever I want for however long I want without any restrictions."

"You sound like Anita."

She pouted. "Anita is a slut. I'd give up all other men if I received a firm commitment from one of them. Anita wouldn't. Therein lays the difference."

A few moments later, Lance and Eric shuffled into the kitchen. "We're done."

Darcy handed them forty dollars each and two six packs of beer. "Thanks, I appreciate the assistance."

"See you after the holidays." Eric waved.

Lance glanced around once more. "Enjoy your new home."

Charlotte hugged Darcy. "Take care. I'm leaving.

Nice meeting you, Joyce."

Joyce embraced Charlotte. "Give me a call when you're in Marin. We'll have lunch, okay?"

After everyone left, Joyce picked up her car keys. "Shall we go out for dinner, or shall I go shopping?"

"Shopping," Darcy said. "Pick out food you can eat, and I'll cook it, okay?"

"Are you sure?" Joyce arched an eyebrow.

Darcy opened her laptop on the kitchen counter, searching for a good website offering easy to prepare gluten-free, vegan recipes. She looked forward to cooking in her own kitchen without worrying if something might break or if someone might come home too soon. She didn't care if she prepared food she wouldn't normally eat. She just wanted to share dinner with her daughter. "I'm positive."

Forty-five minutes later, Joyce set a bag of potatoes, a bunch of leeks, pears, arugula, polenta, and asparagus on the quartz counter in the kitchen.

Pop music sounded from Darcy's computer while she searched the Internet for the recipes they needed to prepare leek soup, garden salad, grilled polenta, and steamed asparagus.

Joyce diced the potatoes and leeks, dumping them into a broth of almond milk. An aroma of pepper and nutmeg dusted the air.

Darcy chopped the romaine lettuce, tomatoes, green onions, and cucumbers and arranged them in two bowls along with tangy raspberry vinaigrette. The polenta sizzled on the grill beneath a cloud of garlic and olive oil. The asparagus steamed in a double boiler until the stalks darkened and the tips glistened black. Darcy turned up the music's volume and danced.

"I'm having fun cooking with you, Mom." Joyce bounced her head up and down to the beat of the drum. "Tyler doesn't join me in the kitchen. He's always upstairs in the entertainment room watching TV."

"You should get a TV in the kitchen." Darcy removed the steamed asparagus from the stove.

"I try not to watch TV at all." Joyce arranged the polenta on a dish.

Darcy cringed at her black-and-white thinking. "Sometimes, you have to compromise to get what you want—togetherness."

Joyce raised the spatula. "If you're such an expert on relationships, why aren't you in one?"

Darcy shrugged. "I prefer to be alone." She slipped out of the room and returned with a bottle of red wine. "A little wine won't kill you." Pouring two glasses, she handed one to Joyce. "In fact, a glass of red wine is good for your health."

As she sniffed the wine, Joyce wrinkled her nose. She set the glass on the counter and returned to stirring the soup. "I don't like to drink."

Darcy leaned against the counter and sipped the rich wine with a hint of raspberries. "What do you like to do?"

"Tyler and I used to hike Mt. Tam, but when we got engaged, we kind of let everything else slide. Wedding planning has been so much work, even with your help." Joyce wiped her forehead with the back of a hand. "Dad and his wedding planner want to reschedule things for the summer to give Tyler and me more time to decide whether or not we want to be together."

"That plan sounds wise." Darcy nodded.

Joyce stared into the pot of simmering soup and

shrugged. "Besides, the weather is too cold to get married outside in February."

"I agree, but the grand ballroom here would be perfect for an indoor ceremony. I love the coffered ceilings and the murals of Italy." She set the salad bowls on the kitchen table and mused a little bit longer on her broken engagement. "Maybe you're right. If Victor and I hadn't pretended to be a couple, then you and Tyler wouldn't be having problems."

After she turned off the stove, Joyce ladled soup into bowls. "I had problems with Tyler before you broke up with Victor."

Darcy arched an eyebrow. "Really?"

Joyce arranged the silverware on the table. "We both work too much. Tyler's away from home sixty percent of the time. We hardly see each other." She stepped back. "When we do see each other, we spend all of our time either loving or warring, and nothing in between."

A gasp escaped her mouth. "You guys weren't friends first, were you?"

"No, we weren't." Joyce placed the soup bowls on the table. "Did you and Dad break up because you weren't friends first?"

"Dad and I dated in college. We were both young and idealistic."

She tilted her head. "What about you and Victor?"

"We were colleagues and referred business to each other." Darcy carried the polenta and asparagus to the table, recalling the conversation she had with Victor after the wildfires in October. "We're friends," Victor had said. "Friends are family you choose...I choose you." Why couldn't she have said the truth back then?

She chose him and would choose him again and again for all of eternity, if given the opportunity. Frustrated, she sighed. "I guess you could say we were co-conspirators."

"Not friends?" Joyce sat and placed a napkin in her lap.

Darcy leaned back in her chair and sipped her wine. She shoved their genuine friendship out of her mind, choosing to focus on the make-believe romance which plunged them into trouble. "Our relationship revolved around a fantasy."

"Tyler said Victor is dating someone else."

Every time she heard his name, pain cut through her chest. When would the torture stop? "Correct."

"Is it someone you know?"

"Worse." Darcy grimaced. "A former client of mine. I suggested she date him, and she took me up on my advice."

Joyce snickered. "So, you have no one to blame except yourself."

Darcy shook her head. "Who's to blame doesn't matter. We've gone our separate ways." She reached across the table and grasped her daughter's hand. "The important thing is I love you. I know you were angry with me for not telling the truth about my false engagement to Victor. I know in your eyes I'm wrong because I'm not like you. I eat meat. I drink alcohol." She released her daughter's hand.

Gulping a mouthful of wine, she grinned. "I hope you and Tyler work out things and get married, but if you can't, then end the relationship now. Divorce is hard, one of the hardest experiences anyone can go through. I'm lucky to have made my career around helping people through the process." She stared at her empty wine glass. "For the longest time, I never needed anyone or anything after your father. But when Victor proposed on your dad's wedding night, I felt something I never thought I'd ever feel again. Hope. I was surprised all of my dead dreams of a happy marriage resurrected with the proposal." She sniffed. Through her blurred vision, she gazed at her ringless hand. "When I realized what I felt for Victor, I panicked. I didn't want to risk getting hurt again. I didn't want to face the possibility of having my happiness taken away. So I ended our relationship." She sobbed. "And now I'm lost."

Joyce grasped her mother's hand. "You're not lost, Mom. You have me."

Sucking in a quick breath, Darcy folded her daughter into her arms. "I thought I wanted to live in this beautiful home, but I never thought I would feel so alone. Living alone is worse than having roommates."

"Do you want me to stay the night?" Joyce patted her mother's back.

"No." Sniffling, she shook her head. "I want Victor. And not for just one night. I want him to stay forever."

Chapter 31

On Christmas morning, Darcy stood sipping her coffee and listening to Christmas carols in the great room beside the decorated Christmas tree. Then her phone rang. Nathan's caller ID flashed on the screen. She turned down the stereo where "Silent Night" played.

"Merry Christmas to you, Ms. Divorce Planner," Nathan said. "Our daughter and Tyler have officially broken up. I hope you're happy."

Recognizing the sarcastic tone in his voice, Darcy winced. She curled up on the leather sofa and stared at the twinkling lights on the Christmas tree. Last weekend, she and Joyce purchased the tree from a tree farm and hauled it across the foyer into the great room and decorated it with inexpensive ornaments from the Dollar Store. A few times, Joyce stopped to check and respond to Tyler's texts wearing a blank expression. Darcy hadn't pried. If she had, could she have prevented the break up? "I'm sorry to hear the news. I hoped they would have worked out their differences, which didn't seem big, after all."

"Bigger than you imagined," Nathan said. "But you don't care I have to pay the cancellation fee on some of the things we scheduled for the wedding."

"What things?" Darcy knew the cancellation for the June wedding hadn't contained any financial

345

penalties, but she didn't know what terms and conditions Nathan negotiated for the LA venue.

"Caterers, musicians, floral arrangements, the works," Nathan said. "My wedding planner works quickly and efficiently on short notice."

She tensed her shoulders. "I'm sure she can get most of your money refunded."

"Hardly," Nathan grumbled.

She straightened her spine. "Well, she's not as good a planner as me. My cancellation penalty didn't go into effect until six weeks before the wedding."

"You're missing the point." Nathan huffed. "Joyce and Tyler were getting along until you interfered."

Anger bristled hot against her skin. "I'm not taking the blame anymore, Nathan. We're all adults. We all make our own decisions." She tightened her grip on the phone. "According to our daughter, she and Tyler struggled with their relationship long before I got involved with Victor."

"She's not the only one involved. Tyler confided in me."

"And?"

"He wants to marry someone like you."

Her heartbeat knocked against her ribs. How ridiculous! She laughed.

"Canceling a wedding is not funny. What did you do to put him under your spell, Mrs. Robinson?"

She recalled the time she met Tyler with Joyce in Healdsburg, how she appeared formal and reserved, and then when they met again at Nathan's wedding, how carefree she appeared with Victor. "I did nothing wrong by being myself."

"You broke up their marriage."

Pulling her feet from under her hips, she swung her legs to the floor. "They weren't married."

"Close enough."

"You're wrong." She reached for her coffee mug on the table. "When you're married, you've already pledged your commitment. When you're engaged, you've pledged your intention to commit. When you're dating, you're still figuring things out. So, don't tell me the stages are all the same, because they aren't."

"Joyce is heartbroken," Nathan said.

Pain seized her chest, even though Darcy questioned the veracity of Nathan's statement. Joyce didn't call her unless she needed something. When she thought of Joyce confiding in her father first, regardless of how much effort she put into their mother-daughter relationship, a dull ache throbbed in her temples.

"I can't believe you mess up everything you touch, including your imaginary boyfriend."

Jerking upright, she tightened her grip on the phone. "What does Victor have to do with Joyce's break up?"

"He's the reason why Tyler questioned his relationship with Joyce. I'm surprised you didn't know."

"I haven't spoken with Victor since Thanksgiving." If they shared a mutual client, she always gathered any news through the client.

"Oh, but he called Tyler to talk about you after you broke his heart."

"I didn't break his heart." A knot tightened in her stomach. She clutched the coffee mug against her chest. "From what I hear, he's busy dating someone else."

Nathan laughed. "Tell yourself whatever lies you

need to. I know the truth. Victor called to relay what happened. He apologized for your insensitivity and asked us not to hold the lie against you. If I hadn't already lived through your lies, I might have listened, but I know better."

"Stop!" Darcy raised the coffee mug. "You have the story turned all around. You were the liar. You pretended you weren't sleeping with Tanya while we were married. When I found the love letters and receipts for hotels and fancy restaurants, you made up elaborate stories that could never be true. You're the one with the wild imagination living in a fantasy world, not me." She gulped a breath. Her heartbeat pounded in her ears. "I love Victor. I was just too scared to marry him after what you did to me."

An aching silence stretched between them.

"I'm sorry," Nathan said.

Relief flooded through her. Oh, how many years had she longed to hear those words. "I accept your apology."

"Do you want me to call Victor?"

The tone in his voice sounded sincere. A sparkle of hope danced through her. "Thank you for offering, but the answer is no." She shook her head. "Fixing my relationship with Victor is not your responsibility. Understand?"

"I understand," Nathan said. "For once, I just want you to be happy."

Me, too, Darcy thought.

****

The doorbell rang. Who could be visiting on the last night of the year? Darcy placed her book face down on the coffee table, swung her legs off the sofa, and stood.

Chuck and Betty hovered on the porch beneath the flood light.

Darcy opened the door and ushered them inside, noticing the gold cuff links on Chuck's shirt and the flash of Betty's silver heels. "You both look like you're ready to attend a party."

Chuck straightened the bow tie under his chin and glanced at himself in the full-length mirror in the foyer. "We're attending a New Year's Eve party, and we bought you a ticket."

"I brought a matching dress in a different color." After shrugging out of her coat, Betty offered Darcy a garment bag. "Go try it on." She wore a short sapphire gown with strappy sleeves and strappy heels. Her dark hair piled into a bun with tendrils framing her soft face and round glasses. "You might meet someone." She winked.

Darcy pressed her lips together, determined to avoid a party to celebrate the end of another wasted year. She folded the dress over an arm and narrowed her gaze at her friend. "I'll reimburse you for the ticket. I'd rather stay home alone. I don't want to meet someone."

"You can hang out near the dessert bar." Chuck rubbed his belly. "I hear the hotel has the best chocolate mousse pies in whole world."

"I prefer cheesecake nibbles." Darcy arched an eyebrow.

"I'm sure we can find you some." Chuck smiled. "I'll even save you a dance so you won't feel alone."

"I don't dance." Darcy recalled how Victor swept her across the ballroom at her ex-husband's wedding reception. A wave of pleasure tingled up her spine, and she bit her lip and lowered her gaze.

Shaking her head, Betty deepened her frown. "We can't leave you home alone."

Darcy lifted her head and stared at Betty's sad expression, wondering if she felt sorrier for her friend or for herself.

"Let's go." Chuck touched Betty's shoulder.

Darcy didn't want to repeat her Christmas experience, but she didn't want to be a grieving woman at a New Year's Eve celebration either. Obviously, Victor planned to celebrate New Year's with Monica in Las Vegas, and not pine at home. She needed to move on, too, even if she planned on spending the rest of her life alone. "I've changed my mind." She clutched the dress tighter. "I'll go."

Betty widened her gaze.

A slow smile inched across Chuck's face.

Darcy disappeared upstairs into the master bedroom and slipped into the ruby dress and a pair of red heels. The dress hugged her curves, and she reluctantly smiled. I don't look bad for fifty, she thought, although I would look better if I was happy. She touched up the makeup under her eyes and applied a fresh coat of lipstick. She ran a brush through her hair and dashed out into the foyer to grab her black wool coat from the closet.

"You look like a million dollars." Chuck grinned.

"I feel like a hundred." She pouted.

Betty hugged her friend. "You'll feel like a million when the New Year begins."

Fifteen minutes later, they arrived at the Flamingo Hotel ballroom where men in tuxedos and women in evening gowns danced to the live band playing everything from jazz to classic rock. A buffet of dinner foods lined one side and a buffet of desserts lined the other side. Bottles of champagne in silver ice buckets graced each table set for eight. Darcy draped her coat over a nearby chair and scanned the guests, wondering if she might know anyone.

"Let's grab some dinner and wine then we'll dance." Betty linked her arm with Darcy's.

Darcy followed Chuck and Betty to the buffet. She piled her plate with salad, cheesy scalloped potatoes, and a slice of juicy roast beef. She skipped the green beans and bread rolls.

A server fetched two bottles of wine, one red and one white.

Chuck poured everyone a glass of red, and they toasted to new beginnings. "Does anyone have any New Year's resolutions?"

Betty glanced up at the ceiling. "I think I'll work less and play more. This year, I worked too hard to make partner. I'm hoping by the time softball season starts, I can take off Fridays again. What about you?" She turned to Darcy, eyebrows lifted.

"Let Chuck go first." Darcy waved a hand.

Chuck laughed. "My resolution is to learn how to cook better so Betty doesn't have to worry about dinner when she comes home."

Darcy nodded. She didn't like to cook, but she also didn't have the luxury of living with someone who wanted to learn how. "What a great resolution."

"Your turn." Chuck pointed toward Darcy.

Biting her lower lip, she thought. "I'd like to get over thinking about Victor."

"You're not the only one with that New Year's resolution." Betty waved her wine glass. "He still talks about you at the office."

She widened her gaze. "He does?"

Betty nodded. "He says things like 'my old love' when he refers to you in a conversation."

He's so old-fashioned, she thought. Why hadn't he called her his new love when they were together? She shifted in the chair. "Why do I come up in any conversations?"

"He's on the phone with Monica at least once a day. She calls him for petty things like what's he having for lunch and can he pick her up something from the store because she's preoccupied with her kid."

Waving a hand, she dismissed the comment. "Give her a break. Her son's disabled. She doesn't have a lot of time since she works while he's in school. Her support settlement doesn't make ends meet."

"You're missing the point." Betty shook a finger. "He talks about his 'old love' with *her*. I've overheard him say he's unhappy. I don't think they'll last much longer."

She leaned closer and narrowed her gaze. "Are you eavesdropping on his conversations with Monica?"

"He leaves the door open when she calls." Betty leaned back against the chair and sipped from the glass of wine. "He doesn't close the door like he did when you called."

"I wonder if that habit means anything," she mumbled. Did a closed door mean an open heart?

Chuck laughed. "Means he's not over you either. He's still carrying a flame."

"His love for you is more like a torch." Betty raised

her glass higher. "We wish he'd close the door when she calls."

Chuck nudged Darcy. "He wants to let everyone know she hasn't replaced you in his heart."

"Then why is he dating her?" She pinched together her eyebrows.

"Because he doesn't want to be alone." Chuck swirled the wine in the glass. "Some guys need someone on their arm, no matter who it is."

She bit back a scoff. "I'm not that needy." She pointed to her chest. "I'm here alone. I'll die alone. I have no problems being alone."

"You're not alone." Betty waved a hand between them. "You're with us."

"That's right." Chuck lifted his glass of wine. "You're with us."

Darcy sighed. She didn't want to remind them of her status as the third wheel, since they wanted to make her feel part of their intimate family.

As the hours ticked closer to midnight, Darcy thought about the scene in *When Harry Met Sally* when Harry rushed into the ballroom to profess his undying love for Sally just before the stroke of midnight. Darcy sat at the table with a few strangers while Chuck and Betty waltzed across the parquet flooring to the sounds of big band music. Already, she'd turned down Chuck three times when he asked her to dance. She refused another man who looked the same age and had a bad limp from an old injury that was acting up tonight.

Eventually, Darcy stood and ambled around the room. A pang of regret clutched her chest for not staying home. At least, at home, she could be braless in a sweat suit with no makeup, watching the ball drop in

Times Square on TV. She could drink and not worry about getting into bed safely. She could forget about Victor with Monica in Las Vegas, strolling arm in arm along the strip, stopping to watch the water show at the Bellagio, drinking Hurricanes from Fat Tuesday, and taking a romantic gondola ride through the Venetian. She could forget about the possibility of him proposing at the top of the Eiffel Tower and marrying her in a chapel in Mandalay Bay then hearing from Betty about the photos of them gazing with adoration into each other's eyes on his desk at the law office. She could pretend nothing happened while she drank a whole bottle of red wine, ate a box of stale crackers, and fell asleep drunk and satiated with no recollection of the night. Just a nasty hangover would remain, which would occupy her time until the first work day of the New Year.

"Looking for someone?" a man standing next to Darcy asked.

"Oh, no," Darcy lied.

"I'm Jason, as in Jason of Argonaut." The man extended his hand. "I'm a forensic accountant."

Darcy glanced at his tall, lithe frame dressed in an attractive tuxedo with a purple bow tie. She admired his courage to open with a literary line and shook his hand. "I'm Darcy, as in *Pride and Prejudice*, only I'm not a man. I'm a divorce planner."

Jason laughed.

Darcy studied him. From the crinkles around his eyes and the laugh lines around his mouth, he looked close to fifty. He appeared healthy like he watched what he ate and exercised three times a week. His smile seemed pleasant. But no spark ignited between them.

"You must read." Jason nodded.

"I belong to a book club." Darcy scooted closer, hoping she found a kindred spirit. "Are you a reader?"

"No, I'm not." Jason shook his head. "My hobbies are more along the lines of drinking beer and watching sports. I do play basketball with a few guys I attended college with, and I take the occasional photograph, but I haven't the patience or the attention span to read anything other than tax returns."

"Too bad." Darcy took a step back, disappointed she could not talk about wicked exes in *Medea* with her new friend. "Otherwise, I'd invite you to my book club."

The lights flickered to signal the countdown to midnight.

"Want to dance?" Jason waved toward the dance floor.

A flutter of butterflies erupted in her stomach. Imagining dancing with a stranger to alleviate her pain didn't translate well into reality. "Umm…thanks, but my heart belongs to someone else."

"Lucky guy." Jason deepened his smile.

A quiver flickered over her lips. If only he knew the truth…

The countdown began. "Ten, nine, eight…"

Jason grabbed two glasses of champagne from a passing server and handed one to Darcy. "You will toast with me, won't you?"

Smiling, she nodded.

"Six, five, four…"

Jason leaned closer. "How serious are you with this other guy? Because I wouldn't mind if we kissed."

Why not? Darcy thought. We might have

chemistry. "You may kiss me."

Jason chuckled. "Ah, I can tell you are in love by the tone of your voice. Who is this guy?"

"No one you know," Darcy hoped.

"…two, one. Happy New Year!"

Darcy lifted the glass of champagne and toasted with Jason before taking a sip to welcome the new year.

Jason wrapped one arm around her waist and pressed her against his chest for a kiss.

Closing her eyes, she waited for the magic to happen, but the kiss fell flat on her lips.

Chapter 32

The day after New Year's, Darcy's phone rang. Faint light filtered through the curtains. How early was it? She rubbed her eyes and seized the phone on the nightstand beside the bed.

"Mom," Joyce sobbed.

"Hey, sweetheart." Darcy tucked the blankets around her cold legs. "Why are you crying?"

"I will die an old maid."

Darcy bit her lip, suppressing a snicker at her daughter's melodramatics. "Take a deep breath and calm down. Then tell me all about it."

She sniffed back a sob. "What has Dad already told you?"

"What he told me doesn't matter." She leaned back against a pillow. "I want to hear the news from you."

Joyce launched into a long story involving how she failed to compromise with Tyler about what they both needed and wanted in a relationship. "So, we broke up, for good. From his online posts, I can tell he's already dating. Every time I call, he's either drunk or hung over. He's a teenager all over again."

"He might have been a teenager all along, but you didn't know it until now."

"Dad doesn't agree with that statement."

Shifting against the pillows, Darcy stared at the pattern on the sheets and sighed. "I wish you wouldn't tell Dad everything before you tell me, but I doubt that pattern will ever change."

Joyce sighed. "Dad said I criticize Tyler too much."

"Dad's right. But you're critical of everyone, including yourself."

"I just want everything to be perfect."

Oh, my poor baby, you're just setting yourself up for failure, she thought. "Nothing is perfect. The only perfect thing about life is its imperfections."

"I can't live with everything not being perfect, Mom. I'm not you. I'm me. I'm analytical and neurotic and controlling. I'm not spontaneous and fun-loving and carefree. Tyler broke up with me because he wants to marry someone like you."

A slight grin creased her face. She picked at a piece of lint on the blanket. At least, Nathan and Joyce's stories matched. "Dad said the same thing."

"Well, he's right. Tyler and I had everything figured out until he met Victor at Dad's wedding, and they renewed their friendship. Tyler said he realized he had been missing out on a lot of fun. Not the type of fun we were having, but the type of fun you and Victor were having." Joyce sniffled. "I can't have that type of fun."

"Don't try to be me." Darcy shook her head. "Be yourself. Have your type of fun."

"Didn't you hear anything I just said?" Joyce lamented. "Tyler doesn't want the type of fun we were having. He wants the type of fun you and Victor had."

Irritation bristled against her shoulders. Oh, when would her daughter learn? "You need to find someone who needs your type of fun."

"Who would that be?"

"I don't know." Darcy shrugged. Why give advice which would never be taken? She tensed her jaw. "Maybe you should ask Dad. He seems to know everything."

Joyce's sobs grew louder. "That I tell him everything first is just a habit. I don't do it because I love him more than you or our relationship is any better. It's not. My response is just different because you both are different."

Darcy suppressed a smile. A seed of knowledge blossomed in her little girl. Now if she could only get her daughter to recognize the wisdom. "Listen to yourself, sweetie. Do you hear what you're saying?"

Snuffles filled the silence.

"Tyler needs someone like you, and I need someone like me."

Darcy punched a fist in the air. "Bingo!"

Joyce laughed. "You know, Mom, my New Year's resolution is to call you more often. Not just when I need something but just to say hello."

"You have a noble idea, but resolutions aren't kept. Most fall apart within the first month." Stretching her legs on the bed, she glanced at the shadows playing against the curtains. Soon, the sun would rise, and she would have to get ready for work, but right now, she enjoyed talking, and not fighting, with her daughter on the phone. Tenderness filled her whole body. "I'm always glad to hear from you, sweetheart, even if it's only when you need something."

"I've got to stop being selfish, Mom, or I'll never find someone to love me the way Victor loved you."

Pain squeezed her chest. Darcy licked her dry lips,

the lips Victor used to kiss. "I don't know how you can say he loved me. Our relationship revolved around deceiving other people."

"But you guys created the fantasy together. Somehow your relationship, whether or not you choose to call it real or pretend, worked." Joyce swallowed. "Maybe you were too close to see Victor's true feelings, but everyone else did. He loved you with all of his heart."

And I love him with all of my heart, she thought. And most of the time, I wish I didn't.

****

The following weekend, Darcy moved into the office space she leased on the corner of Fifth and E Street. She set up her office in one of the two rooms and hired Sasha, a receptionist from a temporary agency to assist with answering phones and scheduling appointments.

By the second week of January, business boomed. In addition to the annual influx of post-holiday clientele, Darcy received a few referrals from Jason, the forensic accountant she met on New Year's Eve. He asked her out to lunch a few times, but each time, Darcy declined. "I don't like mixing business with pleasure," she said whenever he called, hoping the excuse sufficed.

"It would be strictly a business lunch," Jason reassured her.

Darcy doubted his intentions. After her experience with Victor, she knew the dangers of risking a business luncheon despite the lack of attraction on her end. Later that month, on a Friday night, while jostling through the dinner crowd at Ophelia's Bar and Steakhouse, Darcy spied Jason waiting for a table with another man.

When he noticed her, he crossed the room, touching her arm before she opened the door to the special events room where her book club waited. "Hey, Miss Business, are you here on a date?"

Darcy raised her battered copy of *The Heart of Darkness* and shook her head. "I have my Books and Booze Club night. And you?" She nodded to the man waiting in the lobby.

"My cousin from Atlanta is here." Jason smiled. "I'm taking him out to dinner since my idea of cooking is heating frozen chicken wings."

She laughed.

He stepped closer.

Smiling, she smelled his musky aftershave.

"So, if you're not here on a date, then why won't you go out with me? Am I ugly? Too short? Too tall? Too skinny? Too fat? Too boring?" He pointed to her book. "Too dumb?"

Cradling the book against her chest, she heaved a sigh. Why lie? "I already told you the reason."

"So, who's the mystery guy?"

"No one you would know." She crossed her fingers.

"Are you sure?" He raised his eyebrows. "The way you keep putting me off makes me believe he does not exist." Grinning, he leaned over. "Are you pretending to have a boyfriend to avoid hurting my feelings?"

She cringed. Oh, if only he knew she never wanted to pretend about anything ever again. "Please, believe me when I say he exists. He's just with someone else right now."

He widened his eyes. "What makes you think he'll

become available anytime soon?"

She bit her lower lip. Would Victor be single again? Or would he eventually marry Monica just to be settled? After all, most marriages happened for the wrong reason. The groom needed a green card. The bride had an unplanned pregnancy. He didn't have health insurance. She needed to feel secure. He suffered from loneliness. They were friends. They were roommates. They were together as a couple for ten years, so why not? Darcy believed Victor knew better than to settle for a marriage of convenience. "I don't know if he'll become available, but I'm willing to wait to find out."

"For how long?"

Confident, she lifted her chin. "For as long as it takes."

****

A few days later, Darcy received a phone call from Betty.

"I know we're both super busy, but we have to meet for coffee this week."

"Why can't we just talk on the phone?" Darcy frowned at her cluttered calendar booked with back-to-back meetings with new and returning clientele, including a woman who serially married wealthy men only to divorce them in the hopes of obtaining alimony.

"I have news," Betty said. "It's not the type you talk about over the phone."

"Okay." Darcy relented, wondering what the news could be. "I have an opening this afternoon at three-thirty. Can we meet at Katie's Koffee?"

"No problem," Betty said. "I'll see you then."

As soon as Darcy stepped into the cozy coffee

house, she spied Betty sitting at their favorite table with their drinks already ordered. Darcy scooted back a chair and sat. "You better not announce you've won the lotto and are retiring, because then I'll have to send all of my referrals to Victor."

"Don't worry. The news is not about me." She gazed over the rims of her glasses. "It's about Victor."

Interested, she lifted her eyebrows. Oh, why was she so eager to hear any snippet about him? Wouldn't she ever get over him and move on?

"Victor visited Las Vegas for New Year's, and he returned to the office all moody and grumpy." Betty shifted in the seat and rubbed her hands. "No one suspected anything wrong at first, but then Monica started calling every hour on the hour. Finally, last week, Victor yelled, 'I'm getting a restraining order if you don't leave me alone. How many times do I have to say our relationship is over before you understand we're never getting back together?' Then he slammed his door closed. My partnership plaque almost fell off the wall in my office."

A tiny smile lifted the corners of her lips before Darcy cradled her latte and forced a frown. "Why did they break up?"

Betty crumpled a napkin in her fist. "I don't know. He didn't want to talk about it with anyone. Ever since that phone call, he's started closing the door again, working long hours, and keeping to himself. His behavior is like the whole Monica affair didn't happen."

She leaned back in her chair. She often thought about contacting Victor and inviting him over to the office to discuss the possibility of getting back together.

But each time she stopped herself from picking up the phone when she thought of his relationship with Monica. With Monica out of the picture, she no longer had an excuse not to contact him.

"I think you should call him." Betty grinned and nodded.

A smile tugged at the corners of her lips. "You read my mind."

Immediately after her meeting with Betty, Darcy paced back and forth in her office with hands clasped behind her back. She called Victor's office twice, hanging up each time the receptionist answered. Terror and excitement raced through her body when she imagined the conversation that might follow.

She had to be brave, she thought. Or find someone braver than her.

After two more failed attempts, she asked her receptionist to place the call. "When you get Victor on the phone, transfer the call."

"Of course, Ms. Madison," Sasha said.

Darcy waited in her office, perched on the edge of her leather executive chair. When the phone rang, she almost bolted for the emergency exit.

"He's on the line," Sasha said.

She lifted the receiver to her ear. "Victor?"

"Darcy, I haven't heard from you in forever."

His voice sounded bright and cheerful, as if nothing bad ever happened.

"Is anything wrong?" he asked.

"Oh, no, everything's all right." She leaned back in her chair. "I'm calling to refer a client. Do you have time to stop by my new office?"

"You have an office?"

The tone of surprise in his voice forced a bright smile on her face. She gave him the address.

"I'll be there in fifteen minutes," he said.

With trembling fingers, she hung up the phone. How would she occupy the next fifteen minutes? She couldn't focus on anything other than Victor's impending arrival. What would she say? How would he respond? Oh, why did things have to be so complicated when they were real?

The phone rang. Darcy lurched for the receiver.

"He's here," Sasha said.

Darcy stood, straightening her skirt. "Bring him in." The receptionist opened the door and led Victor inside.

He wore a dark blue suit with a red tie. His black hair swept over his forehead in a luxurious wave. He peered around the room and frowned. "I'm a little confused."

"Have a seat, and I'll explain it all." She motioned to the chairs near her desk.

Victor placed his briefcase on the floor and sat in the chair opposite Darcy's big desk. He folded his hands in his lap and stared.

Darcy snatched a set of keys from her desk drawer. "I know you wanted to start your own firm, but you were waiting until the house sold to buy an office. Well, you don't have to wait any longer. These keys are to the room next door." Standing, she led him to the adjacent room furnished with a big maple desk, leather chairs, and built-in bookcases along the walls. A name plate and business cards on the desk read—Victor Madison-Costello.

"The gesture is quite presumptuous, isn't it?"

Arching an eyebrow, Victor picked up a business card with his new name. "What makes you think I'll accept your offer?"

Darcy didn't know. Because she needed to make things right between them, she had taken a leap of faith. "The biggest mistake of my life happened when I broke up with you. Yes, bigger than my divorce and the challenges I've had with Joyce. When I stumbled across this space, I thought of you. We work so well together." She breathed in deeply and stared into his eyes. "I miss our Monday lunches. I miss our camaraderie. I miss you."

He rubbed a thumb over the embossed print on the business card. "Madison-Costello, Divorce Specialists."

She swept open her arms. "Divorce is what we do."

"But divorce is not who we are." Setting the card on the table, he hunched his shoulders. "I've also had a lot of time to think. I shouldn't have assumed you would marry me. I understand your reservations against the whole institution, and I respect your desire not to marry. I thought I could move on and find someone more aligned with my beliefs." Turning, he lifted his head. Tears danced in his brown eyes. "I tried, but I couldn't pretend with someone else when I knew I wanted something real. With you. However that reality looks."

Her heartbeat hammered in her chest. Stepping closer, she took his hands in hers. "I love you."

He peered closely. "Are you really in love with me?"

"Of course, I am." Relief softened her shoulders. She smiled. "I fell in love with you at the Gala."

He laughed. The moisture in his eyes sparkled. "I

fell in love with you when I walked you to your car."

"Are you sure it didn't happen sooner?" She lifted her eyebrows and searched his face.

"You mean, when I kissed you?"

Glancing away, she blushed. Her heartbeat fluttered in her chest, and her palms dampened.

"I appreciate you offering me this office." He released her hands. "I just don't know if I can work next door to you when I want so much more."

Hope squeezed her chest. She nodded. "I want more, too."

Lifting a hand, he brushed a stray hair off her face and cupped her cheek. "How much more?"

Every nerve in her body felt alive. She bit her lower lip to stop it from trembling. "I want you to come home with me every night. I want to wake up with you every morning. I want to share my life with you."

"Enough to marry me?" He raised his brow and searched her face.

"If the offer is still available."

"It is." Smiling, he wrapped his arms around her waist and kissed her.

The passion crinkled her scalp and curled her toes.

When he released her, he slipped his hand into his breast pocket and pulled out his grandmother's wedding ring.

As he slid the cool metal onto the third finger of her left hand, happiness floated through her body. "This proposal is real," she whispered.

Once more, he kissed her lips. "My love for you is as real as it gets."

Oh, if only she could share this joy with Joyce, then her life would be complete.

Chapter 33

On Valentine's Day as guests found seats before the altar in the grand ballroom of the Tuscany home, Darcy stood in front of a mirror in the master bedroom, getting ready for her wedding.

"This whole transformation is incredible." Joyce spun with arms wide, mouth agape.

Linda nudged aside Joyce so she could pin the tiara and veil to Darcy's hair. "Even disbelievers have dreams come true."

"You're right." Joyce wrung together her hands. "I just feel awkward to be here with Tyler after all that's happened."

Darcy stared at her daughter's reflection in the mirror. "I couldn't pick Victor's best man."

"I understand." Joyce leaned close until their heads touched. "Victor should have been more considerate and chosen Barry since you were choosing me."

Oh, my dear child, Darcy thought, you will always be selfish. She laughed. "Barry's the head of my book club. He's more my friend than Victor's. We asked him to be a groomsman, because I wanted you as my bridesmaid." She shifted her gaze to Betty. "I already promised my best friend she would be my matron of honor."

"She's right." Betty adjusted Darcy's skirt.

Joyce spun and paced the length of the room. "I'm

doing my best to be respectful, but everything about this wedding is odd." She pointed to her mother. "You're wearing white instead of ecru. Your groom is young enough to be my brother. Dad's wedding planner shipped the decorations. Don't ask me how she swapped purple and peach for red and baby blue at the last minute."

As she recalled Nathan's apology, a frisson of pleasure rippled up her spine. "Your dad worked it out, so he didn't lose his deposit." She smiled. "I've already thanked him."

A few moments passed. Joyce tapped her lips. "I'm still stumped about the cake. You said everything gluten-free tastes like cardboard."

Darcy shrugged. "Still does, but Victor and I decided the guests would eat it anyway."

"What about the wedding topper?" Joyce wrinkled her forehead.

Darcy smiled, thinking of the Cinderella and Prince Charming wedding topper. "Victor loves fairy tales."

Joyce shook her head. "I wish I understood your logic, Mom." She counted on her fingers as she spoke. "The caterer is the guy who used to own this house. The DJ is a guy you once dated who still looks like he has a crush. The photographer is a member of your book club. And a guy says he's here to see your imaginary husband-to-be. I asked him to leave, but Sam insisted he's not a wedding crasher."

Without responding, Darcy listened to her daughter's complaints. She no longer felt compelled to appease her daughter at her own expense. She deserved to be married to Victor and to have everyone they both loved at the event. "Sam's right. I invited him. His name is Jason. He's a forensic accountant. He relentlessly asked me out for lunch, and I repeatedly turned him down. He thought I had an imaginary boyfriend, so I invited him at the last minute to show him Victor is real."

A knock sounded on the door.

"Yes?" Darcy glanced over her shoulder.

Anita stepped into the room. "I wanted to see the bride before the big show."

"Well, here I am." Darcy twirled with her arms outstretched.

Anita shuffled over to the dressing table.

Oh, my, she's still on the hunt, Darcy thought. Anita wore a tight ruby red dress decades too young for her sixty-five-year-old body. Her cleavage heaved like a heroine on the cover of a romance novel.

"Who is that hussy?" Joyce asked Betty.

"Your mom's friend, Anita, from her book club."

"I can't believe that woman reads," Joyce whispered.

"I might be old, but my hearing's perfect." Anita widened her eyes and stood taller.

Charlotte knocked on the door before she poked inside her head. "Eric wants to know if you're ready."

Everyone glanced at Darcy.

As she admired her reflection, she stood relaxed and ready. The tiara veil draped over her shoulders. The dress fit her curves, and the train swirled behind her on the floor. Happiness washed over her. "I can't believe I'm getting married."

"If you change your mind, I'll marry him." Anita pointed to her cleavage.

Charlotte snickered. "You wouldn't make a good

wife."

"I'd keep him satisfied where it counts." Anita winked.

Joyce kissed her mother's cheek. "I'm sorry I'm so petulant, Mom. I just thought we'd be sharing this special day together in a double wedding, but we're not. I'm happy for you, but sad for me."

"Better the bridesmaid than the divorcee." Darcy hugged Joyce and kissed her cheek. "Someday, your time will come."

Joyce stepped back and examined her mother. "You look beautiful."

"Thank you." Darcy accepted the bouquet of red roses from Betty. "Onward."

Joyce and Betty led the way down the staircase to the grand ballroom.

Charlotte opened the double doors and signaled to the DJ to start the music.

Over the speakers, Barbra Streisand sang, "Someday My Prince Will Come." Victor chose the song instead of the traditional "Bridal March." Darcy didn't mind conceding, but she refused to let him walk down the aisle. "I might be a man in a woman's body, but I'm still a bride," she teased.

Everyone shifted in their seats toward the back of the room.

For an unpleasant moment, Joyce and Tyler stood side by side, gazing at each other.

Joyce opened her mouth. "I'm sorry," she whispered.

Tyler lifted his eyebrows, but he remained silent.

When Barry linked his arm with Joyce's, the spell was broken. Together, they strolled up the aisle beneath a canopy of red roses.

Tyler gazed at Joyce's back.

She swung her hips back and forth in the ice blue dress that flowed along the length of her body.

"She's not going anywhere," Betty said. "You guys can make up at the reception."

Stiffening, Tyler widened his gaze. "I'm not getting back together."

Betty wagged a finger. "That's what you say now." She linked her arm in the crook of Tyler's arm and proceeded up the aisle.

As Streisand's voice warbled into a crescendo, Darcy embarked down the aisle, alone. Against a mural of an Italian village, a garden burst into life. An archway of red roses led from the back of the room to the altar with deep crimson and baby blue petals scattered against the white carpet. As she gazed at the sea of familiar faces, she hugged the bouquet. She had no living parents and had not invited anyone to give her away. With each step, the tightness loosened within her chest.

At the end of the aisle, Victor stood in his red jacket and black slacks. He folded his white gloved hands in front of him.

Seeing him smile, all of Darcy's nervousness melted away. This time, she was marrying the right man for the right reason. At the altar, Darcy handed her bouquet to Betty and grasped Victor's hands.

"You look amazing." He beamed.

"And you look like Prince Charming." She smiled.

Eric cleared his throat then dropped into his Elvis voice. "Dearly beloved, we're gathered here today to witness the union of Victor Costello and Darcy

Madison in holy matrimony." He swept his gaze across the crowded room. "If there be any suspicious minds present in the audience, speak now for their love won't wait."

Darcy glanced over her shoulder. Through the veil, she peered at the guests, waiting for someone to protest.

But everyone, including Joyce, beamed back with approving smiles.

After the moment of silence, Eric continued. "Victor Costello, repeat after me—It only took one night to get stuck on you. For a long time, I was nothing but a hound dog, crying all the time, but now my wish has come true, and I'll forever love you, my teddy bear."

He twitched his mouth.

She squeezed his hand and grinned. Where else would they find an officiant to marry them in two weeks' time?

Giving a return squeeze, he repeated the vows.

"Now Darcy Madison, repeat after me—It took a hard-headed man to make me queen of the whole wide world. I thought you were the devil in disguise, but you kissed me quick and loved me tender, so I couldn't help but fall in love with you."

No longer fighting against a silly smile, she took a breath and stood still. Slowly, carefully, she repeated the vows.

Eric nodded to the best man and the matron of honor. "Please, take this moment to exchange your gifts of love."

Victor peeled off his white gloves and handed them to Tyler who gave him a gold band featuring two vines entwined together to match the Tuscany theme of their dream home. Victor cupped Darcy's hand and slid the gold band onto her finger next to his grandmother's wedding ring.

Darcy repeated the gesture by wriggling a matching gold band on Victor's finger. Tenderness swept through her. The thick interwoven vines reminded her of their interlocking fingers when they held hands.

Eric lifted up their arms for the audience. "By the powers vested in me, I now pronounce you, husband and wife. You may kiss the bride."

Victor lifted the veil and gazed into Darcy's eyes for a long moment before his lips brushed against hers.

With her heartbeat pounding in her ears, she placed both hands on his chest and let herself sink into the kiss.

When they finally parted, Eric motioned to the audience. "Please join me in welcoming Mr. Victor Madison-Costello and Mrs. Darcy Madison-Costello." He wiped a tear from the corner of his eye. "Folks, I've presided over thousands of weddings in my lifetime, but this one has got me all shook up."

Anita stood and shook a flask. "Viva Las Vegas!"

Darcy laughed until tears streamed down her cheeks. "We're married."

"(I've Had) The Time of My Life" played through the speakers.

Grinning, Victor grabbed her hand and tugged her close. "Now the fun continues."

A word about the author…

Angela Lam, formerly Angela Lam Turpin, is an American writer. She is the author of four novels, a short story collection, and a memoir. *The Divorce Planner* is her third contemporary romance set in Northern California.

Visit Angela at:
http://www.angelalamturpin.com

Thank you for purchasing
this publication of The Wild Rose Press, Inc.

For questions or more information
contact us at
info@thewildrosepress.com.

The Wild Rose Press, Inc.
www.thewildrosepress.com

To visit with authors of
The Wild Rose Press, Inc.
join our yahoo loop at
http://groups.yahoo.com/group/thewildrosepress/